CW00495489

'THE FOREIGN SECRETARY R.I.P'

by

RICHARD HAMILTON

'THE
FOREIGN SECRETARY R.I.P.'
by
RICHARD HAMILTON

The Foreign Secretary RIP' describes a selection of varied political and related occurrences, all of an unexpected nature and of course all of the sort to display the capabilities of those politicians involved. Such is the stuff of the everyday life in any Nation's Government. At the same time there are events in which those involved would prefer not to see the light of day; some people go to great lengths to avoid the revelation of a past family scandal or current catalogue of circumstances whereas the simple act of acknowledging a set of difficulties may not even make the news. However, arouse the media and nothing may stay hidden or private for long. On the other hand, a well-known individual may find themselves so surrounded by scandalous revelations connected with other members of their family and those scurrilous scribes cannot resist the opportunity to muddle the muck to bring about a degree of culpability with no more evidence than writing about someone who simply exists, perhaps in the wrong place and at the wrong time. Throw into the melting pot a prestigious family history with the odd impoverished vagrant in its membership, some inherited wealth with seemingly no source, an individual of status on the brink of a breakdown, a little birth right embarrassment and the total recipe has wonderous potential for the possibility of unseating a notable Member of Parliament or at least send him running for the Chiltern Hundreds.

For my daughter Rachel, my son Alistair, and his wife, Margaret, who have been very supportive of my attempts at writing novels, and who continue to look forward to each new book as it appears.

And for all who have ever suffered from severe depression, an illness which can bring an individual to a total and incomprehensible stand-still as they face a mental health disability which may last for the rest of their life.

Also by Richard Hamilton:

'The Baskervilles Dustjacket'

'The Mystery of the Pope's Private Papers'

'Family Saga From Berlin and Back'

*'Music **is** the Food of Love'*

PREFACE

It must be stressed that all the characters in this novel are fictional and any similarities with known individuals are quite coincidental. That is one reason why I have set the novel for the most part in 2030 or there abouts. If in writing about Government and Parliamentary procedures I have made errors, I apologise, but hope my intention has remained clear. For simplicity's sake I have avoided aspects of Party Politics. I have made a number of minor historical references where names are known and are in the public domain but nothing critical has been added. When I was in my forties I suffered a prolonged period of severe depression, and still do from time to time and it strikes without warning so I can vouch for how it can affect any individual; fellow sufferers have my sympathy, as do their nearest and dearest. For one fictional character I have quoted a Citation for an act of Bravery in the First World War and to be sure of the appropriateness of wording I have copied the Citation given for the award of a Military Cross to my Uncle, Captain James Montgomery Hamilton, who was killed shortly before the end of the First World War.

Contents

Chapter/Page   Title

Characters

Maj. Gen. Sir James John	The First Baronet, Norstead Towers
Lady Evelyn	His wife, died from shock
Captain James St John M.C.	Sir James's Oldest Son, Killed 1stWW
	Two sons of Capt. James also killed
Edward St John, M.P.	Sir James's only Surviving Son
Beryl	Edward St John's Sister-in-Law
Peter St John, M.P.	2ndWW Pilot Edward St John's only son
George St John, M.P.	Peter St John's oldest child
Elaine Rosenthal	Wife of George St John, M.P.
Juliette Quemsby	Benefactor to Members of Her Family
Vincent St John	Oldest Child of George & Elaine, Scientist
Crispen MacPhearson	Solicitor to Vincent St John
Beryl St John	2nd Child of George/Elaine, Writing as Jayne St John
James St John, M.P.	Youngest Child of George & Elaine, Foreign Secretary
Rhiannon Lewis	Wife to James St John, M.P., Foreign Secretary
Edward and Darcey St John	Son and Daughter-in-Law to George & Elaine St John
James St John	Only son to Edward and Darcey St John
Joshua and Celia St John	Second Son to George & Elaine St John and wife
Richard and Amy	Children of Joshua and Celia
Anthony May, M.P.	The Prime Minister
Laurel May	Wife of The Prime Minister, Anthony
John Carpenter	Hospital A & E Trauma Consultant
Thomas Magnusson	Government Chief Whip
Daniel Divine	Home Secretary
Jeremy Lutterworth	Adviser to Home Secretary
David Yardlington	Receptionist Royal Court Hotel
Angela	Girl Friend of Jeremy
Nigel Vauxhall	Step-Brother to Jeremy
Rufus Sutton	Oxford Academic, Senior Civil Servant
Audrey Ponsonby	Linguist, Wife of Rufus Sutton
Miss Tomlinson	{Interviewing Panel}
Mr Ratisbon	{for Civil Service}
Mr Horton	{Applicant – Rufus Sutton}
Aggie	Down and Out Killed in Hit-and-Run

Constable Evans	{Policemen Investigating}
Sergeant Vaughan	{Hit-and-Run}
Mavis Evans	Wife of Constable Evans
Inspector Finley	Senior Officer to Sergeant Vaughan
Ern and Emily Caroldine	Owners of Stolen Car in Hit-and-Run Incident
Mr Banstead	Garage Owner
Alan Struthers	Instigator of Hit-and-Run
Sir Ronan Nicholls	Senior Civil Servant 10 Downing Street
Clive Anderson	Acting Foreign Secretary
Jonathan Venniston	Minister Home Office
Penelope Grimble	Adviser Foreign Office
Angus Barrington M.P.	Minister of State Foreign Office
Inspector Anthea Grange	{Police Officers Investigating}
Sergeant Fellows	{Suttons' Break-in }
Sir Reginald Hewlitt	UK Ambassador to France
Lady Shelagh Hewlitt	Wife to Sir Reginald
Sir Peter Carruthers	Master Oxford College
Inspector Waterton	Senior Police Officer, Vincent's Death
Senhor Joaquim Barbosa	Brazilian Ambassador to UK
Sir Emmett Burton	UK Ambassador to United Nations
Senhor Lucas Barreto	Brazilian Ambassador to United Nations
John Stevenson M.P.	Parliamentary Acquaintance of Angus Barrington
Inspector Ball	{Police who attended}
Sergeant Watson	{failure of Lift Mechanism}
Various Pupils Kemby School	Friends of David & Jeremy
Lucinda Quemsby	Pupil at Kroxby Girls School
Henry Palmerson	Chemistry Teacher Kemby, Affair with Lucinda
George Palmerson	Oldest son of Henry, pupil at Kemby
Frank Palmerson	Younger son of Henry, Boy-friend of Vincent
Sergeant Angwin	Cornish Police Officer
Superintendent Jefferson	Host of his own Retirement Party
Commander Zachary	Scotland Yard Officer – Government Security
Brenda Cuthbertson	Computer Police Data Investigator
Gina, Louise and Diana	Wife and daughters of George Palmerson

{Main Characters – Short Story)

Wens Chalk	Thief
Trent Ravenscroft M.P.	{'*Who would be a Member of Parliament*'}

12

The Foreign Secretary R.I.P.

Prelude

Mid-1990s

Two lads, now at the beginning of their year eleven or upper fourth as Kemby School would so describe it, had rushed off to Great Yarmouth town centre just as soon as the first Saturday that they could get free came round. They were hoping to meet up with a couple of girls from Kroxby who they had got to know rather well the previous summer. Their enthusiasm was hardly surprising; when four rather hormonal youngsters in the age range fifteen to sixteen get together and without any immediate adult supervision they are likely to want to stay together for longer than is perhaps wise. This was not the only quartet whose members were so stimulated. It was thus that they had ended the summer term, but if they were hoping to pick up where they left off our young studs were to be disappointed. In fact they soon realised that none of the pupils from Kroxby High School for Girls were around.

They bumped into one or two local teenagers who they had got to know slightly and from them they learnt that there was planned something of a new regime for the Girls' High School. It was local ancillary staff who were first to spread the rumours, confirmed later by one or two of the younger teachers who lived locally and who were perhaps a shade indiscreet in what they said. It seemed that there had been an emergency meeting of the Governing Body just prior to the school breaking for the long summer holiday and as a result the Headmistress had been asked to leave with immediate effect. The parents of four girls were contacted and firmly but politely they were asked to arrange alternative schools for their daughters. It was also known that one of the girls was pregnant and her parents had already given this information to the School's Authorities. The Deputy Headmistress was appointed on a temporary basis to be Headmistress for the new academic year during which time the Governors would be advertising for a suitable full-time replacement. In this matter the temporary replacement was very pleased as she was only eighteen months from retiring so certainly wouldn't have been applying for the permanent post and for the remaining time of her service she was to be rewarded with a doubling of her salary.

At the time of this appointment there had been urgent but confidential meetings with the Headmaster of Kemby. Our lads, when they returned to school later that Saturday, were met by their Senior House Master and in no uncertain terms they were informed of new rules as far as visits to local towns were concerned and because of their disappearance that morning without permission they found themselves having to complete many hours of detention in addition to a considerable increase in long distance running round the school sports field over the following six Saturdays and supervised by which ever member of staff had the misfortune to be on duty for that particular task. A new regime had travelled from Kroxby to Kemby! Without speaking of their thoughts to each other, our two lads no doubt spent much of their time when running, wondering which of them, if either, might be the father of an unborn baby.

Chapter One

The St John Family History

1870 onwards

W hen Major General James Vincent George St John was elevated to a Baronetcy in the closing years of the C19th he was filled with pride, both for himself and his family. It was an unexpected distinction which arrived in the later years of his military career. He had commanded with success during the Boer War and he presumed this was the reason for his elevation to a Baronetcy. The Major General was born in the small village of Ewell, Surrey, but he adopted as his complete title, Sir James St John of Lower Norstead. Sir James came from a long line of military gentlemen, some more distinguished than others but he was the first and only member of the family to be honoured with a Baronetcy. Although he didn't know at the time, he would be nearly the last of this military line; his later descendants turned to politics. In his early twenties he had inherited from his father a medium sized country estate, Norstead Towers, with sufficient funds to maintain it in an appropriate style and the two farms and various cottages which formed part of the estate provided additional income. It was not far from the village of Lower Norstead. Looking to the future, Sir James felt that his family would retain some sense of distinction in the area.

He had two sons and two grandsons but by the end of the First World War he had lost a son, the oldest, James, and the two grandsons; Sir James's wife, Evelyn, had never enjoyed robust health and with the loss of three members of her family she simply faded away. His two grandsons were both killed very early in the war, not long after each of them had arrived in France. Their father, James, who had acquired the rank of Captain in the East Surrey Regiment, survived until the autumn of 1918; he was killed just six weeks before the Armistice and awarded the M.C. posthumously. Sir James's surviving son, Edward was married and their only child didn't arrive until 1922, still very much a toddler as they moved into the mid-1920s. Sadly death stalked the family again and Edward's wife succumbed to Spanish Flu so the surviving son was left to bring up a very small child.

Fortunately, his sister-in-law, Beryl, was of a very kindly disposition and having recovered from the appalling shock of losing her husband and both sons in the Great War made a determined effort to give as much help as possible to Sir James, her brother-in-law Edward, and her nephew, Peter. They all lived at Norstead Towers. Unlike Beryl, Sir James never really recovered from the loss of his wife and four younger members of his family. As a military man he was proud of his family's sacrifices, but he felt the losses most acutely. He was particularly proud of the award of the Military Cross to James, and from time to time he would sit in his library and quietly read the Citation. He kept a copy, framed, standing on his desk. It was a brief piece of writing but as a military man himself he could easily imagine the horror and chaos which accompanied the action.

Captain James St John

'For conspicuous gallantry and devotion to duty. During an attack on two lines of enemy trenches, this officer was conspicuous for his leadership. His company had twenty-six casualties moving up to the assault, but he led the depleted company to the first objective and carried on with a handful of men to the second. Here he was counter-attacked, being nearly surrounded, but got his men away, showing great initiative and resource.'

Sir James gradually took to spending a great deal of time in his small library and sadly, taking an ever-decreasing interest in the remaining members of the family. Even Edward's victory in an election, becoming the local M.P., failed to raise his spirits. Sir James continued to read of military matters and he followed the news of the 1930s with a growing sense of despair, fearing the out-break of another war. He was spared any knowledge of the horrors of the second world war as he died early in 1939, the result of a fall from his horse.

Throughout the 1930s life at Norstead Towers became livelier, much to Peter's delight. A married couple, Harriet and Bill, who had worked for Sir James for some years stayed on at the Towers, and with orphaned and abandoned children from London, they were able to help Beryl with Peter as he had suddenly acquired four younger 'brothers.' Harriet undertook a lot of additional laundry work and Bill was for ever inventing and creating adventures for five very active boys. When Edward was home at weekends he was happy to join in all these games and activities. With some of the residents from the cottages joining in, Norstead Towers could even field an occasional cricket side. Peter was soon to leave what seemed to be an idyllic existence, home from school most weekends and able to join in all the fun, devised by Bill, as he was called up for military service. Unlike his more famous Grandfather, he joined the RAF, engaged in the Battle of Britain when so tragically many of his fellow pilots were killed. This was a frightening and terrible time for young pilots, many only eighteen or nineteen. They may have successfully assumed an appearance of 'devil-may-care' courage and there was colossal camaraderie; never-the-less, fear stalked them all and never more so than when they experienced the appalling horror of witnessing one of their number, a close friend perhaps, being shot from the skies. When Peter was eventually posted from flying Spitfires the notification was accompanied with the award of the Distinguished Flying Cross. His Squadron Leader assured him that he had nothing with which to reproach himself regarding his new posting, that his service hitherto had been absolutely exemplary and as if to underline this he informed him of his promotion to Flight Lieutenant dating from the beginning of his next posting.

For the last two of years of the war he flew the Mosquito in many photo reconnaissance missions. No longer involved in life and death dog-fights, but his reconnaissance flights were by no means without great risks. They were constantly trying to get within viewing distance, at photographic range, of precisely what the enemy wished to keep secret. He had to keep particularly secret his involvement in flying missions close to the end of the war when attempts were being made to spot the sites from which V2 rockets were being fired. The risk of being shot out of the sky was enormous, so pilot skill in endeavouring to remain undetected was paramount and in this respect his skill was sufficient to see him safely through to the end of the war. In 1943 Peter had married Edith, a sister of a fellow officer. They had two children, a son, George who arrived some six months after the wedding, and a daughter, Jayne, who came along three years later.

Like quite a number of his colleagues, Peter stayed in the RAF until the late 1940s, and was involved with flying Douglas Dakotas during the Berlin Airlift missions, 1948 to 1949. When eventually he returned home with the intention of flying commercial aircraft, he found that his father was planning to retire as an MP and with his distinguished war record behind him, Peter changed his career plans and was nominated for the seat by the local Conservative Party and so succeeded his father as one of the Surrey MPs on Thursday 25th October 1951. His Parliamentary career was very Party orientated if somewhat unspectacular. However, he had spoken loyally in giving his support to joining the Common Market and it was perhaps this which caused him to be recommended for a life peerage in the early 1970s. This unplanned retirement from the House of Commons caused the local Conservative Party to stay with the St John family and so it was his son George, only thirty years old, who took over his father's seat in the House at a by election in 1973. Sadly his father's career in the House of Lords was somewhat short-lived as he died in 1980 and George succeeded to the Baronetcy. There was now money in the family and George was not a new M.P. who, as was often the case with many new M.P.s, rather hard up; he had resources. George was lucky to be able to share his father's London accommodation which he also inherited on his father's death. George kept working as a solicitor and based in London this continued to bring in a good income even though he reduced the number of cases which he took on.

George had a long career in the House of Commons, never part of Government, but he was often involved 'behind the scenes', smoothing over difficulties between colleagues, always ready to speak quietly and in favour of the Government's less popular measures. All-in-all he was something of a 'wheeler-dealer' in the whole business of party politics and managed never to make for himself any enemies. Perhaps it was his previous career as a solicitor which gave him these skills, enabling him to smooth over the argumentative style of some of his Parliamentary colleagues. When George first 'entered the House,' as the expression had it, it was an older M.P., Joshua Rosenthal, who took him under his 'wing,' showed him the ropes so to speak. From this fatherly friendship sprang a marriage and on the first anniversary of George taking his seat, he was married to Elaine, the oldest daughter of Joshua. At the same time as the marriage came some unexpected money. Elaine had recently turned twenty-five and with this significant birthday she was allowed to take control of monies which had been bequeathed to her at birth by a distant aunt, one Juliette Quemsby, and of whom none of the current members of the family had much knowledge. Of course to call her 'a distant aunt' may just have been for convenience as she might have been a cousin or a relative that had 'arrived,' joined the family because of a marriage. There was some rumour that Juliette hadn't seen eye-to-eye with the younger members of her family. The money for Elaine had been invested in a trust fund, a fund which over the twenty-five years of its existence had done rather well, giving her a sizable capital fund as well as a significant income. This income was sufficient for her not to have to work so she was able to devote herself to children, three arrived over the first five years of their marriage, be involved in various charitable activities which many of the M.P.s' wives were very actively involved in. She also wrote and to the envy of others she didn't consider this hard work at all, and successfully and regularly published a goodly number of novels, romantic love stories with sufficient sex in them to hold the readers' attention without her ever being accused of writing anything remotely pornographic; such an accusation would have been thought quite unseemly as far as some of the older ladies of the Party were concerned. Her income was also sufficient for her to be able to help George with various expenses incurred while he pursued his 'behind the scenes' work with his fellow colleagues. Whilst he himself was almost teetotal, much of this expenditure took place in the many bars and restaurants made available to members of both Houses of Parliament.

Chapter Two
Same Family, More Political

1990s onwards

By the late 1990s it was very obvious that Sir George and family had thrived. His father-in-law, Joshua Reynolds, had retired from the Commons and now sat, if somewhat infrequently, in the House of Lords. George was clearly a fixture in the lower House and whose time was much sought by Members of both sides of the Commons, and occasionally by various Members of the Government who from time to time needed to avoid a little personal scandal entering the public domain. His work as a solicitor was very limited and confined to quiet but lucrative cases. His wife had continued to write, producing a successful best-seller every two or three years and between chapters kept up her activities with Parliamentary charities. Their three children entered the twenty-first century having excelled at school and university. Vincent, born 1974, was the oldest, studying for a Ph.D. in a very abstruse aspect of Astronomy; something to do with black holes was all his father could ever say when friends asked, hoping that nobody would ask him what a black hole was. The second child, born less than twelve months later was Beryl and she had taken a first in English Literature and was endeavouring to follow her mother's career as a writer but using her second name, Jayne, after her aunt. As Jayne St John she may have successfully written and published, but the family always called her Beryl. Initially she established herself as a short story writer and found herself taken up by many of the monthly magazines. The first short story which she had published was a Christmas tale, entitled 'Who Would be a M.P.' For a very brief summary, the following suffices - *'An Elderly M.P. suffered the loss of his Rolex Oyster wrist watch which he had inherited from his father who was killed when his Spitfire crashed as he came into land in 1942. The watch was snatched by a seasonal chancer'* - gives the main outline. Her mother's publishers were happy to take Jayne on when she started producing longer works and were more than happy to hang on to her when her first full novel was serialised for television. She managed a successful mix of romance and crime and this made for an entertaining visual presentation helped no doubt by the occasional scene of a sexual nature and on which filming Jayne had very little influence.

James Peter Edward was the third child, nearly four years Vincent's junior and he had completed his education with a first in the traditional sphere of Politics, Philosophy and Economics and was planning a career in politics but as it seemed that his father was intent on staying a member of the House of Commons for a few more years, James knew it would be necessary to try and endear himself to a local Party somewhere other than Surrey and win the seat by his own efforts rather than be the fourth member of the St John family to 'inherit' one. Traditionally, would-be M.P.s often stood at first attempt for a seat where their chances of success were extremely limited but perhaps on this occasion a little of the St John Parliamentary success rubbed off, because with his first application for a seat and where he was one of a short list of six, he encountered success. It was a by-election for a North Lincolnshire seat, safe for the Conservatives, so James Peter Edward St John was returned at his first attempt and so joined his father in the House of Commons in 2004. At the time of this electoral victory James was engaged to be married to a childhood friend, Rhiannon Lewis. She and her parents had moved from Wales, becoming near neighbours to James's family and for a few months Rhiannon and James were in the same class at the local primary school. When James was at Oxford, Rhiannon was at Edinburgh where she studied History. Her original intention had been to become a teacher, but when James won his seat for Parliament she decided that teaching wouldn't make a very convenient career. Quite by chance an alternative career more or less landed in her lap. The father of a university friend of hers worked for a London publishing house which specialised in history and after a few conversations Rhiannon found herself employed as one of their advisers.

For this M.P., James St John, a Government role came his way when the Conservatives were returned to power in 2010, the first time a member of the St John family was thus employed. Initially he performed the role of an unpaid Parliamentary Private Secretary and he moved between departments, acquiring useful experience. He took some time to be appointed to the most junior of paid ministerial ranks, partly because he had been less than enthusiastic regarding Brexit. He had clearly supported the stance taken by David Cameron and then Theresa May. He more than made up for this slow start and by the end of the 2020s he had been appointed Foreign Secretary and First Secretary of State. Rhiannon was thrilled with her husband's cabinet appointment as were their two sons, Edward, the elder, and Joshua, now grown up and both working in different aspects of law, Edward in commercial law and was a young Q.C., and Joshua wasn't that long in becoming a Q.C. They were both married and with families, but they endeavoured to keep a low profile where their father's illustrious career was concerned.

James's father was not in the House to witness his youngest son's splendid appointment, having retired at the 2019 General Election. Some months before he told his local party officials of his intention to retire, he had become worried that he might lose the party whip as he had been voting against the Government on several of the issues arising from the Brexit negotiations and were he to lose the whip, deselection would follow and an ignominious end to his Parliamentary career would be the result. Wisely, he chose retirement instead. Both now in their middle eighties, George and Elaine still enjoyed good health but never-the-less chose to live quietly at Norstead Towers. Fortunately they had sufficient capital and income and could employ a small staff so that the various visits from different members of their family caused them little effort beyond being friendly, enjoying prestigious conversation and staying awake during some lengthy meals.

The Right Honourable James Peter Edward St John, P.C., M.P., M.A., was highly intelligent, made a thoughtful and imaginative member of the Government and certainly helped to steer the Party away from some of its occasional extremist tendencies which were often given unfortunate airings at annual conferences. Without ever being critical of the decision of the British Public in 2016 to leave the European

Union he did manage to make successful and subtle moves with his European colleagues to smooth over long-standing difficulties which had arisen in the early post-Brexit days. His announcements in the House of Commons on any of these particular issues were so low-key in style that they became matters of fact with hardly any M.P.s noticing.

James got on extremely well with the Prime Minster, The Right Honourable Anthony May P.C., M.P., not to be confused in any way with a previous Prime Minster of the same surname and nor were they related. James and Anthony were not close friends but they did meet together frequently to discuss aspects of Government policy and occasionally, Anthony, together with his wife, Laurel, spent a weekend at Norstead Towers. Rhiannon and Laurel got on very well and could chat away for hours. Sometimes they were joined at these weekend gatherings by Daniel Divine, the Home Secretary, a good friend of James from their University days. Daniel was not married but he was often accompanied by his secretary, Angela, or one of his advisors. In the labelling of politicians Daniel would be described as a somewhat more right-wing individual than James although it could be said that had more to do with his being obliged to support a strong ant-immigration policy.

Chapter Three
One Funeral and a Wedding

About 2024

If one had something of an individual spirit, there was much to be said for being almost alone in the world at the age of twenty-one; anybody you knew was very inclined to feel guilty on one's behalf and do as much for you as possible. Although Audrey Ponsonby didn't feel particularly lonely she was very alone in this world. Her parents, both of whom had been only children, were rather elderly when she came into their lives. Sadly her father was killed in a car crash when she was ten years old, and her mother, now in her early sixties was beginning to show signs of early on-set dementia. Living now in the out-skirts of Reading, Audrey had been warned by her G.P. that her mother was fast approaching a point in her health when she would be unsafe if left on her own, and that in a year or so she would probably need residential care. She had noticed some problems, an increasing trend towards argumentativeness, a lessening of personal care, avoiding neighbours and friends of long-standing. The strangest change in her behaviour was that her mother had taken up smoking again, having given up over thirty years previously. Audrey had never known her mother as a smoker and she hated the smell of cigarette smoke. She found this change horrible but if she made any mention, Audrey was soon on the receiving end of a very sharp tongue, something else that she had never experienced when growing up. She took very seriously what her mother's G.P. had said but was at a loss as to know what to do. On the one hand it was very worrying but on the other, she couldn't wait for this long vacation to end and get back to Oxford.

Audrey was about to return for her final year, reading modern languages. She had recently returned from one year spent in Paris and this period of study had really lifted her standard in her chosen study of

French, so she was hoping to crown this with a double first when she completed her finals nine months hence. Her second language was Italian and in this she was also extremely talented. For now, she attempted to put to one side this large worry regarding her mother, hoping that with a watchful eye from kindly neighbours, the local Vicar and friends from the Church, she would get to the end of the academic year without too much difficulty on this particular domestic front. Sadly, she hadn't taken account of friends and neighbours, rather like herself, wanting to avoid her mother's company.

In the end, the problem of her mother solved itself, if shockingly and with considerable horror. Audrey hadn't been back at Oxford but a week or so when she was contacted by local police. In the early hours of that morning, the fire brigade had been called to her mother's address, the house was fully ablaze and although her mother had been brought out alive, her burns were so extensive she was not expected to survive. Audrey did reach the hospital in time to speak to her mother but any response was minimal and she died within twenty-four hours of being rescued from the inferno.

At this point in time Audrey now really did feel alone; she had nobody and apart from her possessions back at Oxford, she had little else and not much money. The fire had caused a total loss and it seemed likely she would inherit nothing but a plot of land. The local vicar and friends from the church rallied round when it came to arranging a funeral; it was a pity perhaps that they had not rallied a little more when her mother was still alive. The funeral service was held at the crematorium as she knew there would be few people attending and in this surmise she was totally correct. A very small number of Audrey's university friends attended along with neighbours and a few members of the church congregation. Giving Audrey most support was her college tutor, Dr Rufus Sutton, and immediately the service was over he drove her back to Oxford. To show her appreciation Audrey took him out for a meal that evening and they were joined by her Oxford friends who had driven out to the crematorium that afternoon. If her late mother's friends thought the lack of any post-funeral gathering was unusual, even rude, Audrey was never to find out.

The family solicitor, an elderly gentleman who was kindly in manner, amused Audrey because he was typical in appearance of any actor who had ever played the part of a tight-lipped and reticent solicitor such as would appear in television murder dramas. The similarity was only in appearance and certainly not in manner as he was exceedingly helpful. Audrey had not attended the inquest so she knew nothing of the details of the fire inspector's report. With his report the coroner had been able to bring in a verdict of accidental death. The fire had started in her mother's bedroom, with the likely cause being that she had fallen asleep while smoking. As well as explaining these details the solicitor was able to inform her that she was the sole beneficiary under the terms of the will of her late father; her mother had only retained a life interest. He was not able to tell Audrey whether there was any insurance as far as the house and its contents were concerned as enquiries were still being made. In any event the land where the house stood was probably worth two hundred thousand pounds, quite possibly more which of course would be hers. Local enquiries had so far led him to understand that her late mother had various bank and building society accounts totalling nearly seventy-five thousand pounds. He explained that there may be other investments which he knew nothing about but appropriate enquiries would be made.

The solicitor assured Audrey that her mother's bank would release money so that immediate expenses could be met and he explained finally that it would take a few months to settle the estate completely. If she were happy for him to do so. he would act for the conveyancing of the land sale and he recommended that she should put the sale in the hands of one of the local estate agents after first obtaining a number of valuations. Finally, when everything had been settled and all commissions paid, Audrey inherited well over half a million pounds and this was after all required deductions had been made. The bank had been able to establish quickly that there had been insurance, paid by direct debit. They also processed the sale of some shares, owned by her late father but passed to her mother. She had been receiving annually the dividend income and this information was also revealed from the bank account details.

The final settlement of her mother's affairs took the form of an amazingly splendid credit to her bank account and this stunning event coincided with Audrey's completion of her degree. As she had hoped and her tutor expected, she was awarded a double first. Two of her friends were awarded similar degrees and suitable celebrations followed. It was a large group of graduates and tutors, who more or less took over a favourite local pub for dinner and much wine. The publican was thrilled with the booking because he had been contacted a day or so before and given a couple of thousand pounds to cover the bill. There was an assurance of more if necessary including additional funds for a tip. The only proviso was that there should be absolute confidentiality and with this the publican was most happy to agree. He explained to the party when they arrived that no-one need open a 'tab' for their individual costs, as a secret admirer of them all had settled the entire bill in advance. It was certainly a case of 'eat, drink and be merry'! It was difficult to determine who was most thrilled, the publican and his staff or the guests.

With no firm plans for the immediate future, Audrey stayed in Oxford. Her friendship with her tutor, Rufus, continued. They had been 'seeing' each other since well before her mother's death. Initially, Rufus had been nothing if not discrete, but once degrees had been awarded, their romance could blossom on quite an open basis and it wasn't long before they each gave up their somewhat meagre individual accommodation and moved to somewhere more comfortable for their joint place of residence. Like many of their friends and acquaintances they were 'living together' in blissful happiness.

Although Audrey didn't return to her home town she did write to the Vicar to thank him for taking the funeral service, and she sent a contribution for the restoration fund. A kindly note of thanks brought to an end their correspondence. Audrey didn't get any employed work but she soon found herself giving private language lessons to undergraduates, local school pupils taking GCE A levels, helping some of Rufus's students as they came up to the exam season. It was while she was talking to him about some of his students she discovered that he was thinking of changing his job.

'What would you say if I left the university and got a different job? I fancy having a go at getting into the upper echelons of the Civil Service. Might try for the Foreign Office.'

'That's a surprise, sounds rather exciting. What about money, shall you drop a bit?'

'No, I would probably earn more and the prospects would certainly be better. I think I'll give it a go. What do you think Audrey?'

'A good idea and you may get some overseas postings.'

'Looking to the future Audrey, how would you like to become Mrs Sutton?'

'First of all Audrey looked totally stunned, then her face transformed into quite the most radiant of smiles and finally she confirmed her agreement in a most demonstrative style.

'That was an exquisitely passionate 'Yes' my darling Audrey,' acknowledged Rufus. With equal quality they kissed again.

Chapter Four
Leaving Academia

About 2025

Will you come through Dr Sutton, please? Do take a seat. I'm Miss Tomlinson and with my colleague Mr Horton, we're both from the Foreign Office. Mr Ratisbon is from the Home Office. We've read various reports which have been made following the preliminary interviews and meetings. You've expressed some interesting ideas and we would like to explore those a little more as well as some more general matters. Mr Ratisbon, you mentioned that you would 'kick-off' if you'll pardon the expression.'

'Dr Sutton, I believe your thesis for your PhD was on Medieval French. Interesting as that probably was, I wonder how you see that as a background to a career in the Foreign Office?'
'I don't actually see it as a background to any career. What was important in that piece of study was the methodology, the nature of the research and the techniques involved. In general terms those are very important skills and useful in so many areas of work. I wouldn't be surprised if my thesis were never to be read again, won't disappoint me, but who knows how I might go on to use the various skills which I acquired and developed. Any new Government initiative always needs detailed study to understand how it might affect those members of the public to whom it is targeted. Such study has to be thorough, original and based on fresh research. To rely on supposition alone can be dangerous. My thinking on this goes wider and I'm not one who feels that university study should be related to immediate career prospects. Three years at university provide great opportunities for young people to broaden their education, experience, understanding regardless of whether they are studying media studies or sociology, to give two examples of the many subjects which often come in for misplaced criticism.'

'Taking the argument a little further many students in my tutorials have been rather surprised to find themselves attending discussions on current news, recent programmes on television. Of course, the discussions took place in French and proved an excellent way to extend vocabulary. Along the way I might have interrupted the discussion to draw attention to an aspect of language – grammar, syntax, colloquialism for example. Sorry, got rather carried away with something I have long felt strongly about; there is too much misplaced criticism of much higher education.'

'And how might you use those thoughts within the Foreign Office, Dr Sutton?' asked Miss Tomlinson.

'Quite straight forwardly I think. I hope that doesn't sound arrogant but basic knowledge and understanding has to be given a leading place. Can I use Ireland as an example? That is a country with a long history of troubles and its partition is closer to the end of that history. It would be an unwise diplomat who didn't make himself very familiar indeed with that country's history before attempting to deal with present day issues and that is a consideration which can relate to many situations around the world. There is no substitute for accurate and informed background knowledge and research.'

'Thank you Dr Sutton. Mr Horton has some questions.'

'Dr Sutton, you are a talented linguist, French, German. Do you have other languages, not necessarily of course to the same level of ability?'

'I have some Spanish, studied it until I was sixteen. In the lower sixth I made an attempt to teach myself Swedish. I had success and my knowledge of German helped. Of course, since my marriage, I don't have to worry about Italian. It goes without saying that behind all my language skills is a sound knowledge of Latin.'

'Have you ever acted as an official translator Dr Sutton?'

'No, not in any official role. Obviously, unofficially I've helped at meetings, international student exchanges, accompanying overseas tours, nothing unusual or out of the ordinary. Anything official on an international government to government basis generally needs two translators. It can be very awkward if any of the participants at international negotiations choose to use a language other than their first language. It's not unknown for such individuals not to be as good as they think they are at the language and this can lead to difficulties especially when colloquial or idiomatic expressions are used. At such level of work subtle nuances in use of language can be extremely important and if the translators don't notice them they can lead to awkward embarrassments later on in negotiations.'

Rufus enjoyed all these exchanges although he found it difficult to evaluate his own level of performance or success. There was some discussion about international news and this brought out the fact that he was familiar with several of the main European newspapers, indeed he used them occasionally in tutorials. There was one question on personal opinions. How did he feel about issues which he might be in disagreement with the Government of the day. His response was to see that as an inevitability which would be difficult to avoid, although he would be surprised if such issues were often on fundamental matters of principle. This led to a question about his opinion on leaving the European Union. Rufus chose to be honest: given his interest in all matters 'European' he thought the referendum had been bad for the UK although he was not surprised by the result. He imagined most Civil Servants were well used to the result long before it became a matter of fact and even then there was considerable time before it actually took effect. Even so, Rufus wondered how many of the sub-issues, matters which never made the press, would be successfully resolved, quietly and away from the head-lines of the media. Likewise, he couldn't imagine that the future would see an end to all European co-operation involving the UK so that there would always be matters requiring a negotiated 'in' or 'out' response. Would such matters become major Parliamentary issues? Only time would tell.

Mr Ratisbon wanted to know how much use he made of computers and this became something of a general discussion. As it happened, Rufus had some strong views. 'My computer is never switched off and I couldn't do my work without one. Obviously the University has its own programs, two main divisions of activity. All information regarding students and their individual progress is recorded, essay grades, examination results, matters individual to subject areas. Our departmental administration is coordinated through the computer. There are strict protocols regarding confidentiality and maintenance so that any technical problems are only handled by University employees; no matter the skill, the likes of me for example must not deal with matters technical and there are potentially serious consequences should the rule be deliberately breached. This side of computer usage is only as good as the program development and this is never allowed to be at a stand-still. System updating is vital and that has to be true in all areas where the use of computers is central to an organisation's progress. Dare I say that I have read enough examples to know that this is an area where the Civil Service doesn't have an unblemished reputation. Because it is a colossal organisation with a great variety of computer usage, and that being so, program and system updating has to be given absolute priority. For example, a change of Government often leads to some changes within or between departments, but the same changes are not always plotted through with sufficient care as far as computer programs are concerned so that within one Ministry individual sections are unable to communicate – that is, the computer systems were ignored when the integration of two departments was planned and implemented. Whenever I have read of these problems it has always struck me that as far any Government's use of computers was concerned, there was something of an uncoordinated piece meal approach. Is that still an area of difficulty?'

The panel replied with nodding of heads and no one member was willing to contradict Rufus beyond a general, 'well, progress is still being made.'

'It doesn't sound as if the progress is in any way ruthlessly successful, I apologise if my response is in anyway unfair.' There was no response from the panel; silence said all perhaps. Not connected with University administration, I use computers in a general way for research and that can be marvellous for cross-referring information so that one can establish an unbiased view-point, very important as I have already mentioned. All information has to be corroborated by using two or more sources.'

'Do you undertake much research in your field?' That question had the tone of, 'I can't imagine a language lecturer does much by way of research.'

'I think you would be very surprised Mr Horton. I never keep my study of language separate from the culture in which it exists and develops so I'm continually looking into the source of different expressions and idioms, regional variants. Just like English, no language stands still. Consider how 'text speech' has influenced made stream English usage in recent years. English teachers will tell you that it has made aspects of their work very tricky, particularly the marking of essays and how to allow for the use of 'cutting edge' idioms, if one can express it like that. I ought to point out that my research is always making use of foreign programs and this causes me to be extra vigilant regarding computer security. I won't suggest that I'm never off the computer but it remains available for immediate use for as long as I am on the premises.'

The interview gradually came to a close and the members of the interviewing panel were very cordial in thanking him for his time, wished him well for the future and pointed out that it might be several weeks before he received any notification regarding the outcome of his application. Glancing at his watch Rufus was surprised to discover that the interview had lasted the best part of ninety minutes. Thinking about it all on his train journey back to Oxford he realised that it hadn't been as intellectually demanding as he had expected and he wondered if that had been his fault, were his responses as erudite as they might have been.

Chapter Five
A Very Lonely Ending

2030

At about 10.00pm one night, an elderly lady was tottering along the middle of a deserted South London High Street. Truth be told, to say that she was elderly was wrong, looked elderly was decidedly more correct, because the accumulated effects of drugs, cigarettes and alcohol added about twenty-five years of unhappiness and left her looking like one in her mid-sixties rather than very early forties. She was well known in the area as one who shuffled about, but as to who she was nobody knew. The name she went by was Agnes but if anyone called out to her then the name was Aggie. Whether that was her real name nobody knew, she possessed no papers which gave any facts about her past, so the Social Services of the area were no wiser than the general public. Only using a first name it was impossible to use official records, so who this Agnes turned out to be was anybody's guess. Staff from Social Services had tried hard to talk to Agnes about her past, choosing times when she seemed sober, but Agnes had a brain which appeared somewhat fuzzy when it came to facts – she was totally incapable of saying anything about her past, no memory of parents or siblings and she knew nothing about previous addresses. Occasionally she had mentioned another name which sounded like Linda but when staff asked her whether Linda was what she said, she would shake her head in denial and say it again but just slightly differently and nobody managed to fathom this additional mystery regarding her name. They tried saying the very few surnames which started with the letters L I N D, there weren't many and Agnes responded to none of them. 'Lindner' was the nearest sounding like 'Linda' but still the mystery remained. Whether she was just a very simple individual or whether her brain had become damaged by alcohol and substance abuse they couldn't tell. All that could be deduced was that she was reasonably content and that she could just about manage a solo existence. Currently she had one of two rooms in the attic of a three- story terraced house with a shared bathroom between the two. Social Services paid the rent for this and from time to time sent an official to check that her existence was at an acceptable level such that she didn't have to be moved into residential accommodation which would have been far more expensive.

There was no particular reason she was tottering along the High Street as she did that every night, her last bit of slow exercise before she climbed three flights of stairs to her attic bed. The narrow bed was one piece of a very limited supply of furniture. In addition there was a wardrobe which wobbled alarmingly every time it was opened, a small table alongside the one very grubby window, a hard and uncomfortable looking chair from which most of the last layer of paint was peeling and finally another chair, a really battered and torn upholstered arm chair through which anyone would feel the springs. One of its four castor wheels was missing so it was unsteady as well as uncomfortable. The bedding comprised one sheet drawn over a very old mattress, an uncovered pillow and two uncovered duvets so when Aggie was in bed she was at least warm. About every couple of months the Social Services visitor had the task of replacing sheet, pillow and one of the duvets – these were sourced from a local charitable depot. The three items being removed were bagged and sealed and eventually found their way to an incinerator. There was no fire of any sort in the bedroom and when the owner of the property was told to provide heat, storage heaters were switched on and the cost of running these was reflected in the rents. Social Services made the decision as to switching on heat because all but one of the residents was another version of an Agnes.

Unknown of course to Agnes, but this particular night of tottering was to be her last. Suddenly, interrupting the silence of the High Street, was the screeching of tyres as a car hurtled round a corner and swept Agnes off her feet and projected her into a nearby shop doorway. The drunken youngster who was the very unskilled driver, immediately lost control and the vehicle went through the windows of the same shop. Infinitely more skilled was the Police Officer who was at the wheel of the following car. He had his siren blaring and lights still flashing as he parked while a fellow officer made radio contact for ambulance and additional support. The immediate outcome of this accident was firstly the switching on of a few lights by nearby residents, secondly the arrest of one youth and another man, a little older, both bruised and shaken and both would be charged with the usual list of offences associated with such an incident. The Sergeant in charge had little sympathy for his two hooligans as he locked them up for the night. A bit shaken up they may have been, but it didn't stop them whispering about money and payments when they were being taken back to the Police Station. The most serious outcome was, of course, the death of Agnes. Later outcomes would include court appearances and punishments for two young criminals. The conversation about money had been quite forgotten. The Magistrate made the usual and expected speech about disgraceful behaviour of the two young men as they were remanded in prison on charges of manslaughter. There was an enquiry into the police chase and subsequently this exonerated the driver of the police car, P.C. Brian Evans.

A further difficulty for the police arose when they realised that nobody knew who Agnes was. They accepted the information from Social Services that 'Agnes' was the name she used, but as to who she really was by birth was a complete unknown. A final search of her bedroom revealed no further information, local people who waved and spoke to her had no real information either, she was just their local oddity and a check through finger prints and DNA data bases also drew a blank. The pathologist said that the state of her teeth was such that almost certainly no dental record would exist. Subsequent to all these enquiries was that the temporary if not final resting place for Agnes was cold storage. The Police Officer in charge, Sergeant Vaughan, had the files put away knowing from experience, that cases involving unidentified bodies could remain unsolved for quite some time, even years. He made a note in his computer diary to review the matter in a few weeks because a decision as to burial would have to be made regardless of whether the question of identification was resolved or not. Running alongside the main investigation was a secondary one, tracing the owner of the stolen car. That in itself was easy enough but curious was fathoming any obvious reason for the theft, as the car was a twenty-year-old Ford Fiesta. No disrespect to Ford Motors or Fiesta models in particular, but the stolen car had a very high mileage on the clock, its interior was fairly worn and there were a few patches of old body-work damage still clearly visible despite the damage from the crash. It was the morning after when the police called on the owners, an elderly couple, Mr and Mrs Ernest Caroldine. They lived on a road some two miles from the scene of the crash and where most residents parked their cars in front gardens or at the kerbside. The only reason there had been a police chase was because the sharp-eyed Constable Evans, driving slowly along Eastern Way was suspicious about two guys fiddling with the car which was at that point in a front garden. He carried on, pulling in a little further along the road and watched. When he heard the noise of breaking glass he got out of his car only to witness the Fiesta being backed out onto the road and being driven off in the opposite direction. By the time Brian Evans had completed a turn and started to give chase it was hardly surprising that the eventual crash was a couple of miles away.

It was Mr Caroldine who answered the door, elderly as he was, he didn't fail to notice that his car was missing.

'Mr Caroldine, I'm Sergeant Vaughan and this is Constable Evans. We have called about your car, a 2010 Ford Fiesta, which was stolen last night and involved in a serious accident in which an elderly woman was killed.'

'I don't know anything about that, but I've just noticed that my car has been stolen.' Turning round he called out: 'Emily, Emily, come here, our car has been stolen. The police are here.'

'What did you say, Ern?'

'Car's been stolen and Police are here. Hurry up.'

'Sir, it's eleven o'clock, have you only just noticed that your car is missing.'

'It's not missing, my Ernest has gone out in it.'

'Emily, I'm Ernest and I haven't gone out in the car. It's been stolen.'

'Stolen? Have you called the police, Ernest?'

'Mrs Caroldine, can I help you, I'm Sergeant Vaughan and I have called to enquire about your car which was stolen last night.'

'But my Ern was out in it earlier.'

'Emily!' Everyone jumped at Ernest's shout. 'Emily, shall you put the kettle on and make some tea.' This was said in a gentle whisper and Emily turned and went in the direction of the kitchen. 'Sorry about that Officer. Sometimes it's the only way. You had better come in.'

Constable Evans thought he would go and find Emily and help her with some tea, perhaps be able to calm the situation a little. He left his Sergeant to continue the conversation with Ernest.

'Mr Caroldine, is there any reason you can think of as to why your car was stolen?'

'No, I can't. It's no more than a cheap run-about, all that I can afford. My previous car got written off a few weeks ago, had a crash on a round-about, not far away, the Banstead Round-about. Me and the other driver only had third party insurance. My car was another Fiesta, very similar to the one that's been stolen, same colour, a few years older but in better condition. Came from Banstead Garage. The other car was a vintage Rover and the owner was very angry, said the crash was my fault. It wasn't as I was already on the round-about.'

'Was anyone hurt?'

'No, we were both just angry. From what you say it seems I may be having to find another replacement car.'

'I'm sorry to say but I fear you are probably correct. With a bit of luck the garage might be able to find you something similar again.'

'It's the money, not sure I can afford to buy another. I can walk all right but Emily isn't too good and I'm always having to take her to medical appointments. I'm very glad my remaining days of driving don't take me into having to start buying electric, wouldn't know where to find that sort of money.'

Just then Constable Evans appeared carrying a tray with four mugs of tea and a plate of biscuits.

'Look dear, this young man has made us some tea. Did you get what you wanted when you were out earlier?'

'Emily, I haven't been out, the car has been stolen.'

'I know you were out earlier because the car was gone, that always mean you were out.'

'This is your tea, Emily, the one you put sugar in.' Constable Evans passed her the mug of tea and also offered the plate of biscuits.'

'Thank you young man. Ern, this man is very kind.'

'Yes dear.'

Sergeant Vaughan knew he had to keep the conversation going long enough to drink the tea, he didn't want to cause any offence. He let Ernest show him the back garden where he grew prize Chrysanthemums. There was also a well-cared for and productive vegetable plot. He and Ernest managed to exchange a few tips on matters horticultural while they finished their tea. When they went back in Brian was just beginning to wash up and they added their mugs to the bowl. It looked as if Brian was washing up from breakfast as well.

'Look Ern, you won't have to do the washing up, he is a good boy.'

After a few smiles and hand-shakes the two police officers were able to leave. 'Drive me to the Banstead Round-about, I want to pop into the garage. You can look round the showroom and I'll chat to Mr Banstead.'

Brian Evans did as instructed and looked at the various secondhand cars on offer, actually he noticed a Fiesta very similar to the one involved in the crash, same colour and similar age. Just then he noticed a mechanic getting out of the passenger side. 'Very good car this if you want something   inexpensive, really cheap actually, beautifully kept but very high mileage.'

P.C. Evans explained himself and mentioned the trouble that Mr Caroldine was in.'

'Old Ern, that's a pity. He needs a car for his wife and they don't have much money. I saw the crash over there when he lost his previous Fiesta. We had the other bloke's Rover in the workshop for a while but the bodywork was going to be just too expensive. Mr Struthers owned it and was he furious. Mind you, it was his fault, didn't look what he was doing. I thought he was going to hit Ern, he was so angry. I promised Ern that I would track down a suitable car for him and then I let him sit in the office for a bit. Mr Struthers went off muttering all sorts of threats, said he would come back when we had worked out an estimate. It was quiet just then, so I told the boss I was going to run Mr Caroldine home.'

'Nice to chat, I better go and wait for my Sergeant. He's talking to your boss about something.'

When they got back to the police station Sergeant Vaughan asked his police constable to run a check on one Alan Struthers. From what Mr Banstead had told him he didn't like the sound of the guy and he had also heard that it was Struthers' fault that cost him his Rover.

'Did you have a hunch about Mr Struthers, Sergeant? He's got a bit of a record, minor acts of violence in local pubs, a drink driving offence a few years back, police called to a domestic incident at his home but no action, complaints from neighbours about bad language and temper. All-in-all, not a very nice person.'

'I wonder if our two car thieves know Mr Struthers, think I'll go and have a word with them before the custody Sergeant bids them farewell.'

P.C. Brian Evans was left to write up a few notes which didn't take long. He found himself thinking about the Caroldines, and the difficulties Ernest must be experiencing with his Emily. The more he thought the more he realised how tough life can be when the problems of old-age strike. He would talk to his wife about Emily, see if they couldn't perhaps organise them some help. His Mavis could be good at that sort of thing. They hadn't got any children and it pleased her to be useful, to help people in need, sometimes cost them money but always money well spent.

'I thought so!' Sergeant Vaughan looked pleased with himself. 'Those two toe-rags were paid to steal that car last night. That was why they were muttering about money. Tomorrow, Constable, we'll be paying Mr Struthers a visit, his vengeful ways might just cost him his liberty.'

Chapter Six
Banana'd Anniversary

Laurel looked up over her first cup of coffee and passed a card to Anthony, 'Happy Anniversary darling. One word of caution, dear, open with care.'

The Prime Minister did as his good wife instructed and slipped from a stiff envelope a lightly coloured illustration, a cartoon sketch, showing Anthony standing near his desk, cup of coffee in one hand and a banana skin just parting company with his other; below was what appeared to be a gold-plated waste-paper bin. Looking on was obviously an exceedingly superior Civil Servant and he was commenting: 'You're a long way from slipping on one of those, Prime Minister.'

The portrait of Anthony was delightful, captured him in a very contented mood. The Civil Servant had just the merest hint of exaggeration to all those facial characteristics of this most senior, of Senior Civil Servants. 'Darling, how did you acquire such a delightful card and what's this small signature across the bottom corner, Jimmy Gillray?'

'I acquired it by giving £250 to an up-and-coming cartoonist who has the very good fortune to own to such a splendid name – quite genuine I might add. I met him at a recent exhibition of some of his work together with items from other rising artists. The fee was my suggestion and as I liked his work and I thought it would all amount to a very good piece of publicity for him.'

'I'm sure if I hold this up at my next Prime Minister's Question Time the cartoon will be worth at least the fee and the publicity should bring young Jimmy several lucrative commissions. It is also very funny and delightful so I presume you're planning to have it nicely framed.'

'He based the sketch of you on various newspaper photographs; the hint of familiarity for your PPS he gleaned from a secret mobile photograph I managed to obtain a few weeks back. The frame is all ready to use, just as soon as you have finished waving the cartoon around the House of Commons.'

'Well, thank you my dear,' and suiting his actions to the sentiment, he stepped round to his wife's end of the breakfast table and gave her the gentlest of kisses.

'What are the more mundane plans for the day, darling? I'm sure the political pundits of Central Office have something suitable arranged by way of photo opportunities and television interviews.'

'You are absolutely spot on but the finally agreed programme has yet to be passed my way, but nothing they do will beat this wonderful gift. When I go down, I shall stand it on my desk for today, so just a few privileged people will see it. Now I must just finish this coffee, tidy up, collect a few things and be on my way, but not forgetting the Gillray.'

Laurel supervised the final check as to her husband's appearance, and so with a copy of The Times under his arm and still smiling at the cartoon image, Anthony went downstairs. That was the plan and it was quite successful until he reached the last flight of stairs. Nobody saw precisely what happened but from the subsequent injuries it was thought that he twisted his right ankle at the top step and not holding the banister, he lost his balance and pitched head first down the whole of the last flight of stairs, landing on his left side all the way. He was unconscious and remained so while all around him pandemonium broke out and whatever the assembled group of party pundits thought they were going to do when Anthony joined them was lost in this chaos. Whoever had the good sense to summon immediate help was never known but the police officer on duty just outside the front door and who heard the row did look in briefly and was seen to be on his mobile phone. Not knowing whether there was a major security incident on their hands all manner of people, including armed response officers, rushed to the scene. Cutting through the chaos three actions of real effectiveness occurred. Laurel May, on hearing her husband's cry and the ensuing row while still standing on the top landing, rushed down and in the most imperious of tones cleared people away from her unconscious husband. The second event was the arrival of ambulance and paramedics to the front door and with authority equal to that of Laurel cleared their pathway through to Anthony May. The front-door police officer was the source of the third action: with superb courage, unbelievable determination and using his loudest voice, this officer ordered all non-medical personnel to leave the downstairs hallway. He deserved a medal for his effectiveness for only two people dared to remain. He tapped them on their shoulders and spoke within inches of their faces, 'Out!' delivered with a voice such as could quell a football riot. Whoever they were, they have never come forward to acknowledge their disobedience of the police officer's first command, knowing that the second command echoed the length of Downing Street.

It didn't take the paramedics long to realise that the Prime Minister had sustained several fractures, a cluster related to his left shoulder area and at least one fracture to his left leg, probably his hip. In all probability there were cracked ribs and severe bruising elsewhere down his left side. Responses to immediate checks on heart, blood pressure and oxygen were satisfactory, stabilising and showing no cause for immediate alarm. Eye responses to light indicated that he was not deeply unconscious, in fact he was stirring a little and likely to come round. The Prime Minister had landed such that there was little difficulty in immobilising him and placing him on a stretcher for transfer to ambulance. Provision of oxygen continued, leads were connected to enable all vital signs and responses to be monitored. By the time Laurel May appeared, ambulance and accompanying police escort were ready to leave for St Thomas's Hospital where the emergency trauma team were on special alert.

From the first police car following the ambulance, Laurel telephoned her good friend Rhiannon, wife of James St John, the Foreign Secretary. She gave Rhiannon the briefest of summaries and told her to contact James, as he was First Secretary of State. As she finished that call they were arriving at St Thomas's so she left the police car just as soon as it stopped and immediately took up a position such that she could accompany her husband wherever he was taken, and nobody, but nobody, would tell her to move aside. Anthony was taken to an emergency room where the team awaiting his arrival started to listen to all the hand-over information while other personnel attached leads from Anthony to the fixed monitors and carried out an immediate check on all of his vital responses, which check seemed as satisfactory to them as it did to the paramedics when they first checked at No. 10. Among the group of doctors Laurel suddenly recognised her regular physician, Anthony's as well. She was surprised but impressed with somebody's efficiency.

'Mrs May, can I have a word. I'm John Carpenter, Consultant Trauma Surgeon, obviously you know your own doctor, Malcolm Davis, exceptionally good of him to get here so quickly. In view of what we have been told we need to send your husband for X-rays and also a CT scan to check on his head injury, he was unconscious for a while but signs are that he has sustained no internal brain injury. When that's completed he can be returned to a private room similar this, but with better security so that would probably be the best place for you to wait. There is an adjoining room for close family members. While we are speaking security officers are checking the rooms.'

'When we have the X-rays we can determine the best approach for the two sets of fractures, left shoulder and left leg, most probably the hip; it is quite possible that surgery may be required for either or both. The CT scan will tell us if there is any skull fracture or whether there is likely to be concussion which will need monitoring. Your Physician has been able to assure us as to your husband's usual good health and that is excellent information and matches the information we are gathering from the monitors. Mr May is in very good health and well within the range of what we would expect for any male of his age, indeed, all the readings are at a very pleasing level.'

'Mr Carpenter, I'll wait as you suggest. Presumably when he returns from X-ray you'll know about any surgery needs.'

'Yes, I will see the results as soon as the X-rays have been taken and will let you know and we'll be contacting the appropriate surgeons to lead the procedures.'

It was about forty-five minutes later when Anthony May was brought to his room, he was awake and was able to smile and speak to Laurel. 'Now, you're not to worry Laurel. It seems my head is OK, but it's going to require surgeons to sort out my shoulder and hip. I think James St John will have to be acting Prime Minister for a few weeks.

You must tell Rhiannon that she mustn't let him work too hard – the Ministers do all that.'

'Mrs May, I suppose your husband has given you a rough idea of what needs to be done. There are no concerns for any head injury, just monitoring for two or three days. The fractures all need surgery and it maybe that they can be undertaken at the same time. I'll consult with my colleagues in orthopaedics while we are calling in additional specialists, and in this matter we have consulted with Dr Malcolm Davis. We will have two teams of surgeons working on hip and shoulder at the same time with each team pausing to enable the other team to complete a particular part of the procedure without movement. These days complete hip replacement procedures are generally straight forward and take about ninety minutes. Actually, the X-ray of his hip does show marked arthritis so a new hip was on the cards for the not too distant future. When the hip replacement is complete and all is well, the procedures still required for the shoulder fractures can be completed as all three main bones of the shoulder are involved, upper arm, collar bone and shoulder blade itself, the repairs will involve pinning.'

'If we are able to proceed as planned then that will be best for your husband, only the one general anaesthetic. Anthony will be made ready for surgery and when we have the teams of surgeons standing by we'll start. Minimal physiotherapy will be started within twenty-four hours and be increased slowly over the days immediately following. I know it must all sound very complicated but the actual operations themselves are relatively straight forward and with physiotherapy being started soon afterwards I would expect Anthony to be able to return home in about a week, return home, but not, and I must emphasise, not to work.' Turning to the patient, 'If you didn't attend to all that Sir, never mind. The closing sentence was the most important, about returning home, but not returning to work. A month's leisure spent at Chequers, may be a good idea.'

'Thank you, that is all very clear.' Laurel responded quickly to prevent any discussion involving her husband. 'I'm only sorry because the accident is really my fault. You see Anthony was supposed to celebrate having been one year as Prime Minister today and for a gift I gave him this specially commissioned card. Here, have a look. Anthony found it delightful and very amusing and when he went off downstairs he was still looking at it with a copy of The Times tucked under his arm. He wasn't holding the banister so that is how he came to fall. I suppose accidents always have a cause.'

'I think if I were to be given a similar gift, I should be equally amused and easily distracted. You don't need to blame yourself; people in their fifties should always take care to prevent falls! I'll leave you, Sir, in the tender care of your wife and the nurses and we should be ready to move you to the operating theatre within about an hour. I'm sorry to have to announce, no more food or drink, small sips of water are allowed just to moisten your mouth. One of the nurses will fit a drip so that you do not start to dehydrate as I imagine you have had nothing to drink since just before your tumble.' It was one and half hours later when Anthony was taken to the theatre, by then early afternoon, and there being no complications with any of the procedures he returned, fully equipped with a selection of pins in his shoulder bones and joints and a brand-new working hip, just before six o'clock and in time to hear the opening and surprising item on the early evening news!

If Laurel thought she would be able to relax for a few hours she was much mistaken. Fortunately the first distraction was lunch and she was able to enjoy this in very pleasant peace and quiet. She was just finishing coffee when her first visitors arrived, two members of the security detachment who had responsibility for the Prime Minister's safety. They said little, inspected the suite of rooms again, checked the views from each of the windows and even commented loudly that they considered the suite particularly secure. They were pleased to see only one entrance. At some expense to their department they were able to book two neighbouring rooms so that a twenty-four-hour watch could be maintained.

Her next visitor was one of the domestic staff from Downing Street who had thoughtfully selected various items of clothing and other necessary items for both The Prime Minister and his wife for two or three days. Laurel hadn't really thought about stopping over at the hospital but decided then and there that she wouldn't leave until the end of the next day. Laurel was very appreciative of this member of staff's understanding helpfulness, Pauline was her name, and Laurel made a mental note to seek her out when life returned to something near to normal.

The third visitors were a shade less than helpful. Two members of the Prime Minister's Downing Street staff arrived carrying quite a number of files and papers contained within two red dispatch cases. Laurel was a little angry at this presumption on their part as no message had been sent to anybody regarding the Prime Minister's work. First reactions are often the best. 'Gentlemen, is that work for my husband which you have just carried in?'

'Good afternoon Mrs May. Yes, you're quite right, we know that he will want to keep abreast of any developments so...'

'If I can just stop you there. I think you will find that The Foreign Secretary, James St John. as First Secretary of State, is taking over responsibility for the Prime Minister for the next few weeks so I should be obliged if you would not leave those dispatch cases here but take them to wherever Mr St John is currently working.'

'Yes, I understand that but.....'

'No buts, Sir. Please leave immediately, taking with you all official papers. Sorry to sound terse but that is the Surgeon's instruction, an instruction with which I entirely agree, as does my husband. He was able to tell me that himself before he was taken to the operating theatre and where he will be for the next few hours.'

'But Mrs May.'

The door opened then, and a uniformed official entered and was already in mid-sentence. 'Gentlemen, as you are likely to be carrying classified information it is important that my security colleague here escorts you to your car. No papers pertaining to Government business are to be brought to these rooms.'

Two members of the Downing Street Officialdom left carrying with them all that they had brought in. To say that they looked displeased was something of an understatement.

'Thank you Nicholas, most helpful and I appreciate the speed with which you fitted the communicating alarm system. I certainly didn't expect to be using it quite so soon. I'm going to telephone Rhiannon St John now as I know she will be able to let me know what is going on and I will prefer her version to an official one.'

51

'That's quite all right Ma'am. Just hit the buzzer whenever you want something.'

'Rhiannon, is that you? Laurel here, I'm at St Thomas's, how far away are you?

'Don't laugh, not trying to pinch your place, but just at the moment I'm at Downing Street.'

'Well ask someone to call a car for you but don't use the front door. Come and see me. Do you know about the private entrance for St Thomas's Hospital? Oh, good, well get the driver to drop you there, a security official will meet you, bring you up to where I am, and you'll find me holding court. Is that all right, good, bless you Rhiannon.'

Chapter Seven
Post-Operative Matters

Rhiannon, wonderful to see you, I feel I can relax. Just as soon as Anthony is able to sign anything, I shall send for the Chief Whip, ask him to prepare a short but official letter which will instruct all who need to know, that for the time being James St John is carrying out the day-to-day duties of the Prime Minister. Thomas Magnusson and his staff will get such a letter properly worded, signed and then distributed in the correct manner.'

'An excellent and essential idea, Laurel. Now tell me, how is Anthony?'

'I'll tell you what I know Rhiannon and then you can compare it with what you've heard.'

'Anthony is in surgery now, examinations showed a need for full replacement left hip and that part of the operation is first and following that the three main bones of his left shoulder are being pinned. The second operation will start a bit before the hip procedure has finished so there will be an overlap. The CT scan of his head showed no damage, some observation needed for forty-eight hours. He was already conscious by the time he arrived at the hospital. There is plenty bruising all down his left side and there may be two or three cracked ribs. All being well, he should be back here by late afternoon. So, how does that compare, Rhiannon?'

'Rather different, to say the least. This is the grisliest version, put quite briefly: deeply unconscious with high risk of brain damage, multiple fractures, including spine and both legs. There is a likely risk of paralyses. Today's newspapers had varying versions of that description as their headlines. Some have the odd paragraph about Anthony's successor, later issues have paragraphs about temporary arrangements, His Majesty having to make an appointment to oversee affairs until there is some certainty with the political parties.'

'Your 'rather different,' should surely be described as 'amazingly different;' clearly, the press are having a 'ball'. When the Chief Whip issues an official statement there is going to be much disappointment. John Carpenter is the Consultant Trauma Surgeon here, currently part of the team with Anthony at present, and he will be available to make a press statement when the operation has been completed. Now, if I press this buzzer somebody will appear and I can organise tea and biscuits for us both.'

The door opened almost immediately and Nicholas appeared. 'Nicholas, you said someone would come at once and you were almost in before I removed my finger from the buzzer. Can you contact that nice lady who produced food earlier and see if she can bring some tea and biscuits.'

'Not a problem Ma'am, will probably be with you in ten minutes.'

'Thank you, Nicholas. Also, would you be able to get Thomas Magnusson on the phone or arrange for him to telephone me.'

'At once,'

The tea arrived just as Laurel's telephone rang. As she answered, Rhiannon took charge of the tea.

'Thomas? Thank you for ringing back so quickly. I haven't got any difficulty but it is important that a signed letter, or something similar from Anthony gets out quickly making it clear that James St John is acting for Anthony for the next few weeks. Would you be able to get that prepared, correct wording is important and that is one of your department's strengths. Best arrangement would be if Anthony could get it out this evening, if not in the morning then. What do you think?'

'I think in the morning is best Laurel, just gives me enough time for staff here to get it right. I could come in with it, say at ten o'clock if you think that time will be suitable. Don't want to find the Prime Minister having a bed-bath.'

'I'm sure that will be fine, Thomas, but I'll let you know if that clashes with any hospital plans. Am I right in assuming that what Anthony is doing is understood and known about among your senior colleagues. It would be a bit awkward for all concerned if I'm seen to be playing the part of an intermediary regarding a very important political matter if several key players are unaware of Anthony's intentions. My position is completely neutral, but circumstances alone, Anthony's accident and its serious consequences, are forcing me to take the initiative.'

'I understand you, Laurel and I don't think you need have any worries. You're right though to make sure it is handled correctly, so easy to cause quite unintended trouble.'

'Thank you Thomas, we'll speak again and I look forward to seeing you in the morning.'

Rhiannon passed a cup of tea to Laurel and they both sat back and relaxed. 'Tell me, Rhiannon, has your James been having any difficulty with the officialdom which exists at Downing Street, 'proper' announcement not having been made?'

'Just a little, Laurel, James was holding his own I felt and he was simply ignoring the various interruptions being made along the lines of: 'well when the Prime Minister sees this later' or 'one of us will be visiting the Prime Minister this evening and this can be checked' or 'in the morning matters will be clearer and we can await the Prime Minister's call and subsequent instructions'. Here's a typical conversation.'

'Gentlemen, I fear you have not listened and understood the key instruction. The Prime Minster is at this moment in the operating theatre and receiving skilled treatment regarding the pinning and setting of several bones. He will not be working for a number of weeks, he has already said this in the presence of his wife and the main Consultant over-seeing his treatment. There will be an official statement coming from the Department of the Government Chief Whip, possibly this evening or early tomorrow morning. I also understand that the Consultant will be making a statement to the press assembled at the main entrance to St Thomas's Hospital.'

'But Mr St John, it may not be wise for him to make a statement without it being vetted by ourselves.'

'I really don't think anyone here is competent to add anything to a medical bulletin regarding the Prime Minister's current health, the results of the emergency surgery and the prognosis for the next few weeks. In all probability Anthony May and his wife are likely to move to Chequers for a while. Now can we get on please? I need to know what requires 'action this day' as the PM would say, and what can be left for a while. I also need to get out a statement regarding the temporary over-sight at the Foreign Office. In that respect I wish to appoint Clive Anderson as temporary Secretary of State at the Foreign Office.'

'Sir, probably right, but presumably the Prime Minister will be in a position to endorse that appointment later today or tomorrow?'

'Why?'

'What do you mean, Mr St John?'

'You obviously didn't listen to a word I said, three answers back I believe. The Prime Minister is currently undertaking no work.'

'Yes, but even so, on an important matter such as this surely he.......'

'If, Sir, you are unable to understand my very simple and straight forward instructions, I may have to ask you to leave so that staff remaining are those I know who will be able to carry out the instructions of the 'Acting Prime Minister. Perhaps I ought to advise you that an appointment has been made for me to attend an Audience with His Majesty tomorrow afternoon at two-thirty.'

'We haven't been informed or consulted about that.'

'It was a private conversation between me and His Majesty's Principal Private Secretary.'

'Rhiannon, I am impressed, I can see James asserting himself quite successfully especially with the hint that he will only deal with officials who are not questioning his authority.'

'When I left to come here I felt he was more than holding his own.'

'Perhaps it would help if one of his Officials could temporarily move with him from the Foreign Office.'

'That might put a few noses out of joint.'

Hearing noise from the patient room next door, Laurel glanced in and was surprised to see her husband being wheeled in. 'Good gracious, all finished?'

'Yes dear, come and see, I'm fully awake.'

Laurel walked over, found Anthony attached to various leads and pieces of monitoring equipment and he was wearing a mask as he was taking oxygen but he could lift it on and off. Just then John Carpenter came in. 'Anthony brought you up to date, all the surgery successfully completed. Twenty-four hours bed rest and then some gentle physiotherapy can be started. Overall, Prime Minister, you are in excellent shape, need to be for how you always manage to slag each other off in the House of Commons.'

'Well, thank you John, you have been very attentive to Anthony's needs, very kind.'

'I'll see you in the morning Anthony, nurses will be in frequently and attend to all needs. Remember, do not attempt to get out of bed, the new hip has to settle and it would be easy to cause a dislocation in the first few hours.'

Once John had left, Laurel explained that Rhiannon had kept her company for most of the afternoon and she told him about James St John attempting to be acting Prime Minister in the face of much aloof and official number ten opposition. 'Thomas Magnusson will be in to see you in the morning, about ten o'clock and he will have an official letter for you to sign indicating your approval for James to act in your stead, to be the Acting Prime Minister. That should make it clear to all concerned especially the officials at 10 Downing Street.'

At six o'clock John Carpenter stood in front of the main entrance to read a statement regarding the accident to the Prime Minister, The Right Honourable Anthony May, PC MP, statement approved by the Hospital Management.

'As you know, the Prime Minister had the misfortune to fall down the last flight of stairs at 10 Downing Street this morning. It is thought that he tripped with his right foot and in falling he hit his left side throughout the whole fall and in the process fractured the main bones in his shoulder, bruised and cracked two ribs and broke his hip. For about fifteen minutes he lost consciousness but by the time he was admitted to hospital he had regained consciousness. A CT scan showed that there was no bruising or damage to the brain nor any fracture of the skull. There may be slight concussion and he will be kept under observation. During surgery lasting about three hours this afternoon, he underwent a full hip replacement procedure and at the same time the fractures in his shoulder were all pinned. All the surgery was completed very successfully, and the Prime Minister is now making an excellent recovery. In twenty-four hours' time physiotherapy will be

started and it is expected that he will be able to leave hospital in seven days. It is expected that he will move to Chequers to recuperate for a period of a few weeks.'

When John Carpenter finished, he took no questions and he returned inside the hospital.

Back inside the Prime Minister's suite of rooms, Rhiannon was just taking her leave, wishing both Anthony and Laurel well for Anthony's first night of recovery. She had telephoned James and they expected to meet at their London residence by mid-evening. They had already decided that they would not take up residence at 10 Downing Street as far as they were concerned it was Laurel May's London home.

To her surprise Laurel slept well, despite knowing her husband could be in some discomfort. She woke once or twice and realised that one of the nurses had been in to check all the monitors. She was not too surprised to wake fully at about six-thirty, knowing how early hospitals got started each morning. She went into greet Anthony, found him semi-seated and looking quite perky; he was enjoying his first cup of tea for the day and he pointed to a cup that had been left for her.

John Carpenter was in soon after eight and was seemingly very pleased with how he found the patient. 'Late this afternoon two of the nurses will help you get out of bed and using elbow supports, although you may not manage with the left side one, you can walk round the room once or twice and then sit in a comfortable chair. You will have had enough laying in bed by then and be pleased to be on the move just a little. Tomorrow, you'll find that you can manage much more but what ever you do you will have to be very careful with your shoulder. That will need some very carefully arranged physiotherapy and you will need to use a sling for some time. The nurses will explain how you should and should not move your leg so that you do not cause a dislocation of the new hip – something which would lead to immediate surgery and cause some additional damage as well.'

Almost to the hour, Thomas Magnusson arrived and at ten o'clock presented the Prime Minister with a short letter to sign informing all those concerned that The Right Honourable, James St John, PC MP was acting as Prime Minister while Anthony May was recuperating from his recent injuries and that the period of deputising may well last four weeks. Should it prove necessary, a further instruction may be issued. Thomas explained that his department would ensure that it was copied to all concerned, Members of the Cabinet, other Ministers, Senior Ministry Officials and Officials at 10 Downing Street, The Speaker of the House of Commons and the Lord Speaker of the House of Lords. A statement for the press would be issued confirming the temporary hand over of Prime Ministerial responsibility.

After a short conversation of a less formal nature Thomas left and Laurel felt that she could relax that little bit knowing that the correct procedures had been undertaken and that for the time being her husband had no responsibility, could concentrate on getting better and enjoy some relaxation.

Chapter Eight
Questions to the Deputy Prime Minister
An Unexpected Sequel

Τhe Deputy Prime Minister,' intoned the Speaker.

One of the first members to be called was John Smithson. 'Mr Speaker, may I also on behalf of many of us congratulate The Right Honourable Gentleman on his recent and most distinguished promotion, albeit if only of short duration and given the Prime Minister's tough constitution the duration could be very short, but however, Mr Speaker, may we know if there is any truth in the rumour that the current Deputy Prime Minister owes his promotion to the intervention of Mrs Laurel May and further, that this intervention brushed aside concerns voiced by officials from the Downing Street office?'

'Mr Speaker, may I thank the Honourable Gentleman for his congratulations and I'm sure he won't mind if I set aside the humorous reference to the duration of the appointment. I am sure he and his colleagues will be very pleased to hear that the Prime Minister is enjoying his relaxing stay at Chequers where he continues to recuperate and his doctors remain very pleased with his progress. As to the rest of his question regarding rumour, my answer is quite brief, there is no truth in the rumour.'

There followed another veiled criticism. 'Could the Deputy Prime Minister confirm that the appointment of Clive Anderson as Deputy Foreign Secretary over ruled the Prime Minister's own choice.'

'Mr Speaker, the simple answer to the Honourable Member's question is to tell you and the whole House that the Prime Minister had nobody in mind for the appointment to which he refers.'

The final question of a critical nature referred again to unnamed officials from Downing Street. 'Will the Deputy Prime Minister please explain why no officials participated in the final decisions made by the Prime Minister before his operation commenced?'

'Again, Mr Speaker, the answer is simple. Officials were not involved because the Prime Minister made no decisions immediately prior to his operation. To clarify further, the only decision the Prime Minister made was on the day after his operation when he signed the letter which had been prepared by The Right Honourable, Thomas Magnusson, The Government Chief Whip, a letter which was solely concerned with my appointment and which has been published for all to see.'

Most of the remaining questions struck a gentler tone, some humour expressed about the Prime Minister's bones, their suitability for the insertion of pins. Other questions hinted at the scale of the bill regarding the delivery of spirits to the private flat at 10 Downing Street, another wanted to know who had prepared the jug of milk put out for pouring over cereals. One Member even asked how the Prime Minister took his coffee. With all these questions The Deputy Prime Minister met humour with humour.

The penultimate question was unexpectedly very serious and came from Sheila Tomkinson, 'Mr Speaker, while it wholly to be expected that the appointment of the Deputy Prime Minister will be met with a degree of light-heartedness and some humour, I should like to raise the serious matter of international terrorism which has been developing in recent months, terrorism associated with some of the more frightening aspects of the effects of climate change, where countries are experiencing loss of land to rising sea levels with large numbers of people losing all their possessions, uncontrollable health problems for thousands of people, especially the very young and the very old and of course the loss of crops and consequent shortages of food, so can the Deputy Prime Minister assure the House that all appropriate measures are being taken to monitor such terrorism, and in particular, any groups which may be developing in this country?'

'Mr Speaker, the Honourable Member has rightly raised a very serious international problem, indeed any increase in terrorism for whatever reason is something for which all Governments should be on their guard. As far as groups associated with aspects of climate change, these are fairly recently formed groups but rest assured that Ministers at both the Home Office and the Foreign Office are working together and with relevant senior staff and security officials are monitoring all these acts of terrorism. Should anything develop which is clearly a threat to the UK it will be brought immediately to the attention of myself and the Cabinet and if necessary a meeting of COBRA can be called at almost instant notice.'

The final question was rather different from anything else. 'Mr Speaker, can the Deputy Prime Minister confirm that he will be recommending to His Majesty that an award should be given to the as yet unnamed Police Officer who took such speedy action in summoning emergency services to Downing Street and furthermore took action to clear from the stairwell the many people who were preventing the Prime Minister from receiving the emergency treatment which was so vital?'

'Mr Speaker, the Honourable Member will be pleased to learn no doubt that all appropriate recommendations regarding awards will be made by the Committee in charge of such matters and I have no doubt that will include them looking favourably upon the Nation's favourite Police Officer and his uniquely powerful voice.' With much waving of order papers, a smiling Deputy Prime Minister was able to leave the House and he was immediately driven back to Downing Street, a destination he had yet to get used to.

Much to his very great surprise, James was greeted by Rufus Sutton when he entered the hallway of Number 10 Downing Street. 'Rufus, a pleasant surprise, surely you are not a messenger for the Foreign Office today?'

'No Sir, the Civil Service Powers that be, thought a temporary move for me would be a good idea and your Sir Ronan Nicholls has gone over to the Foreign Office to work with Clive Anderson, perhaps a case of experience with less experience.'

'Tactfully put by someone. How about the rest of the staff here, are you acquainted with any or all of them?'

'All of them, some better than others, getting on very well.'

'That's pleasing, it is nice to have a more familiar face about the place. What is the task of the moment.?'

'Tedious but vital, the regular diary meeting.'

'Yes, we will get onto that first but you had better put out a request to both the Home Office and the Foreign office for a briefing on the matter of climate change terrorism which was raised as a question just now. Fortunately I was aware of what has been put in place but I am also aware that not much has been done and perhaps it is time for that to change.'

'At once, Sir. Excuse me while I just get that put in motion so to speak and then I will return for your diary meeting.'

The diary meeting high-lighted occasions when No. 10 was to expect visitors who had been invited to particular meetings, there were two occasions which involved ambassadors calling at No. 10. There was an evening reception for representatives from the major London based orchestras and other related groups. Statements being made to the House requiring the DPM's presence included an Economic statement from the Chief Secretary to the Treasury and a Defence Statement regarding aircraft procurement. An industrial tour to the North East had been arranged some time back for Anthony May, scheduled for ten days' time and it was thought it should not be cancelled but undertaken by James St John, so briefing papers would be presented to him two days before.

'Would I be right in thinking that diary list would have been typical for the PM?'

'My understanding is that the schedule we have just gone through is considered light.'

'Goodness, I shall need a holiday just as soon as Anthony takes up the reigns again. By the way, how is he doing because I had absolutely no idea just now when I was speaking in the House about his health.?'

Just then the telephone rang and Rufus answered, said nothing for a minute or so and then made some comment of agreement. 'Sir, regarding the matter of climate change terrorism. Apparently there has been activity involving those required to meet, one of whom was Clive Anderson but he has said he will continue with that work alongside his other work as Acting Foreign Secretary. His opposite number from the Home Office is Jonathan Venniston and it seems that, despite short notice, they can both be here at three o'clock this afternoon. If you're agreeable, I need to ring back confirmation, as they would both bring their senior officials with them.'

'Yes, I'm impressed, so get that meeting confirmed and cancel anything that was scheduled for me this afternoon.'

'Just now, Sir, you asked about Anthony May's health. It would seem that what you said in the House was absolutely correct. I'll just go and get the confirmation for this afternoon out to the two departments.'

The three o'clock meeting was very interesting as it turned out. James St John was pleased to meet Jonathan Venniston, somebody he didn't know particularly well, he also congratulated Clive Anderson on his appointment as so far it had been carried out by brief letter and a telephone call, there being obvious time restraints. Jonathan was on his own, he would have been accompanied by an old acquaintance, Jeremy Lutterworth who apparently worked with Jonathan as well as Daniel Divine, but he was on holiday. Accompanying Clive Anderson was Penelope Grimble, Foreign Office advisor but James had previously only encountered her on a few occasions.

James gave words of welcome to all and opened the meeting. 'You may have picked up on the question to me in the House this morning regarding climate change terrorism, my answer was fortuitous and amounted to all I know, but I gather something has been developing. Who wants to make a start?'

'I think it needs to be me,' said Jonathan Venniston. 'The particular piece of information initially came through our security officials. Have you heard of a group which calls itself 'RAFT'? It has existed for about three years, a pressure group arguing about the danger posed to the whole world from deforestation. The title 'Rafts' stands for 'Replant all Forests' and uses the word 'raft' as something that suggests rescue, in this case, achieved by replanting the Rain Forests. All sounds very laudable but more recently they have been making statements that if there isn't real remedial action soon then the campaign needs to become more aggressive. They also suggest that without a negotiated solution to the problems of climate change, then it could even lead to war. It could all be innocent, language just extreme to underline their point but some of the members seem quite angry, potentially aggressive in a violent way.'

'Thank you, Jonathan, as you suggest could be very laudable intentions but could be violent. Anything from the Foreign Office researches?'

'Yes, there is, but can I ask Penny to outline matters as she has been more involved.'

'Thank you Clive. On receiving the Home Office information our attack was to see if there were overseas links, similar groups, and there are, several in fact, all round the world but mainly confined to what might be loosely described as Western Developed Countries, mainly intellectual groups but increasingly using more aggressive language. We haven't yet spotted many links between groups but some of the members of 'Rafts' are in touch with members of a group in Canada, a group using the same name. Like the one in the UK, formed only a handful of years back. Security Services wish to keep a tight watch. If such groups develop and become really aggressive it may need us to have people placed internationally for more effective monitoring.'

'Thank you Penny, and although I didn't say when you came in just now, nice to meet you properly, I feel a little remiss in the matter, sorry. Are these groups large in membership numbers?'

'No, the groups we have found around the world are small in membership and that may well mean we haven't found anything like all of them. Security will keep looking.'

'Thank you. Look, what should be our forward plan on this, continue to be proactive or wait on events?'

'Can I come in on that? So often something dreadful happens, a murder by a terrorist suspect or similar, and then it comes out that he was known to security services and makes it appear as if nothing has been done. So, do we respond to Parliament in a way which is more detailed than the Deputy Prime Minister could be this morning although we may then incur the wrath of what might turn out to be a genuine non-violent organisation. The alternative, as I suggested, always makes us appear to have done nothing.'

'I do agree with you Clive, we so often look as if nothing is being done. We could of course issue a written answer to Sheila Tomkinson and then all who wish to read it may do so. I'm not quite sure of the correct procedure, do we privately advise her that we wish to issue a written and therefore more detailed answer?'

'I think what you have just suggested is the way forward,' offered Clive. Shall the FO prepare an answer, seek Jonathan's opinion and then pass it to you for issuing. How would you feel about that Jonathan?'

'Fine, I'll mention it to the Home Secretary.'

'Good. Well thank you for making the time and at such short notice. Hope this 'new boy' hasn't kept you too long.'

Chapter Nine
A Romantic Getaway

2030

Several thousand miles away, Jeremy was resting on an extremely comfortable sun lounger, a nicely chilled beer to one side and a beautiful woman to the other; eye-candy, to say the least. February was an excellent time of the year to visit any of the Caribbean Islands and this exclusive beach-cabin in a very quiet resort of the Dominican Republic suited them both perfectly. Jeremy had just completed his first duty with the sun-tan lotion and Angela was now suitably relaxed. Jeremy may have been relaxing and a long way from home but he never let matters concerning his work at the heart of Government escape from his thinking for too long. He knew only too well that he was a little bit older than many of those who were employed as advisors to the various members of the Cabinet and he was rather keen to hang on to this particular post. He had aspirations for getting elected to the House of Commons. He had been on two short list panels, thought he had interviewed quite well but there being no feed-back he wasn't sure how well he had done. He felt it important to remain in his present post until he had been chosen to fight an election. He was hopeful about another short list and he would hear about that soon.

'Jeremy, not being nosy, but how did you get to be an advisor at the Home Office?'

'Oh, you know, turned a few wheels.'

'What do you mean?'

'Background, education, my old man, mum's dad still has influence – lots of wheels to spin there.'

'I thought you said your education was pretty awful.'

'That was my early days really. 'Manners Maketh Man' didn't make me, and my manners as a youngster were somewhat lacking so my Hampshire school decided to off-load me when I was fourteen. I got sent to a rather lesser establishment in Norfolk and only just scraped a few low-grade A levels by the time I left four years later. My life changed a bit then, dad married again and I acquired an arse-hole for an older step-brother, only a year up on me but did he look down his nose. He was at home a lot because he had a year off between school and university. I took something of a shine to his younger sister, Emily; she could twiddle me round her little finger and she soon taught me how to deal with 'the brother.' Turn the tables was her advice, achieve more and then you can do the looking down your nose. That's what I did, went to a local comprehensive school to repeat my A levels (and that bit of state education has stood me good stead) and dad paid for examination cramming, far cheaper than school fees as he pointed out, and one year later I had three A levels at grade A and went to Durham University where I got a first in history. It all rather put brother Nigel in his place.'

'And what happened to the odious Nigel, and what's his surname in case I come across him. There are thousands of Nigels.'

'Vauxhall, our Nigel Vauxhall went into banking, at what level I have no idea and I haven't heard anything of him for years. Never at home when I called and that's an infrequent activity these days.'

'How did the other wheels turn for you?'

'Well, I soon learnt to value education, especially when I realised I was quite bright and could actually pass examinations. It's strange how you can go through school and not actually know how able you are. I didn't really know until I started passing examinations at top level and I've met others who've had similar experiences. I met interesting people at

Durham, began to understand the idea of 'gaining influence.' I joined one of the political societies, rather right wing for my taste. Dad's a barrister who meets many powerful people; step-mum's father or uncle, his name is Vauxhall, not sure quite about the relationship, he's an M.P. and she has a great Uncle, a bit old now, but was quite influential in the House of Lords. Then I got money.'

'Explain, where from?'

'From a Great Grand-Mother, who always had a soft spot for me. She died soon after I finished at University and she left to each of her four GGCs half a million pounds.'

'GGCs, Jeremy?'

'Great Grand-Children.'

'You certainly fell on your feet.'

'Actually, really falling on my feet took me back to my local Comprehensive School a couple of years back. I was invited to present the school prizes. Somebody had told the Head there that I had done rather well, got a very good degree and then a post in Government circles. He thought I sounded rather prestigious but he wasn't the Head there when I was a pupil so he didn't have all my details to hand. Anyway, I quite enjoyed speaking there and made myself sound very pro-state education. Pointed out that one famous public school had expelled me and that another, very minor, had achieved nothing for me. You must understand that I was really speaking to the pupils and they were probably pleased to hear somebody spouting on about how they had been a failure. Then I spoke about motivation – I didn't say anything about wanting to get one over my step-brother – but I did stress the need to find some goals, anything that might just spark an interest in something they were doing at school so that they could get better at it. In my case I was ashamed to mention that it was money, hadn't had my inheritance at that time, but told them how I realised that if I didn't achieve something with education I may well end up in any sort of work which rarely provides much in the way of money. I managed to insert the odd bit of humour so all in all my little bit of prize-giving work went down quite well.'

'Really, you're nothing but an old fraud. How did the odd member of the House of Lords help and the M.P.?'

'I don't know, but 'who you know' still works quite well. People are always willing to speak favourably about people they know, especially relatives, they like think it might boost their own standing as well.'

'I thought that sort of thing was history now.'

'Angela, don't you believe it. Do you read Agatha Christie? She was a knowing sort of old bird. She has her character, Miss Marple, say one or two pertinent things on this topic. Obviously it is Agatha speaking her opinion probably, but Miss Jane Marple, when talking about strangers moving into the village, says that it is all very worrying in modern times. People come, say something about themselves but you only have their word for it. She goes on to explain that in times past, people arrived with introductions. They had friends in common, knew someone who knew somebody else. Letters were exchanged. Well in that sort of way, that's how 'who you know' works.'

'Jeremy, I don't know which amazes me the most: your quoting Agatha Christie at me or your admitting to reading her books.'

'Everybody still reads Agatha Christie, she's not described as the Queen of crime fiction for no reason. They keep showing the serials on television and they still keep making fresh ones. In my life time I think I can remember at least four different 'Miss Marples.' When other people talk about the books, it doesn't do not knowing what people are talking about. Looking at someone with a blank expression can be disastrous, especially in my line of work.'

'Something like that happens in my work as well. When it is just me taking down short-hand with a Minister they often want to talk 'shop,' they like a bit of gossip so it is important to keep ones ear to the ground.'

'This is all being too serious. I'm going in for a swim, coming Angela, or will it spoil your hair or the sun lotion that I've just worked in for you, very sensuously to, if I might say so.'

'You swim, I'll stay here and when you come back we'll go and have some lunch and then something of a sleep.' She reached over and smacked his chubby backside. 'Go on, off you go and I want to see you charge into the sea, looking all macho and sexy.'

Later that afternoon, he of the 'chubby backside' found a copy of the previous day's 'Times' and discovered to his amazement that the Prime Minister had fallen down the stairs at 10 Downing Street and was in hospital with serious injuries including several broken bones and concern for a possible head injury. 'Here, Angela, you better read this, our ultimate boss, the Prime Minister, has had a serious accident,' and so saying he dropped the newspaper on to her very beautiful tummy.

Chapter Ten
A Country Weekend

2030

A warm weekend, a few weeks after the Prime Minister's tumble and return to work, the embarrassment quickly forgotten and James St John and his wife Rhiannon were now entertaining Anthony and Laurel at Norstead Towers. Daniel Divine, the Home Secretary, was expected down for some of Sunday but they were not sure who he would bring with him; they never knew until he arrived and occasionally it was a complete stranger. There was something of the 'I'm not predictable' about the current Home Secretary, but he impressed the Prime Minister. Rhiannon made sure to be well involved in organising the weekend as her husband's parents, whilst enjoying the prestige of the visit, were very elderly and not up to planning detailed entertaining.

Since becoming Foreign Secretary, James St John and his wife had the official residence, of Chevening House in Seven Oaks at their disposal but in practical terms it wasn't particularly convenient. Whenever they felt the need for a relaxing weekend they preferred to use it as an opportunity to visit James's parents and often his sister, Beryl would be there. It would be a rare event were Vincent to visit as he was far more inclined to keep his own company at Oxford. Just occasionally James would use Chevening House if he had a large number of official visitors to entertain and such an event might be combined with meetings and discussions. But for the most part, James preferred to stay in London, make use of the many Government facilities in and around Whitehall for meetings and conferences. From the moment he had taken the post of Foreign Secretary he had made it clear to his Cabinet colleagues that they should feel free to make use of Chevening House, it was permanently staffed, so only needed a phone call to make a 'booking,' so to speak. Once or twice James took official visitors to meet his parents at Norstead Towers and such visits always pleased his father as he had enjoyed a lengthy career in politics even though he had never held a Government post.

James was keen to make this weekend visit relaxing but he always made sure to build in a little key 'policy' time as he liked to think it. Having the Prime Minister's ear was an opportunity never to be ignored, especially as he had been acting Prime Minister himself only a few weeks back. For most of the time Anthony would be accompanied by one of his principal secretaries, but this weekend he was without, an unusual exception. Private Secretaries to the Prime Ministers liked to know what he was saying and to whom. Evenings were good times for very private moments as Laurel, the Prime Minister's wife, would entertain the party in the main reception room. She was a talented pianist and never failed to make use of the small Steinway grand piano which graced the corner. If it were a warm evening, James could open one of the French doors, stroll along the patio and still appear to be listening to the music. He even affected to enjoy the occasional cigar and this gave them another excuse to be outside. With or without private secretaries Anthony liked to be fairly discrete.

It was the middle of Sunday morning when a smart car drove up. Those who knew their automobiles would recognise this as an exceptionally well kept metallic blue Jaguar XF, nearly ten years old. Jeremy was driving and his boss, Daniel Divine, sat in the passenger seat and in the back and looking very attractive and exceptionally elegant was Angela. There were obvious signs of recent sun-bathing and it was Daniel who explained to his hosts that he was accompanied by two of his staff who had recently enjoyed a hot, spring break in the Dominican Republic. Their arriving together to pick him up from his London apartment caused him to realise that they were an 'item.' This was a relationship of some months apparently but Daniel had only just become aware of it, slightly annoying for him as he liked to know who was sleeping with whom. Like most thoughtful politicians, he was only too aware of the dangers of 'pillow-talk'.

Daniel admired Jeremy, liked his style, admired his intellect and respected his input to the many discussions he sat in on, but the odd hint had come his way that his trouser belt was not always kept as well buckled as might be expected. Angela Rosemary was the perfect secretary and Daniel was always at his most relaxed when she was on duty and when it was just the two of them there was always some idle chitter chat, political gossip passing between them, who had said what, how somebody had reacted, whose marriage was a little rocky, who was thought to be on the way up and who was perhaps moving in the opposite direction. These scintillating nuggets passed between them on the unspoken assumption that they didn't pass anywhere else. The origin of all these hints was never easy to pin down but Daniel was never too surprised to note their accuracy when unexpected events happened a few months later. He never asked but he supposed some of his Cabinet colleagues had similar experiences.

Just as the Jaguar came to a halt Anthony was walking from the opposite direction and was at the exact spot such that he could open the rear door and offer his hand as Ms Rosemary stepped out of the car. The Prime Minister may have normally been used to being in receipt of such niceties, but he was more than equal to smiling at a beautiful young lady and behaving with impeccable courtesy.

Laurel, who was just coming out through the front door was able to add her welcome. 'Good morning, Daniel. Angela, Jeremy, lovely to see you both, and congratulations on your 'togetherness,' is that an acceptable way to express such matters. I'm very jealous of how you've acquired your lovely colour, it may be but a memory now but your tan is still looking very good. I could do with warm seas and hot sunshine. Now he is Prime Minister, I find it very difficult to pin Anthony down to any sort of holiday planning. Of course, his accident a few weeks back did lead to a rather pleasant country holiday and I managed quite a bit of walking around the countryside surrounding Chequers.'

'You have my sympathy about trying to find a date for booking a holiday,' added Rhiannon. 'Seems to be just as difficult for James.'

'Jeremy, last time we met you had a similar but different car. Am I right?'

'Quite correct Prime Minister. I have a Jaguar F type coupé, same colour. Only two seats and Angela didn't fancy the small boot. I bought them both at the same time, just after the Covid pandemic. A small company, seemingly quite successful, folded, and the two directors were forced to trade their Jags in for cash. I was lucky enough to spot them and hit a very attractive bargain with the garage as I was buying both and the new owner didn't want to be hanging on to them for too long. I don't do a high mileage and I'm happy to keep them in excellent condition so I expect to own them for some time to come. I'll probably have to go all electric when I next change cars. I'm not sure what will happen to these two good friends when motoring is entirely electric but at least I'll have had the pleasure of them for fifteen years or so, For more everyday use I do have one of the all-electric small Mercedes models.'

'Two very attractive vehicles, more so than my official car, but changing that is outside my control. My present car is relatively new but that is because the entire fleet is being changed to all electric and my car was deemed to be at the top of the list. Another Jaguar, very elegant, but I would prefer one of yours. No doubt hundreds of thousands of motorists are getting very nostalgic over the cars that they had to part company with.'

'It is amazing the things a Prime Minister can't do.' Jeremy smiled as he offered this notion, 'on the other hand, Sir, you managed to get your bones well repaired, I see.'

'Shoulder still aches, especially at night, but I can live with that.'

'You have my sympathy Sir, I broke my collar bone some years ago now and the doctor in A & E was pleased to tell me that I could expect to be aware of it for many years to come, 'It'll trouble you like an old war wound,' was his parting shot. 'Sad to say, he was absolutely right.'

'Well, come in everyone, plenty of coffee on the go and James is around, just sorting a few papers.' With that, Rhiannon shepherded her guests inside, through to the patio at the back where one section was in full sun and where she proceeded to pour coffee.

James appeared then and helped himself to the last cup as Rhiannon finished. 'Good morning everybody. Sorry I wasn't at the front just now to add to the welcome party. By the way, has anyone met my new Private Secretary, Rufus Sutton, linguist, something of a high flier, hasn't been with me long yet. He has just completed a spell at the Paris Embassy, has come with glowing reports. He's not down this weekend.'

Silence for just a brief moment which was broken by Jeremy and that didn't surprise anyone, as they realised amongst themselves, someone always knows, and often it was Jeremy. 'Yes, I think his name has come in my direction and we have met once or twice. Been an Oxford don for a few years, married one of his students, also a highly talented linguist, Audrey Ponsonby as was. Think I heard a very sad tale about her: father died when she was young, mother developed early onset dementia, family home caught fire and Audrey lost her mother and all her possessions apart from what she had with her at University.'

'What an awfully sad story.' Rhiannon looked quite tearful. 'Did she have no other family?'

'No, I believe she was left totally alone, an adult orphan, if one can use that expression. On the other hand, I believe she and Rufus are quite a close couple.'

A hush descended on the group while they sat and drank their coffee. Rhiannon raised a little cheer by passing round a plate of plain chocolate hobnobs. They all sat drinking more coffee, plenty in the pot as Rhiannon pointed out. They chattered about nothing of any great consequence, enjoyed the sunshine and looked very relaxed. Rhiannon popped in and out, keeping a discrete eye on lunch preparation as she was good at that kind of multi-tasking.

Eventually she invited them in for lunch, at which meal George and Elaine joined them. Despite doing two things at once, Rhiannon had managed to serve quite a successful Sunday lunch: already on the table were some crab and shrimp cocktails. One of the local ladies who helped from time to time brought in a main course of roast lamb, vegetables which together with potatoes had all been roasted – such an arrangement was easier to manage. James was required to organise the wine and he had opened a few bottles earlier and passed these round for the guests to help themselves. George sat fairly close to Anthony and the Prime Minister was kindly bringing him up to date on various Governmental matters. Elaine just enjoyed listening to the conversation, made the odd comment, but otherwise kept fairly quiet. Concluding lunch, a selection of different fruit flavoured syllabubs were brought in together with an open box of chocolates.

Keeping her eye on how people would entertaining themselves, Rhiannon asked in a general way what everybody was thinking of doing, after lunch was finished. James responded to that by mentioning an idea for strolling round the gardens, he wanted to show Anthony and

Daniel the spring bulbs which were a little earlier than usual. 'You'll join us Jeremy?'

Laurel laughed. 'I suppose that's a discreet way of conducting a Government sub-committee. We ladies could walk in the opposite direction and also look at the spring bulbs and the men could become hush hush as they pass us by.'

'My dear, you mustn't mock us.' If the Prime Minister was proffering a little criticism of his wife's facetiousness, his face suggested otherwise. Never-the-less, four men went in one direction and three ladies the opposite.

'James, my PPS has been telling me of a little disquiet on the bank-benches, some concern that you are cosying up to our European leaders a little too enthusiastically.'

'Perhaps so Prime Minister, so should I fire off a few 'anti-Europe shells', it's always easy to find something to argue about and if it comes from me the leaders will spot the subtext which will tell them not to take it too seriously. I get similar complaints when I entertain the same back-benchers to lunch. While being generous with the wine I point out that the Europeans are our nearest neighbours, and that we simply cannot ignore them.'

'Gracious, I hope making your case is not costing you too much.'

'Quite manageable, Prime Minister, quite manageable.'

'I have mentioned to the Home Secretary, Sir, something of the same disquiet but perhaps hinting at some loosening of immigration rules.'

'I take it Daniel that the anti-immigration faction in our Party leaves you in no doubt as to how closely they are watching you.'

'In absolutely no doubt, Prime Minister. Jeremy described it as 'disquiet' but it is decidedly stronger. I don't treat my fellow Parliamentarians to lunch very often, but when I do and if immigration is mentioned, all comments are exceedingly pithy. I endeavour to look and listen sympathetically but some of the remarks made about foreigners make my blood boil. Nothing in my upbringing has ever made me want to adopt such attitudes.'

'Women coming.'

Sounding as if he had been talking matters horticultural for the last half hour, James added the following comments, somewhat loudly. 'Oh, just over here, amongst these young trees, is a splendid patch of snow-drops. They may all look the same but you have to bend down and look inside the flower head to see the many differences. At last count there were over twenty different varieties in just this small area. Hello my dear. Do draw your fellow walkers' attention to this patch of old snow-drops, so many varieties.' Rhiannon and James smiled at each other and the two groups slowly increased the gap between them.

'By the way, did I tell you that Thomas Woodcroft telephoned me a few days back? Seems he has not been well lately, and his doctor has told him to rest for a while. Problems with high blood pressure, I believe,' said Anthony.
'I did hear, I believe his wife, Joanne, mentioned it to Rhiannon.'
'Something I hadn't heard about,' remarked Jeremy. 'Will that cause any difficulties in the Defence Ministry if he is absent for more than a week or so?'
'No, some good Ministers of State there and a very experienced PUS. Nothing for advisors to get too concerned about.'
'I will bear that in mind, Prime Minister.'

The group strolled on, little more was said and they were soon joining the ladies for tea and cakes. 'Darling, telephone for you,' called Laurel. Anthony wasn't absent from the group very long but when he returned he was looking rather sombre. 'Very bad news, I'm afraid. That was Joanne Woodcroft to tell me that Thomas died this morning. It seems he suffered a severe stroke and was gone before any medical help could even be called. Obviously what I mentioned earlier gentlemen has been quickly overtaken by events. I wonder if Thomas had any knowledge that his condition was so serious. He certainly didn't seem at all concerned when he spoke to me last week.'

The news of Thomas Woodcroft's death rather brought the weekend to an abrupt end. The Prime Minister telephoned for his official car as he felt he ought to be back in Downing Street. It was very straight forward for the remaining three to gather up their few belongings, Jeremy brought his car round and they made a speedy departure. Anthony and James spoke for a while but it wasn't long before the Prime Minister's car arrived. By tea time, James and Rhiannon found themselves on their own, pondering the unexpected turn of events and felt somewhat bereft. During the early evening Rhiannon telephoned Joanne to offer sympathy with a promise of giving help if possible. The call was helped a little as they both knew each other quite well. Rhiannon mentioned that she would like to attend the funeral if that was all right and Joanne promised to let her know when she had finalised the arrangements. She could sense how upset Joanne was, to be expected obviously, but it made Rhiannon realise just how tenuous ones hold on life's events can be.

Chapter Eleven
Home from Holiday

2030

Well Audrey, sorry to remind you but we have to drive back down to London tomorrow. I have to be back at the Foreign Office first thing the following morning. It has been an unusual month or so with James St John only recently back at the Foreign Office and I got quite used to being over at Number 10 with him. I enjoyed that stint, most unexpected, and I hadn't been working with him for that long. Clive Anderson, having been in charge, a good person to work with, is now back in his previous role within the Department and Sir Ronan Nicholls has also returned to Downing Street. Anyway, lovely as it has been to spend a few days in the Lake District and recover from our move back from Paris, sudden as that change was, the 'few days' are now over. Perhaps it wasn't the best arrangement for me to come a little in advance and leave you to organise the final departure.'

'Nonsense, that was all fine, I just missed you. I understand darling about getting used to being in London, but I shall miss Paris and it was lovely to work part-time at the Sorbonne as well as tutor some of your colleagues' children. We made good friends; London just isn't quite the same. Anyway, I'll do all the packing before dinner tonight and you can do the first stint of the driving.'

'You like where we're living, Robert Adam Street? My friend Jonathan and his wife off to New York for three years and looking for folk to act as caretakers and look after their apartment enabled us to really fall on our feet. When I mentioned it to a few of my new colleagues they were amazed. 'What, just behind Portman Square' shouted one, don't think he could believe it. Most of them are doing a sixty-minute commute every day. Certainly pays to stay in touch with University friends. Anyway, down to the bar for a couple of drinks and then dinner?'

'No, you go down, I'll join you in a little while, just as soon as I've finished some of the packing.'

When Audrey found him, he was finishing a phone call. 'Well thank you officer, chaos you say, no actual damage, nothing to repair or things to replace. That's fortunate as it is not our apartment, we're acting as caretakers for friends. We'll be there by early to mid-afternoon and you would like us to ring you when we get there.'

'What was that all about Rufus?'

'Here's a gin and tonic darling and we need to sit down. Our apartment has been burgled, that was the police. They want us to contact them when we get back. They have assured me that there has been no damage, but the place has been turned over, terrible chaos. I shall have to ring the security department at the FO in the morning. It's fortunate I had left no papers from the office.'

'Well, we can be ready to leave quite early if necessary, all packed apart from the last few bits and pieces. Breakfast is available any time after 7.00am so we'll easily be on the road by 8.00.'

It was not to be their day. Before they could even leave Rufus discovered a flat tyre but fortunately one of the hotel porters was able to change the wheel very speedily; a generous tip brought a smile. Once on their way they made timely progress, little traffic about to hold them up. Audrey was just contemplating her turn at the wheel when a farm vehicle started to pull out from a field on the left, didn't stop quite soon enough and before Rufus could move out the way, he struck the tractor on the forks protruding from the front. The force of the collision flipped the car over and it skidded on its roof to the far side of the road and fetched up against the verge bank. The tractor driver was quickly across to see what had happened, very relieved indeed to find both passengers alert and able to get out through the door facing the centre of the road. The farmer was not slow to take action, telephoned his wife to bring their car to the scene of the accident. He also explained to Rufus that if he used the tractor forks he could right the car so that it was left off the road and resting the right way up on the verge. While that happened Rufus was telephoning the police in London who wanted to see him urgently.

84

The upshot of what might have been a very serious accident indeed, was that Rufus and Audrey were able to retrieve their luggage and drive with June, the farmer's wife, back to their farm house. Her husband stayed at the scene and called the local police and Rufus spoke to the London police again. June prepared restorative tea and she and Rhiannon jotted down the formal information that they would each require of the other regarding any insurance claim. June explained that her husband, Harry, had told her that the accident was his fault so the insurance claim should be off the farm insurance. A little while later a police officer in London rang Rufus again and was able to inform him that the local police would send a car and get them back down to London just as soon as possible. Rufus and Audrey both felt quite all right after the shock of being in an over-turned car, seemingly unhurt, not so much as a bruise. Seat belts and air bags had proved completely life-saving. Harry appeared in a police car quite soon and its driver was able to update them on the time to expect their courtesy car for the onward journey to London. Local police would also arrange the recovery of their car. Amazingly, in less than an hour since the accident, Rufus and Audrey were on their way, brand new all-electric Mercedes with police officer to drive them. They were able to sit in great comfort in the back and slowly draw breath after their ordeal. This car made Rufus realise that if his recently smashed car got written off, very likely he supposed remembering all the damaged body-work, he and Audrey ought to consider switching to an all-electric model. This vehicle was supremely quiet and comfortable and they even managed to sleep for some of the journey, waking up when the driver pulled up outside the London Police Station where two officers were waiting to interview them and then visit the apartment.

'I'm Anthea Grange, Police Inspector and this is Sergeant Fellows and we have been investigating the break in at your apartment. Very sorry indeed about your dreadful day but by all accounts you have had a lucky escape. We had thought to send a helicopter for you but decided that that might not have been comfortable enough, not knowing how bruised you may have been. I expect the Mercedes was more relaxing.

'It certainly was Inspector, in fact we both fell asleep, a tribute to both car, a brand new Mercedes electric, and police driver.'

'Because of your senior position at the Foreign Office we need to make more enquiries to be sure that this break-in has no connection with your work. If I understand the situation correctly, you've only been at this address a short while, that the actual owners are in New York, friends of yours. We have made a thorough search of the property and forensic experts have taken a number of different finger prints so we need to get yours and also those of the owners. We'll need DNA specimens as well. We haven't got their details yet.

It was Audrey who spoke up. 'Friends of my husband, Jonathan and Marian Wellington, don't think we have their address to hand, at the apartment though.'

'Initially we can send them finger print and DNA kits and they can self-test. Should any court case arise we will need witnessed prints and DNA samples.' She continued. 'Can you think of any reason why you might have been a target regarding this break-in?'

'No, definitely no reason. We're not known there and have only been back in this country about three months, after a spell of some years in Paris.'

Before they left to visit the apartment, Rufus and Audrey supplied finger prints and DNA samples.

'Don't be shocked when you go in to the apartment. It looks worse than it is.' It was the Sergeant who offered this word of encouragement.

'I'm willing to believe what you said just now Sergeant but this is just terrible.' Audrey and Rufus both looked appalled. 'Is all the damage done out of spite, frustration at not finding what they were looking for?' Rufus looked quite puzzled. 'It's all rather outside my range of experience.'

'We have done a close inspection, and have found nothing broken and nothing soiled, deliberately made dirty. It is sometime the dirtying of premises after a robbery which can be the worst of the experience. We've nearly finished here but before we leave we will have a couple of our ladies in who will tidy up, place papers etc neatly on table surfaces, generally put things straight. If you have two or three nights at a hotel then we can be in touch as to the time for your return.'

'We have assumed the need for a hotel and before we fell asleep in the car coming down we did book a room at the Regal Crown Hotel. We've chosen to go there because we have attended the odd function there in the past and often stayed there when we were over from Paris. I've written their telephone number on the back of a business card of mine and this is the address for the owners of this apartment who are in New York.'

'Thank you Dr Sutton, we'll keep in touch and of course let you know immediately if there are any developments regarding the investigation. If you don't want to stop here any longer we can drive you to the hotel before we return to the station.'

'Thank you.' Without doubt Audrey and Rufus looked very relieved to be leaving.

Chapter Twelve
Cathedral Obsequies For
The Late Thomas Woodcroft

Thomas Woodcroft and family had lived in Greenham Close, Southwark, for most of their married life, and they attended St George's Roman Catholic Cathedral regularly and so it was expected that his funeral would take place at the Cathedral. What was not necessarily expected was that the service would be presided over by the Archbishop himself!

Thomas was from a large family, one of six himself and he and his wife had five children all of whom were married and all had children. Given that he was the most famous member of the family it was no surprise that as many who could, wanted to attend his funeral. Probably at least one hundred relatives were attending. The Prime Minister and his wife were present and this caused nearly all of the cabinet to attend along with several Ministers as well. Thomas Woodcroft was M.P. for a constituency in East Anglia so many of his constituents and representatives from local associations were able to attend. A large number of M.P.s also wanted to be there and they were from both sides of the House as he had been a popular M.P. Because he had been Secretary of State for Defence all three of the Armed Services were well represented and there was a United Armed Services Guard of Honour. Six individuals from the Services, in Full Dress Uniform, acted as Pall Bearers. There were many civilians from the Defence Ministry also in attendance. Thomas was an individual who had made lots of friends over the years and many were to be found in the congregation.

With such a large crowd attending her husband's funeral it might have been thought that his wife, Joanne, would have been over-whelmed with the required organisation. Anyone who thought that, reckoned without the Armed Services being on hand. With little difficulty two members of the Services were made available and Joanne found them invaluable; they were friendly, exceptionally efficient, liaised on her behalf with the undertakers, organised a reception for the family together with particular guests for immediately after the funeral in one of the many buildings in Central London connected with the forces, in this instance not far from St George's Cathedral. In another large venue was the provision of more simple refreshments for anyone not going to the family gathering; strategically placed officers seemed to know instinctively just how to shepherd those who were unsure.

Before anyone could consume any refreshments there was the Funeral Service itself. It almost had the trappings of a State occasion there being so many uniformed individuals. In addition there was a substantial number of ecclesiastical participants, all of whom were ceremonially robed. For those of the congregation who were Roman Catholic, the Service probably posed no difficulties but for those who were totally unfamiliar with Catholic Ceremonial or were infrequent attendees of any Church, then the Service may well have left them very confused. With the Archbishop presiding there were taking part in the complex service a significant number of priests, each with their specific part in the ceremonial. In addition there was a full choir so that parts of the service, which in smaller local churches were said, were being sung, and sung quite elaborately. All the participants were robed, from simple cassocks and surplices for the members of the choir to the most ornate: embroidered brocade robes worn by most of the priests; some of the robes were black and white but anything black was embroidered so that the white shone through; other robes were black on purple, again the black was embroidered. The first appearance of this large ceremonially robed group was in the procession, led by the Cross Bearer, Acolytes carrying candles and two thurifers, one to each side of the processional leaders. These five were wearing full length white albs with a black cross front and back. Down one side of the nave they processed and then back up the middle aisle to take their places in the sanctuary area and choir stalls nearby. The last member of the procession and last to take his position was the Archbishop holding his crozier and wearing his mitre. There was singing accompanied by the organ for the whole of the procession. Immediately following the procession but in total silence was the ceremonially arranged funeral group, the uniformed pallbearers followed by a small number of the immediate family led by Joanne and her oldest son. The silence remained until the coffin was placed on the velvet cloth- covered bier, the family had taken their places and then a family friend who was also a Priest at the Cathedral made a short announcement including words of welcome and condolence. This was followed immediately with the organist introducing the first hymn, *'Immortal, Invisible, God only wise.'* Thereafter, the Requiem Mass followed the order given on the service sheets. For those who are enthralled by magnificently robed ceremonial then it must have seemed a vision of heavenly joy, others perhaps less enthusiastic about it all, some may even have been quite bothered without understanding why.

The first lesson was read by the Prime Minister. It was taken from St Paul's First Epistle to Timothy, chapter six and starting from verse eleven but with a small adjustment to the words to take account of the earlier verses of the chapter: *'But you, dedicated to God avoid wrong, aim to be upright and religious.'* The lesson ended with verse sixteen, the concluding phrase, *'To him be honour and everlasting power. Amen.'* The bible in use was the New Jerusalem version. As Anthony returned to his seat he was very pleased to see his Cabinet colleague, Adil Khan two rows behind. He knew he was a Muslim and so wondered whether attending this service had caused him any personal difficulty. Adil was a quiet individual, constituency in the Birmingham area; he was a very effective Justice Secretary, not typical of MPs but he imagined his success came from quiet thoughtful argument and great sincerity. The second lesson was read by the oldest grandson, Christopher Woodcroft and it was taken from The Gospel according to St Mark, chapter six, verses thirteen to sixteen, one of the most famous passages about children and concludes with words, *' He laid his hands on them and gave them his blessing.'* Anthony thought Christopher read exceptionally well, an excellent representative for the whole family.

It was the Archbishop who delivered the address or homily. It was quite short, eloquent and sincere. He spoke briefly of Thomas's early life and education, his early awakening to the idea of a political career, his sense of dedication to do good for his country and its future. With this theme he was able to incorporate the key aspects from both readings, the nature of the good fight and looking to the future, the importance of the nation's children. Anthony May, still thinking about various people and aspects of the service, leaned towards his wife to whisper that unexpectedly he had enjoyed listening to the sermon. Laurel's smile suggested her approval of his comment.

After the homily the Mass continued and the prayers incorporated some for Thomas Woodcroft's family and other prayers offered thanks for his life's work in the service of his country. It was not expected that that the whole congregation would take communion, this was confined to Joanne and her immediate family. When the Mass ended the Blessing was pronounced by the Archbishop and followed a number of versicles and responses given in the service sheet. Silence reigned while the coffin was lifted and led by the cross bearer and followed immediately by the family, the procession made its way slowly down the main aisle towards the west door. At the same time the clergy and Archbishop processed in the opposite direction to the main vestry. As the family reached the west door the organist commenced his concluding voluntary, at full and glorious volume, the opening phrases of a Prelude based on the hymn tune for 'Now Thank We All Our God.' This hymn had been sung after the Archbishop's address. 'Nun Danket Alle Gott – Marche Triomphale' by Sigfrid Karg-Elert is a gloriously rich and uplifting piece of music and especially suited to the size and range of organs typically found in cathedrals. Given the range of contrasts required for the Prelude's interpretation, it is an exceptionally appropriate piece of music with which to conclude the kind of service that nearly a thousand people had witnessed that day in St George's Cathedral in honour of Thomas Woodcroft.

As the two crowds dispersed, assisted by particularly thoughtful and tactful ushers, roles undertaken by those astute and thoughtful members of the armed services, the undertakers drove away taking the coffin to their chapel of rest until late afternoon when Joanne and a small number of her family would attend a short cremation service taken by one of the cathedral priests, a close friend of the family.

As Anthony May and his wife Laurel were driven back to Downing Street he couldn't refrain from making the comment that it took something for one member of the cabinet to bring to a total close for one day the business of the Nation's Government.

Chapter Thirteen
The Regal Crown Hotel

2030

The Regal Crown Hotel was a prestigious establishment with a history stretching back to the Edwardian era. Their Majesties, King Edward the Seventh and Queen Alexandra were known to have dined there on more than one occasion; less well known were the occasions when His Majesty had dined in a more private capacity. Such historic Royal visits were very much of the past and these days the Regal looked to a more international clientele, the business and political worlds were well represented as were famous members of the more 'jet-setting' celebrity classes. It was a hotel with several large function rooms so was able to host a wide range of events, conferences, business meetings, political gatherings, concerts together with the 'one-off' celebrations which often required grand facilities. An important 'watch word' for this establishment was discretion and its managers took great care when allocating staff to particular events.

In common with other organisations in the varied fields of the hospitality industry, the Regal Crown Hotel had noticed that obtaining staff in the post-Brexit era had become something of an issue. One of the managers, fortunately, had had the foresight to predict this particular difficulty, even before the referendum, and he had persuaded his colleagues to face this likely problem with one or two unusual measures.

The Regal Crown Hotel employed many staff from overseas, particularly Europe. Such staff often had a reputation for arduous work, they were frequently experienced in the hotel business and it was common for many of them to speak several languages. It was quickly understood by the senior staff of the hotel that to lose staff of such calibre would cause considerable difficulties because it was clear that there would no longer be the incoming pool of overseas employees. Their solution was to do everything possible to encourage such staff to apply for the EU Settlement Scheme and the Hotel employed a solicitor to offer advice. They actively encouraged staff to consider staying and this was achieved by quietly improving working conditions, gradually increasing pay, offering more training leading to UK qualifications and with the older members of staff who had made something of a family life for themselves, they looked to encourage the employment of the next generation. Whilst the Hotel's Management Board would always be looking forward in developing and establishing its international business, when it came to staff development it was also looking back in time just a little, to when it was not uncommon for staff to be related to other members of staff. The Hotel's personnel department even went so far as to establish connections with a number of London based estate agents with a view to helping in a small way with the problems of accommodation, not an easy problem to solve with employees of large families.

These staffing initiatives caused a younger member of staff to comment to his manager on how he had noticed during a spell of university vacation work, that the DIY store where he had spent his summer, employed a large number of older staff. At first he found them all a bit intimidating until he discovered that many of them were new recruits like himself. They were people who had retired or been made redundant but who didn't want or couldn't afford to stop working. The manager was interested and took it upon himself to visit a branch of this well-known outlet. He was surprised to discover all manner of people working there but with several factors in common: they were mainly part-time, retirees from previous careers, shop assistants, bank clerks, teaching assistants, even former hotel workers, widows and widowers, lonely and looking for a little companionship and much needed extra money. He also noticed that they were hard-working, good with customers and actually enjoyed what they were doing.

This was information he took to the Regal Crown Hotel's next management meeting and where the potential was immediately realised so a trial was launched using their favoured employment agency. After a few months they had added to their part-time staff a group of people who were willing and keen to acquire new skills and who also brought to the hotel unexpected talents. There was a fifty-five-year-old lady who was superb at any aspect of flower arranging. They acquired two staff from the world of high-speed quick turn-around over-night accommodation, who were more than happy to share one full-time job between them in arranging the hotel's more high-end luxurious suites. Most unexpected was a butler who had recently retired from a well-known London City organisation; within the Regal Crown his skills were unique and he thought he could train a small group of butlers to attend the needs of their most prestigious clients. They welcomed to their midst two very specialist chefs, one whose expertise was with curries and another who had designed cake decorations for a famous supermarket chain. Alongside these unexpected specialisms was a pool of employees who were happy to undertake the everyday needs of the hotel, offering hard-work but on a part-time basis.

So as the hospitality industry generally lurched in the early 2020s with a great need of staff, the Regal Crown found itself in a very encouraging position as the Nation's economy began to recover and the important travelling business-world started flying again. By contrast with all these new initiatives in staffing, one new and unusual member of staff with the Regal Crown Hotel was currently in the middle of his first month's employment. David Yardlington was working with the team of three at the main reception desk. He had recently moved back from Paris where he had been for the last fifteen years. He had followed a somewhat varied career since leaving school aged eighteen. His A level results had been such that a university place was out of the question. His parents were decidedly unimpressed with that distinct lack of success especially given the cost of seven years at boarding school. They suggested that he spend a year or so at the local technical college with a view to obtaining some sort of vocational qualification which might enable him to start earning.

His mother had been particularly miffed that he had managed to fail A level French given that she was French by birth and that as a youngster David had been brought up bilingual. He could speak French to some extent but beyond that he hadn't bothered. However, by the end of two years at the local 'tech' he had obtained some recognised hotel qualifications and a spell of compulsory work experience had been sufficient to convince him that his ability with spoken French was actually rather useful. Before taking a full-time post in hotel work he had been employed in a variety of short-term jobs until his mother successfully persuaded him to work in France.

He had enjoyed Paris, made friends, became fluent in French, and had indulged in a number of romances. He hadn't maintained any links with old school friends, indeed Kemby School was way back in his past and by the time he decided to return to the UK, having obtained a good post with the Regal Crown Hotel, he had no friends in the UK. He found a couple of rooms in the Earls Court area and proceeded to throw himself into his new career. He saw little of his parents as they had retired and were now living in Yorkshire. Much to his mother's pleasure the last time he had spoken to her from Paris, the entire conversation had taken place in French; which of the two was most skilled was open to debate.

Senior colleagues were impressed with their new employee, found him very unflappable and of all their staff who worked on reception his French was by far the best, very unusual as far as English staff were concerned. He also had some reasonable German and Spanish, more or less unavoidable skills to have acquired having worked in Paris hotels for nearly fifteen years.

Chapter Fourteen
Rufus at the FO, Audrey Out and About

The following morning found Audrey and Rufus well rested. They had enjoyed a delightful dinner before retiring for the night somewhat earlier than was their habit. They took their time getting up, enjoyed coffee in their room so by the time they went down for breakfast the initial rush had passed and all was a little quieter and more peaceful. Audrey had called at reception to ask about staying extra nights should the need arise. She was very surprised to find an old friend looking up. 'Bonjour David. Etes-vous bien?'

'Merci, je vais très bien. Oh Audrey, quelle surprise. Qu'est-ce qui t'a amené ici?'

'Rufus est de retour au Foreign Office et nous sommes donc returnés.'

'En es-tu content? Paris va te manquer.'

'Paris me manque déjé mais je n'y peux rien. David, je suis veni demander si notre chambre peut être réservée pour une quatrième nuit. Cela pourrait être nécessaire.'

'Pas de problème Audrey et si vous changez d'avis il n'y aura pas de frais supplémentaires.'

'Merci David, c'est très bien.'

They exchanged greetings in a typically French style, smiles all round with Audrey promising to send Rufus to see him. Catching up with

Rufus at breakfast she really did surprise him by telling him about bumping into David Yardlington who they last saw at the Hotel Auguste Rodin, not far from the Paris Embassy. 'I'll pop round to say hello, you must remind me Audrey. Now what are you having for breakfast, everything or just a delicate lady-like selection?'

'I'll go up to the counter with you and choose a few items ending up somewhere between the two extremes you've suggested.'

'Well, I shall have nearly everything, feel I might need plenty of energy for today. Before very long I must telephone the PUS and bring him up to date on our happenings and then have a word with the security department. I'll probably be able to stay away from the office today, ought to go in tomorrow though. I'll leave it until this afternoon but I shall ring Inspector Grange, may have something to tell her from the Foreign Office's perspective. I do hope nothing is impinging on our security, shouldn't think so but strange things do happen. Just then a waiter appeared, with quietness and discretion to the fore. 'Can I get you tea or coffee?' was his murmured request.

Audrey spoke for them both. 'One of each please.'

Audrey was a little flustered when the waiter offered about half a dozen different teas from which to choose. Unfortunately she hadn't really progressed from tea just being tea. Rufus rescued her. 'A breakfast tea, I think, with lemon, please.'

'Thank you darling, I really must learn my teas. It is easier at hotels where they place an elegant wooden caddy on ones table and you simply choose.'

'Worry not and don't let them think that they have got one over you. Come on, the food counter beckons and we will judge them by their bacon.'

An hour or so and a couple of pots of tea and coffee later, they sat back, Rufus definitely feeling the fuller of the two. If asked he would probably say he was absolutely stuffed! 'I think I'll find a quiet corner in the lounge and ring the office, on my way I'll give David a wave and a hello. Shall you go back up stairs or do you want to join me in the lounge.'

'Oh, you don't want me listening in Rufus, I'll be in our room.'

It was just as Rufus expected. Neither the PUS, Sir Bartholomew, nor the security officer could think of any good reason to suppose anything had occurred other than a random break-in. 'Get matters sorted today, Rufus, and we'll expect you here tomorrow.'

'Thank you Bart, that's very helpful, I should like to spend another day with Audrey. When she saw our place late yesterday afternoon it reduced her to tears. Fortunately, as the police were keen to point out, there had been no deliberate soiling of the place. They are finishing their investigation this morning and then with other staff they employ for this kind of situation undertaking a basic tidying job, picking things up from the floor, putting furniture straight, leaving papers and books neatly on the table. We'll take a taxi round late this afternoon and I expect it will look much improved. So, if that's all right I'll see you tomorrow.'

As planned Rufus and Audrey let themselves in to their flat and were very pleasantly surprised with what the police had achieved. The apartment was clean, very tidy if one or two items were not in their usual places. On the table were several neat piles of books and papers which only they could put away and that wouldn't take them too long. In the morning Rufus would give Inspector Grange a ring and suggest that they might take up residence if the police had finished their investigation.

That evening and back at the hotel, Rufus and Audrey sat in the bar and planned the next day. Rufus knew that he was expected back at the Foreign Office, he would ring Inspector Grange from there. 'How shall you spend the day my dear?'

'Knightsbridge, a day of 'window-shopping' and lunch in The Grill, Harrods. Never know who I might bump into there. Don't worry, my love, I shall keep a close guard on my purse. 'Window-shopping' and actually spending, are very different activities. What time will you be having breakfast in the morning.?'

'Very early I'm afraid, you needn't come down with me, really no need for you to be up and about at the crack of dawn. As I'm quite unfamiliar with the underground journey from here I'll call a taxi so I'll get to the office for eight-thirty. I don't suppose anything will have changed as far as the police are concerned and it's most likely we'll never really know what the robbery was all about.'

Audrey was still dozing lightly when Rufus kissed her good-bye the following morning, promising to be in touch if there was anything to report. Wishing her a nice day he was off to get his taxi. As he expected, Sir Bartholomew had nothing to report nor had the security officer. Later he had a call back from Inspector Grange who confirmed it would be all right for them to move back to their apartment.

Rufus was also brought up to date on some Government Ministerial changes following the death of Thomas Woodcroft. There were to be no moves within the Cabinet as the Minister of State, Clive Anderson of the Foreign Office, was being promoted to the post of Defence Secretary. Most likely there would be a promotion within the Foreign Office, probably two or three side-ways moves among some of the Junior Ministers. In fact the first notification which came to Sir Bartholomew via the Foreign Secretary was a swap. Edgar Shrewsbury, Minister of State at the Defence Department was moving to the Foreign Office to replace Clive Anderson. Other moves would take a day or two to sort.

By the time Rufus had caught up with what was on his desk awaiting his return and hearing about the various Ministerial shuffles it was time for him to join some colleagues for lunch where a little more catching up would take place. Such situations made Rufus very pleased to know that his memory was excellent. About three miles away Audrey was just ordering her lunch in The Grill, Harrods. Opting for a fairly light meal she chose a Pesto Soup to be followed by a mixed shell fish salad to which she added a bottle of still water and a glass of dry white wine, French, a Harrods recommendation. Just as the waiter was walking away with her order she found herself accosted by two old friends from her undergraduate days, one a fellow linguist, the other a historian.

'Gosh, Audrey, haven't seen you for a year or two. On your own?

'Why Jessica, Susannah,. How lovely. I'm only on my own because of unusual circumstances. If you care to join me I can explain unless you have other arrangement.'

'We can join you, splendid suggestion. Jessica and I are enjoying a women's day out and secretly spending a fortune.'

Just then the waiter reappeared. Madam, if your friends are joining you, would you care to take the table just nearby, it will provide a little more space. They all stood up, the waiter rushed about, moved a few things and left a table for three beautifully arranged. I'll give my friends a couple of minutes to choose what they would like and then you can put through one complete order for the table. The waiter left with her the water and glass of wine. She took a sip, found it divine even though she didn't know its origins. At £14.50 per glass she expected it to be quite good.

'So when did we all last meet?' asked Jessica once they were settled with food and drink.

'That party, after the degree day ceremonies were over, five or six years back.'

'When the publican announced the entire bill was in the hands of a mystery benefactor. Did anybody ever know who did that?'

Susannah shrugged her shoulders. 'I never heard, how about you Audrey, I wondered if Rufus might have known.'

'It was me.'

'You, Audrey, what an amazing thing to do! Why? Sorry, that was very rude, it was a lovely, kind and very generous thing to do.'

103

'Several reasons actually. That week the solicitor dealing with my late mother's affairs had placed in my bank account a very large credit which covered all her savings which amounted to more than I ever realised and added to which were the proceeds from the sale of the wrecked house and land and a quantity of shares which she had inherited from my father. That made me feel like celebrating. Getting a double first was another reason and being with Rufus on a permanent basis and although he hadn't proposed I sensed he intended to so, that provided an excellent reason. In fact, the proposal followed only few days later. Paying for the meal was a 'spur of the moment' decision which I did by post to the publican. I suspect he was staggered. Above all, I really enjoyed doing it but not a gesture I have ever repeated. You are the only ones who know, I never even told Rufus; can you keep it that way, please.'

'Now, why are you here?' asked Jessica, 'you were going to tell us.'

'You may have heard that Rufus left Oxford and joined the Civil Service, was posted to the Foreign Office and soon after sent to the Embassy in Paris. That was lovely. A few weeks ago he was transferred back to London, we'd been in Paris for a few years though. When we returned from Paris we moved into an apartment in Central London, free, courtesy of an old university friend of his while he and his wife are in New York. Recently he had a week's leave so we went to the Lake District but just before we came home the London accommodation was burgled and wrecked. The police contacted us, needed us to return to London, which we did. On the journey back though, we had a serious crash and wrote the car off. Farmer's fault, nobody hurt, local police took care of everything and the London police arranged with the local police to provide a car and driver so we continued our journey south in a brand-new luxury Mercedes. We've stayed in a London Hotel for two or three nights, Rufus has finally gone back to work and I'm having a 'Harrods' day. We were wanted back in London rather speedily because the Police didn't know whether there was a security connection, given the nature of Rufus's work.'

'Well, what an eventful time you've had. Was there a security issue?'

'No, all clear as far as that's concerned. Police don't seem to know why there was a robbery and nothing was taken. Burglars just seemed to want to create chaos.'

'A sweet anyone?' Susannah had caught sight of the sweets' trolley and was drooling.

Chapter Fifteen
Hotel Observations

Audrey and friends sitting in the Grill, Harrods, enjoyed much reminiscing, drank several coffees and finally went their various ways with little shopping time left. Not wanting to go home empty-handed, Audrey treated herself to fresh items as she wasn't really sure what state her clothes had been left in. The thought that someone had interfered with her things made her feel a little sick or was she just being silly. However, buying a few nice luxury items made her feel much better. Finally, getting back to the Regal Crown at about five-thirty, she promptly sat in the lounge, ordered a pot of tea and when asked to specify which, simply replied with the merest hint of hauteur that something quite normal would suffice. The waiter didn't repeat his question so she assumed that similar such replies had been given by other inexpert tea-drinkers.

She was just sipping her tea when in strode Rufus, back a little earlier than expected; They greeted each other with a kiss and the same questions: 'How was your day, darling?'

'Well colleagues at the Foreign Office are more than satisfied that no security issue has been involved and they have confirmed that with the police. It would seem then that it was just a random burglary. Perhaps they caused the chaos out of frustration because they didn't find any money, no small things of high value which they could easily sell on, jewellery for example. As we keep saying, we have been out of the country for the last three years or so, nobody has fresh knowledge about us or my work at the Foreign Office.'

'Not having issues such as security and burglary to contend with I had a gentle day which included an unexpected surprise at lunch time. Two old friends found me in the Harrods' Grill. You'll remember one, Susannah Beveridge, as she was in the same language tutorial group as me. The other was her friend, Jessica, don't think I ever knew her surname, she read history and Susannah brought her to the degree day party. They were having a 'girls' day out' but ended up spending the best part of three hours nattering with me.'

'Yes, I remember Susannah, I expected her to get a first but in the event she just slipped into the two-one category. Now Audrey, more serious matters. When do you want to resume living at the apartment? I have one idea, and that's to take a taxi there in a little while, taking with us all that we don't need from our luggage but leaving enough clothes here for tomorrow. Tidy the place as far as books and papers are concerned, perhaps change the bedding, check the fridge for milk and other essentials and then come back here for a final night at the Regal Crown. It would mean that you could go back to the apartment whenever you wanted tomorrow and I would get there when my day at the Foreign Office finished. I should endeavour not to be late.'

'You have been planning. I think I can manage to fall in with those ideas. It has the advantage that when I go back tomorrow I'll find it as it should be, how it would have been had we been able to return from the Lake District in the expected way without having a burgled apartment. I like the idea of getting the final sorting out of our bits and pieces done this evening. I hope that doesn't make me sound a bit feeble.'

'Good gracious, not for one moment do I think that of you. Come on, let's go and get our stuff from the room and sort the apartment out and then we can enjoy a relaxing meal back here for the rest of the evening. Perhaps find a film on the television to watch, they make available quite a selection here. We had better let reception know that we won't require a fourth night here.

Putting Rufus's plan into operation turned out to be far less stressful than either of them expected. Restoring papers and books to their rightful places was quite straight forward and like most people this included tucking odd papers behind the coffee tin in the kitchen, spare keys and other bits to the dish on the hall table and other quirky storage spots were restored to their rightful use. Audrey checked the fridge and made a little list of essentials and while Rufus took it upon himself to change the bed sheets she popped out to a small but quality supermarket which was less than five minutes away. When she returned she was able to assure herself that the breakfast for the day after their return was catered for as well as sufficient food for an evening meal which she would enjoy cooking. Audrey watched Rufus smoothing down the freshly covered duvet and calling a taxi, they were soon off back to the Regal Crown Hotel.

They arrived before they intended to eat dinner but called at reception where they found David on duty. Exchanging smiles and pleasantries they let him know that the possible fourth night booking was not required and then they went into the bar for a drink. From where they sat, the reception counter was in full view so they saw David greeting somebody who was obviously another old friend. Not somebody they knew but he looked a similar age to David. They got quite loud with their reminiscences and from the odd remark that floated over, it seemed they were sharing experiences from school days. In which case they had perhaps known each other for over twenty-five years.

While Rufus went to the bar for refills, a third man of similar age joined the two at the reception counter. David appeared not to know him but the other certainly did.

'Good God, what on earth brings you here Nigel?'

'No law to prevent my being here Jeremy.'

'But isn't it a little out of your league, a little too upmarket perhaps.'

'Not for me. I've been at a banking conference for investment departmental managers. It was held here as befitting the importance of the occasion and if you are around tomorrow you may see me again.'

109

'Step-brother, you haven't changed one bit since we first met, still some arrogance and an attempt at superiority. Do customers entrust you to look after their investments? What a frightening thought. Good to have seen you David, must catch up some time.' With that Jeremy nodded at Nigel and went on his way.

When Rufus returned to Audrey he found her quite enthralled by the exchange she had just witnessed. 'I don't know quite what was going on but David was obviously talking to an old school friend. I got the impression that it was an unexpected meeting but they seemed happy with bumping into each other. Then a fellow called Nigel appeared and Jeremy, David's school friend, referred to him as a step-brother but it was very unpleasant, clearly no love lost between the two. Like the first meeting, this one was unexpected. It ended with Jeremy making an unflattering remark about what Nigel, who is an investment banker, probably didn't achieve for his clients. All quite entertaining in a strange sort of way.'

'It's got you fired up darling. You sound just as if you're describing a short scene from a stage play.'

'In a funny sort of way, it was like a tiny piece of theatre.'

'Well now, what shall we eat, and drink?'

'Entirely your choice my love, use your imagination and decide what will please my palate most, choose romantically.'

As Rufus showed Audrey through to the dining room for what turned out to be a glorious dinner, clearly Rufus excelled himself, and their last evening at the Regal Crown was to prove a prelude to a successful return to their luxury apartment in Robert Adam Street, just close to Portman Square.

The small piece of theatre which Audrey had been enjoying immediately before dinner continued playing but not to any particular audience. Trying to leave the hotel with his reputation intact, Nigel bumped into a friend and fellow delegate, Garry Compton. And he was keen to know who Nigel had been arguing with.

'He's one of my least popular relatives, Jeremy Lutterworth, step-brother, the result of my mother's remarriage.'

'It's possible that I know him. Some time ago I was at a school prize giving event at our local comprehensive school where my nephew is a pupil and he was also receiving a prize. Jeremy was the main guest and was quite an amusing speaker, kept the pupils' attention successfully but as time went on I felt I recognised him. I think he was a fellow pupil at my boarding school in Norfolk, Kemby School. This was not the most successful of schools but was all my parents could afford and they were determined that I should have a private education. I never knew this Lutterworth guy when I was there, year above me if I remember correctly. When I was in the third and moving up there were lots of rumours flying around about some of the older boys meeting up with girls in Great Yarmouth who were pupils at Kroxby Girls' School. It was said that one of the girls had to leave because she was pregnant and I seem to remember that your step-brother was one of this group of older boys. It sticks in my memory because at about the same time lots of new school rules were brought in, regulations about when we could leave the school premises, things like that, general tightening up. His connection with the Comprehensive School where he was speaking was that he had repeated his upper sixth year to improve his 'A' levels which apparently he did with stunning success.'

'Please don't remind me of his stunning success, that's when he overtook me scholastically and didn't he let me know. Revenge probably, because I had crowed at him about my 'A' level results which at the time made him look distinctly inadequate. He's quite high powered at the Home Office, adviser to the Secretary of State I believe. Food for thought.'

'Did you know the man on reception? He also looked slightly familiar and I wonder if they were old school pals.'

'I wouldn't know. Just the reception guy as far as I'm concerned but Jeremy called him David. It would be easy to find out his surname when we're here tomorrow. Thanks for the information Garry, possible ingredients for something of a scandal but knowing my luck it won't materialise. Might even be worth money. Unbeknown to Nigel and Garry, David had caught a glimpse of Garry and it was as he was finishing his shift and about to go home that he remembered him as an old pupil of Kemby. Seeing him, and talking to Jeremy, David's Kemby school-days came back to him as if it were all as yesterday. For just a fleeting moment he also remembered the girls that they used to meet in Great Yarmouth, one in particular, Lucinda Quemsby, had a beautiful face, or was he just being fanciful. He must remember to ask Jeremy about it when he next bumped into him.

Chapter Sixteen
Plan Changed, and Other Matters

Whatever David hoped to talk to Jeremy about when he next met him was not to be. Returning to his place in Earls Court after his shift at the Regal Crown Hotel had finished he and an acquaintance from his floor, Paul, experienced the absolute horror of the lift failing including the secondary safety device. Some people are perpetually frightened of using lifts, David was not one, but this thought and others flashed through his mind as the lift hurtled down to the bottom, plummeting nearly three floors. Fortunately people were about, emergency services were called and the fire-brigade was able to winch the lift up to the ground floor allowing access for the paramedics who were relieved to find both residents alive but David was unconscious. Both appeared to have suffered broken legs, probably internal injuries and spine and neck injuries as well as they had each suffered a terrific body jolt. With David being unconscious it was very difficult for the paramedics to get both men out of the small space and at the same time avoid causing further injury. Paul needed an immediate injection to reduce his pain and nothing could be done to immobilise their broken legs until there was sufficient space. Police had also attended and when both men had been got out and placed in ambulances, they, together with the fire officers were able to begin an inspection to see if there were obvious reasons that had led to the lift's complete system failing. There would have to be a thorough Health and Safety check to determine cause and responsibility.

David was still unconscious the following morning and it could be seen by the bruising that he had taken quite a knock to the side of his head.

Various neurological tests seem to reveal no internal head injury and it was thought that time alone would bring him out of unconsciousness. Paul had been able to answer a few questions about their getting into the lift and what they had noticed immediately before it fell. He had also thought to get a member of the hospital staff to contact the Regal Crown Hotel so that staff there knew what had happened to their employee. The hospital staff also added their opinion that the hotel management should expect him to be away from work for at least two months as he needed extensive surgery to repair the complex fractures to his legs. It was David's immediate manager who contacted his retired parents who lived in the north of the country. Very kindly, he made available a room for a couple of nights as he knew them to be elderly and would almost certainly not want to make a return journey in one day.

When Mr and Mrs Yardlington arrived late the following morning they found David still unconscious but not still, a certain restless could be seen, some shaking of his head, quiet mutterings but nothing understandable. They didn't stay too long and hoped to find him a little better when they would visit later in the afternoon. They were warned by staff that he would need to stay in hospital for several days and his being discharged would depend on how much he understood about what had happened and where he might live. Clearly his Earls Court flat was absolutely unsuitable. His parents saw little improvement in the afternoon and they returned to their hotel room feeling rather depressed. Very kindly, they were offered an evening meal by the hotel staff but they were too bewildered to accept. They managed a little breakfast the following morning and returned to their son's bedside where there were encouraging signs, albeit rather slight, of some improvement. When they returned for their second visit of the day they found that David was not alone. Another man, similar age to David, was sitting trying to talk to him but having little success. He stood up when he saw them arrive.

'Hello, you must be Mr and Mrs Yardlington, David's parents. I'm an old school friend of his, we only met up again recently and quite by chance as I was attending an event at the hotel where he was on reception. I had a little time on my hands this afternoon so I thought I would come and catch up just a little on old times only to hear about this terrible accident. Sorry, my name is Jeremy.' They exchanged hand-shakes, and Jeremy fetched additional chairs.

Mrs Yardlington reached over and lightly kissed her son. 'He seems little improved.' She more or less whispered this to herself.

'I'll see if I can find a member of staff, love.'

'No, let me do that, you stay here with your wife and David. I can ask staff to come and speak with you.' With that Jeremy was off, returning quite quickly. 'The staff-nurse says that a doctor will see you quite soon.'

In fact a doctor was with them very quickly, Jeremy moved away so as to not appear nosy, being only recently reacquainted with David. The news wasn't too encouraging, they were concerned at David's prolonged unconsciousness and were arranging for him to have a brain scan to check for any internal head injury. Nothing was said again about the need for suitable accommodation. The doctor also explained that if they thought David was sufficiently calm as far as the head injury was concerned, they would operate to set his fractured legs. It was agreed that the parents would return late the next morning by which time a result of the scan would be available. Jeremy only stayed another ten minutes or so, gave David's parents his contact details, wished them and David well and then he left.

Jeremy returned to his apartment to meet up with Angela for a while. It was a luxurious pad in the newly restored and revamped docklands area, actually often referred to as 'newly restored' but the docklands had been an upmarket residential area for many years . He told Angela about his day and what had happened to his old school friend, David, who he had only met up with again in the last few days. 'Difficult to know what's going to happen to him as I shouldn't think his parents are up to being able to help care for him.'

'He may well need professional care and that can be very expensive.'

'That's very true love. Shall we send out for food this evening as I have to be back at the Regal Crown Hotel for a somewhat hush-hush meeting. I'm there keeping an eye on matters on behalf of my boss. He gets a little worried about our Foreign Secretary's hankerings for pre-Brexit times and there are plenty of pro-Brexit MPs watching James St John very closely.'

It was mid-evening when he returned to the hotel for his meeting which was taking place in one of the less public rooms, suitable when something of a low profile was required. On his way through the hotel he noticed his step-brother, Nigel in the bar talking to another guy who he thought was vaguely familiar, from where or when he didn't know. He was surprised to see them, wondered what they were up to. When Jeremy got to the meeting room he found the Foreign Secretary as expected together with his PPS. He was surprised to find representatives from both the German and French Embassies. There were no official interpreters, dangerous ground was being trodden. James looked up as he entered. 'Ah Jeremy, Daniel mentioned that you would be sitting in. Let me introduce you to our overseas representatives, Monsieur Dubois and Herr Dietrich. Greetings were exchanged and James offered drinks, ordered by telephone, and quite soon a waiter came in with a tray of drinks. Conversation flowed, a bit slowly to start with. Both visitors were keen to mention some of the difficulties which were being experienced by different parties involved in the many and varied aspects of import and export. There was a second interruption when the same waiter reappeared with a repeat of the order. Jeremy didn't need to make any notes, didn't hear anything which he thought would cause much concern for his boss; in that respect he was a 'little' wide of the mark.

This was evident at the following week's questions to the Prime Minister. At about half-way with questions containing little to ruffle the Prime Minister, one of his own back-benchers was called.

'Can the Prime Minister confirm that there are no plans for the Government to make any attempt to renegotiate any of the provisions agreed at the time the United Kingdom came out of Europe and could he further tell us what knowledge he had of a meeting being held by the Foreign Secretary at the Regal Crown Hotel one evening last week which was attended by representatives from the French and German Embassies.' Quite a gasp of astonishment passed across the Government benches as the significance of the second part of the question sank in.

'I'm sure the Honourable Member will pleased to hear that the Government has no plans for any renegotiation of the details which led to The European Union (Withdrawal Agreement) Act 2020. As to the meeting he refers to I'm sure he will understand that I am not always aware of every meeting which may be taking place and no doubt what was probably a small social event will be reported to my office in due course should it be felt that anything of significance emerged.'

Plenty of perturbed faces among the bank-benchers but one or two decidedly more worried faces on the front bench. When the Prime Minister left the chamber he was followed fairly quickly by the Foreign Secretary and after a little more time elapsed the Home Secretary also left the chamber. What conversation took place in the Prime Minister's room was known only to the participants but later in the evening the Home Secretary gave Jeremy to understand that the Prime Minister was livid, pointing out that no matter how unofficial and low key the meeting was, the fact that it appeared to be secret would cause considerable concern and even anger among the critics of the Foreign Secretary. The Prime Minister considered there had been a serious error of judgment in that his office was not informed about the meeting and had he known in advance he may well have stopped it.

Chapter Seventeen
Further Police Investigation

When David's parents visited the hospital the next morning they were surprised to find two police officers in attendance. But before they could enquire as to their reasons for being there, the doctor they had met the previous day was waiting to see them.

'We have received the results of the scan which shows some bruising of the brain and this may well be responsible for the prolonged period of unconsciousness, although any swelling is slight. Obviously we are monitoring him for the fractures but our Neurological team is also on his case and they will watch carefully for any signs that may indicate the unconsciousness is lessening. At present, then, I'm afraid it is just a waiting game if you'll pardon the expression. We may well operate later today, as the surgery cannot be postponed any longer.'

'Thank you Doctor. My husband and I, we must return home today but we will telephone regularly and the ward staff here have our contact details. We will visit again in a day or two. The hotel where David works, very kindly are making a room available for us as we can't manage to undertake a return journey and a hospital visit in one day. Before we move to our son's bed do you know why the police are there?'

'Only that they have discovered some information about the state of the lift that failed and that they hope to have a word with you, as well as see for themselves the extent of David's injuries.'

When Mr and Mrs Yardlington met the police, they were appalled to hear from them, Inspector Ball and Sergeant Watson, that the Management responsible for the building where their son lived had failed to have the lift inspected, that the mechanism was in such a state of disrepair that it was an accident waiting to happen. The police told them that the Health and Safety Executive would be conducting a formal enquiry which would most probably lead to a court case. It should lead to compensation.

'While we have been sitting here, we have heard David speaking, only very slightly.'

'Yes, I heard something like that yesterday afternoon but I couldn't make any sense of it.'

'We've written down some possible words. They may perhaps be names or part names but these are the words which we have written down: Luce, Lucy, Quem, Kim or Kem, Queen, Jer or Jerry. Do any of these mean anything to you?

'One or two might mean something. I think Kem might refer to Kemby as that was the name of the school he was at until he was eighteen. Lucy is obviously a girl's name but I don't recollect him ever referring to her, don't think he had girl friends then. Jerry might be short for Jeremy, an old friend of David's from school days. He was here yesterday visiting. Apparently they had met by chance in the hotel a day or so ago because Jeremy was attending an event at the hotel. They had been out of touch with each other for many years. He gave us his contact details, my husband has it in his wallet. Henry dear, have you got the card that the young man gave you yesterday, you put it in your wallet.'

Henry was obviously a very quiet husband, he just nodded to his wife and got the card from his wallet and passed it over to his wife.

'Jeremy Lutterworth, I remember now having read it. He only used his Christian name when he introduced himself. We need to keep this so do you want to jot the information down for your record.' She handed it to the police officer.

'We have your contact information, so thank you for this. Mr and Mrs Yardlington, we'll get out of your way now. Do hope your son's health improves soon. If the need arises we can telephone you.' Hand-shakes and the police left, leaving David's parents keeping watch for a short while before they had to leave in time to catch their train. They would ring the hospital the next day to find out how the surgery went.

As the police enquiries at David's bedside came to a close, quite different enquiries were unfolding at a London area Police Station.

'Sir?

'Yes Sergeant, how can I help?'

'Developments on that 'hit-and-run' a while back.'

'And, come on, out with it.'

'We appear to have a DNA match, only just come through.'

'That's a surprise.' Inspector Finley continued, 'I didn't have much faith in that DNA test being matched. Well, tell me the details.

"Yes Sir. There was a robbery along Robert Adam Street, near Portman Square. It involved a Dr Rufus Sutton, he is a senior official at the Foreign Office so there was concern about security issues. Because of that, DNA samples and finger prints were taken for elimination purposes. Our match is with Dr Sutton's wife, Audrey Sutton. The match in question indicates that the dead woman is the mother of Mrs Sutton.

'If that's the case Sergeant, it is a little odd that she is not aware of her mother's accident, presumably they were not in touch with each other. We had better telephone them and arrange a time to call. Can you set that up Sergeant?'

'Yes Sir.'

'Have we got a reasonable photograph now, such that it won't cause any upset when people are asked to view it.?'

'Yes Sir.

'By the way, has the owner of the car come forward? Is anything known about him or his car?'

'Yes Sir, I left a report on your desk, silly business really, but will lead to manslaughter charges.

'Sorry, I did read that, I must be getting forgetful. Now. Sergeant, we ought to contact the police who investigated the robbery which led to the DNA test, result of which we are using. They might like to know even if it doesn't help them with their enquiries. Find out who they were and I'll get in touch.'

'Sir.'

It was the following afternoon before they were able to meet the Suttons. Inspector Finley introduced himself and Sergeant Vaughan. 'We're sorry to bother you, Mr and Mrs Sutton. May I suggest you sit down. You will recall that when the police investigated your break-in you were asked to supply DNA test samples. Currently we're investigating a hit-and-run crime involving an unidentified middle-aged woman, sadly she was killed in the incident. What I have to tell you may come as something of a shock but your DNA test result Mrs Sutton, indicates that you are the daughter of the woman who was killed in the hit-and-run accident. Of course the tests will have to be repeated to ensure their accuracy but at the moment we must work on the assumption that the result is correct.'

'But Inspector, what you say cannot be, I attended the funeral of my mother a few years back. She died following a house fire. Sadly, I have no other relatives and my father was killed in a road accident when I was a child, about fifteen years ago.' Audrey had been reasonably calm at first but now she was showing some signs of distress and Rufus moved closer and took hold of her hand.'

'Are you all right to answer just a few more questions?'

'Yes, go ahead Inspector.'

'Your mother's funeral a few years back, did you have her remains cremated?'

'Yes, we did.'

'Have you kept anything of hers? I'm thinking about the possibility of further DNA tests.'

'I hardly have anything, papers that also concern me, nothing of a personal nature. I have a small quantity jewellery. Would earrings be suitable?'

'Possibly, for pierced ears? A pair which you haven't worn might do. I'm not an expert but I could enquire about suitability. What about your father, do you know if he was cremated?'

'I don't think so because I remember my mother taking me to his grave occasionally. Why do you need to know about him?'

'This is a little awkward Mrs Sutton.'

'Please, let me interrupt Inspector. Audrey darling, the Inspector is wondering whether there is a possibility that you may have been adopted but never told.'

'Thank you Mr Sutton, most helpful of you.'

Mrs Sutton was quiet for a few moments as she thought about what her husband had said. 'I'll get the jewellery, I know I have two pairs of earrings which I have never worn, too heavy. Excuse me, won't be a moment.'

When she returned Sergeant Vaughan placed the earrings in specialist bags. Mrs Sutton provided another DNA test specimen and soon after that they left. Rufus and Audrey felt the need for a large gin and tonic so that they could sit and relax. Rather than pursue too many 'what if' unanswerable questions they just sat quietly.

Other police enquiries still continued which led to a visit to Jeremy Lutterworth. The officers who had visited David Yardlington and spoken to his parents decided that the friend Jeremy might have some insights into David's mutterings. It was early evening when they called and found both Jeremy and his girlfriend Angela Rosemary present. Inspector Ball and Sergeant Watson introduced themselves, explained the reason for the visit and then mentioned the muttered names spoken by David. Jeremy agreed that 'Kim' or 'Kem' probably referred to their old school Kemby. He couldn't remember anyone called Lucy and he had no explanation regarding 'Queen' or 'Quem.'

'Mr Lutterworth, remind me, would I be right in thinking you left Kemby School in about 2006 and that you went there in 2001?'

'No, not quite right Officer. Those dates are correct for my old friend David but I didn't go to Kemby until 2002.'

'Any particular reason, may I ask?'

'Yes, got chucked out of my previous school, not something I make any secret about.'

'Oh dear, still happens to quite a number of lads every year I imagine. You obviously knew David quite well, any other names you recall, pupils you knew equally well.'

'Sorry, all just vague faces now and I probably wouldn't have recalled David but for meeting him at the Regal Crown Hotel.'

'Well thank you for your time, Sir, Miss, we'll be on our way.' As they drove back to their Station the Inspector surprised his Sergeant by saying that he thought Mr Lutterworth was a little glib regarding the amount he didn't remember. 'Hiding something, I think. I'll give it all some thought but I think I might have some research for you to start on in the morning. I'm not sure how it fits our current enquiries but I don't like it when a witness is lying.'

Chapter Eighteen
James St John and Rufus Sutton

At a more famous building in Central London, the Right Honourable James St John, the Foreign Secretary, was rising from his seat to take questions on foreign affairs. There were pleasant exchanges between himself and the Shadow Foreign Secretary which didn't amount to much but the first back bencher to be called was a familiar voice, the Honourable John Smithson; he had recently asked awkward questions of the Prime Minister which had tricky implications for himself. Expecting further questions about his recent meeting at the Regal Crown Hotel he was surprised to hear a different matter being raised, that of himself and Rufus Sutton

'Mr Speaker, can the Foreign Secretary assure the house that a recent robbery which occurred at the apartment of one of his senior civil servants had no security implications and further can he assure the house that no secret documents were in the property at the time?'

'Mr Speaker, should I be alarmed at the Honourable Member's repeated concern regarding matters at the Foreign Office, a question to the Prime Minister a few weeks back and now one to me? However, in the matters to which he alludes I can assure him that there were no security implications whatsoever and nor were any confidential documents of any sort at the premises concerned. He will understand I'm sure if I do not mention the member of staff involved by name, it could be a security issue. At the time he and his wife were on holiday in the Lake District. As soon as the police were informed about the robbery by neighbours they contacted the hotel in the Lake District, and my senior civil servant and his wife made immediate plans to return to London, a journey which was not without incident as they were involved in a serious road accident. Fortunately no one was injured and local police were able to arrange for a car and driver to take the couple to the London Police Station where officers were able to tell them about the robbery. After further investigation the police came to the conclusion that the robbery was a chance affair and whatever the criminals were after, they failed, nothing was stolen but the place was left in a terrible mess. As yet, though, the perpetrators have not been apprehended.' Mr Speaker went on to call the next M.P. who had caught his eye.

At the end of questions the Foreign Secretary returned to the Foreign Office in King Charles Street where he had a meeting planned with his PPS, Rufus Sutton. They were getting on quite well, although only acquainted for a few weeks. He was intending to sound him out on the fall-out from the recent meeting which so upset the Prime Minister when he had heard about it. The Foreign Secretary did sympathise; nothing worse for a Prime Minister than to be very wrong-footed during question time. He may have answered the question with considerable aplomb, certainly not without dignity, but it was obvious to most MPs that the meeting was something the Prime Minister should have known about.

'Good afternoon Sir, I was in the House just now, so can I thank you for the manner in which you answered the question about the break-in at my apartment. Actually, there has been an unexpected development over that, somewhat of a personal nature which affects my wife.'

'Yes, Audrey, have I remembered correctly. All right is she, not ill or something?'

'No nothing like that. A few weeks' back there was a hit-and-run in London and the victim, a women who looked very old but who was probably in her forties, was killed in the collision. Initial inquiries failed to identify her so finger prints and DNA were taken but there were no matches. However, after the break-in both Audrey and I gave finger prints and DNA for purposes of elimination and it turns out that the victim in the hit-and-run was Audrey's mother. At first we thought there must have been an error because Audrey's mother died some years back in a house fire; I accompanied Audrey to the funeral and

126

cremation. The DNA comparisons are going to be checked but they'll be correct, the laboratory will have checked before releasing that information to the police. Fortunately I realised what the police officer was about to say and I managed to speak first and suggested to Audrey the possibility that she may have been adopted at birth but had never been told. She took that suggestion quite calmly but I could sense her mind whirling ahead, thinking about her father, had there been an earlier marriage. I wouldn't be surprised if there doesn't have to be an exhumation order for her father's body if only to clarify matters. It would provide evidence one way or the other as to Audrey's parentage; she may even feel the need to undertake some research.'

'Well, Rufus, that must have been a very unsettling meeting for Audrey. What about documents, birth certificate and such?

'As they stand, Audrey appears to be the individual born to the couple she knew as her parents. The police are going to follow-up at the hospital where Audrey was born and make other enquiries to see if there was an adoption of some sort, perhaps unofficial, incorrectly recorded. But I'm sure back in the nineteen nineties these matters were very carefully recorded.'

'Will you keep me posted just in case something problematic crops up? We were going to talk about a number of European issues but we'll leave that for now, in fact another matter has come about. You will be aware that our Ambassador in Paris and his wife are arriving this afternoon, in fact about now, and I've got myself double booked for this evening, can I blame my wife, or else it's my memory. You must know Sir Reginald and his wife, Sheelagh.'

'Yes, indeed, great friends, shared many short holidays around France. Audrey rather misses Sheelagh.'

'That's rather useful, do you think you could take them out to dinner this evening, somewhere very up-market? I'll be seeing him in the morning.'

'With pleasure James, Audrey will love that and it will take her mind off other matters. If we're finished here, I can make arrangements straight away and then contact whoever has met them at the airport. I'll give Audrey a quick ring and book a table at the Regal Court Hotel. We stayed there for a few nights after the robbery and it's a very nice London hotel.'

'How efficient, hotel already vetted. Rufus, don't get our Sir Reginald drunk; need to be able to pick his brains tomorrow.'

'Worry not Foreign Secretary.' Rufus went back to his office, knowing that he and Audrey would have a very enjoyable evening ahead of them. He knew that Reginald and Sheelagh were being met by one of his colleagues using an official car. It didn't take him too long to track them down. In fact they were already on their way back to Central London.

'Rufus, Reginald here, nice to speak to you. Jonathan in the front has passed your call to me.'

Hello Reginald and Sheelagh of course. I'm speaking on behalf of James St John, something of a mix up this evening. He's blaming his wife or his memory, perhaps both, but he has got himself double-booked and as he knows you and Sheelagh are well acquainted with Audrey and me, we're to take you out to dinner this evening. If you're agreeable to that I'll book a table at the Regal Court Hotel, 7.30pm suit you both all right?'

'Excellent suggestion and Sheelagh agrees, I've had the phone on 'speaker' so she's fully up on what you've suggested and why. So how haven't you been blamed or as Principal Private Secretary are you above such mundane matters as the Foreign Secretary's memory?'

'No comment; how's that for 'Civil Service speak'?'

'Reginald laughed. I'm just being told that the driver will pick us both up soon after seven so we'll meet you at the hotel. Let's not worry about predicting time for finish, Sheelagh and I can get a taxi. Ah, OK. That's not allowed Rufus. Driver says he only needs about fifteen-minute warning and he can be back at the hotel. Sheelagh says love to Audrey, we'll see you tonight. I'll get my London-based dinner-suit out of the wardrobe, give it an airing.'

'That sounds fine Reginald, till this evening then.'

Chapter Nineteen
'A Terrible Shock'

Whatever matter the Foreign Secretary mentioned to Rufus as having caused him to be double-booked for the evening never materialised as a phone call from Rhiannon threw him and his family into terrible turmoil.

'James darling, is that you?'

'Rhiannon, everything all right, you sound very distressed?'

'It's your brother, Vincent. I'm sorry James, he's been found dead in his rooms. The Master has been on the telephone, the police are there. Your parents haven't been told yet and your sister is away. Are you able to go, James? It must be you I feel.'

'Did they tell you what happened, how did he die? I know Vincent and I weren't in touch often but he would have told us if he had been seriously ill.'

'The police are suggesting that he took his own life.'

'My God, what has happened to cause him to do that? Obviously I'll have to go, I'd better let the Prime Minister's office know, just basic facts. I'll have both my mobiles so all necessary numbers are available. I'll be able to use my official car, reimburse the cost. I don't know when I'll get back but I will ring my dear as soon as I know anything.'

'All right James, I'll text police and college numbers for you and you can ring ahead, contact the police would probably be best.'

James called for his car and he was on his way quite soon. He rang back to his office and organised for staff to ring the police at Oxford to let them know when they could expect him. The police would be able to contact his car and arrange to meet him when he got to Oxford.

He was on the outskirts of Oxford when he was met by a police car and an Inspector Waterton joined James St John in his car. 'I am very sorry about your brother's death, this must be a difficult journey for you, Sir.'

'Are you able, Inspector, to tell me anything of the circumstances of my brother's death?'

'It would seem that he asphyxiated himself by covering his head with a plastic bag, tied it round his neck having inserted in the bag some cotton wool soaked in something like a cleaning fluid. He would have lost consciousness very quickly. He has left a note but that is addressed to his family and as yet it has not been read. There is another letter addressed to the Coroner. At present the family letter is with officers at the scene of your brother's death. When we get to the college the Master will meet us. I've only met him very briefly as I was about to leave the College when he came to your brother's rooms. He may be able to tell you more. Obviously there needs to be an official identification and then there will be a post-mortem and an inquest. I'm sorry to say that it is not going to be possible to prevent the media getting hold of this news item so there will probably be a considerable amount of publicity.'

'Thank you Inspector, I understand the difficulties.'

They lapsed into silence but it wasn't long before they arrived at the Master's Lodge. He had obviously been on the lookout and was waiting at his front door when James and the Inspector arrived. 'James, I am so sorry to welcome you under such terrible circumstances. Come through and can I offer you a drink, a brandy perhaps?'

'That would be very welcome Sir Peter.'

'Anything for you Inspector? Do please sit down, both of you.'

'Thank you Master, but nothing for me.'

'Inspector, I'm sorry, forgetting myself. This is Sir Peter Carruthers. Master, Inspector Waterton.'

'How do you do Master, sorry I left so soon earlier.'

The Master passed a generous measure of brandy to James and then handed over the letter which the Inspector had mentioned. 'I thought you may prefer to read this here rather than in your brother's rooms.'

'To my family,

I'm sorry, there seems no other way. I cannot face public humiliation but nor will I give into blackmail. Some of my colleagues may be willing to tell you about aspects of my private life; it will perhaps explain why I am nearly always on my own. Recently I have found myself in a compromising situation with a young research student, not for the first time. It has become a little more than private knowledge and one of his 'friends' wants money. This is as good a solution as any other. Please tell mum and dad that I am very sorry for the hurt that this will cause.

I hope this doesn't cause James any difficulties, newspapers might make something of it.

Vincent'

'No reason you both shouldn't see this. Read it aloud Peter. His last sentence is something of an understatement I think. Has what my brother refers to as 'private knowledge' reached your ears?'

'I'm sorry to say I had heard. In fact I had known for a while. Modern times, one tries to accept all relationships provided nothing seems to be illegal or abusive or behaviour which seems to be as if an older person is taking advantage of somebody much younger. Vincent never fell into such categories. Never mentioned by him, but I had heard that he was losing his sharpness of mind as far as his research work was concerned. His original Doctoral Thesis was considered outstandingly brilliant, but now, not quite as good. Sorry James, but can't keep information like this confidential, the press will find out everything.'

'Do I need to make a formal identification here or has my brother's body been removed to the mortuary?'

'I'm afraid he has been removed, usual procedure once initial investigation has been completed and the pathologist or doctor has made an examination. Investigation will have included photographs. I'm sorry if that's not what you expected,' explained Inspector Waterton.

'No, no, that's all right. The identification can be made later this evening or in the morning. That being so, Peter, can I make a confidential call to the Prime Minister, it is important he hears the circumstances before the press find out.'

'James, through there, my study, you won't be over heard.'

James smiled his thanks and walked through to make what he felt was going to be an uncomfortable call. 'Prime Minister, James here. Look, I'm still with the Master of Vincent's College together with the Police, Inspector Waterton who joined me for the last part of the journey. This call is confidential. If you are uncomfortable with that you could ring me back on my Foreign Office issued mobile.'

'That would be best, ring off and I'll get my secretary to connect us. Angela can you......'

James lost the rest of the call and he suspected that in any case he shouldn't have heard the first phrase. Angela? James's memory clicked in and he wondered if she had been transferred from Daniel Divine's office. Curious but before he could give the matter anymore thought his mobile rang.

'Prime Minister, look I need to tell you about the circumstances of my brother's death as there are implications. I'm afraid he took his own life because he was being threatened with blackmail over his private life. Unbeknown to the rest of his family, Vincent was gay and it seems

134

he has been somewhat indiscrete and someone who has compromising evidence wanted money. I imagine that because Vincent is my brother the blackmailer thought he was on strong ground and that's why you need to know the circumstances before it all hits the press, possibly tomorrow, certainly the day after. The Master has also told me that opinion among the College Fellows was that Vincent's research was in decline. I won't be able to make a formal identification until the morning. I'm hoping that the post mortem doesn't reveal anything embarrassing. I expect to return to London by mid-day but I ought to visit my parents as my sister Beryl is away and I haven't been in touch with her yet.'

'James, you mentioned implications, but we will not worry over them. They may prove serious or no more than embarrassing. You need to take all the time that your family needs, just keep me posted. Remember me to your father, one of the grand old men of the 'House'.'

'Thank you Prime Minister, you've been very kind and understanding.'

As James returned to the other room he felt decidedly better about matters. 'Gentlemen, can I go to where my brother was found. Is it likely that Police Officers will still be there and are they likely to want to ask questions?'

'I don't know the answer to that, it depends on how far their investigation has proceeded. We'll only know when we get there.'

'James, let me lead the way, we can go via a quieter route than some. As far as I know there are no media representatives there.' With that the Master led the way.

Chapter Twenty
Audrey

At the time of her mother's death Audrey remembered having felt very alone although at the time she didn't mind and anyway the feeling of loneliness soon passed with Rufus coming into her life. Now, the day following the visit of the Police Officers and Rufus having left for the Foreign Office, she felt very uncertain as to who she was and that thought left her feeling frightened, over-whelmed by a sense of uncertainty about herself, as if she had been cast adrift. As to whether her adoptive parents should have told her she was puzzled, easier if they had. She realised that although the police were carrying out repeat tests they were unlikely to obtain a different result. There were two possibilities, she had been adopted and the parents she thought were her parents were not blood related to her. The other possibility, unless a DNA test ruled it out, was that her father had had a daughter by a different woman. Somehow she thought the second of these possibilities was least likely, actually she really hoped that was the case because it would be almost impossible to find out the circumstances of such a birth. Audrey feared that this news and the uncertainty, no, changed or fresh certainty, was going to cause her a great deal of emotional disturbance and worry. She also had a horrible thought, might the police want to exhume her father's grave, would she even want that. Fortunately, Rufus seemed quite unphased by it all and she was struck by his immediate kindness when he realised the direction in which the Police Officer's thinking was moving. Being told by Rufus that she may have been adopted as a baby seemed so much more acceptable to her than being told through the mouth of authority. Audrey knew that the best solution for current feelings was to go out, visit a museum and she wasn't far from quite a selection, she could go for a walk in one of the London parks, she could even telephone her regular hair salon and see if an appointment was a possibility.

Pondering this array of choice her thoughts were interrupted by the telephone and she was delighted to hear Rufus's voice. 'Darling,' he said. 'Have you any plans for this evening?'

'No, nothing my love and I haven't started to cook some slow, low heat, four-hour recipe.'

'That's good. It's just that our Ambassador, Sir Reginald Hewlitt and Sheelagh are over from Paris for a couple of days. The Foreign Secretary has another engagement for this evening and as you and I know them well, it's suggested we take them out for dinner and I've got the Regal Court in mind. What do you think?'

'Wonderful, darling and that will take my mind off other matters. Gives me an excuse to ring my hair salon and see if they can fit me in. You'll be coming home first and then what, we all meet at the Regal Court?'

'That's the plan and I should be home easily by five o'clock. I'll telephone and make a booking with the Hotel.'

Phone call ended and Audrey's mood was transformed and she became even more relaxed when the hair salon receptionist said that her regular hairdresser had just been notified of a cancellation for later in the morning. That gave her time to call at a favourite coffee bar just a long from the salon, read the newspaper and indulge her taste buds with a couple of cappuccinos. With a bit of luck David might be on the reception counter at the hotel and he can renew his acquaintanceship with the Hewlitts.

Audrey was really looking forward to the evening as the four of them had become good friends during their stay in Paris. They often went to the theatre or opera together and occasionally when work commitments permitted, they travelled together for weekend breaks. Much of their touring of France and visiting famous places were all done in the company of Sheelagh and Reginald. It was almost like being on

138

holiday with close friends, rather than with a senior colleague. She got on with Sheelagh particularly well and they could talk for hours on just about any topic one could think of. As planned, they met in the bar of the Regal Crown Hotel, Reginald and Sheelagh were already there and as a welcome gift they already had a bottle of champagne on ice. As soon as the waiter spotted the arrival of their friends he was over to open it. With a friendly pop of the cork, bubbles poured and all was well with this friendly quartet.

'Do you remember David Yardlington who worked at the Hotel Auguste Rodin. I met him the other day, he has returned to the UK and works here. He is their senior reception guy and I gather the management here are very impressed with him. I'll just see if he is on duty this evening.'

'That was quite a co-incidence for Audrey, bumping into David the.....'

Seeing the look on Audrey's face Rufus's sentence remained unfinished.

'Terrible news about David, he and another resident at his block of apartments were using the lift when its safety mechanisms totally failed. They are both in hospital but David is still unconscious, brain has been bruised and is a little swollen. He's broken both legs badly and he has been very shaken up, a lot of internal bruising. They have had to operate to set the fractures. The hotel people here are being very helpful, allowing a room for David's parents to use when they come down from North Yorkshire to visit. He is in St Thomas's Hospital so perhaps I'll visit tomorrow. They say that people who are unconscious can be aware of people talking to them, I'll tell him what we've been doing. Well, that was all something of a shock, but this champagne will help, I think.'

Audrey pulled herself together and as they sat down in the dining room she made a very determined effort to jolly everybody up. Reginald made himself responsible for all the wine. At Sheelagh's suggestion they opted for a giant shell-fish platter and this had available just about every kind of shell fish imaginable including a circle of oysters running round the edge. It looked absolutely sumptuous and it was every bit as delicious. The dish had been placed on a small rotating device so that each of them could get to the tasty bits that each fancied as well as having some fun by rotating just as one of them was about pluck from the dish that 'tasty morsel' that they had spun the dish for. Still, if they had to wait their turn because there was too much spinning of the dish they could sip the magnificent Chablis which had been the first of Reginald's choices from the Hotel's cellars and this made for a wonderful start to their dinner.

By contrast they all opted for individual dishes for their second course. Rufus went with a well-known French dish, Entrecôte à la Bordelaise. Shelagh who was very fond of salads opted for thin slices of rare roast fillet of beef. Reginald who obviously had a good appetite went with an individual Beef Wellington. Just to be different, Audrey opted for a less expensive dish, Navarin of Lamb. Rather than take a number of individual orders for vegetables the waiters brought two large dishes with a wonderful array of different vegetables. Even though Audrey's Navarin of Lamb was cooked with many vegetables she was happy to help herself to more. To accompany all of these meaty dishes, Sir Reginald's second choice were two bottles of Nuit St George. 'They would all be drunk,' thought Audrey, and she made a mental note to drink more slowly.

When it came to sweets Sheelagh could have placed a bet on Reginald's choice, especially when she saw on the menu that the restaurant maintained a good selection of his favourite Italian ice-cream and she could have doubled the bet by saying that his choice would be a mixture of Chocolate, Coffee and Vanilla flavours topped with some whipped cream; Sheelagh won her own bet! Men keep together and Rufus went with his favourite, trifle. Sheelagh may have known with absolute certainty Reginald's choice but for herself she was quite undecided. In the end she stayed with savoury food and chose camembert served with crackers and grapes. The last to choose was Audrey and she opted for a hot summer pudding. When they had all finished, they strolled through to the lounge where coffee and chocolates awaited them, not the usual mint chocolates but a box of the

Hotel's own selection box of chocolates. Sheelagh and Audrey still had plenty of wine to drink and brought their glasses with them but Reginald and Rufus selected vintage brandies. Audrey made another mental note to ensure that she reminded Rufus to drink plenty of water over night or he would be facing his day at the Foreign Office with a serious head-ache. In the event Audrey was quite wrong, because when the car called for Rufus, Reginald having already been collected, they both went off to the office as if they had consumed nothing more intoxicating the previous evening than a tonic water. Sheelagh and Audrey were not in the least 'over-hung' and had promised themselves a day at the shops, something they both knew would be a great pleasure even if they spent not a penny.

While Rufus and Reginald were travelling to the FO Rufus received a call from the Foreign Secretary telling him of the dreadful news from the day before and also pointed out that the arrangements for the day would have to be changed. Further information would be available when they arrived. 'That's a terrible thing to have happened, likely to cause some press speculation, Rufus?'

'Almost certainly, can't keep matters like that out of the newspapers these days, Reginald. I'll just call Audrey, let her know that my plans for the day may have to change.'

Chapter Twenty-One
A Terrible Shock Continues

James was surprised to find that he had slept quite well. Perhaps the extraordinary events of the previous day had tired him mentally more than he realised and this thought caused him to 'revisit' some of them. He had visited his brother's college rooms, found little to concern him, the investigating team had left and all that was to be seen was police tape across the doorway and a single police officer standing outside, he supposed as a cautionary measure to warn students and other staff of the situation indoors. The Inspector who had accompanied James also left, promising to contact him regarding any arrangement that he needed to know about for the next day. Very kindly the College Master invited James to spend the night at his place, several spare rooms at the Lodge. Obviously James did not want to eat formally in hall and the Master arranged for a meal to be sent over. Fortunately, thanks to the efficiency of his Foreign Office staff, James had arrived with sufficient luggage to keep him going for a couple of days.

It was his mobile which caused him to wake early. Beryl had turned up and had heard the bare outlines of what had happened from a telephone message and decided that a call to James was the first necessity. She also telephoned Rhiannon and they had both decided that all three of them should call on their parents in the morning. Any arrangement for James to make a formal identification or learn details of a post-mortem if that had been completed would have to wait until the afternoon or even until the next day. He used his mobile to listen to the 7.00am news broadcast and was relieved to hear no mention of his family's tragedy. All being well they might be able to break the news to their parents before they heard it on the television. When he met Peter for breakfast soon after 8.00 o'clock he was pleased to discover that the news had not changed and that nothing was in the newspaper, well, certainly not The Times.

'Peter, I am going to have to ring for my car very soon as my sister has come home and she and my wife both think that the three of us should visit our parents before doing anything else. It may perhaps be that I will have to come back to Oxford this afternoon to make the formal identification.'

'James, just do what you feel is right as I can let people concerned know where you have gone. Have you a telephone number which you can leave so that I can make contact if necessary?'

James took out a card and added a couple more numbers and passed this over. 'There is nothing confidential in those numbers so feel free to give them to the police.'

'Thank you. You had better get your car called if it is coming out from London. Then we can have a leisurely breakfast.'

James couldn't help but notice that Peter led quite an old-fashioned existence as Master. Being unmarried he had a house-keeper who came in daily and as well as keeping the Lodge impeccably clean and tidy she also prepared a very substantial breakfast and it was obvious that Peter really enjoyed this meal. 'I make the most of breakfast, James, rarely eat at lunch-time, might have a cake with a couple of cups of tea mid-afternoon and that keeps me going until the evening meal. I do a lot of walking around college, rarely use my car, preferring to walk into town, so I manage to avoid putting on weight. I have to watch my drink consumption because if I'm not careful I can consume far too many glasses of sherry, not forgetting port or brandy in the evening. Enough of me going on about my eating and drinking habits. How do you think your parents are going to take this dreadful news of your brother?'

144

'To be honest I don't really know what to expect. Father has a reputation for calmness, found it very useful as a solicitor and when he was an M.P. He used to help fellow members get out of tricky situations and it wouldn't have done if he had been prone to react badly to what ever he was told. But Vincent's death, his oldest off-spring, I'm not sure. Probably he'll retreat into himself and be very quiet. With my mother, floods of tears are very likely to be the first reaction, but she will recover quickly and be extremely practical, organising funeral and such matters. Of course, I have no idea if Vincent made a will, could be there are precise instructions for his final departure. I must find out if he had a solicitor. I wonder if the police searched all his private papers yesterday, I must ask. Oh dear, I can see that there is going to be much to do in getting everything sorted. There is a limit to how much time I can be away from Government. The Foreign Office Department has a reputation for throwing up the unexpected. I must telephone my principal secretary soon.'

'James, I hope you don't mind my saying but you are in danger of trying to do just too much. I'm sure your wife and sister will take on many of the tasks which in normal circumstances you might have been expected to undertake. You can't ignore the fact that you are Foreign Secretary. Use your family and some of your staff if you feel you can trust them sufficiently. In my experience people will rally round when individuals find themselves totally overwhelmed. Make that one essential phone call and then perhaps have a rest while you wait for your car. I can deflect any incoming calls, especially if they are media in origin.'

'Wise words, Master and I'll take your advice.'

James made one brief call to Rufus Sutton, found that he was on his way to the F.O., told him about his brother and that he had heard that matters concerning the Ambassador's visit had been passed to his Minister of State and that his meetings had been either cancelled for the next three days or handed over to other staff. Rufus explained that he and the PUS could keep most cabinet colleagues at bay but perhaps the Prime Minister wouldn't be so easily put off.

'Rufus, thank you. I'll give the Prime Minister a call each afternoon. I think you can assume I'll be away from the F.O. until next week.'

Not forgetting Sir Peter's wisdom, James lay back on his bed and dozed.

It was about an hour later when there was a light tap on his door and his driver came in. 'Shall I take all this luggage out Sir?'

'Thank you Tony, I had better keep everything with me then there shouldn't be any problems.'

'In addition to whatever telephone numbers you have with you, your staff handed me a pretty comprehensive list before I left.'

'That's good, at least someone is organised. I must just bid the Master farewell and then I'll come round to the car. Where is it parked, his private drive?'

'Yes Sir.'

The drive over to Norstead Towers was fairly uneventful. Beryl had telephoned their parents to confirm their plans and told them when to expect them, and that James would be just a little later. One surprising call to James, was the Prime Minister, but in the event he uttered just a few general and soothing platitudes. He did tell him that he would entertain Sir Reginald to lunch, have Rufus along as well, possibly one of the Ministers. James was pleased to hear of that plan, thought it would suit Sir Reginald nicely, make him feel his visit was worthwhile. There were no more interruptions to the journey and it didn't seem long before they were pulling up at Norstead Towers. To his amazement, it was his mother who stepped out to welcome him.

'Darling James, this must all be so difficult for you. I can't think what Vincent thought he would achieve, must have really taken leave of his senses or had too much to drink. Your father is in his study, doesn't want to be disturbed but he'll come out when he's ready.'

'Hello Mother let's get in doors. Tony, can you drop everything off just inside the porch?'

'No problem, Sir.'

He and his mother went through to the drawing room where Beryl and Rhiannon were waiting. Rhiannon came straight over and gave him a giant hug. 'James this is just terrible, I don't know what to say but I hope there won't be any more unpleasantness to learn about. I suppose you haven't had any results of a post mortem yet?'

'I doubt it will be done until this afternoon at the earliest, so I'm afraid we will just have to wait.' Still holding Rhiannon, James looked across to his sister. 'Beryl, thank you for coming.'

'James, what do you know so far?'

'I have this letter, addressed to the family. This is a photocopy as I have left the original with the investigating officer. Vincent also left a letter for the coroner but I have not seen the contents of that.' He passed the family's letter to Beryl who read it quite quickly and then passed it to Rhiannon. 'As you can see there is still information to come out, at the very least a name, perhaps several.'

'It doesn't surprise me.'

'Beryl, how do you mean, did Vincent confide in you?'

'No, put it down to intuition. In all his teenage and adult life Vincent never mentioned women, girl- friends, nothing to remotely suggest a straight life style. Remember, he and I over-lapped at Oxford for two years, I did see him around, always with men, perhaps rather 'pretty,' can one say that?'

'I'm not surprised either.'

They all seemed staggered by their mother's comment.

'I think mothers can sense these matters. It doesn't sound as if there was a long-term love-based relationship though, that's sad.'

147

'Should I take this letter through to show father, or wait for him to join us?'

'I think you should wait James. When do you expect to hear anything more?'

'I'm not too sure mother. Certainly in the next couple of days. I have to go over to make the formal identification, probably do that tomorrow. If I'm staying here tonight I ought to tell Tony so he can return to London.'

'Stop over please, not sure when your father will appear.'

'I'll tell Tony now. Can I ask somebody for coffee?'

'Good idea, brother dear and perhaps we can eat something simple for lunch.'

It wasn't until the middle of the evening that his father appeared. James thought he looked a shade ashen and he seemed very terse when he spoke. He shook hands with James and took the letter when offered. 'As a former M.P. and a solicitor nothing about male sexuality surprises me. This seems no worse than other similar matters I've encountered. Because it is going to be a very public affair the unpleasantness will be worse.'

'I fear you are absolutely correct Father.'

Without saying anything else Sir George took himself back to his study. There was a loneliness about his stooped and rather slow departure and it caused James to feel that they were all very much aware of this sudden appearance of age in their father.

It was the middle of the evening when James received a call from Sir Peter. 'James, I have a message for you from the police. Can you be here for about 11.30am and then later in the day, towards 2.00pm to make the formal identification? If those times are all right with you I don't have to take any further action.'

'Those times are fine. I'll ring about the car in a while, shouldn't be any problem. Thank you Peter.'

His last phone call of the evening came from the Prime Minister. 'Thank you Prime Minister for making another call today. I am with my family at present but father is keeping to himself, but tomorrow I have to return to Oxford for a meeting with police late morning. I have no news of whatever information they may have; I just have to wait.'

'Well, James, just to let you know that many people are thinking of you and your family. Perhaps in a few days I can speak with your father; we've been acquainted for many years.'

'I've only spoken to him briefly today. Obviously he is very shaken and has retreated into his shell and wishes to be on his own.'

'I imagine he will open up a little in a few days, not an unusual reaction, James.'

' Yes, you're probably right, thank you Prime Minister.'

'Did you hear me talking to Sir Peter earlier, Mother? I have to leave for Oxford in the morning. Will you be all right? Rhiannon, Beryl, what are your plans if any?'

'I can stay for a few days, how about you Rhiannon?'

'I have nothing pressing. There are proofs of my next book and I need to check them, but I have plenty of time for that. Am I likely to be useful here.'

'Rhiannon, dear, you're always helpful and welcome of course. I doubt there is much you can actually do at present. I imagine it maybe at least a week before the police release my son's body. George and I will have to talk about a funeral but I doubt he is up to that just yet. Difficult to know whether it should be here or at Oxford, after all that's where he's been for the last thirty-five years or so. What do you think, James?'

'Not really sure, Mother. It may be that Vincent left a will and that might contain instructions. I haven't had an opportunity to look for a will or enquire of any solicitors in Oxford. If he did have views on a funeral I can't imagine what they might be. We never really had the kind of conversations which would give me any idea what he felt about such matters. By the time I was up at Oxford, Vincent was completely immersed in his research, so we didn't meet very often. Sorry, I know that doesn't sound very helpful. Now, if nobody minds I am going to make an early night, accompanied by a whisky. I need to be up early in the morning in case arrangements have to be changed.' Giving Rhiannon a smile as he poured himself a scotch, James was on his way.

Chapter Twenty-Two
Ghastly Information

James was about quite early but found there had been no overnight messages so he was able to enjoy a relaxing breakfast together with his wife and Beryl; Rhiannon had been the kindly soul working the magic in the kitchen even before James appeared. 'I'll telephone when I get any information or discover there is nothing to learn. I'll come back here or, if you prefer, return home darling, when I have completed all I need to do in Oxford. If I get the opportunity I'll sound out Sir Peter regarding Vincent's funeral and see if there is any College expectation.'

Tony arrived soon after 9.00 o'clock and they were at the Master's Lodge well in time for the meeting with the police. It was Inspector Waterton who arrived to meet him and they exchanged pleasantries, James asked if Sir Peter would stay, and Inspector Waterton started.

'I'll give you the facts as we know them and in chronological order. It was Vincent's secretary, Janice Etherton, who found the body, called the police, and then alerted key staff, including Sir Peter. Police were in attendance from 10.30am and the police doctor arrived soon after. He conducted a brief examination and established that Vincent was dead but did no more, so that a pathologist could examine the body in situ and have photographs taken. Police officers examined the room but there had been nothing untoward noticed, no damage to doors or windows. There was no sign of external violence to your brother's body which soon after was taken by undertakers to the mortuary for the post mortem and this has been completed.'

'The plastic bag which your brother had tied tightly around his neck contained a liquid substance including formaldehyde and this would have brought about unconsciousness quickly, with fatal asphyxiation following speedily. The pathologist has calculated that death occurred between mid-night and 2.00am. He has also established that sexual activity occurred not long before death and he suggests that Vincent may have been raped. At this moment in time we have no other names to link with your brother but given how aspects of college life can be like a closed community it will be surprising if names do not emerge in the next two or three days. The pathologist has sent various specimens for laboratory analysis and samples have been taken for DNA comparison but results will not be available until the beginning of next week.'

'Thank you Inspector, that's been very clear. My mother was talking vaguely last night about funeral arrangements and wondered how long it would be before the body could be released.'

'I can't give you a precise answer but you should think in terms of two weeks, almost certainly not sooner.'

'Now I still haven't made a formal identification, is it convenient to do that this afternoon?

'Yes, let me make one phone call and by the time we're there all will be ready.'

'Sir Peter, when I return can I have a little of your time, two or three matters to discuss?'

'Not a problem James, I'll be here for the rest of the day.'

The Inspector finished his call and looked up. 'If we go now we'll arrive just right.'

James had never made a formal identification of someone who had died and he had no idea what to expect other than what he had seen in various dramas on television. In the event James found it a surprisingly gentle process. He was shown into one room, occupied by an official known as the Coroner's assistant and to whom he showed his identification. There was a window looking through to another larger room and as James looked a stretcher trolley was being wheeled in. The white cloth which was covering Vincent was folded back and James was told that he could enter. He and the Inspector did so. He recognised his brother immediately noting that his face appeared clean and uninjured and that his hair had been made tidy. He perhaps inclined his head, paused a moment, turned and left the room and told the Coroner's assistant that he could confirm the identity of his brother, Vincent St John. It was probable that the whole formality of identification took less than two or three minutes and Inspector Waterton drove him back to the Master's Lodge. James gave him his thanks, made sure he had any necessary phone numbers and the Inspector went on his way and James joined Sir Peter.

'James, what did you want to ask?'

'It's on behalf of my mother as she doesn't know whether to arrange Vincent's funeral locally, at Norstead, or whether there is an expectation that it ought to take place here in Oxford, even at the College. At the moment my father is silent on everything and neither my sister nor my wife have any clear thoughts on the matter.'

'I don't think I can give you a straight answer, sorry, James, because that is most unhelpful. Vincent has been known here for over thirty years and in the normal course of events, family in agreement, his funeral would be expected to take place here. But given the circumstances of his death and what further information may come to light, there is perhaps no certainty as to what should take place.'

'I get the picture, Peter, and I had been thinking along similar lines. A private funeral at home may be the best arrangement, family, close friends, college representatives. Look, you've been immensely helpful over the last few days, much appreciated. I think I can leave now, Tony is nearby and with a bit of luck I'll be able to have a quiet evening at home with Rhiannon. I'll perhaps telephone our two sons and bring them up to date.' They shook hands and James met Tony outside and they were off. James took the opportunity then to telephone Rhiannon and arrange to meet her at their home.

A quiet evening at home didn't really materialise. There seemed to be endless phone calls, family and Government staff as well as a call from the Prime Minister and just when he thought there was a lull Inspector Waterton was on the line. 'Sorry to bother you again so soon but we've had a confession, not quite the right word, but a College research post-graduate student has been into the police station to talk about Vincent. He wanted it known that he and Vincent had been seeing each other regularly, was last with him on the afternoon of his death when he thought Vincent was his usual self so he has been in something of a state of shock since he heard. He's an Alan Corbynsky, scientist, and his area of study is something to do with molecular plant biology, that's as best as I can remember what he said of his work. He also said that he didn't think he and Vincent shared an exclusive relationship but he was unable to say more. From what he said we don't think there was anything like an act of rape between them. DNA tests may reveal more.'

When the Inspector rang off, Rhiannon produced a bottle of red wine and finally they both felt a degree of welcome relaxation. For a while they sat in companionable silence but then James told his wife what Peter's opinion was on the matter of Vincent's funeral. Apparently she, Beryl and their mother had talked a little more about it and had come to a similar conclusion so unless their father felt strongly otherwise, that was probably what would happen. All that remained was to plan the form of the ceremony.

Just before they went to bed there was a good-night call from his mother and James was pleased to hear that his father was up and about, seemingly more his usual self. Beryl had stayed and he sensed that his mother was pleased to have someone else to talk to.

It was most fortunate that James and Rhiannon both enjoyed a peaceful night because the following morning brought with it several rather ghoulish newspaper head-lines with some hinting at further revelations yet to emerge. The Prime Minister's spokesman had done his best to ensure that everyone knew that the Foreign Secretary retained the total confidence of Anthony May and that Vincent's death was a very sad occurrence but had nothing whatsoever to do with government, a deeply upsetting time for the St John family and it was to be hoped that the press would be respecting their privacy at such a time. It was a 'hope' in vain because when James looked out he saw a crowd of reporters just beyond the front gate; he was pleased to see that there were two police officers in attendance. He telephoned his mother and he learnt of a similar circumstance at the family home. It made him even more thankful that Beryl had stayed with their parents.

Soon after he had finished reading the newspapers he received a call from the Prime Minister so he was able to bring him up to date on how matters stood and that nothing else could be done until they received a date for the release of his brother's body. He explained that he didn't know what further information would come out about his brother's life style. The Prime Minister made the usual and expected kindly remarks, and then went to say that the visit of Reginald Hewlitt had been successful and that the lunch party had been very pleasant and enjoyed by all. Rufus Sutton had attended, two other officials and also one of his secretaries, she had been rather helpful in keeping some short-hand notes.

'Prime Minister, was that Angela Rosemary who is engaged to Jeremy Lutterworth, both at the Home Office?'

'Quite right, James. Angela has made a transfer and is with me. You'll remember I met her when we were at your place that weekend earlier in the year. She is exceptionally efficient. Daniel didn't mind as he is not too keen on having couples working in the same department.'

'Understood, Anthony, can lead to difficulties of confidentiality. I think I can say that I'll be back at the Foreign Office after the week end. I shall have to miss a day for the funeral, probably in a couple of weeks, possibly sooner. I don't intend being at the inquest as there will be nothing of any evidential nature I can contribute. I intend to telephone Rufus later today and get myself up to date.'

'That's good, James. I will see you next week then. Regards to Rhiannon.'

Chapter Twenty-Three
Further Police Investigations

Sergeant Watson had plenty of work to get on with which required some careful thought and planning. He wasn't quite sure why Inspector Ball wanted to follow-up on these enquiries as he thought the work centred on what had happened with the failure of the lift and the injuries to the two men; it was a case of the inspector and his hunches. He wanted his Sergeant to inspect pupil lists for past pupils at Kemby School and Kroxby School so his first important activity was to obtain warrants as he didn't want to be blocked by somewhat guarded responses which would thwart his efforts. Thus armed, he telephoned both schools and made appointments. He would need to stay the night somewhere as both schools wanted him to call during a morning. He had also pursued enquiries at the Regal Crown Hotel regarding who knew David Yardlington and had had confirmed the name Jeremy Lutterworth, somebody he knew about anyway. One of David's colleagues had heard two men talking who had attended a Banking Investment Seminar and one of them seemed to know either David or his friend Jeremy Lutterworth who was talking to him at the same time. The only name this colleague had noticed was a Nigel. That was sufficient to cause Sergeant Watson to make a few more phone calls. First of all he tracked down the Banking Seminar organisers and with a bit of persuasive 'Police Talk' he obtained a list of the delegates and as luck would have it there was only one 'Nigel,' Nigel Vauxhall, who he traced to his place of work. As soon as Nigel knew that Sergeant Watson wanted information about Jeremy and the name of the other former Kemby School pupil he was happy to oblige. Nigel explained to him how he and Jeremy were step-brothers and Sergeant Watson tucked this piece of information away. To this information he added the name, Garry Compton and from the list of delegates he was able to trace him via a mobile phone number. This proved helpful because Garry was able to explain a little more about how the boys used to visit Great Yarmouth on Saturdays, having absconded from school sports and other such activities that they should have been engaged in. Garry wasn't too good on remembering boys' names, as he pointed out it was well over twenty years back. They ended the conversation with Garry promising to be in touch if he remembered more.

For his first journey he managed to set off quite early hoping to arrive at Kemby School at about ten o'clock. Presenting himself at the school office, he was pleased to discover that he was expected. He explained his purpose in greater detail, that because of certain police enquiries which centred on a former pupil, David Yardlington, who probably left in the summer of 2006, he wanted to ask about some other pupils. He knew that David had been a close friend of Jeremy Lutterworth. He also mentioned that another name had come up in the course of their enquiries, Garry Compton, but he thought he was a year younger.'

'Sergeant Watson, can I stop you for a minute because I want you to meet one of our older secretaries, Miss Davenport, who has worked here over forty years and her memory of faces and names of former pupils is legendary. We have very clear records of past pupils, years attended, address as known at the time, a photograph and a brief note of external examination results.'

'For a police officer making enquiries your Miss Davenport sounds like a gift from heaven.' Sergeant Watson smiled.

'I'll take you through to her office and the records you want to see are in the room next to hers.'

Miss Davenport was fairly typical of an unmarried lady in her middle sixties, as Sergeant Watson supposed was her age, neat and precise in her appearance, quietly and discretely dressed and very attentive to whatever was being said.

'Sergeant, have I understood you correctly, you want me to look up records for three former pupils and then tell you what I can remember about them, their associates and anything else that comes to mind.?'

'That's perfect, Miss Davenport, thank you.'

'Let me start with the name that I remember most, Jeremy Lutterworth. He came to us having been expelled from his previous school and we used to joke that 'Manners Maketh Man' had done little for him. He didn't achieve much while he was here but I seem to remember he was involved with some trouble which involved a group of girls from Kroxby Girls' School, Great Yarmouth. When I say trouble it coincided with the sudden departure of that school's head mistress and a number of girls were asked to leave and one was thought to be pregnant.'

'And that's all before you pull up the record, Miss Davenport.'

'At the time of the Head Mistress's sudden departure the rules at this school were not being enforced sufficiently as was wise for the pupils. Jeremy Lutterworth was often out in town with a group of four or five other boys, David Yardlington was one of them. Let me pull out some records and see what else I remember.'

When she came back from the room next door she was holding about half a dozen old school records. 'I have records of David, Jeremy and Garry here, Garry was in the year below the others but by only a few weeks. I have pulled out records of three other pupils in the same year as David and Jeremy, Peter Norton, Thomas Wolverton, and George Palmerson. Now as I remember, this group of lads often used to take themselves off to Great Yarmouth on Saturdays when they should have been here for different sport activities. Perhaps one reason they got away with this rule breaking was because George's father was on the staff, he taught science, chemistry I think. George had a much younger brother, Frank, who also became a pupil ten years later. Staff got a small discount if their children became pupils here. I don't know why I have remembered all that detail though. After the crisis at Kroxby Girls' School the Headmaster at the time here, tightened up the rules regarding permission for leaving the premises. Unfortunately prior to that things had got a little lax. Looking at these records I can see that none of them achieved inspiring results. Once they had left school I have no idea what they went on to achieve, do you know anything of that Sergeant?'

'Well I have some information. Jeremy went on to repeat his A levels and achieved high results and went to Durham University and currently he is a Government Ministerial Adviser. David spent fifteen years at a Paris Hotel and he is fluent in French as well. Garry is a Banking Investment Adviser.'

'That is very impressive. Now one other thing I remember about this group of lads was that they were physically a bit more grown up than most of their contempories, could easily be taken for eighteen. I imagine that made them more attractive for the girls about whom you are asking questions tomorrow.'

'That's the plan, Miss Davenport. You've been most helpful and can I just say that your memory is absolutely stunning. I'm going down my 'memory lane' this afternoon as I haven't been to Great Yarmouth since I was a boy so I intend to go and eat something like a pizza and then stroll about with a large ice-cream cone. I'm stopping the night at one of the hotels looking out to sea.'

'I'm sure you will enjoy yourself. In case your memory is not quite as good as mine, I have made photocopies of the records for you to keep. I don't think anyone will mind, they are twenty-five or so years old. We're only a two-form entry school so we can keep records for a very long time, but the bigger five or six form entry establishments must have to dispose of records frequently.'

'That's exceptionally helpful of you and I'll give those a good look before I visit Kroxby School. For now I can rest my mind from matters policing because it's a rare treat for me as far as Police work is concerned to get the opportunity to spend a day at the seaside. Provided I return to my Inspector with some useful information, and you've enabled me to make a very good start, no questions will be asked as to how I spent any leisure time which came my way.'

In fact his afternoon proved extremely enjoyable as he was able to catch the last boat trip out to Scroby Sands and see a large colony of grey seals, the weather was perfect and he delighted in such a mini-cruise on a calm sea and with magnificent views. Earlier he had really gone down memory lane as he bought his promised ice-cream cone, took off his shoes and socks and strolled along the water edge wondering whether his ice-cream's flavour lived up to the one in his memory. Probably not as he then recalled how he loved sea-side rock as a child, something which he knew he would hate now! Later, when he checked into his chosen hotel, one which didn't manage to include 'sea-view' in its name, he found himself in a beautifully appointed front room with breath-takingly stunning views out to sea. He might have preferred rougher seas, some stormy atmosphere because he had brought with him for his 'busman's holiday' reading, 'Devices and Desires,' by P D James, a great piece of detective fiction reading. He had read all her novels and never minded re-reading them, a sign for him that it was a good book. Sometimes if he read something which he found really brilliant he would go straight back to the beginning and start again.

It was a pleasant hotel, modest in size and not very busy. Unusual for him, he took his book with him when he went down for his evening meal as he thought he might be able to continue reading without causing offence. His thinking was right, he occupied a small table to one side of the room and there were just two couples the other side. They were obviously all friends and beyond initial pleasantries our Sergeant was his own company, along with a very senior and fictional colleague, Commander Adam Dalgliesh.

Chapter Twenty-Four
Further, Further Investigations

His start the following day was perfectly leisured. As was his usual habit he was up quite early and finding the previous day's pleasant weather had continued he went for a lengthy walk along the front. It successfully blew away a few cobwebs and thoughts of Adam Dalgliesh because he had read until very late to finish his book. He probably walked three or four miles, he wasn't in any hurry as he was not expected at Kroxby Girls' School until eleven-thirty. When he returned for his breakfast he realised that perhaps he had been out for a little too long as he found the proprietor looking a little anxious, perhaps not even sure that he intended to have his breakfast. He apologised suitably for this tardiness, didn't take too long over his breakfast, paid his bill to which he added a good tip, and returned to his room to focus his mind on the police work which was soon to engage him for later in the morning. He re-read all the records that he had been given the previous day and reminded himself of the girls' names and bits of names on which the enquiries at Kroxby would be based.

As planned, he arrived at Kroxby School at eleven-thirty but unlike his reception at Kemby School, Sergeant Watson realised immediately that his next enquiries would be handled far more formally. He was shown into the Head Mistress's office and introduced to Miss Frosby and before anything was said she asked to see his warrant and Police identification.

She explained, 'I'm sure you realise Sergeant that as Head Mistress it is important that I check thoroughly the paperwork attendant upon any enquiry such as yours. Can I make a copy of these items?

'It is perfectly in order for you to make a copy of the magistrate's warrant but not my police identification. Feel free though to make a note of my name, rank and number.' It was at this point that Sergeant Watson realised that he was feeling very nervous, the sensation that he recalled from school days when he was sent to see the Headmaster on account of bad behaviour. He supposed it was because he had had to contradict the Head Mistress's request; he would never have contradicted his Headmaster. She must have pressed a button because just then her secretary came in and was asked to photo-copy the Magistrate's warrant.

'Now, Sergeant, I understand you wish to ask about some former pupils dating back to about 2004. Actually that was when I was appointed and I imagine your enquiry date is not a coincidence. Am I right?'

'Yes Ma'am. I believe that just before your appointment four pupils were asked to leave and that it was rumoured that one pupil left because she was pregnant. It is those pupils, rather their names which interest us.'

'Can you explain why?'

The Head Mistress's abrupt questions did nothing to make the Sergeant feel any more relaxed. 'We have an individual in our area who has suffered badly in a lift failure and currently he is in hospital, unconscious and has multiple fractures to his legs. He is David Yardlington who was a pupil at Kemby School at the same time as the pupils from this school were asked to leave. He has recently met up with an old friend from the same time and we know that they were involved with meeting the girls from this school along with others from Kemby. The man who is unconscious keeps muttering bits of names and it is quite unclear what he is trying to say. One name sounds like 'Lucy' and another sounds like 'Queen' or 'Quem.' We don't know whether these part-names or words are important but when my Inspector mentioned them to the former acquaintance, of the man in hospital, Jeremy Lutterworth, he gave the distinct impression of clamming up and lying.'

'It all sounds a shade tenuous if you want my opinion and had you not arrived in possession of a Magistrate's warrant our conversation would have come to a speedy conclusion. However, because the business of the pupils who were asked to leave this school and the one pupil who became pregnant led to a number of extraordinary meetings of the School Governors and the dismissal of my full-time predecessor, I do have much of the information to hand. I have four names to give you one of which will explain your bits of names uttered by your hospital patient. The key name is Lucinda Quemsby and I can say that she was the pupil who became pregnant. No mention was ever mentioned of the father, not even if he was a pupil of Kemby School. The remaining names are June Fretton, Prudence Tomlinson and Henrietta Allumbie. Do those names help at all?'

'Indeed they do Ma'am. The one which explains David Yardlington's mutterings is very important and if she is the one who became pregnant it begs the question as to why it has come to his mind. The other names have not arisen in any of our enquiries but they are all names which we can probably track down if necessary, fairly unusual names as far as births, marriages and death records are concerned. Should any information come to light which may be of importance to your school, we will of course let you know.'

'Well Sergeant, I am pleased that the school has been able to help you. It is amazing how far back in time some police enquiries go. I hope it all turns out to be relevant.' Miss Frosby stood up at this point, Sergeant Watson was speedy to stand as well and proffered his hand.

'Sorry Sergeant, just take your seat again, perhaps I have been a little hasty. I noticed in the record which I glanced at, a note about Lucinda which may be of interest. It seems that it was her parents who arranged for her to be withdrawn from this school but the original admission a few years earlier and the payment of all fees was undertaken by her Grandmother, a Mrs Daphne Quemsby. Older relatives paying school fees is not unusual but in this case it seems that the relative had taken much more responsibility for Lucinda, that is until she became pregnant. I'm not sure why I have thought to provide this additional information but perhaps it will prove relevant.'

'Well, thank you ma'am, in our work it is not uncommon for information which at first glance may seem irrelevant but later assumes greater importance. I mustn't trouble you further.' They both stood up again and not needing to shake hands again, Sergeant Watson was soon on his way. He didn't drive far before he stopped, bought himself a newspaper, and strolled into a nearby café for a snack lunch together with a large pot of tea; his visit to Kroxby School had left him decidedly thirsty.

He had a good drive back, but found his Inspector was out when he reached the Police Station. This time enabled him to write up a report which he left for his boss to read and then wrote up his expenses claim and left that as well for his boss to counter sign.

He thought about the names he had received from the Girls' School. The most important one was Lucinda Quemsby and he did a search for that. A reference to a birth came up dated 1991, an address in the West Country. It seemed straight forward and he printed off the information. He tried Henrietta Allumbie next as it was the most unusual name. There were several listings and if they were correct as far as 'his' Henrietta were concerned she was a writer, short stories which appeared in magazines. Newspaper articles were also listed. Usefully there were contact details. Having printed all the information which came up he tried June Fretton's name next. There was nothing more than a straight forward listing for a birth, several in fact but only one which had a correct date. Her address was for somewhere in the north. Strangely, when he tried Prudence's name nothing appeared, further attempts using different ways of keying in her name also drew a blank. He left that for the time being and tried the surname 'Quemsby' again. The response was interesting in that it brought up information about a trust fund set up early in the twentieth century. He printed off what was on the screen but didn't have any more time to pursue it. Plenty to talk over with the Inspector when they met up in the morning. He wasn't at all sure where it was going to lead them, if anywhere. On his way home it did occur to him that he or his Boss must ring the hospital and check on David Yardlington, they needed to know what might be planned for his immediate future and also they needed to be informed if he remembered anything more when, hopefully, he recovered consciousness.

For now Sergeant Watson needed some food, a beer or two and probably an early night, at least he oughtn't to stay up late reading yet another crime novel. Crime novel reading won the day and Sergeant Watson turned up to talk to his boss yawning yet again.

Chapter Twenty-Five
Links

Well, Sergeant you seem to have had a very interesting couple of days and but for the suspicion that Jeremy Lutterworth was lying to us when we questioned him I don't think we would be at all interested in this. After all, clearly it has nothing to do with David Yardlington's accident and that is what caused us to visit him in the first place. I take it we have received no further information about how he is doing in hospital?'

'Correct Sir.'

'Any thoughts on why his old school friend should be so cagey about telling us of his past? He knew we had only called because of the accident and the strange things David was saying.'

'I can only think that something happened all those years ago and that it still worries him or causes embarrassment. It may just have been petty crime, something stupid that teenagers get up to, who knows. As you have said, Sir, our concern was the accident. We know that those responsible for the safety of the lift failed to do what was required of them and there may be police action as far as that firm is concerned but it has nothing to do with when David Yardlington and his friends were fifteen or sixteen.'

'Absolutely correct. We'll put it all to one side other than to check on David's progress in hospital and any action required by us in connection with the firm responsible for the lift.'

'I'll telephone the hospital later today to check on the patient, meanwhile I'll get on with other work.'

'Thank you Sergeant.'

'Sir.'

In fact there had been developments regarding David. A member of staff from the Regal Crown Hotel's Human Resources Department had gone to visit him in hospital and by coincidence found that over night he had recovered consciousness and that his elderly parents were visiting as well.

'Good morning, I'm Joan Clarkson and one of my responsibilities at the hotel is to check on anything connected with staff welfare. If this is a bad time I can come back later but it may be helpful as your parents are here if I let you know how the Hotel can help with your immediate future.'

'That sounds a very good idea.' It was Mrs Yardlington taking the initiative. 'Are you up to this David, it may be important?'

David nodded and muttered something, perhaps a 'yes' or 'good idea,' his speech still wasn't very clear.

'Joan, can we call you Joan, it was only late last night that the hospital telephoned to tell us of David's coming out of unconsciousness, but they warned us that his speech wouldn't be too clear for a few days but at least now the worry is mainly connected with his physical recovery, how well he gets over the surgery from a day or so back.'

'Well, that's why I have called David. Most of the staff, certainly those on full-time contracts, are covered by an insurance policy in terms of health and accidents. Not just accidents at work so this policy will enable us to make a claim on your behalf. When the hospital decides you are fit enough to be discharged the insurance claim will cover you until you are able to look after yourself. You're certainly nowhere near fit enough to be at home on your own so they will pay for nursing home or convalescent care. I'm going to speak to the ward staff here, if that's all right with you David, as we need to be kept informed of your progress. Back at the hotel I can arrange for the claim to be made and make some enquiries as to where you might go for the additional period of recuperation. Do you want to stay down here, London based, in touch with friends or do you want to be in your parents' area where it will be easier for them to visit?

'London, down here. Hospital visits.'

'I understand you David. You will need to attend hospital for out - patient visits so to stay in this area would be best.'

'Yes.' David and his mother both said that at the same time.

'I'll be off now, quick word with staff before I leave and of course, David, I will keep in touch with you.' Smiles all round and Joan Clarkson was away.

David's father spoke just then, generally a man of few words normally. 'Your employers seem to be extremely helpful son. That insurance deal will cost a lot of money and that takes a lot of worry away knowing what can be done for you.'

'Yes dear, and David, it is such a relief to see you conscious again. I hope it makes you feel a lot better.'

'It does mum, thanks.'

A phone call later in the day between Sergeant Watson and the ward's staff nurse brought him in to visit David Yardlington for what he expected to be his last visit. He was very pleased to see him conscious at last and able to speak reasonably well. He explained to David that because he had muttered names and bits of names they had undertaken a few enquiries but were not sure how relevant they all were. He explained that their enquiries centred on the accident involving the lift.

'I'll start with some girls first and the name you nearly got right was Lucinda Quemsby and when I enquired at her old school the following names were mentioned, June Fretton, Prudence Tomlinson and Henrietta Allumbie. Why was Lucinda so much on your mind?'

'You'll think I'm mad but the other day I thought I saw her and as Jeremy knew her so well I wanted to tell him. I know it couldn't have been her because she would be in her forties now. Somebody must have just reminded me of her. The other girls you have mentioned we used to meet in Great Yarmouth. I haven't thought of them for years. June Fretton had a bit of a thing for me but I wasn't very keen. Going back to Lucinda, she was the one who was rumoured to have left because she was pregnant.'

'She certainly left and the other three were asked to leave. The school had a new Head Mistress and there was much tightening up of rules. If Lucinda were pregnant could you have been the father?'

'No, I might have fooled around with June a bit but nothing like that with any of them.'

'How about your friend Jeremy?'

'Could have been, he used to boast about what they got up to but boasting is one thing, doing is another.'

'What do you remember of the other boys whose names I have been told about, Peter Norton, Thomas Wolverton, George Palmerson and Garry Compton?'

'Nothing, old mates I think. They used to be in Great Yarmouth with us on Saturdays. I think Garry was in the Hotel some time back. Did you say you had a photograph?'

174

'Yes, this is him.'

'Difficult to say if that teenage face became the guy I saw, but I think so.'

'You are correct, he attended some investment banking conference.'

'I remember that because Jeremy met a step-brother who was attending as well. Nigel was his name I think.'

'Your memory has done extremely well Mr Yardlington, obviously your bang on the head has not damaged that bit of your brain. One final query. When you were still unconscious and we didn't know how relevant or important what you were trying to say might be, my Inspector and I called on your old friend Jeremy. He seemed very cagey about your former friends and just said he remembered nobody from his school days. He was quite unhelpful.'

'Can't help your there unless he didn't like reminding himself about Lucinda and the baby. As far as I remember none of us ever heard anything more about those girls.'

'Thanks for your help. I don't think anymore enquiries will arise from your unconscious mutterings. What happens to you now?'

'Well, I had an operation on my legs a few days back now, and when the doctors think my legs have set sufficiently I'll be discharged. As of this morning I discover the Hotel has an insurance for the majority of the staff for accidents, on or off the premises and that will cover me for as long as I need to stay in residential care of some sort until I can fend for myself. Hotel welfare person is making arrangements for me to stay somewhere down here, so that I can get back to the hospital for out-patient visits. Eventually I'll go back to my flat and start work again. I hope the lift has been mended correctly.'

'Keep asking about that because there is likely to be a court case. The lift was not properly maintained, a case of gross negligence. The Health and Safety Executive are still completing their enquiries. I'm no solicitor but there could be compensation. Your hotel will have a solicitor, he'll know I should think.'

'Thank you for that, I'll make enquiries. Some good compensation will be very useful.'

'Goodbye then and thanks for answering all my questions.'

'Cheerio.' They shook hands and the Police Officer left.

All his visitors had left David quite worn out and before he'd even realised, he had fallen asleep and it was only with the arrival of the evening meal that he woke up. He found he had been kipping for over three hours. The catering staff brought him a helping of Lasagne and peas and that was followed by a chocolate sponge pudding with chocolate sauce. It wasn't at the standard of the Hotel's Chefs but it was tasty comfort food and he ate the lot. He could have drunk a beer but all that was on offer was water or coffee; he had both.

When visiting time started he was surprised to find Jeremy coming into his room. 'Hello David, feeling a little better. Certainly good to find you conscious.'

'Jeremy, nice to see you. I had the police here earlier, the Sergeant was talking about you. Apparently when I was unconscious they were concerned about my incoherent mutterings.'

'Yes, I know, they came to see me.'

'They've done some research and tracked down names that I was trying to mention, in particular they are curious about Lucinda Quemsby. Do you remember her?'

'Vaguely, not sure.'

'You amaze me Jeremy. I know it's years ago but there was a time when you couldn't get enough of her, to coin a phrase.'

'Teenage boastings, David.'

'I had a strange experience a few days ago, I thought I saw her, Lucinda. It was only a momentary thought, must have seen her double, doppelgänger – that's the expression isn't it?'

'My, you have a vivid imagination David or you are still suffering from your bang on the head. Anyway, can't stay long, see you again no doubt. Cheers'

'And you, Jeremy.'

Jeremy may have walked away seemingly quite cheerful, but he certainly didn't feel cheerful, in fact he was quite worried that his youthful sexual experiences, such as they were, amounted to very irresponsible behaviour, or was he confusing boasting with reality and was something from his past going to return with most unexpected and unwelcome consequences. Then he started to wonder about David and his mention of seeing Lucinda; he didn't want to think about that as he could easily guess at the source of his doppelgänger.

Chapter Twenty-Six
Politicians Try Not to Panic

There is a truism with which politicians are familiar, the need to be able to cope with the unexpected, and by definition the unexpected can only ever happen, never planned, lands from nowhere; but according to Sod's Law, it will always come at a very inconvenient moment. The kidnap of the Brazilian Ambassador to The Court of St James, Senhor Joaquim Barbosa was no exception to these everyday pieces of wisdom.

At the moment when this stunning piece of news broke, the House of Commons was in session but just at that moment was between different pieces of procedure and the best description would be to say that the 'House' was in a state of pause. With the hurried exchange of notes along the front bench the Leader of the House stood to make a statement.

'Mr Speaker, My apologies for interrupting the matters in hand, but I have to tell the House that as the result of a deliberate collision between three cars in South London earlier today, Joachim Barbosa, the Brazilian Ambassador, has been captured, we presume kidnapped, but as yet we have no information regarding who was responsible nor do we know what their demands, if any, will be. From eye-witness accounts he seemed uninjured but he was thrown into the back of an escape vehicle which left the scene at very high speed. It was a black saloon car, thought to be a......... Senhor Barbosa's wife and children have remained resident in Brazil although they have visited London on a number of occasions. At present they are in Brazil.' The Leader of the House paused to read another note which had been passed to him. *'We now know that the escape vehicle was abandoned and left in an*

179

enclosed complex of garages. There have been no reports of eye-witnesses to this exchange of cars.' A further pause, a further message. *'We have been further informed by Scotland Yard, that all their desk-top computers have been bombarded by repeated emails, one message only,* **"You will be hearing more from the members of RAFTS"** *I am able to tell the House that this terrorist organisation is known to Security Services as are similar groups around the world, their intention is to use force to bring about immediate implementation of measures to halt Climate Change. We understand that the particular intention of RAFTS is to force key countries, Brazil being one, to replant the rain forests. We will bring more information to the House when we receive it, but as to action, Mr Speaker, other than to say that there will be a meeting of COBRA later this afternoon, I'm sure all honourable members will understand if we refrain from indicating the current measures being taken by the Police and Members of the Security Services.'*

The Leader of the House sat down, had a hurried conversation with the Prime Minister and they both then left the Chamber, joined by the Home Secretary. There may have been calmness in the House as the Leader made his statement, but back at Downing Street activity was decidedly more energetic. The Prime Minister sent for the Foreign Secretary, and he was joined by Edgar Shrewsbury. Daniel Divine, already with the Prime Minister, telephoned Jonathan Venniston to join them. The Prime Minister also asked for Clive Anderson to attend. The urgency of the situation must have been felt for everybody arrived with exemplary speed.

Anthony May opened the discussion. 'I don't want there to be any sense of panic about this kidnapping, not suggesting of course that it isn't immensely serious, it is, but panic and knee jerk reactions won't achieve anything. Initially I want the Security Experts to complete their opening investigations and of course we haven't heard the last of 'RAFTS.' I can't see the demand being anything to do with money, so what might it be. Any thoughts?'

'Yes Clive, you look keen to speak.'

'Thank you Prime Minister, the demand has to be an undertaking or a commitment by the Brazilian Government, but to whom will the commitment be made and how can it be verified remains to be seen. Of greater importance is the opinion of the general public, a sizeable chunk will support RAFTS, won't they?'

'Does that mean as The Home Secretary, I may want the Police and security forces to fail? That puts me in the role of supporting an illegal public kidnapping.'

'That is going to be a very real dilemma Daniel. What do you think James, are representatives of the Brazilian Embassy are going to come banging on the door of the Foreign Office very soon?'

'It is going to attack the principle that has governed us for all time, that Governments must uphold the rightness of obeying the law. Do I say one thing but believe another?'

'Well, gentlemen, you are all at the heart of the problem. We have to face various scenarios: What should we do if the Ambassador is found very quickly? What do we say to the Brazilian Government if the kidnap lasts a long time? What attitude should we take in the event of public opinion being much in favour of the kidnap – a real possibility I fear?'

'Returning to an earlier point, I think the only demand and action in response worth anything will be a public commitment made to the United Nations and agreement for United Nations Forces to be allowed to inspect progress without giving notice to the Brazilian Government.'

'Thank you Daniel, probably the only valid request worth making. With the speed of social media these days, public opinion will be clear within twenty-four hours. How will this be reflected in the House of Commons? Newspapers will be clear by the morning. I wonder how long it will be before RAFTS make their demands public. We also need to consider what we are going to say when asked for individual opinions – are we going to try and remain neutral although I doubt that is even possible. When we have finished these purely political ponderings, serious as they are, I shall ask the Security Services to tell us what they know about the group by way of hard facts, they have been monitoring them for some time now. Daniel you had better remain for that, I'll get staff to organise some refreshments.'

Just then the Prime Minister's exclusive high security phone rang. 'Yes…………..yes………..I understand…………..strange………….right,' He put the phone down.

'You were right, Daniel, information just in, 'RAFTS' demand released. An unequivocal undertaking by the Brazilian Government along the lines you suggested. But, as the kidnapping has taken place in the UK, it is for us, the UK Government, to initiate the request with the Brazilian Government. So we certainly won't be staying neutral and we need to have important discussions with our U.N. Ambassador, Sir Emmett, and very soon.'

By the time evening news bulletins were being broadcast it had become very clear where public opinion lay as far as this extraordinary issue was concerned. Around the world it was being seen as an example of people power, especially as it was on issues which many many people thought individuals and small countries had been ignored. Former politicians, experts on aspects of global warming, scientists studying particularly the effect of rain forest loss, anybody who felt they had relevant expertise – all were queuing up to be heard, and also keen to be 'on board the 'raft'. Some back-bench M.P.s who found themselves being bombarded by their constituents were bravely coming out with remarks also in favour of the Brazilian Government being forced to take action but whether that was really what they believed or was their concern for their future career as an M.P. was perhaps uncertain. Anything to do with re-election always focusses the minds of M.P.s.

Downing Street had put out a fairly neutral statement regarding the international situation now facing the Government but that at present the Foreign Office was in preliminary talks with representatives from the Brazilian Embassy. More specific was a statement from the Foreign Office to the effect that so far, The Right Honourable James St John had been unable to make contact with his opposite number in the

Brazilian Government but that ministerial contact was expected soon. The Foreign Office also announced that the Foreign Secretary would be making a further statement to the House late the following morning.

There were various calls from around the world, from precisely who was less clear, that the United Nations should be taking action, what action was also unclear and it was not seen as an issue in which the Security Council could be involved. Overnight, matters did not quieten down as seen by the UK newspaper headlines as well as early morning news broadcasts. The newspapers were totally unanimous in principle if not in tone.

'Shafted by a Raft'

'Brazil Shamed'

'Brazilian Government Silenced'

'Sympathy for the Protesters, Concern for the Ambassador'

'UK Dilemma over Law and Order'

'Search for Ambassador Continues'

'Can People Power Win?'

'UK and Brazil to Negotiate'

Some of the lesser headlines, supplementary thoughts, pointed to the dilemma being faced by the Government, not wanting to be seen giving support to illegal actions but also not wanting to be seen unsympathetic to what was becoming a major issue as far as ordinary people all round the world were concerned.

News broadcasts were different, influenced by actions occurring overnight in the Brazilian Capital as large crowds were beginning to mass outside Government Buildings and outside the Presidential Palace. At first these crowds appeared calm but as time went on and more people gathered it was clear that although it was their own Ambassador who had been kidnapped, sympathy was with the demands of the protesters; Reforestation had to replace Deforestation. Here in the crowds were people who knew what it was like to be working in unbearably hot conditions, where crops were failing because of climate change. As one Brazilian put it: *'Why clear vast areas of forest if the land made available becomes too hot and dry to use?'*

When the House of Commons gathered to hear the Foreign Secretary's statement there was great uncertainty as to what he might be able to say.

Mr Speaker, further to the statement made by my Right Honourable friend, the Leader of the House, I am now able to make clear the Government's immediate concerns and actions. Whatever individuals may think privately about climate issues which this protest group wish to address, it must be right that we remain mindful of the fact that an accredited Ambassador to the United Kingdom has been kidnapped, an action which is wholly illegal, both Nationally and Internationally. The protest group responsible has made no further contact since yesterday. The demand is that the Government of the United Kingdom should negotiate with the Brazilian Government regarding the issue of deforestation and that the release of the Ambassador, Joachim Barbosa, will only occur when a commitment in line with the protest group's demands has been made in unequivocal terms to the United Nations. At present representatives of this Government are endeavouring to make contact with the Brazilian Government to start negotiations. The House will understand that at present I am unable to predict any time scale for these vital matters. The process is further complicated for the Brazilian Government because of large scale protests currently taking place outside Government Buildings in Brasilia and also outside the Presidential Palace. It is to be hoped, Mr Speaker, that the situation will become clearer in the next twenty-four to forty-eight hours, certainly once there is a response from the

Brazilian Government, and at such time I will make a further statement and take questions.'

The Foreign Secretary took his seat, spoke to those nearest to him and then left the House. To say that he left behind a couple of hundred M.P.s feeling calm as a result of his statement would be a gross exaggeration and Mr Speaker had to work very hard to bring about order and close the session. When James returned to the Foreign Office it was to hear Ministers and Officials all saying versions of the same thing, that nothing more had been heard from RAFTS, nor from the Brazilian Government and that there had not been so much as a hint as to where the Ambassador had been taken. Of those three situations the most serious was the silence being maintained by the Government of Brazil, as apart from anything else it underlined the impotence in the current position of the British Government. For a moment there was silence, indicating if nothing else, nobody knew what to do; silence and optimism don't make good companions.

Joined by Edgar Shrewsbury and Rufus Sutton, James St John went through to his office to telephone the Prime Minister.

'Ah, James, I believe you left the House in uproar, if what I have heard from the office of the Speaker is true.'

'Yes Prime Minister, hardly surprising, as I really had nothing to tell them. Presumably Mr Speaker requires my return to the Commons?'

'Indeed he does, tonight was his suggestion, I have delayed it until this time tomorrow.'

'And if the Brazilian Government maintains its silence?'

'We must hope for inspiration, James.'

'Thank you Prime Minister and I presume you mean 'Divine' inspiration, pun intended or not, I'm unsure.'

Chapter Twenty-Seven
Politicians Not Panicking

A s it happened, before the night was out the Foreign Secretary was to find that no inspiration was needed, events obliterated need. He was telephoned by the Prime Minister at five o'clock in the morning and not just for an unusually early greeting.

'James, have I disturbed your sleep? You need to know that there have been riots throughout Brasilia and that this has prompted the President to telephone me to arrange for our respective Ambassadors to the United Nations to meet as soon as can be organised for later today today, New York time, about late afternoon for you and I. Together with appropriate officials they will consider possible ways for meeting the demands made by RAFTS. In the light of that I will contact the Speaker to delay the statement by yourself to late afternoon but we must make sure that before you speak, we have up to date information, all the facts.'

Later, when James was listening to the morning news as he was driven to the Foreign Office, he discovered that around the world there had been a number of attacks on Brazilian Embassies. Rightly or wrongly, the protest centred in the UK, but against Brazil, had certainly found its supporters. The newspapers he had with him continued with the previous day's approach of sympathy for the protest movement but there were several comments, editorially and otherwise, which expressed displeasure at the performance of a certain Foreign Secretary. He knew for himself that the wisest approach to take when you have nothing to say, is to say nothing.

'Have you been following the news in the last couple of days, Tony?'

'Difficult to avoid, Sir. It makes a change when a kidnap doesn't lead to a demand for money from the victim's family.'

'That's certainly true. The group leading the protest seems to have found supporters all round the world so we'll see what today brings.'

'No news, Sir, of the Ambassador's where abouts yet?'

'Nothing.'

James enjoyed his occasional conversations with Tony, gave him useful tiny snippets of how the general public might be thinking.

When he got to the Foreign Office he found the place agog with amazement and activity, that sense of something momentous about to burst upon the world, confidence was breeding confidence, so James could only hope that some of that confidence would find its way into what ever he had to say to the House when the time came later that day. In his office he asked Rufus if he knew whether Sir Emmett Burton had been briefed?

'Not as yet, but I believe the Prime Minister is going to speak with him in about an hour's time. I suspect the briefing will be about negotiating techniques as against policy issues based on facts.'

'A case of waiting on what Senhor Lucas Barreto says, given that his Government is making the running on the issue. Dangerous thing for me to say but I feel there is a chance that this crisis may be over sooner rather than later. I presume we are to expect RAFTS to make a response when they hear what has been agreed at the UN? I take it Rufus, that we will get warning of whatever is agreed before the UN make some general announcement.?'

Before any answer was forthcoming the telephone rang. 'Not too tired, James?.'

'Good morning Prime Minister, I hope you had a little more sleep after we finishing talking in the middle of the night.'

'No need, James, once I'm up and about I keep going. I need you over here now as I want you to be in on the briefing of Sir Emmett. After yesterday and the newspaper reports this morning it is vital that we are all clear on what is being said. You know, only one hymn sheet for all the performers.'

'I'll call my car now and be with you in a few minutes, Sir.'

James St John, joined by Edgar Shrewsbury and accompanied by Rufus Sutton were with the Prime Minister twenty minutes later. 'Morning Gentlemen, do sit down, we all know everybody here?' Agreement was shown with general muttering and nodding of heads, among the Civil Servants mainly. 'We have a few minutes before this call will come through. I think the main approach is to let the Brazilian team talk themselves towards a position favourable to everybody, everybody world-wide if that's not too much of an exaggeration. Any thoughts James?'

'Only one, can the UN take on a great level of responsibility in something like the reforestation of a large area on the immense scale that we are assuming?'

'We were talking along similar lines before I called you over and we can put it to Sir Emmett when his call comes. The critical factor is the degree of co-operation between the United Nation's team and the National team withing the Country concerned.'

'Prime Minister. Sir Emmett Burton is on the telephone, switched to room speaker so that all can hear.'

'Prime Minister, good morning, Sir.'

'Sir Emmett, good that you are able to make contact before your meeting. Do you have any strategy as far as your approach to the meeting with Mr Barreto is concerned?'

189

'Well, Prime Minister, I usually do approach such meeting with some idea of what to expect and hope to achieve but in this particular case I feel it important to do a lot of listening, become clear on what is on offer. One of the unintended advantages of using official translators is that you do get time to consider each point as it is made, conversations proceed at a more helpful speed. With this particular issue it is to see if there is a viable proposition which the United Nations can monitor in such away as to be acceptable to all the international agencies involved, and there are many, hence I need to hear exactly what is being suggested before anything is accepted, let alone agreed to.'

'If I may say so, Sir Emmett, that's all very good to hear. This kidnapping is exceptionally unusual, none of the usual demands nor any threats but it has had the effect of arousing public opinion, all round the world.'

'Any knowledge of precisely who is responsible?'

'No, and we haven't managed to name any individual from the group. RAFTS may be responsible but as to where they are, how long they have existed, these are still matters of which we are ignorant'

'It would seem Prime Minister that they have calculated the expected response with great skill and they must be delighted with the particular response in Brazil. Effectively brought this evening's meeting about.'

'Hopefully that will work in our favour when you hear what Mr Barreto has to say. I will be available with colleagues and officials at the same time so that you may raise anything with us directly if you think that will help.'

'That will be about nine o'clock UK time, 21.00. I'm not sure why I'm thinking so, but I don't expect this meeting to be lengthy. There seems to be a sense of 'need to get this problem solved' which is one reason why I am quite hopeful for a good outcome.'

'That's good to hear, Sir Emmett. May speak later this evening then.

When the Prime Minister had concluded pleasantries he turned to the group who had joined him. 'Is Sir Emmett's optimism justified?'

'To coin a phrase, Sir, only time will tell, even if it is only a few hours.' That was the Foreign Secretary's final thought on the matter.'

'Except for a Statement from you, late this evening.'

'Prime Minister, wouldn't it be better to delay that until tomorrow morning, it would be inconvenient for many if we cause M.P.s to hang around to no effect.'

'No, James, I feel we must endeavour to keep to the arrangement, even if it is no more than offering apologies and a requesting of patience while we await developments from the meeting taking place in New York. I don't want anyone to be able to say that we're not working flat out on the matter, not good politics.'

'As you wish Prime Minister.'

Later in the day, James St John let his immediate staff know that he would be out for a while; he didn't specify where. 'I don't need my car, I'll hail a taxi.' If Rufus thought it strange he certainly didn't show it.

Without bothering to say anything to other staff who were around, James walked back through the ground floor of the building complex until he found himself in Great George Street. He hailed a taxi very quickly and asked to be dropped near Tottenham Court Road Underground Station. Here he took the tube east to The Bank, changed, and travelled south on the Northern line to London Bridge. When he emerged from the underground he could be seen wearing an old-fashioned pac-a-mac and a pair of glasses, lowish on his nose so he was looking over the top of them. From London Bridge he wandered along a series of roads towards the west until he reach Southwark Bridge Road, turning up towards the River Thames he strolled along until he was outside the May Hotel. 'Hello Tony, your Molly about, I sent her a text a while back.'

'Good morning, Sir. Yes, I can find her for you, in the kitchens I think.'

'Mr St John, how lovely. Don't see you often enough.' Molly gave him a friendly smile and then said she would get coffee and she showed him through to the lounge to wait.

'Here you are, you just want to pass a few hours, Sir.'

'Yes please, Molly, feeling rather low again.'

'You'll have to see your doctor one day, you know.'

'I know Molly, but when doctors begin examining Secretaries of State, they start asking themselves searching questions as to competence to be at work and should they let anyone know.'

'I suppose that might be a little embarrassing. I can make available one of the bedrooms if you want to pass a few hours, read for a while, have a sleep.'

'That'll be perfect, Molly. I'll leave about five o'clock if that's all right.'

'Not a problem, Sir, just make yourself comfortable.'

After yawning somewhat James went in search of Molly, settled up with a generous quantity of cash, left the Hotel, then again turned towards the river and when he reach Upper Thames Street he hailed a taxi and took himself to Harrods. Thirty minutes later and looking like the Foreign Secretary once more, he hailed another taxi and returned to the Foreign Office. Smiling at various members of staff he went through to his office. Rufus tapped on his door and came in. 'Pleasant afternoon, Sir?'

'Yes thank you, Rufus. Any news in likely to affect the plans for this evening?'

'No, nothing has changed, it's all still topical news around the world, lots of popular support. Downing Street staff have organised food for mid-evening so that we can be available if anything new comes in.'

'Change of work for a while. I presume you have a pile of correspondence for me to plough through and initial, other papers to read and initial, documents for the next Cabinet Meeting.'

'Indeed Sir, boxes prepared and available now if you're ready.'

'Thank you, Rufus, need to get through as much as possible.' When James took on a very single-minded approach to work he could shift a great quantity. It reminded him of his Oxford days when he might have put off the completion of an important essay for far too long until he was forced to cut himself off from all distractions, apply total concentration and a couple of hours later he may have written an essay of 'first class degree' standard. He now applied the same techniques to his Government papers and at 7.20pm when his colleagues were getting ready to go round to Downing Street, he closed his boxes, contents read completely, understood and initialled to that effect.

Chapter Twenty-Eight
Politicians Pleased

Quite a quantity of ultra-classy sandwiches were served, as appropriate for the address in which they were to be consumed. Whether all the attendees enjoyed them with equal enthusiasm was quite another matter, but the selection included prawns and smoked salmon, rare fillet beef, guinea fowl with truffle paste, a rare Welsh blue cheese from Anglesey, Camembert and all the sandwiches had small pieces of salad to accompany them. It wasn't known if the Prime Minister had a free hand in choosing fabulous bottles from certain cellars but it must have been a stunning experience. The 'said' cellars were thought by some in the know to hold many wines of great vintage and in total valued at several million pounds. Anthony May's selections were all wrapped in large napkins so nobody really knew what the vintages were, other than they were superb, and it was to be hoped the important recipients of this cellar largesse, as they waited to hear what their Ambassador to the United Nations had achieved, were really able to appreciate the choices made by their boss. Playing the part of a genial and generous host the Prime Minister urged all to eat and drink; so easy to be extravagantly generous when the bill is covered by agents of convenient anonymity with addresses at the Treasury.

It was just after nine o'clock when Sir Emmett made his first 'appearance,' filling a large television screen with his voice delivered through four very high-quality speakers. 'Prime Minister, Gentlemen, good evening. A short break has occurred, earlier than expected and that augers well I think for the rest of the discussions. First suggestions would indicate a willingness on the part of the Brazilian Government, they want to be seen in a favourable light. There is also information circulating regarding the amount of civil pressure building up to force the Brazilian Government's hand on the issues and this is coming from schools, universities, armed forces. There is also a very considerable degree of unity across political parties. There could be other more subversive forces at work but we are unlikely to hear about those. There are other worries beyond this particular issue coming from countries who feel that they are vulnerable in the same way, obviously not connected to the Rain Forests situation but countries with other non-green activities in which their record is not what it should be. I will leave it there Sir, people returning.'

The Foreign Secretary was looking pleased with the situation. 'That seems particularly positive, Prime Minister; I may even have something of purpose to say to the House later.'

'And you may be right James but we must wait for the last word on these matters to be uttered before you offer so much as a syllable.'

Daniel Davies was at the supper and his concern remained with the approach to the kidnap. 'I wonder when there may be sufficient response from the United Nations for this RAFTS organisation to release the Ambassador. It is extraordinary, that for a relatively new pressure group taking direct action, we have absolutely no information about it.'

'Could it be, Home Secretary, that their newness is its strength? With a small number of active members, very clued up when it comes to using technology, may well help them seemingly to disappear. Might they also have spies, to use an old-fashioned term.'

'Jeremy, do you mean from within the Government or security forces?'

'I feel something like that has to be considered. Of course, should the issue be resolved at speed, we may never know.'

'I sincerely hope we will know.' The Prime Minister looked rather determined with this remark and for a while an uncomfortable silence descended over the group. It was only the second appearance by Sir Emmett which brought conversation back to the group.

'Prime Minister, I think we may have achieved all that is possible this evening, indeed, possibly sufficient to resolve the crisis completely. With the approval of his Government, Senhor Lucas Barreto has put forward the following: Total agreement for the Reforestation of the Rain Forest area which has been cleared, provided the cost is borne by the United Nations and that being so, his Government will agree to United Nations Supervision. There are suggestions about international work forces, involvement of international environmentalists and other scientists needed for such an undertaking. The final suggestion which will need specific detail to be thought through, would be their agreement to internationally and legally binding agreements by all parties, overseen by a neutral power, rather in the style of the Canadian General who acted during the long negotiations which led to the Good Friday agreement in Northern Ireland. That is my summary of where we are at this moment. It will be reviewed and written up in the morning, presented to United Nations Officials on behalf of the Secretary General for consideration. If it all goes through it will be remarkable for its speed quite apart from the specific achievement and the release of Senhor Joaquim Barbosa.'

'Sir Emmett, thank you for your report. Unless you feel it to be premature we propose to make a brief statement in the House of Commons tonight followed by a more detailed written statement to be issued in the morning, both statements to be based on what you have told us in the last few minutes.'

'I think that if we just keep to the basic points, all should be well.'

'Thank you Sir Emmett and of course we will make sure you see what is said just as soon as it has been prepared, especially the written version for tomorrow.'

'Thank you Prime Minister.'

While these concluding remarks were being made there was a flurry of activities by various advisers and between them a statement to be read to the House in the next half-hour was more or less agreed.

197

At 10.00pm The Foreign Secretary, James St John, took his place in the Commons.

'The Foreign Secretary.'

'Mr Speaker, with sincere apologies for keeping the House so late, but I'm sure all Right Honourable and Honourable Members will be pleased to hear that agreement has been reached between the two sides involved, represented by the two Ambassadors to the United Nations as far as the rain forest issue is concerned and that tomorrow, details will be presented to the United Nations Officials for ratification by the United Nations Secretary General. In principle, Reforestation of the Rain Forest Areas which have been cleared will proceed just as soon as the scientists and environmentalists have the plans ready. Funding and supervision will be undertaken by the United Nations. Legally binding international ratification is to be overseen by a neutral power.'

'Mr Speaker, I appreciate that this statement is but the merest outline, the hour is late, so now perhaps is not a suitable time for questions. A written and more detailed statement will be available for the House by mid-day tomorrow.'

Much to the relief of James, this was agreed and in a short time the House was deserted.

At three-thirty a.m., the following morning, two police cars were driving in opposite directions along the Victoria Embankment, both heading towards New Scotland Yard. As they drew level, lights flashed and sirens blared and as this distraction got going, two large sacks were pushed out from the near-side rear doors. Cars leaving Scotland Yard just then, stopped, officers got out and as they went to the two sacks, the first cars drove away at phenomenal speed, were soon out of sight, never to be seen again. By the time a very startled Senor Joaquim Barbosa was staring at the Police Officers surrounding him and another group of Police Officers were peering at a full-size tailor's dummy, the quiet of the night returned. Attached to the Ambassador was a luggage label carrying the simple message:

'We have kept faith'

About three quarters of a mile away a tramp was just stirring, grunting and groaning he got to his feet and after a little rummaging he relieved himself against the nearby tree. Rather than sit down for a bit more sleep he shuffled across a couple of roads, leaned against the safety railings, and looking down into the waters of the Thames he 'inadvertently' dropped the component parts of a very new 'pay-as-you-go' mobile phone.

Police cars driving in the capital in the early hours of the morning was not an unusual sight and when at different times, two police cars were each in different deserted areas the driver and passenger got out, removed their uniforms, just a jacket and its appropriate attachments, and nobody was about to see. Other unseen activities occurred, working from the front and back of the car at the same time they appeared to be peeling off the outer finish of the car to reveal a middle of the range family saloon, and added to these peelings were two thin plastic surfaces from each number plate. Later in the day all these unwanted bits and pieces were boxed into a small parcel, given over to Royal Mail and on arrival were found to be at a destination where nobody would notice the odd bonfire.

Success all round was the considered opinion of the morning news broadcasts – 'Success at the United Nations,' 'Brazil Agrees', 'Ambassador Released,' 'Rain Forests Saved,' - some of the Newspaper headlines. For the Government a written statement was prepared for issue by mid-day, couched in suitable terms but based entirely on what was reported by the United Kingdom Ambassador to the United Nations, Sir Emmett Burton. It may have sounded more suitable with its parliamentary style of phrasing but added no more facts to what the Foreign Secretary had said the previous evening. Before its release the Prime Minister had been in discussion with Mr

Speaker and there was Government agreement to questions and debate following the next occasion of Questions to the Prime Minister.

Written Statement - The House of Commons

'Mr Speaker, Right Honourable and Honourable Members will be pleased to learn that following discussions between Sir Emmett Burton, The United Kingdom's Ambassador to the United Nations and Senhor Lucas Barreto, The Brazilian Ambassador to the United Nations it is now possible for the Brazilian Government to put forward to United Nations Officials their proposals for the reforestation of the cleared areas of the Rain Forests but this is subject to the cost being borne by the United Nations and that being so, the Brazilian Government would then agree to United Nations Supervision. There are particular issues involving International Work Forces, Environmentalists and other Specialist Scientists still to be worked out and quantified bearing in mind the need for very careful and scientifically planned planting. The final suggestion to emerge from last night's discussions and one which will need careful international agreement was that all the legally binding agreements by all parties concerned should be overseen by a neutral power, in the style of the Canadian General who had acted during the long negotiations which led to the Good Friday Agreement in Northern Ireland. Mr Speaker, this is a summary of what the Brazilian Government felt able to present this morning to the United Nations Officials on behalf of the Secretary General for their consideration.'

When James St John was being driven home from the Foreign Office, having left a little earlier than usual, he realised he felt totally exhausted. He needed to speak to Rhiannon about it, something wasn't right.

Within a day or so this news about the kidnapping and high-powered goings-on at the United Nations became stale and the general public was soon distracted by other events which filled their screens and newspapers. However, in important circles, matters were not so easily forgotten and this was revealed by one of the questions to the Prime Minister the following week when Mr Speaker called Mr Knowlesey.

'The Prime Minister will know that in a previous career I was a Senior Police Officer so I would appreciate his thoughts on the recent kidnapping of the Brazilian Ambassador and in particular, whether those employed in upholding the rule of law, as I was for twenty years, should ignore such a crime simply because the motives behind the kidnapping are seen by the general public to be worthwhile and in the public interest, or as in this recent case, seen by the world-wide general public to be worthwhile.'

'Mr Speaker, the Honourable Gentleman's question goes straight to the heart of a very difficult and moral question, one which has been exercising a number of minds since the kidnapping, to which he referred, took place. To kidnap somebody to satisfy some ridiculous fad would be wholly wrong so the question must be, can it ever be that the 'fad' becomes such a serious matter that the kidnap can be seen to be justified. The answer to that must be a resounding, 'no,' and so I can inform the Honourable Gentleman that the police and other forces concerned never stopped searching for the missing Brazilian Ambassador. Regrettably, even now, we still do not know the identity of the kidnappers nor where the Ambassador was held prisoner but investigations are continuing.'

Later that day, Angus Barrington, Minister at the Foreign Office, was enjoying a very rare moment of relaxation in one of the quieter bars. He was sipping slowly a glass of lager while a friend of his, John Stevenson, M.P. for one of the more northern constituencies, walked over to his table carrying a large measure of Malt, probably very expensive, thought Angus.

'Angus, join you for a few moments. I have to say, unusual to see you in here.'

'You're right, John, just having a quiet moment reflecting on the words from our Prime Minister, about the rights and wrongs of kidnapping. Haven't seen you about for a while, not been ill, I hope?'

'Since you mention it, yes, I have been off colour for a few days, all right now though,'

'Rested up at that Yorkshire place of yours I suppose.'

'No, just at my London flat, with my wife. The Yorkshire place as you put it, not really ready for living in yet. I was up there yesterday just to check on all the decorating my son and a group of his universities chums have been doing. I think they were short of money so were happy to accept my offer in exchange for a fortnight's painting. Actually, they've done a good job, not surprising because one of the girl's fathers is a painter decorator and she always did part-time work for him to earn pocket money. I expect she kept them all in order. Later in the summer there is to be the final work on the heating systems and a new kitchen and then it will be more or less finished. The heating will more or less pay for itself and with solar panels energy bills will be as good as zero. How my ancient mother lived there for so long I'll never know, poor heating, still used open fires in the main downstairs rooms and her bedroom. If people came to stay it meant fires in eight bedrooms. It's a beautiful spot, surrounded by gardens and paddocks and in the middle of very scenic 'nowhere'. We wouldn't have kept it but a surveyor who looked at it, charged me a fortune mind you, said it was in great structural shape and that the roofs had all been repaired within the previous ten years, and at the same time, he thought, the attic windows had all been replaced with wooden framed double-glazed units. Everything above the highest ceilings has been fully insulated. That was probably my father's last big spend on the place.'

'He's a budding environmentalist, your son, have I remembered him right?'

'Yes, that's him, Peter, always cracking on about issues concerning pollution, coastal erosion, soil erosion – nothing new really but he tells me the science is always developing. His crowd, all scientists of sorts,

202

biologists, naturalists, an oceanographer, another hoping to be a zoologist, they were up there for a couple of weeks or so, you know, coming and going, but between them got everything done and managed to enjoy themselves as well, judging by the fires that they had lit, and the remains of a BBQ, stones still just warm to the touch. They were keen on my money but they all seemed to have cars, wealthy parents I suppose but perhaps kept them short of readies. I telephoned him yesterday to pass on thanks to his mates, said I would send some more money as they finished more than I expected. Told me there had been quite a crowd of them, said they had all been there for their last couple of nights. They had had a BBQ and lit a great fire to celebrate the outcome of the kidnapping, you know, what the United Nations is going to achieve, they cheered over that.'

'Now that was an event to capture the imagination of youngsters, students, folk of that age, all round the world if the media maniacs reported it correctly. I know colleagues at the Foreign Office were amazed. Another drink, John, have our own little celebration, and good to see you looking well.'

'Now that's an excellent idea, thank you, Angus.'

Chapter Twenty-Nine
Police Party Planning

Never mind proper police work, crime investigation and the like, Sergeant Watson had been summoned in by his area boss, Superintendent Jefferson, to discuss of all things, social events, in particular, the Superintendent's retirement party which was to be held in the police social room which was attached to the police station where Sergeant Watson was based.

'Ah Sergeant, come in, have a seat, make yourself comfortable and my wonderful p.a will bring in some tea and cakes.'

'Thank you Sir.'

'I expect you are wondering why I have asked to see you but it is just that I have heard that you are one of these clever efficient types who are good when it comes to 'multi-tasking' and it just so happens that you are based where my retirement party is to be held in a few days' time.'

'Yes Sir, although I'm not quite sure whether I'm saying yes to the bit about multi-tasking.'

'Well, I have that bit of praise from your Inspector, but no matter. It's just that I want someone to make several telephone calls for me and it will be better if they are made by a police officer rather than a secretary. Over the years I've obviously met a large number of different guys with whom I have worked, a number have left the force, some weren't that good but quite a few I've kept in touch with, followed their careers, that sort of thing. I have a list here of a few and what I would like you to do is to track them down, give them a call and ask them if they can make my party. I've contacted others with whom my wife and I exchange Christmas Cards but these few are guys I would enjoy just bumping into again before I pack up altogether. Do you get my drift, Sergeant?'

'Yes Sir, and as the party is next door to my station I can easily update the organisers on numbers.'

'That thought had occurred to me as well. This is the list, anyone you know?'

'Well, I've met Sergeant Vaughan, we were on a course together.'

'I knew him as a young P.C., thought he would have gone further up the ranks, perhaps family issues and he didn't want to move.'

'I've read about Inspector Finley recently, something about a 'hit-and-run' on another officer's patch, an old 'bag-lady' if my memory is correct and her DNA led to an unexpected identification of somebody else.'

'I collaborated with him a few years back, I should think there is another promotion for him yet. At present Sergeant Vaughan is his bagman.'

'I didn't know that.'

'Over the years, Sergeant, I have tried to follow the careers of a few fellow officers as we get an interesting selection of guys in the force. That probably explains why the odd one or two of my past associates are at present or have been in prison. No need to raise your eyebrows Sergeant, none of them are on the list.'

'Glancing down the list again I see the name Joshua St John, Q.C. I think I have seen his name in the newspapers, would I be right, Sir?'

'Quite correct, Sergeant. He's an up-and-coming lawyer, became a Q.C. at quite a young age. Well-connected individual, younger of two sons, his father is the Foreign Secretary, James St John. I met young Joshua a few years back, before he became a leading Q.C. He was part of the prosecuting team in a large fraud case, I was one of the investigating officers. The case did young Joshua quite a bit of good as he showed himself very able at presenting aspects of a complex accounting fraud in such a way that the Jury were able to get immediate grasp of the facts. He impressed me and we kept in touch.'

'Will he know any of the other guests, Sir?'

'Don't worry Sergeant, he's a very affable guy, soon make himself at home. After all, it won't be a room full of uniform-wearing guys. Casual dress is the request for the evening, much pleasanter for the ladies I feel.'

'I'll get started on making these calls, Sir, and also make sure to let those running the event on your behalf are updated.'

'Thank you Sergeant, let me know of any problems.'

As Sergeant Watson went off to deal with Police matters of a retirement and   social nature, another Sergeant was on the receiving end of a phone call which took him a little by surprise.

'Hello, is that Sergeant Vaughan. This is Audrey Sutton, you remember, you and Inspector Finley came to see me about the DNA identification. Have you got any further with those enquiries.'

'Good afternoon Mrs Sutton, thank you for ringing. The initial results which caused us to call on you have been checked and confirmed but we have yet to hear about any results arising from the testing of the jewellery. That shouldn't be too long in being sent through to us.'

'Actually I wasn't chasing you on those tests, more, I was wondering if you were likely to track down my father's grave with a view to obtaining DNA. I realise this won't have any effect on your case as far as the identification of the woman who died in the hit-and-run incident, but ever since you startled me with the possibility that I may have been adopted, I realise I want to know whether my father was my real father. The thought occupies much of my time, quite frightening in a way.'

'I do understand Mrs Sutton, these kind of investigations can cause much heart-ache and family distress. I'll have a word with Inspector Finley, as it was our investigation which brought about your distress, we may well be able to arrange a DNA test on your behalf. Can you leave the matter with me for a day or so?'

'That's very encouraging Sergeant. By the way, would you have had occasion to let Inspector Grange know that the DNA tests which were conducted after the robbery at our apartment, led to a result in an entirely different investigation.'

'No, probably not, although my Inspector did say something about doing so. It wouldn't be usual for that to be organised given the thousands of DNAs now logged in world-wide data bases. Nothing to stop you letting know her know should you have reason to telephone her. Nothing confidential from our point of view.'

Thinking that jobs are best not put off and so forgotten, Sergeant Vaughan gave his Inspector a call.

'Sergeant, how can I help?'

'It's about the DNA identification which has led to some concern for Dr and Mrs Sutton. Mrs Sutton has called to ask if there is likely to be any need to follow up the identification of her father, or the person she believes is her father? I think she is beginning to worry about who she really is.'

'Oh dear, not an uncommon reaction. It happens sometimes when people buy as a Christmas or birthday present one of these home kits which enable DNA to be read, leads to some unexpected finds in families where many would wish that the 'finds' had remained, well, 'unfound.' I wonder if we can obtain an exhumation licence as part of an on-going investigation, need to cloud the issue a bit. I imagine a pathologist would be able to obtain sufficient specimens on site and there would be an immediate re-burial. Let's go ahead and see how far we can get before somebody up the chain queries the need. Can but try. Set the ball rolling, Sergeant.'

'Sir, will do.'

With police enquiries continuing it was easy to forget that normal activities for other people also had to continue. No exception to this rule of life was the Foreign Secretary who had had his routine knocked aside very badly, but even James St John had managed to return to work and was getting started on a lengthy catch-up again with letter reading. Fortunately his staff had sorted them according to urgency and high-lighted the key paragraphs. He had a good memory, he was particularly good with names and with the least reminder he could recall relevant previous correspondence or meetings and this enabled him to make quite good progress. However, he had by no means finished when a phone call was put through to him from Inspector Waterton.

'Foreign Secretary, I am sorry to bother you so soon, and am I right in thinking you have recently returned to the Foreign Office for the first time since your brother's death?'

'Yes, that's correct but don't let that worry you unduly, it was a few days back and I have been very involved in the recent kidnapping which you have probably read about. How can I help?'

'It's more in the way of giving you a piece of information. Another 'friend' of Vincent has come forward, more or less repeats what Alan Corbynsky had to tell us. He is a Frank Palmerson, another post-graduate research student, a physicist. He told us about an on-going non-exclusive relationship he had with Vincent but that he hadn't seen him for a couple of weeks. His main reason for visiting the police was to say categorically that he was totally surprised to hear about a suicide, that there was nothing he had seen of him which remotely suggested such an event was likely. He was thanked for his information and as with Alan, he happily gave finger prints and a specimen for DNA analysis. So far and despite collecting a considerable amount of forensic evidence none of the tests so far have identified anybody and so if there was a rape it doesn't seem as if any perpetrator has caused himself to be on any data base or he was careful. We may not be able to solve this aspect of the case, remembering that the pathologist was not one hundred percent certain. When it comes to the inquest it may be best if the word 'rape' is not used.'

'Thank you for bringing me up to date Inspector. Would it be in order for me to ask that now I am back at work you call me with information at the end of any working day unless it is something urgent.'

'That's perfectly all right, Sir.'

'Just so you know, on Thursday I shall be very busy here with an Anglo-Indian event regarding trade negotiations as well as an official luncheon. The following day, Friday, is when the funeral for my late brother is being held. It means that getting hold of me sometimes is going to be quite difficult.' They ended the call then, but James suddenly realised that soon he would be getting very busy again, something he was beginning to find quite frightening.

Chapter Thirty
An Unexpected Result

When Sergeant Vaughan received the notification he really was most surprised and he couldn't wait to see his Inspector.

'Sir, I have some very unexpected information concerning the identification of Audrey Sutton.'

'You had better come round.'

'Well Sir, we appear to have a familial link. Have you been following the recent news concerning the suicide of the brother of the Foreign Secretary?'

'Yes, indeed. Once it hit the newspapers, hard to avoid, somewhat overtaken by the kidnapping now.'

'In the course of the forensic gathering by the police in Oxford and the interviewing of witnesses, one of the DNA results has implications for Audrey Sutton. I should just mention that I haven't got far with the request for the exhumation of the person she thinks is her father, in fact it may not be necessary. A 'Frank Palmerson' has come forward to reveal that he had been one of Vincent St John's lovers. Frank's DNA reveals that a close relative of his, probably his father, is the father of Audrey Sutton.'

'Good gracious, that's a bit unexpected.'

'Yes and no, Sir. We certainly didn't expect the death of the brother of the Foreign Secretary to lead us to this piece of evidence and likely conclusion. On the other hand, Frank Palmerson, mid-twenties I believe, was a pupil at Kemby School, where his older brother, George Palmerson, was a contemporary of the group of lads who knew Lucinda Quemsby. More importantly, their father was on the staff of Kemby School, taught chemistry I believe.'

'So, a Mr Palmerson, with something of a roving eye for young ladies in his area. I think I need to make contact with Oxford CID and you and I better drive over to see Palmerson junior just as soon as a meeting can be set up.'

'Sir.'

It didn't take long for the Oxford Police to pull Frank in for an interview and Inspector Finley and Sergeant Vaughan were on their way early the following morning.

It was Inspector Waterton who met them and took them to the interview room to meet Frank Palmerson. Introductions complete, it was Inspector Finley who took the initiative.

'Mr Palmerson, can I say straight away that we are not here to accuse you of anything, but we think you may be able to help us with another case, one of identity. Can I just check some facts: you are thirty and a former pupil of Kemby School where your father teaches chemistry?'

'Totally correct, Sir.'

'Do you know the name, Lucinda Quemsby?'

'No, I don't think I have ever heard of that name, very unusual, so I would have expected to remember it.'

'A couple of months back we investigated a hit-and-run case in which an unidentified female, a vagrant, was killed. A DNA test enabled us to identify her daughter. This caused a shock and led us to discover that most likely an unofficial adoption took place at the time of the birth.

214

The adoptive parents never told the child, now grown up, that she had been adopted.'

' I hope you are…..'

'No, no Frank, don't jump to conclusions. So far the daughter's real father has not been discovered and the daughter has only known one man as her father, probably adoptive, but he's been dead for about fifteen years. Your DNA test result has given us enough information for our scientists to suggest that you are closely related to the unknown father, possibly your older brother, but more likely your father. I should explain that an important connection is that Lucinda Quemsby was a pupil at Kroxby School at the same time as your brother George and his group of friends, were acquainted with Lucinda.'

'What makes you think it is my father?'

'We would both need to be students of genetics to understand that with clarity, but take it from me, that the scientists who analyse DNA results are very good at sorting the connections. How old is your father now?'

'He's in his early sixties, on his own now as my mother, his wife, died from breast cancer quite a few years back.'

'We will need to see him, can you give us his address.'

'Yes, I will write it down for you.'

'Thank you. I will probably have to explain the circumstances under which your DNA sample was requested. Is that likely to cause a difficulty?'

'No, not a problem, dad knows about me, so does George for that matter.'

'How might he react to this news, not that we should expect you to know?'

'He's always been a very calm individual, not easily ruffled. It's not a situation likely to lead to any court case?'

'I doubt it very much.'

'Shall I telephone him, explain and make an appointment for you, end of school day tomorrow suit?'

'An excellent and very helpful suggestion, certainly tomorrow afternoon will be fine for one or both of us.'

In the event it was Sergeant Vaughan who had the pleasure of driving out to the Norfolk countryside again to make the acquaintance of Palmerson senior. Frank Palmerson's instructions led him to his father's house easily and he found the owner waiting. 'Hello, I'm Henry Palmerson, Frank told me to expect you. Do come in.'

'Good afternoon, Sir, Sergeant Vaughan. Very sorry to bother you.'

'You don't need to tread too carefully, Frank has told me of the nature of your visit.'

'That's very understanding of you. You'll know then that your son's DNA test reveals that you are very likely to be the father of a woman who has had no idea that she may have been adopted at birth. We have established that she is the daughter of a Lucinda Quemsby who was a pupil at Kroxby, leaving in about 2006 because it was thought she was pregnant. For some time we wondered if the father was one of the boys from Kemby School, a group of them, including your older son George, knew her and other girls rather well. However, the test result suggests that it is far more likely to be you. Do you remember Lucinda?'

'Oh yes, I remember her very well, she was a beautiful girl. Please don't for one moment think I forced myself upon her, no suggestion of rape, I assure you. The attraction was sudden and totally mutual, we met in a cafe. The only thing I can say which you may or may not believe is that I didn't hear about her leaving because she was pregnant. I perhaps ought to explain that at about that time I became

216

very distracted, because that's when my wife's breast cancer was first diagnosed, I had to take some time off work.'

'Thank you, Sir, that's all very clear. You do realise that we will have to tell the woman, who is your daughter, what we have discovered. That, of course, assumes that a fresh DNA test based on a sample which I hope to collect from you before I leave, confirms what we believe to be the case. What I don't know is whether the woman concerned will want to make contact.'

'Yes, I understand that and I can see it being a very awkward situation. You can tell her that if she wishes to see me I will certainly not refuse.'

Chapter Thirty-One
More of the St John Family

Since before the time of the first Baronet of the St John family the name Richard had not appeared. Now there was one, a rather precocious lad, oldest child of Joshua, the younger son of James and Rhiannon. He had been passing time one day doing very little and took to leafing through an old family photograph album. Initially thinking it rather dull he began to laugh when he found a group of pre-war children, it was their old-fashioned clothes which set him off and cloth caps which made them look like old men. Of course he came across names which he had never heard mentioned, and he noticed the words 'killed in action' and 'died' under some and followed by a date. He had to ask his mummy what 'killed in action' meant and being a sensible lady, she didn't try to distract the lad or brush the question aside but told him in very simple terms that there had been a war which involved Great Britain and that during the four years that it lasted a very large number of young men were killed. She reminded him about the War Memorial near where they lived and all the names that he had seen engraved in the stone and she told him why the names were there. She then explained that the photographs of men in uniforms he had seen in the album were members of their family from over one hundred years back, and, sadly they had been in the war and had lost their lives in a battle. That was what 'killed in action' meant, lost their life while fighting in a battle.

'I see.' That was Richard's response. She didn't doubt he had understood her, but she knew that the tragedy and enormity of it all was beyond his years. She was pleased that he continued looking at the photographs. Later, when she looked in on him again she found him writing a list and at the top was the name, Major General Sir James St

John. Next to it was the name Evelyn and under those two names was Edward and then under that name was another, Peter.

'Why, Richard Joshua George, I think you are writing out what looks like a family tree.'

'That's right, Mummy. We were looking at one in school which had lots of names, names all over the page. There were four Georges and in the middle of the page was one name in big letters, **VICTORIA**. Miss Jefferson said it was about Kings and Queens.'

'I think you were learning some history, the history of part of the Royal Family.'

'There were lots of short lines, some up and down, some going across. There were signs which we use in sums, = but I don't know what those were doing because Miss said the numbers we could see all over the page, well they were dates.'

'I expect she said, perhaps you didn't hear her. What do lots of men and women do when they are grown up?'

'Have babies.'

Celia St John laughed. 'Yes they do but what do most of them do before they have children?' (Too late, but she really hoped he didn't go down the road needing her to talk about sex!) 'Something like a big family party?' she added quickly.

'Oh, yes, they have a wedding.' His mummy breathed a sigh of relief because the first three or four words might have led to a number of alternatives!

'Well, that's what the equal sign means, the two people whose names are on either side of the sign got married.

'Make one family, is that right mummy?'

'Yes, well done, you could say 'equals one family' because two people from different families have joined together.'

'Miss Jefferson was very interesting.'

'I can show you where to put some more equal signs in your family tree and if you like, we can begin to add more names. At the moment all the names you will find in that album belong to daddy's past family, his ancestors. You would need to look at other albums to find the names from my family. I can show you some.'

'You're good at history mummy. You said so one day.'

'Yes, I learnt a lot of history at University in Edinburgh, in Scotland, your Granny, daddy's mummy went to the same university and we both learnt history.'

'University?'

'Like a very, very big school where all the pupils are over eighteen years old.'

'I'm going to play with my computer, Harry said he would come round.'

'That's all right, means orange squash and biscuits I suppose.'

'Yes please. Harry liked those ones we had the other day.'

'I'll see what's in the tin.'

But Richard had gone and Celia went back to the kitchen.

Later in the week Celia came across her son's list of names which he had been writing on Saturday. She could see that he had added more and it stirred up her interest in history just a little, so taking a pencil she lightly added equal signs and appropriate additional names. Where there was room she went down the list and added a small number of brothers and sisters. She nearly got carried away, but just in time thought better of it and left it with only her few pencilled additions which he could 'biro' over. She hoped he would continue, ask her a few more questions and with the right size piece of paper he could get the main line of his dad's family tree from the first Sir James St John to her Joshua, and their children, Richard Joshua and his younger sister, Amy Celia.

Celia spent a while looking at the same photographs which had caught her Richard's attention. Because of her interest in history she had learnt quite a lot of her husband's family back- ground and she enjoyed looking back at these photographs, especially some of the large group ones, typical of what were taken at weddings before everybody took to using their mobiles. The large ones went back to the nineteen thirties. Under one were many names, typical selection of period names for the most part – Henry, Arthur, Albert, John, Norman, Walter and there were female names which were coming back into fashion – Ida, Agnes, Betsy, Faye, Ethel, Martha, Polly – it was quite enchanting to read all these old names even though she had no idea who most of them were, not necessarily even relatives. There was one which was a bit different, Juliette, didn't seem to blend with the more Victorian styled names. She would have to look the name up but Celia thought it French in origin. She didn't expect that her husband, Joshua, would know much about these old relatives and quite possibly the Grandparents wouldn't know either. It might require a visit to Norstead Towers and talk to the Great Grandparents. And then it occurred to her that she could telephone them at Norstead Towers. The telephone rang for quite a while and then a lady's voice said, 'Hello, Elaine speaking.'

'Wonderful, the very person. This is Celia and my son Richard is your great grandson.

'Yes, I know who you are, married to Joshua, is that right?'

'Absolutely, nothing wrong with your memory. Richard has got a little interested in history as the result of looking at old photographs of your family. Between us we were writing out something of the family tree. Later, I found myself looking at group photographs from various family weddings. Some had names on them, I could place several of them. One name I didn't know was given just as Juliette in a group photograph from your parents' wedding. Any chance that you might know who that is?'

'Yes and no. er, Juliette Quemsby is a relative from the Rosenthal and Quemsby side of the family. You'll remember that my father was the M.P. Joshua Rosenthal, he acted as mentor to my George when he first got elected. Joshua's wife was Daphne Quemsby, my mother and her Grandfather was the first Quemsby we know of on our side of the family. Obviously they go back but we don't know any more names. I have to think carefully here because there were two Archibalds and two Peters, one of whom died as a baby. Now Juliette, we always spoke of her as a distant aunt, probably a convenience expression, may just as well have been a cousin. She was very wealthy, don't know how, none too keen on the younger members of her near relatives, there was a grand-daughter of a niece, no, nephew, who got into various troubles. Juliette set up trust funds for other relatives and I was one. Sorry, I'm rambling, trying to remember, got it now, my Great Grandfather was Peter Quemsby and his brother was Archibald. For such older families there weren't many children, strange that. There were various Quemsby cousins but we never met. The Quemsbys on our side of the family were very few in number and ended with my mother. On Archibald's side there were more but I don't know how many. I think he married a Marion 'Somebody', and they had three children, yes, that's right, a Peter, named after his brother, but, as I said just now, he died at birth, then Juliette, don't know where that name came from, the one you're talking about and who didn't get married, but from her came the money, and finally, Alfred, and from him and his wife, Molly, I believe that was the name, there were children, they're distant cousins I suppose. One was a boy, named Archibald, after his Grandad. I vaguely remember there was a Peterkin, not sure where he fits in. I think I only remember that name because he was a character in 'The Coral Island' which I used to read to the children. I hope that's not all too confusing.'

'I've scribbled it down, probably got the main threads sorted.'

'The Trust funds which came my way arrived on my twenty-fifth birthday and enabled me to continue writing, work with various charitable activities at the House of Commons and be at home with the children as they came along.'

'That was wonderfully generous of her, did you meet up often?'

'Well no, never in fact as she died a year or so after my birth, but the trust was set up when I was born 1948.'

'You have been ever so helpful, can I ring again please if my knowledge fails me?'

'Of course you can dear. Love to your Joshua, Richard and Amy as well.'

Celia knew she would have to be careful when Richard was home from school, she mustn't take over his new interest. Nothing to stop her doing her own family tree of course. If she thought she was going to get started immediately and wallow in a day of family history, Celia was to be disappointed and the first hint came in the ringing of the telephone.

'Oh, Celia, I am glad you're in. It's Darcey, sorry should have said. I'm in something of a panic. You know Dad lives on his own, well about an hour ago he was picked up by police and ambulance-men just wandering around, didn't know who he was or where he lived and he hadn't got anything with him for identification. It was just lucky that when he got to hospital another patient recognised him.'

'That sounds awful, how can I help?'

'Normally I would manage because Edward would be able to change his arrangements and come home but just at present he is up in York leading the prosecution in a major fraud trial and he is on his way to court now and I can't reach him. Obviously I need to get to the hospital but I have no one for James, can I bring him to you? It's not even one of his nursery-school days.'

'Not a problem, Darcey, run him down, bring his favourite things, especially anything that he hates to be parted from. My two will love to

224

find him here when they get home.' And that's how Celia's 'family history research day' became one of toddler minding, story reading and playing games. She wondered about Darcey's father, sudden onset of dementia, could it happen that quickly, Celia had no idea. Just at that moment she couldn't remember his name, not that dissimilar to Edward's. Edmund, that was it, she had only met him once or twice so she could be forgiven for not remembering.

Celia thought she had about thirty minutes before young James would arrive so she gathered up the bits and pieces of Richard's family tree and the two albums of photographs and put them away. She put a kettle on in case Darcey wanted a drink before she drove off and she also hunted out Richard's toys from when he was James's age. Perhaps later in the morning James would like to visit the local shops and pretend to be grown up, drinking milk and chocolate in one of the many cafes which seemed to be everywhere these days. No more thinking time, front door-bell was ringing and when she opened it, it was obvious James was raring to go, charged in with great enthusiasm. 'Celia, thank you so much, this is his bag with everything he might need and this piece of paper has a couple of important telephone numbers. You won't be offended if I don't stop, better get to the hospital as soon as possible.'

'Go on then, be off to your dad, let me know how you get on and if the need arises James can stop over.'

'Thanks, you are kind Celia, bye then.'

'We're meeting at Vincent's funeral in a couple of days, don't forget.'

Celia turned round to see where James had raced off to but to her surprise found him quietly looking at Richard's books so that augured well for the rest of the day.

Much to Celia's relief James seemed to enjoy his day, especially going out in the middle of the morning and being taken into a coffee shop. James didn't drink coffee but he did get a small cup containing hot, foamy milk and a good sprinkling of chocolate on the top. During the afternoon he kept asking when Richard and Amy would come home. Needless-to-say, when they did finally arrive, delight all round, especially as Celia had gone to extra trouble over tea, several favourites of her two children, fruit cocktail set in jelly, ice-cream, chocolate cake and a number of bags of crisps.

Soon after this little feast was over Darcey telephoned. 'Hello Celia, James been all right?'

'Yes, he seems to have thoroughly enjoyed himself and now he is playing with my two, smiling faces all round. So, how's your father?'

'Much better thankfully. In the end it was nothing to do with dementia and his condition is not uncommon. Apparently he has a bladder infection, did nothing about it, took to drinking less than was healthy, got dehydrated and the effect was to cause symptoms just like dementia. He's now taking antibiotics and he's on a fluids drip and will come home tomorrow so if it's all right I can pop down in about an hour and pick James up.'

'I think there may be some tears over that, why not let him stay over and then you come down in the morning.'

'Are you sure, Celia, that's very kind of you and then I can visit dad this evening. What sort of time do you think would be best in the morning?'

'My two will be off to school at eight-thirty so how about nine-thirty.'

'That will be fine, Celia. Thank you so much, love to your two.'

'Bye Darcey.' When she told the three about the plan, cheers all round.

Chapter Thirty-Two
India Day and Surprising Police Information

The Prime Minister for you, Foreign Secretary.'

'Good morning Sir, I was shortly to ring you but you have beaten me to it. Is this about our day of Indian business?'

'Absolutely right, James. At present I see I have an official luncheon in my diary, the arrangement hasn't changed I take it, and will it be the usual buffet style which gets us nicely over any cultural dietary problems.'

'Everything is as planned, Prime Minister. Angus Barrington is more or less running the event, I must say he is an outstandingly gifted individual so I hope you won't be promoting him with a move outside the Foreign Office anytime soon. He will make an excellent Minister of State within the F.O. if a vacancy ever arrives.'

'Yes, his name gets mentioned frequently. Actually I spoke to him yesterday, asked him to invite the Justice Secretary, Adil Khan to the luncheon, thought his presence might be helpful. I know he was born in this country but his parents are from New Delhi. Talking about Angus again, remind me, what's his background.'

'His father is in international banking, his mother is something of a linguist, but not sure of her actual work. Angus himself gained a scholarship to somewhere prestigious and then read languages and history at Cambridge, got himself a double first. Ever since he came to this post in the Foreign Office he has been making himself quite an expert in all matters pertaining to India, particularly with aspects of the country's diverse culture. That's an area in which we often let ourselves down. I think brilliance at languages must run in Barrington's family, he has a lad aged about twelve and I understand he is leaving his teachers standing with his incredible innate skills with languages.'

'Yes, Angus is somebody to watch. Now, what's the main thrust of the day?'

'Primarily international trade, issues over aspects of their developing a non-carbon environment, still a problem area for them. Education is on the agenda, as their population is so vast there are still great extremes in so far as education being available to all, and as time goes on the gap between the well-educated and the uneducated becomes ever greater, basic education is there though. Joining us for the day are experts from Trade and Education Departments, and quite a number of relevant outside people. Angus was hoping that a descendant of Mahatma Gandhi would be visiting, Great Grandson I believe, but in the end his travel plans have had to change. It is all to do with the fact that it is one hundred years since Mahatma Gandhi's famous protest against British Salt Laws, the very early days in the fight for India's independence. Today's conference and meetings can see the two Nations in a spirit of co-operation.'

'It sounds like an event which may have positive results, wish young Angus well for me.'

'I will indeed, he's popping in to see me for a few minutes quite soon. We'll meet at luncheon, Prime Minister.'

Just as they ended their telephone conversation, there was a tap at the door and Angus Barrington came in. 'Your timing is perfect, Angus, the Prime Minister has just asked me to wish you well for today's events. Take a seat, although I know you don't want to be long. By the way, good idea to invite Adil to the luncheon.'

'Thank you James. Adil was the PM's suggestion, very bad over-sight on my part so I have spoken to him, apologised and asked him to sit in on the session discussing education. I haven't had an opportunity just lately to bring you up to date, and also to say how sorry I am to have heard of your various difficulties. Your brother's funeral tomorrow I believe.'

'Yes, thank you, it's been a difficult time. Now where and when do you want me today, in addition to the luncheon appointment which the Prime Minister mentioned just now, at least he knows about that.'

'If you would sit in on the trade discussions, could be very useful. It's not that they are necessarily the most important part of the day, but they could be the most complex.'

'I think you are probably very right. I take it Rufus is involved, can he give me a 'heads up' when I'm required?'

'Yes, Rufus is very involved, has a sharp intellect which comes to the fore with events such as being held today. I'll prime him accordingly. In addition to the trade aspects I just mentioned, feel free to walk in on any of the various meetings, you have the detailed plan showing times and rooms.'

'Yes, here – my essential 'bible' for the day.'

'I think that's all James, so I'll away and just ensure that no crises are poised to envelop us.'

'That's fine, thank you Angus.'

As Angus went off to check on everything, James sat back to read more outstanding mail but found his mind wandering to another aspect of the day, Education and how the UK can help. He thought that the Indian Government knew far more about reaching out to the most remote communities within the vast area and population that was India, but James thought that far more could be done at the level of higher education, exchanges between research students especially in the sciences where mutual co-operation would benefit everybody. It was something he ought to sound Sir Peter on, somebody who had been in his mind just lately. Thinking about this aspect of the day reminded him of the late involvement of Adil Khan. Embarrassing that it was a last minute suggestion, partly the fault of Adil's rather self-effacing personality, but he must have realised that he had been forgotten even if he never took offence.

Letting his thoughts wander to aspects of Trade, a matter in which he engaged in later today, he supposed at a similar level, it would be technological imports and exports which would be of most benefit. He needed to listen to the representatives from the Trade Department.

Now not involved in any close way with the 'India' day, was the Home Office but it hadn't escaped the notice of Daniel Divine that the event was taking place and he was at that moment just mentioning it to Jeremy Lutterworth. 'Jeremy, have you been in any way involved in the Foreign Office and their large 'India' event taking place today?'

'No Sir, not involved, brief summary papers about it have 'crossed' my desk but I feel the Home Office has been kept well clear of the detail of the event.'

'Are there likely to be issues arising which will affect any H.O. policies, situations we need to look out for?'

'Most probably immigration. You must be aware how quite a sizeable group of your own MPs watch immigration numbers like many people check their 'pools' each week. If the groups meeting today start talking about training initiatives, exchanges of information, you can be sure that aspects of immigration will be hanging in there somewhere. When are you next in the Commons for questions?'

'Next month and there is always at least one question about immigration, often in connection with activities generated by my good friend James St John, although he's been a little distracted of late. Family sadness with the death of his older brother and the various embarrassing revelations. I expect the press are watching closely. Anything else I need to be warned about Jeremy?'

'No, things are quiet just at present. Can I ask you something, a little personal though?' With a nod from Daniel, Jeremy continued. 'My Angela, did she sort of get pushed in the direction of the Prime Minister? I never knew, and Angela's been a little reticent on the matter, all I know is that she's working very long hours.'

'No, certainly no pushing from this end. I didn't want to part company with her, far too efficient. It came about more by request, not from the PM directly of course, but via two or three individuals who have as part of their brief, various matters to do with personnel.'

'Thank you, I understand. I'll away for the time being, but I expect I will see you before the day's out.'

To say that James St John was a little tired after his very busy day at the Foreign Office was something of an understatement; yet again he was shattered. The kind of day which 'The India Event' brought about was such that Angus Barrington could thrive on but for James, nothing but worry and irritability as he thought of all the little things which could go wrong. He had managed to relax a little at lunch and he went out of his way to speak to Adil without so much as hinting in any way that his presence was not expected.

In the end he persuaded himself that he had urgent business at home which couldn't be put off as it was his brother's funeral the next day, and so, convinced by his own thinking, he called his driver and went home a couple of hours early. 'Urgent business' was the need for some sleep; his wife took one look at him and sent him upstairs clutching a large malt whisky.

A couple of days after Sergeant Vaughan's return from visiting Henry Palmerson, his Inspector telephoned Rufus and Audrey Sutton and arranged to visit them early that evening, when Rufus had returned from the Foreign Office, somewhat tired but he pulled himself together for Audrey's sake.

'Thank you for seeing us,' Inspector Finley started. 'Our need to speak with you continues our previous conversation and information obtained from DNA test results. On our last visit I had the awkward task of suggesting to you, Mrs Sutton, that your blood mother was the woman killed in the hit-and-run accident which we had been investigating. At the end of last week we received another surprising piece of information. You will have read of the death of Vincent St John no doubt, and while the police of Oxford were working on that case a young man who had known him well, a post-graduate research student, came forward to talk about how he had come to know Vincent. For identification purposes this young man provided us with a DNA test sample and the result was very unexpected. It suggested that your blood father, Mrs Sutton, was somebody closely related to the young man who had come forward, possibly an older brother, more likely his father. I need to explain that this young man attended Kemby School in Norfolk and that his father was on the staff. When we spoke to the father he admitted to having had a short love affair with the pupil from Kroxby School, Lucinda Quemsby, who we now know to be your blood mother, Mrs Sutton. I realise that this is probably another shock but can I just let Sergeant Vaughan tell you about the man he met the other day.'

'I found him very friendly, approachable and kindly in manner. He made no secret of having known Lucinda about thirty years ago. The attraction between them was mutual, he knew it was wrong, offered no excuses for his behaviour which he realised was totally inappropriate. At the time he and his wife were having a difficult time because she had just been diagnosed with breast cancer. For a few years the treatment appeared successful but she died, twenty years back now. It was while he and his wife were coming to terms with her diagnosis that Lucinda left Kroxby School, he never heard the rumours that her leaving was because of a pregnancy.'

'Just before I came away I explained that I would be seeing you regarding the new information about DNA results. Needless to say I was maintaining confidentiality about you, just as I am now about him. When I left he asked me to tell you that should you wish to meet, he wouldn't mind in the least, the choice would be entirely yours. It was a very encouraging conversation for once, as sadly many police conversations are certainly not amiable or encouraging.'

'Well, thank you, both of you, that's all very clear. Unlike the last time you called with similar information, but about my mother and which came as an enormous shock, this time it comes more or less as expected other than learning the identity in due course. Whether I shall want to meet the person you believe to be my father, I really can't say, something Rufus and I will have to talk about. Another distressing aspect of the whole saga is what happened to my blood mother, Lucinda, between giving birth to me and her death four or five months back now? She obviously followed a terrible downward path but it surely didn't start straight away. I wonder what her parents were like, what influence they exerted over her to bring about a secret and unofficial adoption and then how they looked after her when it was all over.'

It was Inspector Finley who responded to this. 'Sadly, without a very specific investigation into the Quemsby family it will be very difficult to find out. Such an investigation would require considerable research and need several interviews and meetings with various members of the family.'

'It could be something for a private investigator.' This was Rufus Sutton's only comment during the whole meeting.

Chapter Thirty-Three
Cornish Paperwork

Sergeant George Angwin was born and bred in Looe, on the South Cornish coast, likewise all the known generations of his forebears. On the other hand his wife was foreign; she had been born in Torquay! At present he was following up what might be a time-consuming enquiry which had come down from one of the London Stations. Enquiries which had followed a hit-and-run incident had shown that there had likely been a deliberate attempt to falsify records regarding the birth of a baby girl, Audrey Ponsonby, in 2004. From the information he had received it transpired that Audrey had been brought up knowing only that name, although she was now married to a Dr Rufus Sutton. As the result of DNA tests taken subsequent to a robbery at the Suttons' apartment, and others taken after a fatal hit-and-run, it appeared that Audrey Sutton, nee Ponsonby, was the daughter of Lucinda Quemsby, the woman killed in the hit-and-run. The only other information which George Angwin had was that Audrey Sutton was in possession of what appeared to be a perfectly valid birth certificate showing that Audrey had been born at the now closed Royal Infirmary, Looe, parents – Frederick and Christine Ponsonby and date of birth as 6th May 2004. He had investigated the birth certificate but found that the registrar from that time retired soon after and had in fact died in 2015. At the present moment in time George was leafing his way through the records of the Royal Infirmary, Looe.

His leafing was of short duration as success came speedily. He found himself studying the hospital notes regarding Mrs Ponsonby, both for pre-birth visits and then for the two day stay in hospital for the birth. The record showed dates which suggested that Mrs Ponsonby had only started visiting the Infirmary only a few weeks before the expected birth, but no mention of a previous hospital. As before, this looked in order and there was mention of a record book being handed over which would be used to record medical facts of the baby for the first few years, vaccinations etc. He knew about such record books as his daughter-in-law was given one recently, when his first grandson was born, it was called the 'red book'

The only additional point that caught his attention was that a nurse had scribbled a note that the mother seemed very young for her age. He also read that the mother-to-be had given as a contact, an Aunt, Miss Ponsonby. George also noted that there was no mention of Mr Ponsonby in connection with any hospital information. The delivery had been normal and no assistance needed, although it had been a long labour. He made a note of the given address and decided that he would make a visit and see if any of the near neighbours remembered anything. Before doing that he checked the electoral roll for 2003 to 2005 and was very surprised to find that nobody of the name Ponsonby was listed. Reference to other available data bases told him that the house where the family were supposed to have lived had changed hands four times in the last twenty-five years. Only one of the neighbouring houses might be occupied by people who remembered the Ponsonbys; in the event he drew a blank as he found nobody who could recall the Ponsonbys, not really surprising.

Sergeant Angwin prided himself on being thorough in his work even when the matter he was dealing with was a little on the tedious side. The present case was a good example, but he decided he would pursue the search a little more for where these people had lived. With a bit of internet surfing he was able to bring up a list of local businesses for the relevant period in time and then refined the search to estate agents, including other terms such as 'property rentals,' 'lettings' and such like. There was quite a long list but he supposed that some of them no longer existed so he thought he could make telephone enquiries, perhaps complete them all in half a day or so. He soon began to feel that he was going achieve nothing as his responses were very negative: 'No we didn't start until 2020, sorry', 'The firm did exist then but we bought them out in 2015, no records from before that date', 'We only entered the rental market about 2018'. After taking a break and fetching a cup of tea he struck lucky. An estate agency under the name of Jones and Son had been running for nearly fifty years. The original 'Jones' was long since dead and the 'son' referred to in the title, was a David Jones and had retired. The present owner and proprietor was Lewis Jones, nephew to David.

'Yes, Sergeant, we may very well be able to help. 2003 was about the time my Uncle David fell in love with computers. Don't get me wrong, the agency had been using them but not in a big way. It was my Uncle who saw greater potential, he was keen on avoiding any work which required information to be typed out, presented, analysed more than once. 'Never delete,' was one of his mottos, rather, save it in as many ways as possible, so that any member of staff can pull a record up should it be required. As our records stand at present I can produce a list of anybody who has rented, or a list of any property address for which we have had letting responsibility. I think we can find the information you want if we have had relevant dealings. Just give me a few minutes, perhaps better, I'll ring you back very soon. You just make yourself comfortable, have a tea-break.'

Sergeant Angwin rang off thinking that Lewis Jones had to be Welsh given the number of words he used! Second cup of tea fetched and the telephone rang.

'Sergeant Angwin speaking.'

'Lewis Jones here, I think I have found what you wanted. 3, Plaidy Avenue is a small, detached house which we let in February 2004. The clients opted for a twelve-month let and paid in full in advance. The clients were Mr and Mrs Frederick Ponsonby, they came from Reading. They only stayed nine months.'

'I think that information is very helpful Mr Jones.'

'You ought to thank my Uncle. The only other information is a pencil note added, I think it is my Uncle's writing, 'short employment contract.' The meaning is probably obvious, Mr Ponsonby was to be in Looe to complete a short period of work.'

'Do you have an address for where they lived in Reading?'

'Yes Sir, 15 Amblecote End, sorry, no post code. The telephone number at the time was 0118 42346791, that's a long number, hope it is correct. We had a reference from a Reading firm, place of work probably, 'Timbersides Constructions, 14 Bath Road Court, Mr John Jones.' Lewis chuckled at that. 'Never know, might be a relative, there's only about ten million of us!'

'I take it that you have no mention of there ever being more than just the two tenants, Mr and Mrs Ponsonby?'

'Sorry, I think I have given you everything we know.'

'Just one more thing, have you had any other clients with an address in Plaidy Avenue?'

'No, just that one, I can answer that quickly because I did my initial search using the address you gave me and the name 'Plaidy' came up only the once.'

'Well thank you very much, Lewis. You've been most helpful. I'll make a note of everything you have told me just in case there is any follow up needed. Anyway, many thanks.'

Sergeant Angwin sat back, looked pleased with himself because he nearly hadn't bothered to pursue the address side of the enquiry. His report would still be on the short side but would look a little better now.

For the attention of Sergeant Vaughan:

With reference to your enquiry, re: Mr and Mrs Ponsonby and daughter Audrey.

I can confirm the following facts:

1. They rented 3, Plaidy Avenue, Looe from February 2004 for 12 months, paid in advance.

They moved away after nine months. Mr Ponsonby had a short-term contract for work in the area.

2. Baby was born at Looe Infirmary, 6ᵗʰ May 2004. Comments made on hospital record by staff:

Mother only started attending Infirmary a couple of months before birth.

Mother seemed very young for her age.

The labour took a long time.

Hospital 'red book' issued.

3. Estate Agent who arranged the let gave as background information the following facts:

'Ponsonbys' previous address: 15 Amblecote End, Reading.

Telephone number at the time was 0118 42346791 - long number, incorrect?

Estate Agent obtained reference from John Jones of 'Timbersides Constructions, *14 Bath Road Court. John Jones was probably a previous employer.*

4. Birth Registration – seemed in order. Registrar retired soon after and died in 2015.

5. Checked electoral roll for 2003-2005 – Ponsonbys not listed.

6. No neighbours in Plaidy Avenue who remembered the Ponsonbys – near houses had all changed hands.

' Just a thought: If the Ponsonbys wanted to bring about a false identity for a new born child then the circumstances which I have detailed here provide most of the necessary ingredients. The 'aunt' mentioned as Miss Ponsonby, could be Mrs Ponsonby and she could have registered the birth as if she was the mother. If the real mother

were Lucinda Quemsby she could have passed herself off as Mrs Ponsonby when in hospital. In these circumstances the only surname which may ever have been mentioned would have been 'Ponsonby.' Lucinda's parents could have arranged the whole scheme with the Ponsonbys, people that they presumably knew who wanted to adopt without anybody ever knowing. Lucinda's parents must have persuaded her to go along with the scheme, convinced her that not having to be a teen-age mum was a good thing and also a way of avoiding an abortion.

Sergeant George Angwin'

Chapter Thirty-Four
Celebrating Coppers and a
Meeting of Greater Moment

The result of Sergeant Watson's work on behalf of Superintendent Jefferson was beginning to show itself and those guests, non-uniformed as requested, who had already arrived to acknowledge the sterling work of this retiring senior officer were definitely enjoying a plentiful supply of beer, their accompanying wives, husbands and partners, men with men, women with women and men with women (all combinations, married and unmarried, allowed for, Geoff was totally up to date in matters p.c.) were looking resplendent in colourful outfits and whilst many were also enjoying a beer others were enjoying the many different drinks available at this event. If any particular tipple were unavailable, no one would moan as no money was required to change hands during the course of the evening. Nobody could complain about any tight-fistedness on the part of Geoff Jefferson as he was paying for the entire evening and one result would be a sizeable crowd turning up to wish him well. Not surprising given that his lengthy and successful career ended at senior rank, a large number of officers would have crossed his path and he was looking forward to meeting up with a goodly number of them again.

Police officers, like any other group of people getting together and who only have their work as a common factor, are inclined to talk shop, latest developments, promotion, pay, humorous moments, senior officers, shift work – the list is long if not endless. Perhaps at a party with alcohol flowing, getting the best laugh might be a good opener. Petty thief caught stuck in the toilet window, another found with his pockets stuffed with packets of cigarettes, caught asleep behind the wheel of a car, reeking of drink with the engine still running, caught with his trousers down – all grist to the mill for a copper looking to capture his audience. Sworn protestations of innocence when found in such embarrassing circumstances provide a further post-script to any reminiscence, usually gains a further bout of laughter and the more the alcohol flows the louder the laughter gets. For one custody sergeant attending this party a recent arrest provided him with a good laugh; a group of four young muggers were brought in to his station recently because one of them didn't realise the incident was taking place outside his grandma's house and to make the lad even more embarrassed the said grandma visited the station and shopped the lot; she knew the families of all four.

Because Superintendent Jefferson had deep pockets the refreshments at this particular bash were of unusually good quality so there was no shortage of the younger members of the guests stuffing themselves as if to make up for the short-comings of their own catering efforts. They may have still been proud of their slim build combined with very large appetites but it didn't put off the portlier guests from endeavouring to keep up with them – and failing.

There was another small group holding forth about spelling problems, in particular the spelling of names. One particular officer had recently been taken to task for failing to spell the name of a witness correctly. To justify his annoyance he spelt out the offending surname and challenged his listeners as to how it should be pronounced – E a s t a u g h f f e. Needless to say this example caused other guests to relay problems with unusual names and between them they had encountered quite a few, including Andilet, Quintrell, Sallow, Zouch and Quemsby.

'Is somebody here called 'Quemsby'? That's not an everyday name although it does occur in my own family history.'

'Nobody here with that name, just a name which has come up in some enquiries I've been making. Hello, I'm David Watson.'

'Nice to meet you, name's Joshua.'

'Joshua St John?'

'Gracious, how did you know that?'

'No great mystery sir, I helped Superintendent Jefferson track down some of the names on his guest list and yours was one of them. Actually he told me you would be someone to make himself at home. Was he right, Sir?'

'No need to call me 'Sir,' not in court now, presuming that you have remembered how I earn a crust. Your Superintendent is right, I generally fit in where ever I am. Actually I need to speak with him because happy as I am to be here, family difficulties mean I ought to be away quite soon.'

'Sorry to hear that. Tell me about the name 'Quemsby.' As David Watson asked this Joshua subtly moved them as a pair slightly away from the rest of the group who had started to talk among themselves anyway.

'An aunt I think, about two or three generations back, fell out with younger members of her family and left her money to other relatives instead, my grandmother being one of them and if my memory is right, her mother's maiden name was Quemsby.'

'Don't want to pry but is your early departure this evening connected with your surname being in the press today? Sorry, perhaps I shouldn't be asking.'

'You're not wrong. Vincent St John was my uncle although I hardly knew him, kept himself rather remote, his younger brother is my father, James St John.'

'Of Foreign Office fame?'

'Quite right, but not for conversation here I feel.'

'Say no more.'

'So how did the name Quemsby come your way?'

'Got called to a lift failure incident, passenger left unconscious and while he was coming round he was muttering various names from twenty-five years back, his school days, and one name which at first seemed rather obscure turned out to be a Lucinda Quemsby.'

'Not one of my forebears, certainly. I better go and present my apologies to your Superintendent. Good to have chatted, David.'

Curiously David wondered to himself how Joshua could be so confident about there being no connection between Lucinda Quemsby and his forebears.

In the same building was a small office where a meeting between Commander Zachary and Ms Brenda Cuthbertson was taking place. Commander Zachary, Zach to a few close friends, had a variety of roles within Scotland Yard, one of which was little known about, but involved him meeting occasionally with Ms Cuthbertson. He brought a combination of wisdom and common sense to the meeting whereas Brenda brought the results of high-quality computer 'surfing,' having had access to the Yard's vast data resources and their purpose, and between them, was the protection of important people. 'PIP' sounded a little silly, useful disguise for a national matter of great significance. The splendid search facilities of the modern computer programs as used for recording all police data was that events, incidents, names, dates all got recorded and all could be cross- referenced. Their concern was to make sure that people of whom the Government had great need didn't get entwined in other people's serious affairs, perhaps by accident, by default or become surrounded by rumour and as a result an important individual could be destroyed by the press.

'Thank you Brenda for coming in this evening, at least you understand the need for discretion and the advantage of meeting at a time when far fewer people are around, avoids awkward questions.'

'Not a problem, Commander.'

'I suppose I'm never going to get you to call me Zach, even at just these meetings. Anyway, who's come over the horizon?'

'You're not going to be surprised and that's before his name entered the press recently, James St John. Two sides to this, one is the most recent, the death of his older brother, suicide, revealed homosexuality, in the reports I've seen, possibility of rape prior to death. The second is in the days and weeks before, various enquiries which directly or indirectly connect with his senior secretary Rufus Sutton and his wife Audrey. Burglary at their flat in London while they were away. Police concerns for security so DNA and finger prints taken. DNA match with a woman killed in hit-and-run which shows her as Audrey's mother. Investigations about her birth are suggestive of possible deception. Other enquiries connect a member of staff, David Yardlington, at the Regal Crown Hotel with the Suttons – knew each other in Paris. Various enquiries via David following his accident in a lift failure where he lives, link him with names from his school days, one of which is Lucinda Quemsby, a rare name but occurs in James St John's family back ground. Lucinda Quemsby was a pupil at Kroxby School for Girls at the same time as David Yardlington was a pupil at Kemby School.

Another set of DNA results have led to the discovery of Audrey Sutton's blood father. One of Vincent St John's close friends, Frank Palmerson came forward to explain his relationship with Vincent and he agreed to give a sample for DNA purposes and this revealed that his father was the blood father of Audrey. It is not as surprising as it may seem because Frank was formerly a pupil of Kemby School, where his father was one of the teachers. He, the father, and Lucinda met quite by chance and an affair ensued.

'My, how complex, but I can see how that can all interconnect, and could set off a large number of threatening rumours. How might the deception regarding the birth registration have occurred?'

'As follows: a 'mother to be' admitted to hospital in Looe, called herself Mrs Ponsonby but there was a comment in notes that she looked very young. With her, was somebody described as an Aunt,

Miss Ponsonby. Birth proceeds normally but takes a long labour – suggestive of youth. Registration is conducted with a Mrs Ponsonby presenting herself as the mother, has the baby with her, her own birth certificate and wedding certificate, she also has with her the 'red book' issued by the hospital. The Ponsonbys, who had taken a short lease on a house in Looe, came from Reading. They were never listed on electoral roll for Looe. With hindsight, one can see how a deception may have occurred. The Aunt is actually Mrs Ponsonby who is adopting the baby unofficially. The mother in hospital, calling herself Mrs Ponsonby, was Lucinda Quemsby. Presumably the adoption was organised by Lucinda's parents and the whole arrangement was kept very secret and of course, Lucinda was persuaded to go along with the plan. What happened to her afterwards is at present unknown. Before the discovery of Frank Palmerson's father being the blood father of Audrey Ponsonby, other enquiries had been made about the contempories of David Yardlington and it was discovered that just possibly a Jeremy Lutterworth, adviser at the Home Office, thought (still thinks?) he may be the father.

'And what is known about the Quemsby name in the St John family tree?'

'I have a genealogist working on it, won't be difficult and I should hear the outcome in a few days. Most probably is a relationship of cousins, possibly not first cousins.'

The Commander was thoughtful for just a few moments. 'The key question is if or when I should approach James St John about these matters. I certainly don't imagine the issues will go away, especially anything to do with the private life of Vincent St John. And since that unfortunate matter when the Foreign Secretary held an ill-advised meeting without informing the Prime Minister, there are MPs keeping a closer watch on any matters which pertain to him. I'll certainly wait until your genealogist reports back.'

Chapter Thirty-Five
Family Tree Complications

It was in fact the next day when Brenda sent a short note to Commander Zachary. 'I have received information about the Quemsby family and how it connects with the St John family. Initially the connection arose from the marriage between Sir George St John (current elderly Baronet) and Elaine Rosenthal as she was the daughter of Joshua Rosenthal MP and Daphne Quemsby. Daphne's father was Arthur Quemsby and he was first cousin to Alfred, Juliette and Peter Quemsby. Peter died as baby, Juliette remained unmarried and had no issue. The Quemsby line continues as direct line from Alfred to his Great Granddaughter, Lucinda and Great Great Granddaughter, Audrey.'

Juliette Quemsby was wealthy but the source is unknown and she left money to various relatives including her first cousin twice removed, Elaine St George, mother of James St George. Rumour seems to have it that she did not approve of her own directly related descendants.

Linking these names by relationships:

Arthur Quemsby was Grandfather to Elaine so Great Grandfather to James St John

Juliette and also Alfred were 1ST Cousins twice removed to Elaine

Elaine and Peterkin were third cousins

James St John and Lucinda were fourth cousins

James St John and Juliette were first cousins thrice removed

James and Audrey are fourth cousins once removed (James and Rufus by marriage)

Although fairly distant it does mean that James St John and Audrey Sutton are related, fourth cousins once removed, I think that maybe the correct description, certainly cousins and same applies to Vincent and Beryl.

There is also the connection that we learn from DNA: James's brother, Vincent, was the lover of Frank Palmerson and his father, Henry, is also father to Audrey. This means Frank and his older brother George are half-brothers to Audrey Sutton.

So far no information has been found on how Lucinda spent the years after the birth of her baby until her death. Based on the pathologist's report it is likely that drugs and alcohol were involved taking her in a downward spiral.

Family lines to show the St John family line
And the two lines of the Quemsbys

Archibald Quemsby - two brothers- Peter Quemsby   **Maj.Gen Sir James Vincent**
had three children   had one son   I

       I   I   **George St John**

       I   I   I

Alfred, Juliette   Peter   Arthur   Edward St John

  I   unmarried died as baby   I   only surviving son

  I   I   I

Archibald Quemsby   Daphne Quemsby =   Peter St John

  I   Joshua Rosenthal   I

  I   I   I

  I   Elaine Rosenthal = **George St John**

  I   _____ I_____

  I   I   I   I

Peterkin Quemsby   Vincent Beryl **James St John = Rhiannon**

Married Lynn Taylor   unmarried **Foreign Secretary** I

  I   _____ I___

  I   I   I

Lucinda Quemsby - - - - - - - -Henry Palmerson   Edward=   Joshua=

  I   I   Darcey   Celia

  I   I   I   I

Audrey Ponsonby=   George & Frank   James Richard &Amy

     Rufus Sutton

When Commander Zachery received this additional information about the Quemsby line in the St John family tree he was not best pleased. It just seemed to place the Nation's Foreign Secretary in the centre of much potential rumour-mongering. Without doubt he was going to have to discuss this with James St John and soon. For once he was at a loss as to how to go about this. Should it be a very confidential meeting between himself and James St John but that wouldn't be easy to arrange. He had heard that the marriage between James and Rhiannon was very good so would it be better to make it a meeting involving her and then he could see them at their house, easier to maintain confidentiality. Gradually it was that option which appealed more and as he had their home telephone number he decided to arrange a meeting there and then.

'Rhiannon St John speaking, can I help?'

'I think you can. My name is Commander Zachary of Scotland Yard and one of my more confidential tasks is oversight of any events which could possibly lead to situations which may cause embarrassment to the Government or to its individual members. Various pieces of information have come my way and I feel the need to share them with you and your husband. In case you might think otherwise, I must stress there is nothing criminal about this. Is there a time when I could come out to see you both. I have contacted you at home as I don't want to go through your husband's private office at the Foreign Office.'

'Goodness, how mysterious you're being. Late this afternoon would be best as later we have to drive over to James's parents for the funeral tomorrow of his brother, Vincent. I can contact my husband to make sure he is home in time. Shall we say 4.30pm?'

'Excellent.'

Rhiannon was fortunately one of those unflappable individuals so she was outwardly quite calm about the Commander, intrigued, certainly. She used her husband's private mobile number knowing that only he would answer it.

'Hello darling, unusual to hear from you at this time especially as I will be home very soon.'

'Yes, that's why I'm telephoning you. Are you alone?'

'Yes, I am.'

'I can tell you more when you get here but I have agreed to a meeting between us and a Commander Zachary for four-thirty this afternoon.'

'I know that name, yes. Would 'watch-dog' suffice?'

'Excellent, James.'

'I'll leave now.'

Tony was able to make good time and leaving at three-thirty they avoided the worst of the traffic. James walked in with thirty minutes to spare before the Commander was expected.

'Rhiannon, so what does our rather secretive Commander want then?'

'He hasn't been clear but he wants to discuss some information, nothing criminal, something he stressed, which has come his way and which may be embarrassing.'

'Well, not so embarrassing that he can't talk about it in front of both of us. Time for a coffee before he arrives?'

'Yes, dear. All ready and I have told him about the funeral tomorrow and our need to be at your parents' this evening.

Commander Zachary was exactly on time and didn't waste any time, other than to accept a coffee, before explaining himself. 'Thank you for seeing me at such speed, very helpful. One of my duties is to watch out for situations which have the potential to cause embarrassment to individual members of the government or the government as a whole. There's a very particular handful of M.P.s who keep a close eye on you, Sir, so it behoves me to keep a watch on other circumstances which may crop up. Can I ask, are you familiar with the name, Quemsby?'

'Yes, there is a Quemsby in our family, my mother's maiden name and goes back to mother's Great Grandfather, four generations back I believe. There is another branch but I'm not sure about them, quite a number of distant cousins.'

'The actual relationship is that three people with the surname Quemsby are your mother's mother, her Grandfather, Arthur, and Great Grandfather, Peter. The other branch to which you referred arises from Peter Quemsby's brother, Archibald. He married a Marion and they had three children, Peter named after his uncle and who died as a baby, Juliette who never married and had no issue, but she became wealthy from sources unknown. She is the one who left money to your mother in trust for when she was twenty-five. The third child was Alfred and he married a Molly Taylor and from them is a direct line for three generations ending with Lucinda. As you suggested, you have several distant cousins. For example, you, Vincent and Beryl are all fourth cousins to Lucinda, and it is Lucinda who is central to the situation which I am describing.'

'In a police investigation two months or so ago concerning a fatal hit-and-run, the woman who died was a vagrant, identity unknown at the time of the accident. However, DNA linked her to somebody of your acquaintance, Rufus Sutton's wife, Audrey. The DNA showed that she was the daughter of the accident victim. This came as a shock as she had no knowledge that she was not the natural daughter of the couple she knew as her parents. In another quite unrelated investigation but involving you as a member of the family, is the death of your brother, Vincent. You will remember that a Frank Palmerson came forward to explain his relationship with your brother. He provided samples for DNA testing and this showed that his father was Audrey's blood father. Further investigations have made it clear how this was not such an extraordinary coincidence as it seemed. Henry Palmerson, Frank's father, was a teacher at his son's school, Kemby Boys' School. Henry admits to having had an affair with a Lucinda Quemsby, a pupil at the nearby girls' school, Kroxby. This would have been at the time Frank's older brother, George was a pupil at the same school.'

'When you look at the descriptions of some of the relationships it transpires that you and Audrey Sutton are related, fourth cousins, once removed I believe is the correct term. Additionally, Frank Palmerson and his brother George are half-brothers to Audrey Sutton. In describing relationships your two sons are fifth cousins of Audrey. I think you can see that in the wrong hands, a scurrilous editor could wreak havoc with such information. It seems that there was a private, possible illegally brought about adoption in the West Country, so that Lucinda Quemsby's baby was brought up as Audrey Ponsonby.'

'I must point out that at present, Audrey Sutton is not aware of Henry Palmerson by name, that will only come about should they choose to meet.'

'George Palmerson, Frank's older brother, and at the time of Lucinda becoming pregnant, was a pupil at Kemby and along with other boys often used to meet various girls from Kroxby and it seems that sometimes relationships were not quite as they should have been. One of the lads is a David Yardlington who works at the Regal Court Hotel and he has recently met up with one of the other lads, Jeremy Lutterworth. Currently he is an adviser to the Home Secretary. From information which has come via these investigations Jeremy may well think he is the father of Lucinda's child, but we know from DNA that cannot be so.'

'Commander Zachary, what you say seems very complicated and involved, but I can see how it could all be woven in such a way as to be very awkward for my husband, certainly embarrassing and likely to be embarrassing for the Government. Do you have a solution to suggest?'

'I have to confess, nothing obvious comes to mind, and nor do I know how far the discussion should spread. Just one question more if I may, is there any connection between your immediate family and the Quemsby relatives?'

253

'No, sorry, I'm afraid there has been no knowledge or connection as far as I know. I don't even know if any of these cousins are still alive. I should just mention that I did know about the DNA result which led to Audrey Sutton being told that she had probably been adopted at birth. Her husband Rufus mentioned it to me in the context of his telling me that his wife was a little upset. This was a day or so before my brother committed suicide.'

'Thank you for that, James. As far as the Quemsbys go, the genealogist who did the research on this case did say that he thought that Lynn Taylor, Lucinda's mother was still alive but address unknown. Lynn's husband, Peterkin, has died and all the earlier known relatives are dead. It was probably Lynn Taylor who arranged the adoption and very likely she ought to be the one who knows what happened to Lucinda from the time of the birth to her death, after all she certainly went down quite a spiral ending up destitute. Going back to my main concern, ought the Prime Minister to be involved?'

'Yes, Anthony May does not like to be caught out with new information because a sensible briefing had not been forth-coming. Like this, it will have to be a private meeting, probably here.'

Little more needed to be said and the Commander left, promising that he would make the arrangements for any meeting between them and the Prime Minister. Rhiannon did the driving over to Norstead Towers and James sat quite silent for a time, pondering all that the Commander had said. That was Rhiannon's interpretation of the silence.

Breaking the quiet, 'Do you think it is very likely that the press will get hold of all that the Commander was saying? What do you think, Rhiannon?'

'There always seems to be some story or other breaking into the news so I imagine there must be hundreds of researchers digging away to see what can be found out about the 'great' and the 'famous,' and I suppose you do fall into such categories.'

'I imagine you're probably right but I do hope this funeral can be quiet enough for the press not to be hovering at the grave-side.'

Chapter Thirty-Six
A Moving Committal and an Unexpected
Ringing of the Front Door Bell

In the country house of Norstead Towers, the St John family was
recovering from the funeral of Vincent. To say that the event had
been very understated would not be an exaggeration. The College
had been represented by The Master, Sir Peter Carruthers, the
secretary who had had the sad experience of discovering
Vincent's body, one research assistant who had been working most
closely on Vincent's recent work, and Frank Palmerson; he at least had
seemed genuinely fond of Vincent. The family was represented by
Vincent's elderly parents, Sir George and Lady Elaine, their daughter
Beryl, youngest and now only son, James. He was there with his wife,
Rhiannon, their sons Edward and Joshua together with their wives.
The young children stayed away, looked after by kindly neighbours.
There were three people from the village, not strangers, but not well
known by the family. Perhaps they were the kind of folk who always
attended a local funeral. The service took place in the Parish Church of
Lower Norstead, conducted by a visiting clergyman, The Reverend
Gerard Alderton.

Gerard Alderton may not have known any of the family, probably
never heard of Vincent, but yet he managed to give a positive and
moving address based in part on the family history, military service in
the nineteenth century and both world wars, political service in more
recent years. Gerard Alderton had taken the trouble to complete a little
research into Vincent's work, had spoken to Sir Peter who knew about
Vincent's early days as a research student. He had obtained a copy of
the Ph.D. thesis which he had read and from which he managed to

tease out a little understanding, sufficient to impress the small congregation as part of a short address. Equally impressive, he held the copy aloft. He made no pretence that Vincent had been a Christian but from the Master and also Frank Palmerson via a late evening phone call, he was able to assure those attending the service that Vincent had been known for his kindness and loyalty amongst a small circle of associates.

Without doubt the Reverend Gerard Alderton conducted the service with a sense of personal conviction and spoke in such a way that each person attending could feel that they had been spoken to individually; that was a wonderful spiritual gift. Vincent's brother, James read one lesson, taken from the Book of Genesis, Chapter one, to the end of verse eighteen, 'And God saw that it was good.' Beryl read two of the prayers, both of which drew attention to the work of scientists, prayers which gave thanks for the many discoveries which helped the whole of humanity, both in the expansion of knowledge and the increase in medical discoveries. At the graveside the Reverend Gerard Alderton delivered the concluding prayers with warmth and in particular managed to read the final blessing as if it were delivered by Almighty God in person, if such a thought was not sacrilegious.

From later conversation it seemed that Beryl was the only one to have noticed a stranger at the funeral service. Her expression for him was that he appeared to hover, hovered in the background, hovered back from any movement until he felt that it would be all right and that he would remain unnoticed, staying on the edge of matters. When the party moved round to the graveside he stayed near the west door and when everybody had driven off to Norstead Towers he delayed his departure by five minutes or so.

When he rang the bell the party had moved into the main room to partake of what ever Elaine had ordered to be put out for tea; there was tea or coffee to drink with the alternative of sherry or a glass of wine. It was one of the staff helping with the refreshments who answered the bell and opened the door to a middle-aged man, very slight of build, about five foot six inches tall, dressed in charcoal grey and to which the only relief was a white shirt; even his cuff-links matched the grey.

In quiet but confident tones he asked to speak to Sir George St John. The individual who received this request was uncertain as to what to say or what action to take. In the end she fell back on the time-honoured phrase – 'one moment please, Sir,' left the door ajar and went in search of help. It was to James that she delivered the request and without any comment he took himself to the front door.

'Good afternoon, I'm James St John, Sir George's son. How can we help?'

'I am Crispen MacPhearson, solicitor for the late Vincent St John and I have driven over from Oxford to read the will.'

'The will, what will?' We didn't know there was one, no copy was found among his papers and Vincent never mentioned such a document to anyone in the family.'

'If I could come in for a few minutes and be shown to a small room I could explain matters to you quickly and then you could advise your family of my arrival and be able to tell me how you wish me to proceed. At the moment I am still carrying out your late brother's very precise requests.'

'Yes, follow me,' and James showed Mr MacPhearson to a very small room, little more than an alcove with a door at the end of the passage leading from the front door. Mr MacPhearson sat down on one of only two chairs and James remained standing.

'Your late brother had this will prepared only a few years back and he was at pains to stress that nobody but myself and the second witness were to know of its existence. In addition to that instruction he insisted that in the event of his death, nothing was to be said by myself or the witness until after his funeral and interment or cremation.'

'This is preposterous, we've been going through papers and other items in his College rooms. What appeared to be rubbish has been disposed of and we have started to think about what to do with the small amount of furniture which belonged to him as against that provided by the College. He had a large quantity of books, many were scientific and we expect to give those to the College, some others were connected with the family, even some from his childhood.'

'That is perfectly all right Mr St John. Vincent said to me that that was what he expected to happen and that it would make no difference to his will.'

'I find that very strange and I'm not sure I quite understand, but if it's as you say, then so be it.'

'Rest assured, that when you hear the will you will understand. Can I suggest you go and mention my arrival to members of your family and then return to me with one of two instructions. That I should wait until the post-funeral gathering has finished, actually that may be the best arrangement as I am in no particular hurry. Alternatively I could read the will to your parents, sister and yourself without further wait.'

'Mr MacPhearson, I will show you to a more comfortable room, provide you with refreshments of your choice, and then in about forty-five minutes or so the family will be able to gather and hear what you have to say. Follow me through to the dining room, where there is room for us all.'

'Thank Mr St John. A pot of tea and a few biscuits will be ample for me while I wait.'

James returned to the funeral party and gradually moved round speaking first to his father, then to his mother who was standing with Beryl, and then to his two sons, leaving them to explain what was happening to their wives. James then decided to pick up another cup of tea and circulate among the various guests, privately hoping that they wouldn't be staying too long. The Vicar was first to leave closely followed by a small group of village folk; they had cars between them and their departure caused no difficulty. He was unsure what to say to the party from Oxford but in the end decided to give Sir Peter Carruthers a clear explanation of what had happened and hoped that they could occupy themselves for short while. He couldn't imagine that there was much in his late brother's will to keep them long.

The nine of them, the members of the St John family who had attended the funeral, went through to the dining room. sat down and waited for Crispen MacPhearson to start. 'I appreciate that I imagine you have found my arrival here today somewhat strange, but in my defence I can only say that I have been carrying out my client's instructions as to how and when I should arrive. I have to say that the late Vincent St John was a curious individual, had something of an unusual sense of humour and he also led something of a very split life style. Vincent St John's work and appearance at College represented only half of his life's activities. That brings me to the actual will, drawn up only a few years back and signed by himself in my presence and witnessed to that effect by my clerk.'

'I don't need to read every word. The first paragraph refers to all he possessed in Oxford including the content of his rooms, any monies found in his rooms or pockets of his clothes and his bank account which he used exclusively for his time in Oxford. The current balance for his Oxford based current account amounts to £15066.43p All Oxford possessions are left to his parents and/or descendants.'

'The second paragraph is more important and I'll read it exactly as it has been recorded: I leave my cottage which is owned by myself exclusively (The Seagull Cottage, Sea Front Road, Eastbourne), its entire contents including books, furniture, paintings, floor coverings, garden furniture and contents of garage and out-buildings; the monies held in any bank accounts based with institutions in Eastbourne; documents and what they represent currently held by my solicitor, Crispen MacPhearson in an envelope marked – Will, Vincent St John, – to my very good friend Frank Palmerson, c/o The Lady Isabel College, Oxford. I wish to explain, Frank is the kindest individual I have ever met, he is my best research assistant even though he understands that my powers for original work are in decline, yet he does nothing but encourage me as best he can. He also understands my somewhat unusual ways when it comes to matters of a sexual nature. I am able to trust him absolutely with any information that he has come to know about me. From time to time he has travelled with me to Eastbourne and yet I can confidently say that only three people know about my ownership of 'The Seagull Cottage,' myself, Crispen

MacPhearson and Frank Palmerson. What Frank chooses to do with this inheritance is entirely for him to decide. Up to date bank statements have always been copied to my solicitor and he can tell Frank the current balances. Any documents which may represent value will have to be researched to ascertain their current value. I do hope my family will not be upset with my intentions but it is currently my firm impression that my parents, my sister, Beryl and my brother, James, are all in possession of considerable resources.'

'Ladies and gentlemen, that concludes the reading of the will. I have with me statements for all the bank accounts relating to Eastbourne, referred to by Vincent St John and can say that the total balance for all, as at the last day of last month amounts to £219043.58p and to the best of my knowledge there has been no activity with any of the accounts during the last few weeks.'

'I will contact Frank Palmerson at the earliest opportunity, although I thought I saw him at the funeral service. May I ask, has he come back to the house?'

'Yes, he is here,' said James, although might it be a little awkward if you speak to him in any detail while he is here? Perhaps it would be better for you to make an appointment to see him at your office in Oxford,'

'To make an appointment was my intention.'

It was Vincent's mother who spoke after something of an uncomfortable silence. 'I'm not sure I know what to make of all that you have read, Mr MacPhearson. Clearly I understand the content and intentions conveyed by the will but it makes me realise how little I understood my own son. Did we keep apart or did he choose to keep apart from us, I simply don't know.'

'I can't answer you mother,' said James. 'Vincent and I were never close all our lives.'

'Speaking for myself,' said Beryl, 'I think I admire his independence of purpose. He has written of Frank's qualities but the writing also shows Vincent's qualities and I can admire that.'

'My son was right in one respect, your mother and I have quite sufficient resources for our needs. It shows that he gave positive thought to his family. It is not for me to criticise how he chose to live his life or to whom he chose to give his wealth. Thank you Mr MacPhearson for your clarity and diligence in conducting our son's wishes. James, when you go back to the other room will you ask Frank to come through.'

When Frank came to see Crispen MacPhearson he was feeling a little apprehensive, in fact he didn't expect to be asked to see him.

'Do take a seat Mr Palmerson, may I call you Frank.'

'Yes, please do, more relaxing.'

'If I tell you that I am in a position to inform you that you feature in a will which I drew up on behalf of Vincent St John, the news will come as a surprise?'

'It most certainly will. He never gave me any hint of such an intention and nor would I have expected it. What has he done, left me his books and research papers?'

'No, not those. He has left you his cottage in Eastbourne, its entire contents and the balances of any bank accounts or similar which are based in Eastbourne and as of this moment those monies amount to something over two hundred thousand pounds. I imagine the cottage is worth something in the order of half a million pounds, as to the contents I have no knowledge regarding their value. There will be inheritance taxes but I imagine you will still be left a fairly wealthy individual.'

'I can't..... don't know what t.......that can't be.......What about his family?'

'Vincent has written of you in a very kind manner and clearly held you in considerable esteem and affection. You needn't worry about his family, they actually had no knowledge of the Eastbourne possessions. They receive all possessions and monies associated with his Oxford address. He also says that he knows that all the members of his family are quite affluent and that none of them would have been dependant on anything that he had to leave as far as their own future security is concerned. I imagine that Vincent was very fond of you and that you were also fond of him.'

'That's very true. I loved him, that may sound odd as he was much older than me but I did love him. I knew all about his other relationships and they never worried me. He treated me differently and I think I was the only person to know about his cottage in Eastbourne, a beautiful place and we enjoyed going there together.'

'You're right about the cottage. Vincent mentioned how discrete you were about it, that you never mentioned it to anyone.'

'He didn't ask me to say nothing, but I simply felt that was the right thing to do.'

Chapter Thirty-Seven
New Relatives

Hello, Audrey Sutton speaking.'

'I'm sorry to bother you, Mrs Sutton. I'm Commander Zachary, Scotland Yard, and it is important that I should be able to speak to both you and your husband on a confidential matter, nothing to do with policing or crime, I assure you. I have chosen to telephone you as it concerns you more than your husband and also, I didn't want to go through people in the Foreign Office before I reached your husband on the phone.'

'I can understand that, fortunately I have a private number for him.'

'I'm certainly not asking to use that but it would be helpful if you could contact him and see if any meeting for later today, perhaps early evening might be possible? At your place would be most convenient?'

'Today may well be possible because the Foreign Secretary is absent, so my husband might be able to come home earlier than usual. If you care to hold the line, I can ring him and arrange something quite quickly...Yes?......won't be a moment or two. Darling, is that you?...good, is it possible that you could be home a little earlier than usual, it is just that a senior officer from Scotland Yard needs to talk to us both, and confidentially?......He hasn't said yet, probably about my background and family connections.......Excellent, love, I'm sure he will agree to that time, hang on.........Commander? yes, how about four-thirty today?...All right you say........will see you later then, good bye........Rufus, still there? I'll have coffee and a selection of nibbles ready for your arrival, 'bye then.'

In the event, Rufus was home with sufficient time to consume two coffees and an exquisite slice of a coffee and walnut gateaux, whipped cream and sliced almonds; the combination made for perfect late afternoon relaxation, not forgetting to gaze on his lovely Audrey. 'So, no knowledge of this policeman's purpose. Who did you say he was?'

'I didn't, not on the telephone as I didn't know whether you were on your own. Commander Zachary and if I'm not mistaken he's ringing the bell now.'

'I know of him, very shrewd operator, deals with difficulties arising from confidential information. I'll go and let him in and introduce myself at the same time.'

'Commander, I know of you but we haven't met, I'm Rufus Sutton, do come through and let my wife ply you with some coffee, and if you have a sweet tooth, some home-baking as well.'

Introductions completed and as the Commander wiped his lips after enjoying the slice of gateaux, he accepted a further cup of coffee, cleared his throat, 'I'd better make a start. Mrs Sutton, your husband may well know all about me but I'll introduce myself anyway. I have a number of roles within Scotland Yard, one is for the Prime Minister and Government and it is to follow up when pieces of information come to light and in such a way as to have implications for any member of the Government which could interest a Member of Parliament via an awkward question in the House or be the basis for a difficult newspaper article leading to unwanted and/or unfounded speculation.'

'Good gracious, how do we land in that category, surely my recently discovered adoption at birth doesn't in anyway connect with a member of the Government.'

'Well, the answer to that is the famous 'yes and no.' The only people who know of the circumstances which I am explaining to yourselves are the Prime Minister and the Foreign Secretary, and his wife, Rhiannon St John. They will receive remaining details in a few days. I

266

gather you know that your mother's name was Quemsby, an unusual, in fact, quite a rare name. Until it was mentioned to him, James St John knew that the name existed somewhere in his family tree but beyond remembering that it was the surname of two or three forebears of his Grandmother he had no further detailed information. I believe no one from the family is in touch with the Quemsby branch itself. As yet we haven't researched the previous generation to Lucinda, the blood line that is. In terms of relationships, James St John and Lucinda are cousins, fourth cousins if we have got the terminology correct and that means that you are also related in the same degree, 'once removed.' It connects your husband by marriage and he is a senior official working closely with the Foreign Secretary. In itself, not a difficulty, except that we have no knowledge of how your blood mother led her life after giving birth to you. Clearly there was some sort of downward spiral in her circumstances, probably involved drugs, eventually leading as you know, to very impoverished circumstances. People in the press would be very good at probing all that.'

'Is that really going to cause James St John great difficulties, after all.….'

'Darling, I think you ought to let the Commander finish the story, there must be more, I suspect.'

'Thank you Sir. Mrs Sutton. I believe you have recently come to know about your blood father, Henry Palmerson.'

'Yes, school master, had an affair with my mother when she was still a school pupil.'

'Quite correct, but the information came to light as the result of police investigating the circumstances of Vincent St John's suicide. It seems that Vincent, brother of the Foreign Secretary, led a sexually 'adventurous' life style, involving quite a number of male research students from his own college, one being Frank Palmerson, Henry's youngest son. I'm breaking confidentiality by giving you names but it makes easier the process of explaining the whole situation. With further information having come to light it appears that Vincent and

267

Frank were long-term lovers, not exclusive on Vincent's part, but of Frank, he was exceptionally fond. Unknown to Vincent's family he had well hidden wealth which he kept exclusively in Eastbourne. There was a valuable cottage where he and Frank used to stay, he kept various saving and bank accounts in the Eastbourne area and until his will was read the relationship between Frank and Vincent was not known about any more than the family knowing about a will. Under the terms of the will, the 'Eastbourne' wealth, comprising cottage, contents and various bank accounts, was left to Frank – in all, about three quarters of a million pounds. So far the press haven't probed the Vincent St John situation in any detail. Wills get published so someone will pick up on it.'

'I can see a certain sordidness in Vincent's life style and that has implications for his college and also for his family, but again, I hardly think the press will worry about my connection.'

'You may well be right but through your blood father you and Frank become half-brothers, similarly with his older brother, George.'

'Please don't tell me George comes into the picture.'

'Again that famous answer, 'yes and no.' At the time Lucinda became pregnant there was a group of lads of similar age from Kemby School who used to abscond on some Saturday mornings to meet a group of the girls from Kroxby, Lucinda and her close friends at the time. The boys included George Palmerson, a few others of less significance, David Yardlington who you and your husband knew quite well in Paris and in recent times have met up with because he now works at the Regal Court Hotel.

'Yes, we have spoken with him, very pleasant fellow. I have heard sadly something about an accident involving him.'

Yes, there was a failure of the lift system where he lives and he and another resident were very seriously injured; David will be away from work for some weeks. There is one more pupil from Kemby School, friend of David's, Jeremy Lutterworth.'

'That's a name I know, adviser to the Home Secretary, Daniel Divine.'

'That's correct, well thought of and influential I believe.'

'I've met him at quite a number of meetings at Cabinet level.'

'Well, as we understand the information from the time of their school days, Jeremy was the most forward of the boys and, so it is said, enjoyed Lucinda's company rather closely. In fact, until the DNA match came through, opinion at the girls' school was that one of the boys I have been mentioning was thought to be the father of Lucinda's baby.'

'I begin to see, Commander, that you have a very complex spider's web and with the power and strength to ensnare all sorts of innocent people, including us.'

'Yes, indeed, Ma'am. There has also been a very large number of people involved in the enquiries, certainly three separate police investigations, staff from two schools, and other individuals on the periphery of it all. No crimes have been committed, no wrong doings – except some under-age sex from twenty-five to thirty years ago. But your choice of word, 'ensnare' is very potent and all this information, were it to find itself in the wrong hands, much damage could be done. The individual at most risk is, I feel, James St John, the Foreign Secretary.'

It was Rufus who responded to that. 'His position becomes very vulnerable.'

'I think I have told you all the relevant information and of the people involved. If anything further emerges, of course, you will be told as soon as possible.'

'Thank you Commander, without doubt, you have been very clear indeed. Would you care for more coffee before you depart?'

'No, I need to be away quite promptly now, but thank you anyway.'

Later that evening, while preparing for bed, Rufus mentioned to Audrey, 'I wouldn't be surprised if James St John were to have some sort of breakdown soon, his behaviour has been a little strange of late.'

Not replying to that but Audrey suddenly announced that she intended contacting Henry Palmerson. 'Better I do that as soon as possible lest it seems that I have been forced to make a move because of press interference.'

Chapter Thirty-Eight
He Went Wandering

J ames's driver collected him as usual, 7.30am on Monday morning and the drive was usually fairly easy and James could expect to be at his desk at about 8.15am.

'Tony, would you mind dropping me in Great George Street, I could do with achieving a quieter arrival this morning.'

'Will do, Sir.'

James alighted clutching his well stuffed brief case for the day, watched Tony drive away and then promptly hailed a cab. The National Gallery, please.' He walked around Trafalgar Square and hailed a second taxi, can you drop me at a very old street called The Clink. The journey didn't take this driver long and James soon stepped out into this particularly historic part of London where it was amazing to think that a famous old prison dated back to the twelfth century and which gave a word to the dictionary still in regular use to this day. From there, The May Hotel, Southwark Bridge Road, was but a pleasant stroll.

The May Hotel was a modest looking establishment, a little larger than first appearances suggested as the buildings went further back from the road than expected. James had only entered it once or twice. Going in, he knew to expect, a warm and cheering welcome.

'Mr St John, how lovely to see you again.'

'And you Molly, you're looking well, everything going according to plan here?'

'Couldn't be better.'

'How's your Anthony? Pity he's the wrong shape or he could earn good money mimicking the real Anthony May.'

'Do you mind, Sir, at this address, my Anthony is the real one, mind you, he can do the voice all right.'

'Of course, Molly. You got my message.'

'Yes indeed, Sir. Everything is ready, a quiet room and well out of sight.'

'Excellent Molly. I may be here a week, possibly longer, depends just how I feel. Anyway, this envelope contains enough for a week in advance.'

'You didn't have to do that, Sir.'

'I know, but I insist. How is Douglas keeping?'

'Much better now he knows he has us here looking after everything and him as well. It was so sad when his health deteriorated and he couldn't run the hotel, but he couldn't believe his good fortune when his brother was able to step in.'

'I'm sure you both do marvellously, although I won't pretend that you are not sorely missed in my office at the Foreign Office. I'll go up to my room for a little while and then I need to pop out for about an hour. Is it fairly easy to pick up a taxi on the road outside?'

'Oh yes, Sir, you won't wait above half a minute. Now, let me show you up. Thank you for what you said just now, I do miss my early mornings at the F.O.; always gave your desk an extra polish.'

As he stepped into Haroldson's he was hailed, 'Good morning Mr St John.'

'Ah, Thomas, thank you, a need for a little discretion today.'

'Understood, Sir. How can we help?'

'I have a need for a full-length light weight summer coat, perhaps something in a dusky sort of green, see what you have. Also a spare pair of trousers, nothing particularly special.'

'Right away, Sir, and might a hat be necessary?'

'Something in the style of a cap, perhaps.'

'Try this, Sir?'

The choice was perfect and the fit quite splendid and the same applied to the cap and trousers – garments to blend anywhere.

'I also need some shirts, half a dozen, single cuff, easy to blend as far as pattern and colour are concerned, shirts that I won't be wearing ties with.'

'I understand, Sir.'

Again perfect choice achieved.

'Opticians next door?'

'Yes Sir.'

'Would you oblige me with a visit.'

'Certainly, how can I help?'

'Take these reading glasses which fit me fine. I want a pair of glasses with plain glass lenses such that I can wear all the time. Nothing too striking, don't want to look like Harry Palmer. Give who ever you see this money, don't want any change.'

'Fine, back in a couple of minutes.'

As good as his word, back, holding out a perfectly normal everyday pair of glasses such that anybody might wear and they fitted perfectly. 'My acquaintance said that there was far too much money so he has contributed it to the international appeal for children with cataracts.'

'Excellent. Well, that's all I need to buy. Can you bundle this lot up and book a taxi to take it to this address, asking for a Molly May. I'm using cash for everything just at present. What's the tally for my instant wardrobe?'

'Here we are Sir, £595.'

'Take this £750, use what is necessary for the taxi and hold some on account in case I need to telephone for anything.'

'Fully understood Sir, make sure you relax for a few days, the parcel will be at this address by mid-afternoon.'

'As usual, Thomas, you've been exceedingly helpful.'

'The firm's pleasure, Sir.'

James stepped out and immediately caught the eye of a taxi driver who performed a smart 'U' turn and he was very soon back at the Clink and from where he walked, back quite quickly at The May Hotel.

Molly obliged him with a pot of coffee and James lay on his bed and relaxed with his E-reader, intending to catch up with various downloads he had purchased but had never found time to read. Not surprising, sleep took over within twenty minutes and he didn't wake until a tap at his door heralded the arrival of some clothes. Instead of reading, he switched on the television and relaxed with one of the many episodes of 'Midsomer Murder.'

Before James started with Chief Inspector Barnaby, Rhiannon took a telephone call from Rufus Sutton. 'Good morning Rufus, how can I help?'

'Rhiannon, this is a little tricky, but we were expecting James at the Foreign Office this morning. Have we got our wires crossed or is there a difficulty?'

'I don't understand, Rufus, Tony collected him as usual, 7.30am so unless he went somewhere else he should have got to you. I haven't had occasion to try his mobile numbers, just give me a few secs and I'll try them via my speed dial. Hello, no, both switched off and that's a little unusual. He has another one but I know nothing about it, not even the number.'

'Strange, don't worry, Rhiannon. I'll ring the car pool and check where he went, perhaps something in the diary which missed the copy kept here. The third mobile is a security one for cabinet members but I have tried that and got no answer, it is set up to be difficult to switch off so I imagine he's left that somewhere so as not to be disturbed by it and also so nobody else can hear it.'

'Let me know when you track him down. He's been a little stressed and tired of late. I will ring his parents and his sister just in case they have heard something, but I'll only contact you if I have actual news.'

Rufus decided to telephone the car pool himself. He didn't want needless rumours flying about. 'Hello, Rufus Sutton here, Foreign Office. Would you be able to find Tony for me or get a message to him.'

'Yes Sir, just one moment, I think he is in the staff lounge.'

'Good morning Mr Sutton, Tony here.'

'Ah Tony, just a quiet call if you understand me. Did you bring Mr St John to the Foreign Office this morning?'

'Yes Sir, just as usual. No, not quite, he asked me to drop him in Great George Street, said he wanted to achieve a quiet arrival, those were his words.'

'Did you see him enter the building?'

'No, not actually enter, just dropped him at the door and drove off along the road, turning first left to go round to the front of the building as one of the senior secretaries had telephoned for me. I'm often booked for just as soon as Mr St John arrives. May I ask, Sir, is there a problem?'

'Discretion is the word, Tony. Yes, there is a problem, the Foreign Secretary has not arrived and we don't know where he is and there has been no message. Mrs St John had no information either, she said you collected him as usual.'

'Yes, that's correct. Anything else I need to do, Sir?'

'No, not at the moment Tony, say nothing to anybody unless I or a representative from security contacts you.'

'Right you are, Sir.'

This was a new situation for Rufus, a missing Secretary of State: gone for a walk, had a nervous breakdown, lost his memory, kidnapped, terrorist activity – the list was endless. He called through to the general office and summoned the senior secretaries and advisors. He decided a brief general discussion might help before he telephoned security. Other than to look surprised nobody had any suggestions to make or had knowledge of other events. The consensus was to hand it over to security and let the Prime Minister know. As usual, Anthony May was quite calm when apprised of the news that his Foreign Secretary had disappeared. They mentioned to each other the obvious things but Anthony assured Rufus that the security service would sort it and he promised to give Rhiannon a call.

'Rhiannon, Anthony May here, just ringing to assure you that everything is being done to trace James. The security services are very good at this sort of thing. Has James been himself lately, he's seemed a little tense to me?'

'Yes, certainly very preoccupied, but he has had much to worry him of late and I put it down to that. The other day when he came home he was so tired I made him go and lay down, he slept for about four hours.'

'Rest assured, we'll stay connected. The security services may call you, they'll want to ask a large number of what may prove to be irrelevant questions but humour them. I'm sure James will be with us in the not-too-distant future. One final point, we've had no indication of any sort to suggest that James or any member of the Government is under any sort or terrorist threat, that's reassuring for you I hope.'

Chapter Thirty-Nine
One Foreign Secretary Still Missing – Just

The Security Services went into action and followed various procedures. One was to check on the last matter mentioned by the Prime Minister to Rhiannon so all intelligence information which had been received was reviewed and they came to the unanimous conclusion that nothing that had been heard in recent months suggested any risk to the Foreign Secretary or any other member of the Government. That left the more usual domestic risks, kidnap for reward, murder but body unfound, intentional disappearance. Of those three the third was probably the easiest to investigate; kidnap for reward should lead to incoming contact; murder needs a motive and a body. Both kidnap and murder can be investigated for any witnessed activity in the immediate vicinity but in the present circumstances there was nothing. The security department checked all three mobile numbers known by them and used by James St John and like Rhiannon found the two which should have been on, had in fact been switched off. If James St John deliberately wanted to disappear then he would have wanted to leave the area of the Foreign Office speedily after being dropped by his driver which suggests he arranged to be picked up or he hailed a taxi. With good photographs and a small time scale for the likely hailing of taxis, any investigation could be relatively straight forward. As far as murder was concerned James St John appeared to have no known enemies, seemed well liked.

First success was with the taxis, one driver came forward and stated that he had taken his fare from Great George Street to The National Gallery and that was the sum total of the information. They had no conversation, fare paid in cash. Nobody on the staff of the National had any recollection of seeing him at the time in question. There being no further information coming from taxi drivers they diverted enquiries to Mrs St John. Replies to simple queries as whether he had any luggage when he left led to negative responses. When asked about paying for every day spending Rhiannon said that he generally used a card as cash machines were rather few and so obtaining cash became rather difficult. She explained that James kept a large supply of cash in the safe but she didn't have the key. If they knew how to open it they could have a go. A handful of keys and some additional expertise and the safe was open in under an hour.

Rhiannon inspected the contents, said that everything looked as she remembered although it was sometime since she had seen inside. One of the security inspectors dialled the secure mobile number and they immediately solved one mystery as it was responding from the bottom drawer in the safe. There was between three and three and a half thousand pounds in the safe but again, Rhiannon couldn't say if James had taken any, she didn't know how that could be ascertained. She would go on line to the bank and check what had been taken out in cash over the last few months, which might give some idea of how much her husband had with him. When the security staff summarised the domestic situation they couldn't tell whether James St John had a supply of cash on him but there was no evidence to suggest he hadn't; he had no additional baggage when he had left in the morning so if he were absent for more than a day or so he already had spare clothes available or he would have to purchase some. Rhiannon had no knowledge of anywhere her husband might go if he wanted to disappear for a while. As far as buying clothes she said that he had often used a gentlemen's outfitters along the Strand but she couldn't remember the name of the shop. He didn't use the shop exclusively though.

It didn't take the security services long to track down Haroldson's Outfitters, and when reminded, Rhiannon remembered that was the name of the shop which she knew her husband used. On enquiry they showed the staff a photograph of James St John and one member of staff recognised him. Oh yes, one of our regulars, a very good customer. When asked if he had been in recently the answer was a little vague, yes, it had been recent but no purchase had been made, he had just strolled around looking at some stock on display. As to whether that was a common occurrence the answer was also a little vague.

Without wanting to accuse the shop assistant (a rather refined individual who they suspected would have preferred a more superior title for his job description) of lying, they simply decided that James St John had most likely purchased clothes there and then and paid in cash thus preventing anyone from tracking his use of debit or credit card.

Another appeal for taxi drivers didn't bring forward any help, but then The Strand was a particularly busy spot for taxi hire. As it happened it was down to bad luck because the taxi driver of interest had only worked a short day, driven home, picked up his girl-friend, driven out to Heathrow where they had left his taxi, and at the time the appeal for witnesses had been put out, a young and happy looking couple were at thirty thousand feet and half way across the Atlantic Ocean and it would be ten days before they flew back from the Caribbean. The security services' UK search for the nation's Foreign Secretary ground to a halt for the time being.

With Rhiannon's approval two security officers called on Sir George and Lady Elaine at Norstead Towers. 'Sir George, thank you for seeing us. The reason we have called is connected with your son, James St John and his disappearance. Increasingly, it appears most likely that he has chosen to do this himself. We realise that this country house is quite large, many rooms and attics and there is a number of out-buildings, so we wonder whether it might have been possible for him to have come here without your realising and that this is where he is currently hiding.'

'Nonsense, I can't imagine that happening for one moment, what would he be doing for food and drink and how could he be using any facilities here without someone becoming aware of him. You agree with me, Elaine?'

'Yes dear, in the main, but it would have been possible for him to have been here for a short while, perhaps no more than overnight provided he had someone assisting, a co-operative taxi driver, for example. In that way this may have just been an interim arrangement while he waited for a short while, a day or so perhaps, before moving on, just a thought.'

'I suppose that's possible dear, can't imagine why the dam fool is behaving in such an odd way, though.'

'He must have suffered some kind of breakdown, Rhiannon has said that lately he has been working very hard and has seemed rather stressed. But, gentlemen, this is not helping you. I think the best thing for you to do is conduct your own search of the entire house. It doesn't matter where you go. Our bedroom you'll find quite obvious and the same applies to my husband's study. As far as the attics are concerned nothing is locked and the only locked out-building is where the mowers and fuel are stored.

Other officers still with Rhiannon remained interested in the two everyday mobile phones and were working on the assumption that he had them with him so that he could switch on one if he needed to make a quick call. An arrangement was made for one security officer to stay at the St John's home so that if Rhiannon took a call there was some chance of making a trace. James was too knowledgeable about these kind of matters to make any call from wherever he was staying, would probably walk some distance and then use his phone. Even if they could trace him to within a mile of his base it would be something.

Security Officers also asked about James's sister, Beryl and also the two sons and their families. 'Well, of course, I have spoken to them all. Beryl lives in quite a small London apartment so I'm sure James will not have gone to her and Beryl has made no mention of having heard from him. I can't for one moment think that he would have involved our sons, two families, both with very young children so it would have been impossible for him to have hidden with them.' In these matters Rhiannon felt quite confident in being certain; Norstead Towers was the only possibility simply because of its size.

By the evening, with many people now being aware of the fact of the Foreign Secretary being missing, the news could not be kept out of the next day's newspapers and an arrangement was made for the Leader of the House to make a statement to the Commons by late the next morning. Needless to say the presenters of late-night news broadcasts and those editing the following day's newspaper issues had a field day; there wasn't one alarmist suggestion that didn't get an airing so by the end of the second day people were talking about gangs of kidnappers, paid murderers, terrorist cells existing in many parts of the capital – however implausible, if it could be put into words, it was. The statement made to the House of Commons was exceptionally bland, tried to suggest the Foreign Secretary was probably resting but that the security service was involved just to be that bit more cautious. Nobody was convinced by that and several MPs wondered if there wasn't a serious security issue which the Government didn't feel able to comment on just yet.

Over-night between the third and fourth days of this saga, for that's what it appeared to be turning in to, Rhiannon was disturbed from sleep by one bleep on her mobile phone. At three twenty-five in the morning a text of one sentence comprising just two words landed: 'I'm safe.' With its arrival Rhiannon turned over, smiled to herself and promptly fell asleep for the next five hours, her best sleep since the troubles began.

A little late, but at nine o'clock she provided the overnight security officer with toast and coffee and as no more than a throw away remark she just mentioned that she had heard from her husband during the night. The poor guy choked on his toast, certainly dribbled quite a quantity of coffee and was covered in confusion and embarrassment by the mess he had made.

'Ma'am, weren't you instructed to wake me if there was any contact?'

'Oh, but it was only a two-word text message, you surely couldn't have done anything with that.'

Recovering now from his first spluttered question, the officer went on. 'What did he say?'

"I'm safe.' That was all, just, 'I'm safe.'"

'Excuse me, I must let the department know.'

When he returned to the breakfast table he mentioned that some colleagues would be arriving to look at the phone so that they could attempt some analysis. He left it sounding vague. Rhiannon wasn't looking too concerned as she was just pleased to know that he was safe as she had every confidence in the message. In fact she was returning to bed to continue the sleep that she had been enjoying, so she left her mobile on the table. When the 'experts' arrived they were all talking at once, about how James must have reinserted a battery for a very short time and then removed it after sending the message. They had already tried to download some software onto the mobiles in James's possession but failed because the batteries had been removed. Clearly the Foreign Secretary was no novice when it came to knowing how to be really silent.

Since she received the over-night message Rhiannon remained extremely calm, just waited for the days to pass. For various reasons she thought that the coming Monday would be significant but she kept that thought to herself. She spoke to James's parents and tried to reassure them that all was well and she also spoke to Beryl several times, like Rhiannon, Beryl seemed none too worried. The rest of the week passed, she heard little from Rufus or representatives of the security services so she was unsure if any progress was being made. However, at 7.30am Monday morning the front doorbell rang and when she responded she found two large black bags on the doorstep and as she looked up a taxi was just disappearing down the drive. In side one bag was a collection of dirty clothes and in the other, new and also other clean and unworn clothes. With these was an envelope addressed to her and inside the briefest of notes read: 'Dearest, I should see you tomorrow evening (Monday) at the usual time, I shall make my own way to the Foreign Office, James.' Rhiannon smiled and laughed and was so pleased that her confidence hadn't been misplaced.

Monday morning, 8.30am at The Foreign Office, a private hire car drew up, a brand-new Mercedes, almost before it had stopped the chauffeur's assistant was opening the kerbside rear door and out-stepped, The Right Honourable, James St John, P.C., M.P., Her Majesty's Foreign Secretary. He passed through the door, which was being held open as usual, and as he looked around he was pleased to notice just a few 'dropped jaws,' otherwise silence reigned. 'Good morning everybody,' said James, as he made his 'progress,' perhaps not exactly Royal, through the foyer to the lifts. When he arrived at his suite of rooms, he could hear quite a noise, loud conversation, something amounting to argument he thought, but as he opened and walked through the elegant mahogany-framed doorway, the silence was instant. And then Rufus, just for a brief moment forgot his usual elegant phrasing,

'Good God, Sir! Where the bloody hell have you sprung from?'

'Why Rufus,' said a voice with the tone of one who has just stepped out of a brand new two-hundred-thousand-pound car. 'I'm sorry, didn't Tony pass on my message regarding travel arrangements for this morning? Perhaps when you have recovered yourself, Rufus, you had better come through and begin to bring me up to date on recent developments; you can also ask someone to organise coffee and biscuits for the two of us, and one more thing, ask one of the secretaries to get a message to Number Ten, I ought to let Anthony know that all is well and if he wants to know where I have been, tell him I have been staying with Anthony May.'

On his desk he found recent newspapers covering the story of his disappearance and he glanced at just a couple while he waited for Rufus and some coffee.

MISSING FOREIGN SECRETARY

TERRORISM

Security Officers remain baffled by the Foreign Secretary's unexplained absence and are suspecting a terrorist kidnapping. The only substantiated information is that he was collected as usual from his home and taken to the rear of the Foreign Office Buildings where he was believed to have hailed a taxi and been dropped at The National Gallery. After that, nothing is known as to his whereabouts. His wife has assured the authorities that he was in good health, a little tired as he had been dealing with a family bereavement. Government sources have indicated that there were no known threats against members of the cabinet. Recently, his brother, Vincent, committed suicide at an Oxford College where he was a Senior Research Fellow. There have been rumours of blackmail against him arising from homosexual relationships and this death and the rumours have been a shock for the whole family. Officers from Interpol have been alerted and police are keeping a watch on ports and airports. Security has been increased for all the Cabinet and members of James St John's family. Their two sons are both lawyers and a check is being made as to whether there may be any connection between the disappearance and recent court cases involving the two sons.

MISSING FOREIGN SECRETARY

Brother's Sex Scandal Suicide

Foreign Secretary missing, brother committed suicide amidst blackmail threat arising from all men sex-fuelled Oxford College scandal. Police are working to see if the connection involving the two brothers is related to the disappearance. Some who knew the brother at Oxford hinted at recreational drug taking. The blackmailer is not known although Police have suspicions based on information given by other research students.

When Rufus came through, carrying a tray of coffee and biscuits, in itself a rather unusual activity for this member of staff, he was still looking a shade flustered, that embarrassed expression which can smother some men on discovering that their trouser zip is undone.

'Well, Foreign Secretary, can I say how delighted we are to welcome you back, unavoidable but I'm sure you will understand that there has been something of a panic in the various departments where there is responsibility for staff security, yours included. May I ask if Mrs St John is aware of your return?'

'Yes, Rhiannon knows I am here but I will telephone her in a little while, just to assure her that all's well. Tell me, is there much awaiting my immediate attention.'

'No, very little in fact as the Ministers of State have taken it upon themselves to avoid leaving files for your attention, not being sure when you would be available to work on them. May I ask, sorry for repeating myself, but when you came through to this office you made a rather cryptic remark to the effect that you had been staying with Anthony May. What did you mean?'

'I expect any internet search will tell you how many individuals alive in the United Kingdom have the name 'Anthony May' and that quite possibly more than one of them resides in London.'

'Yes, I quite understand. Tell me, is facetiousness to be the name of the game for the whole of today or might there be some serious Matters of State with which to occupy our time?'

The telephone rang before James had time to phrase a suitably pithy rejoinder; Rufus picked the hand-set up.

'Yes Sir, he's here. The Prime Minister for you, do you require me to leave?' With an appropriate nod of his head, Rufus felt compelled to take a seat.

'Good morning Prime Minister, James speaking. Yes, Prime Minister, Immediately? Of course Prime Minister, At once, Prime Minister.'

James looked up. 'Sorry to disturb you Rufus, could you ask for my car to be brought round?'

'At once, Foreign Secretary.'

If James smiled at that, Rufus didn't notice.

Chapter Forty
At No. 10

James, good morning, very pleased to see you looking so well and unharmed. You may be interested to know that I am not the least surprised at that. In fact I was one of the very few people at work in this particular location who managed not to indulge in any massive hysterical panic and you'll be pleased to know that I ignored everything the press said about you and your disappearance. I came to the conclusion that you felt the need for a week's rest with a little bit of amusing mystery thrown in for good measure, anywhere near the truth?'

'Something like that Prime Minister.'

'The point is James, what are we to do with you now? I mean, can I leave you in charge of the Foreign Office and if I do, what will the press have to say, not forgetting of course, a handful of rather right-wing M.P.s who don't always have your best interests at heart when they start asking questions. Do you see my dilemma, James?'

'Indeed I do, Prime Minister.'

'And on another matter, I have received privately from Commander Zachary a request that I should meet with him together with you and Rhiannon at your house, that this is an extremely confidential meeting and nobody outside the four of us are to know about it.'

'That is correct Prime Minister, it is at my suggestion and when you hear what has to be said you will understand why it has to be totally confidential. I know it all sounds a bit mysterious, although it is all potentially very serious, but be assured that absolutely no dishonesty is involved. Regardless of what date you suggest to Commander Zachary, Rhiannon and I will be available as it is obviously easier for me to adjust my diary of events than it is for you.'

'This evening if that is not too speedy, then it won't be in my diary. About four o'clock. Commander Zachary will drive me over in his car.'

'That will be fine, Prime Minister. I shall go home early, perhaps a migraine as that is my usual reason for leaving early.'

Warned in advance, Rhiannon was ready with coffee for this most unusual meeting. Fortunately she had not been doing anything special so had no event to cancel. The Prime Minister had got an evening event booked but he would be back in Downing Street in very good time. It was an informal event which Laurel was also attending and she would have everything ready for him.'

Leaning back and appearing to relax somewhat, Anthony May glanced at the other three. 'Now, tell me if I have got anything wrong. DNA tests have shown that Audrey Sutton, formerly Audrey Ponsonby, was adopted at birth, something she was never told about and her blood parents are Henry Palmerson and Lucinda Quemsby. Henry is also the father of Frank Palmerson, who was a lover of your late brother, Vincent, and to Frank, your brother has bequeathed the bulk of his estate which may amount to three quarters of a million pounds. Henry's love affair with Lucinda Quemsby took place when the older son, George, was a pupil at Kemby School when he and friends used to meet the girls of Kroxby School and until the crucial DNA test result came through, any one of a group of teenage lads could have been thought to be the father of Audrey.'

'Now, James, via the cousin of your Great Grandfather Arthur, Alfred Quemsby, there is a direct line of three further generations to Lucinda Quemsby making the two of you cousins to some degree. It also just happens that a sister of Alfred, Juliette Quemsby, inherited a large fortune and that via trust funds she created, has bequeathed money to various members of the family, including your mother, Elaine, but Lucinda's line didn't benefit.'

'Finally, looking at Audrey's relationships in all of this, she is a half-sister to Frank and George Palmerson and also a cousin, of some degree, to you James. At the present moment the Palmersons and the Suttons have not met but Audrey does know that her father has been traced by a DNA test result, a test arising from a different investigation.'

'I imagine a few youngish middle-aged men, from the original group of lads who used to meet up with girls from Kroxby, contempories of George Palmerson, are still around and might any one of them perhaps be thinking that they were responsible for the baby, is that a possibility, Commander?'

'Yes, that could have been of some concern to them. Of the group, David Yardlington works at the Regal Court Hotel and is a former friend of the Suttons from their Paris days and recently David has met up with a couple of guys from the original school group who were attending an event at the hotel. One of the group is Jeremy Lutterworth, advisor to the Home Secretary.'

'Presumably nothing has been said to Daniel?'

'Nothing has been said.' James thought that perhaps there should have been by now.

'Commander, have I got it all correctly understood because I have made no notes?'

'Prime Minister, your summary is flawless.'

'Thank you. Now, the concern, or at least your concern, James, is what might people in the media make of all this were the story to become public knowledge. At present, the knowledge is limited, but we have yet to give the Palmersons a few more details, and the Suttons, and you will be informing your parents, James, and also your sister Beryl. And will you be telling your two sons and their wives? If and when all that is complete then the story will become public, simply too many people will know.'

'To continue, the question is not when to make this matter public, but how? The 'how' is dependant on some agreement between three groups of individuals: Audrey and Rufus Sutton, Henry, George and Frank Palmerson, and finally, James and Rhiannon St John and immediate relatives. I think Commander, you need to fully inform the first two groups of individuals of everybody involved and then there needs to be a meeting of an extended family sort comprising Mr & Mrs Sutton, Frank and his father, James and your wife Rhiannon to finalise how whatever is agreed, is made public.'

'Of course, the media will have a stunning time with the whole story, it being so amazingly convoluted. It would make a wonderful plot for a stage play; James, does your sister, Beryl still write? So much material for her in all of this. I don't suggest that what the media have to say will lead to resignations, but some individuals are going to have to change their posts.'

Silence followed this Prime Ministerial summary.

James broke the silence. 'My recent behaviour gives me the perfect excuse to resign. I have probably had something close to a nervous break-down, so, Prime Minister, you shall have my letter of resignation just as soon as you think appropriate.'

'Agreed, sad to see you leave Government, James, but there isn't really any alternative. It will mean a personal statement to the House so correct timing is crucial. I had better release Angela back to the Home Office; that will please young Jeremy. I don't want Rufus to suffer as a result of all this, given that he and his wife are the most innocent of 'victims' and I use that word not in any legal sense of guilt and innocence. He is, by all account, brilliant at his work; I think he could join the Downing Street team, it's in need of new blood. James, if you are going to be able to use your recent absence as an appropriate excuse, you need to go on immediate sick leave and in a few days, a week at most, resign on your doctor's advice. You can adorn one of the back benches for a while, looking suitably wise, full of political sagacity. Can you manage that role, James?'

'I can play that part, not many words to learn.'

'Has that got the ball moving sufficiently, Commander? If so you need to have two or three meetings at some speed?'

'As you say, Prime Minister, although I'm nearly up to date with essential meetings. I'll get started tomorrow on other matters. Do you and I need to return to Downing Street in a few minutes?'

'No, slight change of plan, Zach. You gave me a convenient lift as I needed, unexpectedly shall we say, to see James regarding his health. I can telephone now and return using my official car. You can leave just as soon as you feel you have completed everything at this meeting to your satisfaction. Is that all right?'

'Yes, Sir.'

'And James, I hope you don't feel I have sacked you because no such action could be further from my intentions. You have been a brilliant and thoughtful member of the Government.' With that final comment, a most unusual Prime Ministerial meeting drew to a close. The Commander left within five minutes, Anthony followed just as soon as his car arrived, about thirty minutes later, and finally in just under an hour, James and Rhiannon left to visit his parents and Beryl, who was already with them.

Chapter Forty-One
A Very Strange Meeting

Courtesy of Sergeant Vaughan, and three or four phone calls, a meeting was set up for Henry Palmerson to meet Audrey and Rufus Sutton. Where, exercised the mind of Audrey until she hit upon the Royal Court Hotel for lunch. A Saturday was agreed, Henry Palmerson could get to London during the morning, well in time for lunch and would have plenty of time to fill in the various gaps in Audrey's knowledge of her mother, Lucinda Quemsby. Together with Rufus, there would be just the three of them. For reasons which were quite unclear to her, she was very optimistic and was looking forward to meeting Henry.

Well in time, Rufus and Audrey were in the lounge bar of the Royal Court Hotel, looking out for Henry and as the time passed eleven-thirty, he arrived. He was fairly tall, white haired, slim build and wearing a slightly old-fashioned blazer for which they were to look out. Audrey's father came over in response to their wave. Hand-shakes, a chaste kiss from the daughter and they all sat down to a round of coffees with the promise of alcohol with their lunch.

It was Audrey who spoke first. 'Henry, welcome to London and this hotel, a favourite of ours as we stayed here for a few days after our flat was burgled when we were on holiday earlier in the year. By coincidence there is a member of staff here who is an acquaintance of ours, from when we lived in Paris for three years. We've only recently returned, a few months back.'

'I'm delighted to meet you both although I am rather nervous, worried that you will be wondering just what sort of predator I was when I knew your mother. Thank you for calling me Henry, I was a shade embarrassed that you might have felt obliged to use a more familial term which really wouldn't have sounded at all right. Sorry, I'm gabbling on, as both my sons would say.'

'Henry, please don't worry about a bit of gabbling. As you must realise, I'm Rufus, and I can tell you that Audrey here is very excited as well as having been over-whelmed by all the information about her past which has come to light and by an amazing collection of circumstances, terrible that two deaths had to be part of those circumstances. I suppose the incredible thing about all this history which we now know about, is that none of the discoveries could have been made pre-DNA analysis days.'

'When all this started, Henry, it was my blood mother about whom I heard first, although the circumstances were very sad. I never had any knowledge whatsoever that I had been adopted at birth. The person I knew as my father, died when I was a child. My mother used to take me to his grave occasionally. When I was in my very early twenties, my mother, my adoptive mother of course, began to show signs of dementia and sadly she caused her house to catch fire and was killed. I was at Oxford at the time, with Rufus by then, but I suppose I still became an adult orphan.'

'We were married by the time we first met with the police who were investigating a fatal hit-and-run accident to inform us that the dead woman, a down-and-out sort of individual, was my blood mother. It was very hard to believe at first, but gradually the evidence fell into place. Nothing has ever been discovered about the time between my birth and the time of her death, so what had happened to her over the years is still unknown. At least we know her name, Lucinda Quemsby.'

'Audrey, I can't imagine for one moment how much of a shock that must have been but I suspect when the information about me surfaced, it was a bit less of a surprise, perhaps had a little less impact.'

'Yes, I had just got to the point, curiously, of requesting an exhumation of the person who I thought was my father so that DNA could be used to check whether or not he was my blood father, when the police came with news of your existence. And what an amazing set of circumstances caused that information to come to light. Tell me, what did your son think about that?'

'All three of us were equally stunned, but I must tell you soon about the Lucinda I remember, and the circumstances which brought us together, something that my boys knew nothing about nor, I ought to add, did my late wife.'

'Shall we save that for lunch or later?' suggested Rufus.

'Let's go in then, I'm sure conversation will continue to flow.'

'I'll organise some wines, you two start ordering food.' Rufus was all action, probably covering some nervousness. Audrey went for crab and salad while Henry opted for chicken soup. They both chose something rather exotic involving fillet steaks. After quick decisions about the wine, Rufus joined Henry with the choice of soup but rather than go with fillet steaks his choice went for the lighter option of Dover Sole. Choices all made, the conversation resumed.

'Henry, please tell me about Lucinda, as you remember her.'

'She was absolutely lovely. I met her quite by chance in a small café one Saturday afternoon, she was on her own as was I. Our differences in age didn't really occur to me, yet I was close to forty and she was fifteen coming sixteen. Frank was just a small boy then, George was about to start sixth form as I remember. I was bewildered by news of my wife, Diana, her very recently diagnosed serious cancer, which was likely to be incurable, as was the case. Lucinda liked to talk, a kindly sort of chatter, as I said she was lovely, beautiful and she spotted my loneliness straight away, really very sensitive for her age. How can I best express it, the sound of her voice, so soothing. To say that I had an immediate crush would be an understatement; I found her completely entrancing, but I was lost between two extremes, shame at having a relationship with an under-age girl from a neighbouring school, but on the other hand, the sensuous love of an all-consuming passionate love affair, an exultant romance – can't really find the right words, sorry, I'm getting carried away with my memories, and my emotions. Our affair, if that's the correct description, lasted for a few weeks, coming to an end with the conclusion of the summer term. Soon after that my wife's health deteriorated markedly and I had to spend a lot of time with her at home, I was unable to return to teaching when the Autumn term started, in fact I think I had a whole term off. Actually, I didn't return to teaching until after her death which was very early the following year.'

'Lucinda had mentioned the boys she used to meet, teased them she said, unmercifully, what kind of relationship she had with any of them I wouldn't know, anything serious I imagine was more in their minds than in reality. I'm ashamed to confess that I knew nothing about her not returning to Kroxby School in the Autumn, I never heard about the rumoured pregnancy and of course that was when matters regarding discipline got tightened up at Kemby and the boys stopped going into town on Saturday mornings. I remember George moaning about it, saying how it made the weekends dull. I ought to explain that although the fees paid by staff for their sons to attend Kemby were much reduced, the boys had to be boarders so during term I saw much less of George.'

'After Diana's death, I did wonder about Lucinda, thought about what she might have been doing, did she go to college. It was my impression that she was very clever, probably the sort of pupil who found school studies pretty easy, shouldn't think she was stretched. I gather, Audrey, that you're a linguist, well that is most certainly a skill that didn't come from me, must have been in your mother's genes. Lucinda was talented, so wouldn't be surprising.'

'Thank you Henry, you have given me a lovely image of my mother. Now, you've talked non-stop for a while yet have managed to empty two plates. You must look at the sweets trolley, I know Rufus will. I'll probably stick with this wine and perhaps have a coffee.'

'I have something else for you. When I first heard from the police about my probably being your father, I charged up an old mobile phone of mine and managed to find these photographs, just a small number of Lucinda and one or two selfies of both of us. And there is this, a print

300

of the one photograph which I think captures her beauty and personality, well in my eyes it does and it was the best photograph anyway. I've had this old silver frame for many years, something from my mother's belongings and it seems to suit the print quite nicely. I hope you like it.'

'Now, as you mentioned a certain trolley just now, I'll opt for the trifle, how about you Rufus?'

'Has to be something with chocolate, let me look.'

After the eating was all finished Rufus noticed how quiet Audrey had become. 'Are you all right, my love?'

'Yes, yes, just looking at this lovely photograph and wondering what it would have been like to have known her, grown up with her, had her in my life and then with those thoughts I wondered what did happen to her, how did she end up, what, just one step up from a tramp?' That's when the tears started, very quietly, sobbing, nothing hysterical, quietly crying. Rufus took her hand, said little, a soothing touch, warmth of love and understanding. Henry managed to withdraw, not physically, but his presence didn't intrude. The quietness lasted a while, nobody interrupted and slowly Audrey came back to herself, kindly and charming, just as she was, when Henry had first arrived. She shivered, looked up, 'I think, darling, a brandy might be welcome.'

Back in the lounge and exceptionally comfortable in some rather beautifully reupholstered traditional sofas, three vintage brandies suited the mood just perfectly. 'Henry, when you arrived this morning you were worried about a bit of gabbling and although Audrey didn't so much as hint of any nervousness, I know that there was certain amount of apprehension, but in the event a pleasant calmness has enveloped us all. So excuse me for offering a small toast. Here's to new relatives.' Rufus smiled and raised his glass. Audrey and Henry raised theirs and echoed the sentiment, and with smiles all-round the relaxed calmness continued.'

Audrey looked towards Henry. 'We know about you, obviously, and Frank, but tell us, what does George do?'

'He's happily married, to a Georgina, fortunately very pleased to be called Gina and very beautiful, perhaps reflects something of her Egyptian background as her mother came from Cairo. Gina and George have two girls, both troublesome teenagers, in the nicest possible way. Louise is the oldest and just beginning to think about choosing a university, a couple of years younger is Diana and just as bright as her sister. I think both will be scientists of some sort. Science was not George's thing, better at mathematics and he studied surveying, but now he is an estate agent, near Cambridge and spends a lot of his time dealing with groups of students involved in multiple renting arrangements, houses which are owned by people living abroad, or more frequently these days, purchased for the sole purpose of letting to students. I don't think George loves his work particularly, but it is lucrative, pays for their golf and keeps him in art materials. Gina is a P.E. teacher, runs the hockey teams where she teaches. Mind you, she fell out with hockey for a while recently, as she took a blow to the side of her head from the ball a few weeks back, slight concussion so kept in hospital for a couple of nights. Golf can be equally dangerous; George got his glasses smashed last year when he was hit in the face by a golf-ball travelling full pelt. The daughters have not taken up either of those sports, both preferring to swim.'

'When I knew we would be meeting and had heard that you had two sons, I soon worked out that they would be my half siblings or half-brothers, As George has two daughters does that make me their aunt or half aunt; I need to study more genealogical terminology.'

'Either way, Audrey, I'm sure they might like the idea of having some sort of aunt, because Gina is an only child so at present they just have one uncle.'

'And if eventually Rufus and I have children that will create some half-cousins, what do you think, darling?'

'Highly amusing and potentially very complicated, like the family tree of some ancient Royal family somewhere, East European, perhaps.' Quietness descended on trio just then and it was Audrey who broke the silence by suggesting some more coffee and Rufus went to organise it.

'May I ask you, Audrey, would you be interested in meeting my two sons. Rest assured, I won't be in the least offended if you don't wish to or want to think about it for a while.'

'I have been mulling it over, and one aspect which makes me feel it might be a good idea is that I have no relatives, certainly nobody was ever mentioned by my adoptive parents and Rufus is an only child, parents now quite elderly.'

'Coffee on its way,' announced Rufus as he plonked himself down. 'What have I missed?'

'Henry was just wondering if I, but that means we, would like to meet Frank and George. I had got as far as saying that the idea appealed partly because beyond your parents, neither of us has any relatives.'

'Good idea, something to look forward to, and you are right as far as we are concerned, we're rather light on the relatives front.'

'Er, look, I need to be making a move soon, there's a convenient train in about forty minutes so I'll ask at the desk if they will call a taxi for me. I've promised the boys to give them a ring this evening, you know, reporting back to the family.'

'Favourably, I hope.' Audrey offered this with a great smile.

Rufus went over to the front desk to organise Henry's taxi and when he came back it seemed time for farewell handshakes, a slightly bolder kiss between father and daughter and they all went over to front entrance for further hugs and waves.

It was early evening when Audrey and Rufus were just switching television channels having finished with the news. 'Can you hit 'standby' for a moment Rufus, something to tell you.'

'You sound very mysterious, Audrey, come up on a lottery?'

'No dear, but I have come up with a plus.'

'What do you mean? Using some new piece of text speak?'

'I have been thinking of using one for a few days now, but some of this afternoon's conversation with Henry put it in mind, so when we came in just now, I used a home pregnancy test and for a positive result this particular test shows a plus sign in the window, and that's what I came up with, a 'plus'! Now, don't move Rufus, love, just sit still! I'll pour you a whiskey, Glenmorangie be all right?'

Chapter Forty-Two
The Chiltern Hundreds

James St John's first step on his 'Parliamentary' stroll to the Chiltern Hundreds was via a telephone call from Rhiannon to their G.P., an understanding medical man who was always willing to make a home visit where James was concerned, although such a call was a rare occurrence, as James had generally enjoyed excellent health. However, as Rhiannon pointed out to her James, matters couldn't be ignored when he took to running away from work. Disappearing for a week and causing the security services to have a combined apoplexy was a step likely to cause a degree of worry in all political circles. When Dr Griffiths arrived he conducted a quick once over as far as James's vital responses were concerned, heart rate, blood pressure, and for good measure he extracted two lots of blood samples. 'Now, James, what's this about not being able to stay at work, finding excuses for leaving early. What else have you been doing, or not doing, which isn't exactly what is expected of a Secretary of State?'

'Avoiding document reading and then having a blitz at a large quantity, avoiding evening events where possible, delegating more than I should, waking up early in morning and then thinking how to avoid more work. When I was Acting Prime Minister, I found it over-whelming, and but for my senior civil servant I would have gone under. Sometimes when I'm being driven to work I have an almost uncontrollable urge to ask the driver to turn round and take me home, yet when I get there all seems all right. I used to thrive on everything political, party conferences were meat and drink for me, now I have to use headaches so I can spend more time in the hotel room; hand-shaking fund-raising events have me wanting to run a mile. The stupidity of all this is that when I just can't avoid whatever it may be, I go along and quite enjoy myself or a meeting I'm making excuses to avoid but I go and come up with some good contributions. It all sounds so silly when I tell you.'

'No, it isn't silly, not at all. How's the alcohol consumption as politicians can find themselves drinking too much?'

'I try to be very strict but it isn't easy, people don't like to feel their hospitality is being rejected. I like a scotch when I get home.'

'So, are you drinking more or should I ask Rhiannon's opinion?'

'OK, it's increased.'

'James, I'm not a specialist psychiatrist and you may care to talk to one, but in my practice I diagnose depression frequently, certainly every week. Sometimes it's fairly mild and the individual can bounce back after a few days' rest, a course of anti-depressants for two or three months. On the other hand it can be more severe, as is the case with you, because other factors are working against you, high-powered and exceptionally responsible job, always in the public eye, constantly having to contribute, produce ideas, make key decisions and for which the price of failure can be enormous.'

'I ought to tell you that I have discussed my mental health problems with the Prime Minister.'

'And?'

'I'm going to have to step down, very reluctantly on his part.'

'That makes my task easier James. But can I just mention three other factors, two of which I think don't apply in your case, but be honest, tell me if I'm wrong. Money and marriage are the first two and in your case am I right in thinking, no problems, although with politicians it's frequently not the case.'

'I can honestly say you are totally correct and you're also right in suggesting many politicians get in a mess with both. What's the third issue?'

'Sudden bereavement.'

'Ah, yes, it's been a difficult time. I seemed to have to do a lot, it was very embarrassing hearing about my brother's life style. I suppose it was a great shock, not losing my brother, as sad though as that was, but all the revelations that came out. There has also been something else you perhaps ought to know about. There is a distant branch of my family, all second and third cousins surnamed 'Quemsby' and about whom we know virtually nothing. It turns out that a middle-aged woman, almost a 'down-and-out', killed in a hit-and-run a few months back, was the blood mother of my most senior civil servant's wife, Audrey and she had no idea that she had been adopted at birth. Further research has revealed that the woman who was killed was a Lucinda Quemsby, a distant cousin of mine and that means that Audrey, who is a lovely person by the way, is also a distant cousin of mine. I hasten to add, nothing unpleasant in discovering these 'new' relatives, just a bit embarrassing perhaps, especially if it gets into the press.'

'James, what you tell me just shows how great a load you have been bearing, and your body, your mind, your system – take your choice of words – is refusing to carry it any further. Here's a few suggestions: I sign you off sick for a month, prescribe a course of anti-depressants, most likely for several months, if not years, but they take two to three weeks to start working, refer you to a specialist but that will mean your telling another person all about yourself, and in great detail. Finally, you take two letters to the Prime Minister – one from yourself, handing in your immediate resignation and one from me explaining briefly why. I take it your constituency work can be covered for a while.'

'Yes, no problem with constituency work, neighbouring M.P.s always help in such circumstances and I have a very good local agent. I agree with all your suggestions except for one, I don't want to see a specialist as you seem incredibly knowledgeable. Also, I may choose to resign my seat in about six months.'

'Ah, the old 'Chiltern Hundreds,' probably wise. My knowledge of depression comes partly from surgery experience, obviously, but also from my father; he was a doctor and suffered from depression for many years. Can Rhiannon call at the surgery pharmacy in an hour or so to collect the prescription, I'll email it through to them now and mark it urgent. Tomorrow afternoon I'll drop off the letter I mentioned, will somebody be here?'

'Yes, tomorrow afternoon will be fine and Rhiannon will be able to call at the surgery. And Doctor, thank you very much, just talking about it all has helped enormously.'

'Thank you. Just two more things, from time to time you will suddenly feel very well, full of 'get up and go,' treat that as some kind of remission, short-term I hasten to add, so whatever you do don't suddenly stop taking the anti-depressants, vitally important. Today fortnight, about this time, I will see you again.'

James watched as his doctor sent off his email and then he walked with him to the front door, meeting Rhiannon as they got there. Darling, can you go to the surgery in an hour or so, to collect some pills.'

'Of course I can, you look better already. Dr Griffiths, you must have worked some magic.'

'Griffiths! Dr Griffiths, you must have thought me terribly rude as I haven't used your name once, couldn't remember it and didn't like to say, sorry, silly of me.'

'Worry not, just another symptom to add to the list. I'll allow you to let your lovely wife, Rhiannon, pour you a measure or two of something of quality and you can tell her about our little conversation. I'm off, see you in two weeks.'

'I'll pour one for myself as well! Come on, fancy us having a doctor who prescribes alcohol. Is that a post-script to part of your earlier conversation when he told you I had got to lock up the booze?'

'No dear, but I did admit to drinking a little more than I used to.'

'Yes, I had noticed, but not in any excessive way and I haven't been aware of your having been drinking during the day.'

Comfortably ensconced on their largest and most squashy sofa, whiskeys to hand, it was Rhiannon who started. 'Well, what's the verdict, just a half-sheet precis, even just a one sentence summary.'

' Here you are, in one sentence - Severe depression, lengthy course of anti-depressants, illness not uncommon, resign immediately from the Government, one month off from all work, gentle constituency work on return and 'Chiltern Hundreds' in about six months.'

'How very wise is our Doctor Griffiths; he has my total approval.'

'I should have referred myself to you. Are you sure you won't mind, pulling away from all the public life, big events and the like?'

'Good heavens, no. I shall relish it. I don't mean that I'll put my feet up and start crocheting blankets. Lots of interesting local things to do, I might even start reading some history again. But, James, one thing which hasn't been mentioned is 'sunshine.' I should like to visit Italy, I don't mean tomorrow or next week but soon, so I'll make some enquiries.'

'Agreed, and as I mentioned to the good Doctor Griffiths, we're not beset with money problems.'

'Good, glad that's settled. Now in case you hadn't noticed, I only poured you one measure together with a large ice-cube, so I'm allowed, according to our local medic, to pour again and unlike you, I'm not on rations!'

By the following morning James had made a number of important phone calls: to the Prime Minister, mainly to confirm his suggestion that he should have to resign and that he had seen his G.P. He was going on extended sick leave and he also confirmed that he would be sending his letter of resignation later that day together with a letter and certificate from his doctor; another call was to Rufus Sutton and James was a little taken aback by Rufus showing such surprise as he thought he would have known about his intentions, no matter but he was really surprised at the depth of Rufus's concern and sympathy. His final call was to his mother who remained quite calm, almost unconcerned and that certainly didn't surprise him because he had long since come to know that no matter how important or startling his news, his mother would remain unruffled. Until he got used to this aspect of his mother's personality he found it disappointing, especially if he had come home from school to shout out that he had been placed first in a school examination. After a while, sadly, he didn't bother to announce any of his news unless it was of vital importance. Even so, he thought that when he announced that he was resigning from the Government because of ill health, his mother might just have expressed a little surprise and sympathy; he knew his father would be more worried.

A little later James telephoned Rufus again to request that he gather up the few personal things to be found in his office and to ask that Tony drive them out to his home and collect two letters of some importance to be given to the Prime Minister. Rufus again commiserated over his illness and also sent greetings to Rhiannon; James appreciated these touches.

The next call was one to him for a change. 'Hello James, Beryl, just checking in on you as I thought mummy didn't seem too bothered for something as serious as your resigning immediately from the Cabinet. To me it all seems very dramatic.'

'Thanks Beryl, that's kind of you, yes, mum was a bit low key but then she's always been like that with anything I've ever had to tell her.'

'I have another motive for ringing, it's just that all your happenings and events involving various people close to you and the family, all sound so extraordinary, it's causing my brain to blast out the next book, obviously not wanting to involve you or any identifiable political individual but I fancy an aspiring Bishop wanting to beat himself up with his Crozier.'

'Sounds fun sister, dear, but you will have be careful or you might just land yourself with a defamation case, a very pricy error to make. Actually the Prime Minister mentioned something along those lines.'

'Thank you for the warning, yes, as soon as a character is recognisable as an identifiable individual then anything you write has to be positive and complementary. I'll jot down a few ideas and see if it might get anywhere. I'll let you have a look if it seems as if any of my 'brain-blastings' have possibilities.'

'Sounds fun Beryl, will be in touch.'

'James, James? Ah you're there. Look when Tony has been can we go away for two or three days, even if we just pop over to your parents?'

'Good idea, love, I should like to have a chat with my dad, want to know what he really thinks about my resignation. I haven't forgotten about Italy just in case you think I'm agreeing to this alternative with some ulterior motive.'

Chapter Forty-Three
Letters Exchanged and other Thoughts

*D*ear Anthony

It is with much regret that I find that I must resign from your Government; my health is such that I can no longer give the role of Foreign Secretary the detailed attention that it inevitably needs. It has been a great privilege to be a member of such a team as you have brought together in Government and I wish you and your colleagues the very greatest of success for the future, confident in the knowledge that you will be leading the country with honesty, integrity and great imagination through the difficult times which are enveloping all nations at present.

With very best wishes

James St John

This and the Prime Minster's warm reply were released later the same day.

Dear James

I am saddened to receive your letter of resignation. Without any doubt you have made a very significant contribution to all our Cabinet discussions and have led your department with flair, imagination and great skill. Your presence in Government will be greatly missed. On the other hand I look forward to hearing wise and thoughtful contributions to Parliamentary debates in the not too distant future, profound wisdom delivered from the more elevated benches of this 'House.'

Laurel and I count you and Rhiannon as very good friends and we both wish you well for the future.

Yours

Anthony

Just for once these important and formal letters between Prime Minister and one of his Cabinet were unusually short and not in any way unnecessarily padded out with remarks concerning the privilege and honour of serving in Government together with lists of achievements; such remarks were at a minimum. In the same vein of brevity was the letter from Dr Griffiths to the Prime Minister, short, formal, and to the point. It confirmed that he had made a professional examination of James St John and that he found him to be suffering from severe depression with personal circumstances exacerbating the condition. He enclosed a medical certificate to cover James for one month, further ones to follow if necessary although he was none too sure if such documents were even required for members of the Government; providing such a certificate was not an everyday occurrence! Dr Griffiths also indicated his approval to James St John's decision to withdraw from Government on a permanent basis.

The Government reshuffle brought about by James's resignation gave the Prime Minister the opportunity to surprise the political pundits of the day by moving Daniel Divine from the Home Office to the Foreign Office and in the opposite direction, the little known Angus Barrington was promoted from his post as Minister of State at the Foreign Office to become the Home Secretary. Privately, James was thrilled by the promotion of Angus and thought his knowledge of matters multicultural would stand him in great stead in his new role. There were some other hidden moves of which James got immediate knowledge, Jeremy Lutterworth and his partner, Angela Rosemary, both travelled with Daniel Divine and his former senior civil servant and good friend, Rufus Sutton, found himself working very closely with the Prime Minister at Number 10. That was a move which greatly surprised Rufus, but afforded James very great pleasure indeed, as he hadn't expected the Prime Minister's very recent suggestion to be so immediate. He made a mental note to suggest to Rhiannon that they should invite Rufus and Audrey to dinner one evening.

A day later than planned, but with knowledge of all the latest Whitehall moves, James and Rhiannon drove to visit his parents, and Beryl, who they knew was also to be there. For once James's mother showed a little more sympathy and understanding of the situation in which he found himself and was pleased that they were thinking of a little holiday, pleasant relaxation, a change of scene.

'You'd better go and give your father all the latest Whitehall news, it never fails to perk him up these days. When you've finished I need to ask you something.'

His father, probably because he had been an M.P. for many years, had more understanding of the stresses which were to be faced by M.P.s, constantly in the public eye and the barrage of criticism which they often had to endure via social media. He mentioned to James that he remembered with horror the emails he used to receive until he made the decision not to read them until they had been sifted by one of his staff. They began to get so awful that this pre-reading of emails had to be a task shared by all his staff, too depressing left totally for one person.

James was amused to hear from Beryl how he, James, had inspired her to produce a character for a possible new novel, who was a senior Bishop within the Church of England. 'Beryl, before I determined to become an M.P. I thought of several different career possibilities but never one requiring me to wear a Mitre and weald a Crozier. I might have enjoyed the theatre of the role but little else. What do you have in mind for your Bishop?'

'I intend to start him off very traditionally, in terms of education, background and a speedy advance through various ecclesiastical appointments in the Church, happily married, two daughters one of whom has also been ordained. I want to develop some oddities of behaviour, yet to be decided. Swimming in the nude is one, wild water swimming. Perhaps saying the unexpected in sermons or missing out a key word when reading a lesson from the bible. I have yet to work out the nature of a scandal which he might find himself embroiled with, possibly getting too close in an advisory capacity to an Archdeacon who has found himself somewhat compromised with a female parishioner, link it all back to his school days and some animosity between a couple of characters from the past who also knew the Bishop as a teenager; other possibilities are beginning to reveal themselves.'

'All sounding very readable, quite tabloidish in the manner of a bit of muck-raking.'

James found his parents in need of further detailed explanation about the additional relatives the family now had. He never got a clear understanding of why his mother couldn't remember who the Quemsbys were, after all, it was his mother, born Elaine Rosenthal and her mother, his grandmother, who was Daphne Quemsby. Was this the beginning of some form of dementia, not something he wanted to think about. He would talk to Beryl, she would have some common sense to bring to the matter. His mother interrupted his thinking just then, made him wonder if she realised what was on his mind.

'James, pour me a sherry and then sit here with me. Need to ask you something.' They were soon settled.

'So, what's bothering you, mother?'

'Yes, that's the right word, 'bothering.' I'm worried about my mind and how I behave.'

'Goodness, mother, no worries on that score, surely?'

'I went shopping the other day, I don't go that often but it was a nice day so off I went. I bumped into an old friend, three or four years older that me, still sharp of mind and very proud of being able to do everything for herself.'

'That's good, isn't it?'

'Yes, I thought so. She was in the queue just in front of me and there was a youth on the till, probably a sixth former earning pocket money. He was newish to the work, seemed nervous.'

James laughed, 'Probably nervous of the line of 'old biddies' about to descend on him.'

'That's as maybe, but it was how my friend spoke to him which caused me the worry. She could see his name badge and addressed him by name, but very sharply. I remember it word for word. *'Mike, is it? Do you like working here, pleased with what you do/'* There was nothing likeable or pleasing in her tone of voice at all, and Mike looked quite terrified. It made me feel very sorry for him. *'Well, what is it, yes or no lad?'* The young lad nodded, quite nervously, managed to mutter a 'yes.' *'Well, try looking as if you do. It's a pity nobody here has told you about smiling. I suggest you start and then you'll get on better.'* By this time she had bagged up her items, got some money out, slapped it down and told the poor lad to put the change, 10p I think it was, into the charity pot. *'Don't forget what I said.'* With that she stomped off.'

'A particularly 'vinegary' old friend, if you don't mind my saying so, mother.'

'Feel free. I felt I should have slapped her one. Anyway, it was my turn next, so I said as much as I thought was necessary to cheer him, he managed a smile, at least. The supervisor appeared then.'

'Everything all right Mike, did I over hear some trouble?'

'You certainly did. I interrupted and didn't allow Mike to answer. If things people say can be described as an assault, then young Mike here has just been assaulted, badly, and with absolutely no justification whatsoever. It was the previous customer, she seemed to think it was her place to give Mike a lesson in customer courtesy and she was absolutely horrible. Mike, you need have no worries, not all old people are like that.' He managed another smile.

'Thank you madam, we are aware of that particular customer, but you are the first customer to have witnessed an entire incident. Very good of you to speak up. The next time she is in we'll have a member of management follow her round. She thanked me again and sent Mike off to his tea-break and she took over the till.'

'Well, mother, what's the worry, unpleasant incident I grant you, but you seem to have done all the right things.'

'Yes, thank you for saying that. The old lady, Pru, is her name. Did she realise how awful she was being or was it how her aged brain was causing her to behave; will I know if I get like that? That's what I'm worried about, James, will I start doing that sort of thing?'

'No, I don't think so as I'm sure we would have seen hints of it by now. Get Beryl's thoughts on it all, she has a great deal of wisdom where such matters are concerned, comes from all the weird characters she keeps dreaming up for her novels. She's produced an errant Bishop for her latest, based on or inspired by what I've been doing just lately, bit of a cheek so I shall demand some royalties if it's a success.'

'Oh, it will be, she has a great following these days, James.'

Beryl would know exactly what to say to her mother, but as it happened, she also had some possible understanding of another matter to speak to her brother about, what happened to Lucinda. 'James, you mentioned at one point the concern over what may have happened to Lucinda Quemsby after the birth and adoption. Without revealing any names I did ask a doctor friend of mine, a psychiatrist and she has worked with women in the kind of position in which Lucinda may have found herself. She suggested the possibility that Lucinda may have suffered from severe post-natal depression, guilt over giving up the baby and that even though she may have returned to her parents' care, perhaps for a year or so, her depression and guilt may have got so bad that she just left them. Quite possibly there may have been various unpleasant relationships with subsequent men, but eventually what probably happened was an uncontrolled, gradual and inevitable decline and with nobody to help, vagrancy just came upon her. My friend suggested it may have all taken a number of years, including spells of alcohol and substance abuse.'

'How very depressing and to think that may have happened to a member of our family and none of us were remotely aware of what misery was occurring. If I can mention all that in slightly less gloomy terms I might try and tell Audrey if there is ever a suitable opportunity.'

Chapter Forty-Four
Thread Ends

Mavis Evans, the kindly wife of P.C. Brian Evans, hadn't forgotten what Brian had told her about the Caroldines, how Ern was having to do nearly everything for his Emily. Mavis had a talent for making discrete enquiries and it wasn't long before she managed to get someone to call on the couple, check what benefits they were claiming, and as was so often the case, it seemed that nobody had picked up on Ern being a carer, and this fact alone led to a useful rise in weekly income as well as a back-dated lump-sum because it could be shown that the officials who had made some earlier decisions were in possession of enough information such that the carer's allowance should have started over two years earlier. That certainly eased Ern's worries and for a while he was able to take his Emily to various appointments by taxi. Help for Ern didn't end straight away because Mavis had a few friends with spare money, the kind of people who wouldn't dream of splashing out on a fifteen-thousand-pound cruise, preferring instead a few nights in a comfortable hotel in the Cotswolds or a nice City, perhaps York, always popular was an elegant seaside multi-star hotel, just slightly out of season. These were the little holidays which gave them something to talk about when they met friends for a mid-week lunch. They were familiar with Mavis's sense of philanthropy and enjoyed supporting whatever current need she had unearthed.

It was a number of conversations amongst these good people which led to Mr Banstead, of Banstead Garage to call on Ern one morning, driving a fairly elderly but beautifully maintained Fiesta. In fact Mr Banstead's mechanic had been responsible for its maintenance since it was eight months old, knew its every nut and bolt. Mr Banstead took

Ern for a drive, Emily sat in the back because just then she couldn't be left. Through various hints and odd remarks Mr Banstead let it be known that the car that he was demonstrating had been reduced to a little over fifteen hundred pounds because the person for whom they were selling it needed it sold in something of a hurry. If that wasn't quite the story, no matter, but it caused Emily to speak up, 'Is this our old car, back from repairs Ern?'

'No, Emily, dear, not our old car, but one very similar.'

'Are you sure, Ern, it's the same colour, feels the same.'

'Yes, dear, I'm sure.'

'It would be better to have our old car back, those taxis cost a lot.'

And that was how a number of kindly local people together with the DSS rectifying their error caused Emily to see their old car being driven into their front garden one morning.'

'Ern, Ern, come and look, our old car has been returned.'

Of course, if the mechanic who delivered the car had had his way, three villainous individuals now serving several years for manslaughter, would have paid for it and kept the Caroldines in petrol for the rest of their lives.

Unbeknown to the official genealogist who had sorted out the Quemsby family tree for the benefit of Commander Zachary, Celia St John, daughter-in-law of James and Rhiannon was pleased with what she saw her son Richard doing as the result of looking at old family photographs. She decided that she would write out the family tree just so she could have a better understanding of the Quemsby line. When she had spoken to Elaine, her husband's mother, she was surprised to hear her say that she wasn't sure whether the Quemsbys were blood related, yet Elaine's mother was a Daphne Quemsby, some confusion there. Like the genealogist, Celia hadn't found any mystery over the family tree but what she really wanted to know was how Lucinda got forced into the illegal arrangement regarding the adoption of her baby and then so neglected afterwards. The other mystery she wanted solving was the source of Juliette's inherited wealth. Short of one day discovering a copy of a relevant will and a solicitor's letter amongst old family papers, it was likely to remain a mystery; why not, many families had them. Perhaps she could have a hunt among the books and papers in Sir George's small library.

Once her father-in-law, James, had told all the family about his resignation from the Cabinet, she had then heard all about Audrey Sutton and who her real parents were, discovered as the result of DNA tests arising from various police investigations, and that led to her becoming familiar with relatives that even her husband Joshua didn't know he had, certainly not an everyday occurrence. Being of a friendly disposition she felt the need to suggest to Joshua that they should have a family get-together, a party, so that they could meet the newcomers. In this matter, Celia was to be 'pipped at the post' as the friendly Audrey already had the matter in hand; the known members of the family were soon to receive nicely printed cards inviting everybody to a 'family bash' at the Regal Court Hotel.

In planning this event Audrey, now just beginning to show that the family would increase in number again in a few months' time, had decided to call at the hotel and was thrilled to discover David back at work and looking not too bad considering the awful accident he had suffered. While he was waiting for their event organiser to appear, David suddenly asked Audrey a question.

'I hope this won't offend you, Audrey, but for some time now you have been reminding me of somebody I once knew when I was at school. This thought apparently was much in my mind when I was unconscious because I kept muttering parts of a name. Is there any possibility that you are related to somebody by the name of Quemsby?'

'How extraordinary that you should think that. If you had asked me a few months back the answer would have been no, but in fact I have recently come to know that I was adopted at birth, and I never knew anything about that, my adoptive parents kept it a complete secret. My real mother was a Lucinda Quemsby.'

'Good God, I knew her when she was a pupil at Kroxby School for Girls. A group of us lads used to meet up with Lucinda and some of her friends on Saturday mornings.'

'Yes, that's right but what you probably don't know is that an old teacher of yours, Henry Palmerson, taught chemistry I believe, is my father.'

'Bloody hell, that'll put Jeremy's mind at rest.' Words out of the mouth can never be put back and David immediately regretted mentioning Jeremy.

'And would you be talking about one Jeremy Lutterworth?' Audrey offered this follow-up with something of a quizzical expression.

'Er, yes,' replied a somewhat uncomfortable, David. 'Do you know him?'

'Not actually know, more a case of 'knowing of', if you get my meaning. Are you still in touch with him? Had something of a reputation didn't he, bit of a 'lothario,' or was it all a bit of boasting? I think Lucinda might just have been winding the famous Jeremy round her little finger, some of his friends as well perhaps.'

'Oh dear, I'm sorry I mentioned it all. Yes, I am in touch, but only in recent months as he has been here for the occasional political meeting.'

'Yes, I had heard, adviser in Government I believe. Well, when you next see him, David, you can tell him that my certainty as to Henry Palmerson being my father rests on a DNA test. I think I might like to meet this Jeremy and perhaps try and spot something of the teenage Jeremy.'

'Right, oh, well maybe, yes, thank you, Audrey. Ah, here is Thomas, he'll be able to arrange the party you mentioned.'

As Audrey went off with Thomas she was amused to reflect on how discomforted David had appeared, so far removed from his usual level of confidence. Perhaps one day she would have the opportunity to have a similar effect on the famous Jeremy, which would be a lovely tease in which to indulge herself.

And so it came to pass, that a few weeks later, Henry, George, Gina and two beautiful daughters, together with Frank, were able to meet with the current members of the St John family, all twelve of them and presiding over this gathering was Rufus, being quietly restrained but accompanying a radiant Audrey, looking just that little more, 'great with child'. Audrey had noticed David was in reception so rather than anymore leg-pulling she invited him to look in and meet up with George and his one-time chemistry teacher, Henry Palmerson. David immediately recognised his old chemistry teacher and yet the greeting was very warm, almost like old friends, much to do with the passage of time he supposed, and the nature of the occasion. He and George recognised each other and David was introduced to Frank. Conversation was not in anyway slow to go down the 'do you remember old.......' route and much laughter ensued.

Just then David felt a tap on his shoulder, turned and found Jeremy Lutterworth standing behind him. 'Jeremy! Where have you sprung from?'

'Just called by to see how you are now you're back at work after your accident. Didn't occur to me that you would be at a function, but they said at the reception desk I would find you in here.'

'This is something of a very unusual family do, not that I'm of the family, just acquainted with several members. Audrey and Rufus - I expect you know of them, well certainly Rufus - are hosting a little party to meet new relatives – that's how they expressed it on the invitation card.'

'Yes, I have heard via other sources, about the discoveries that certain DNA tests have led to. Who are you talking to at present?'

'Gosh, Jeremy, use your memory! Surely you remember George Palmerson, he hasn't changed that much, this is his younger brother, Frank and of course their father, our old chemistry teacher, Henry Palmerson.'

'Chemistry! I'm with you David. Good evening Sir. Hello George and nice to meet you Frank, you went to Kemby but a few years later, am I right?

'Yes, but like you others, it all seems a long time ago now.'

'Jeremy, now your memory is functioning, can I say how nice it is to see you again. Congratulations on your later educational achievements and where they have taken you, Cabinet Office meetings I hear, very grand. Very cutting edge I suppose, and for the record, just call me Henry now. Perhaps in a few moments you will allow me to introduce you to my daughter.'

'No need, Henry, said Audrey, just appearing from behind. Rufus pointed him out to me; heard his voice. So, you're the famous or infamous Jeremy, how do you do, lovely to meet you.' All said with a stunningly radiant smile, and if Jeremy were to admit to the truth of the situation, the smile was as mesmerizing as one he could recall from over a quarter of a century back. It certainly explained how David was immediately reminded of Lucinda. 'Am I right Jeremy, I believe you knew my mother?' This caused a few smiles, very restrained guffaws from those standing about.

'Well, Mrs Sutton, or may I call you Audrey. You mustn't believe all that has ever been said about or by a sixteen year old lad' This last phrase, a speedy mutter and very sotto voce. 'Such are male teenager boastings and I don't suppose for one moment I was any different.'

'Nothing you say is surprising, given the kind of things I used to hear lads at University saying about their final years at school. However, it is very nice now to be able put a face to the reputation. I don't know how long you will be around but when you've finished digging up Kemby memories and putting to rest some stray ones, come and say hello again, talk to Rufus and meet his former boss and my fourth cousin, James St John, who, as you know was, until recently, the Foreign Secretary.' Before Jeremy could make any reply, she kissed him quickly and was off and Jeremy was left nursing a blush which he felt was not leaving his face with any speed; he had been well and truly upstaged, outmanoeuvred, out-witted and as many 'outs' as one could think of, all a giant reminder of events many years ago.

'Hey, you guys, just wipe all your silly grins off your faces, I'm sure I'm not the only one to have made an ass of myself when I was once an over-hormoned-adolescent.'

While they from Kemby, including Jeremy, enjoyed a mini reunion which seemed to involve much mirth while nattering nineteen to the dozen, Audrey was to be seen chatting very animatedly with Gina, and her daughters, Louise and Diana. 'Can I just say how beautiful your hair looks, all three of you, it just glistens so exquisitely.'

That's my Egyptian background showing through. You're by no means the first to make such a comment, thank you, Audrey. Some of the girls' friends are quite jealous.

The four of them had happily given up trying to establish which piece of genealogical terminology described their relationship. Wasn't it perfectly straight forward, fourth cousins once removed for Gina but by marriage, for Louise and Diana, fourth cousins twice removed!

 Sir George and Elaine found themselves comfortable armchairs and chatted amiably with whoever passed close by. Rufus and James found an opportunity to catch up on what was happening at Downing Street and it was very obvious that Rufus was exceptionally pleased with his appointment and got on extremely well with the Prime Minister. 'Am I right in hearing that you are getting a little closer to the Chiltern Hundreds, James? I never said, but I was in the House to hear your resignation speech, both whimsical and serious, is that a fair summary?'

327

'Probably, didn't want to be too sombre or long-winded. I'm not sure the back benches are really going to be my scene, but I've only tried them out a couple of times. On the other hand, perhaps the back benches of another place might be tempting, not that I have any automatic right to such an expectation.'

'I think I might just have heard something of that, probably when I was walking between offices, a possibility but, er, well you know all there is to know about confidentiality, sealed lips and so forth.' Rufus smiled but James knew his lips would definitely be ultra-sealed.

'Perhaps that Jeremy Lutterworth may get lucky this time round?'

'Daniel always speaks well of him. He's around somewhere, turned up by chance to see how David was after his accident, but instead found himself meeting his former girlfriend's daughter, if the term 'girlfriend' is actually correct. He just ended up with something of a red face. Audrey, I suspect, just pricked a balloon of some very old teenage boastings.'

'Audrey will have done that very nicely, I'm sure. Should I have a word with my agent on Jeremy's behalf or would that be the kiss of death? I know that he has a go at most seats that come up for one reason or another and there have been a couple of close decisions.'

'Sort of Constituency nuance James, of which I wouldn't have any knowledge, I'm afraid.'

'Rufus, I'm forgetting myself, so sorry, haven't offered congratulations on Audrey's news, do hope you're both excited.'

'Absolutely and at the last discussion, name possibilities included Anthony, Rufus and Henry, even James at an out-side chance. Anthony is my father's name, don't think I have ever mentioned that.'

'Told you the name was not too exclusive! Whatever the name, your Audrey will make a glowing mother,'

Rufus's smile was all that was needed by way of a reply.

Oblivious to all the 'adult' conversation taking place, the youngsters, James, Richard and Amy stuffed themselves silly and then charged round the room, and occasionally, most of the hotel ground floor as well, until a kindly member of staff ushered them in the right direction; no more than a bit of fun as far as this trio of children were concerned they being of an age when they would never understand the notion that they were causing extra work. When they felt in need of some real fuss, they went and found their Great Grandparents where somebody else would tell them not to be a bother. If on any of these sprints they passed close to the table of food they would grab something, just to keep their bellies topped up.

An unexpected sequel to the international kidnapping which led to the United Nations funding and supervising the Brazilian Rain Forest replanting, was a small article appearing in just one of the national newspapers. Peter Stevenson, son of the M.P. John Stevenson, together with a group of fellow university students appeared before a London Magistrates' Court charged with the kidnapping of the Brazilian Ambassador, Senhor Joaquim Barbosa. The case was referred to the Crown Courts for a later date. It was this newspaper which Angus Barrington found open at the article on his desk when he arrived at the Home Office one morning, a few weeks after becoming Home Secretary. He read the short article, raised a wry smile, but refrained from any comment to his assembled staff. Unlike them, he was not curious as to why only one daily newspaper had picked up on the story.

One further sequel was that James and Rhiannon missed this particular nugget of news as they had both agreed that when they got to Northern Italy for a one month's restorative retreat they would forswear all English newspapers for what they termed as the 'duration.' They could just about manage Italian restaurant menu cards and they purchased English guides to any tourist spots which inspired their aesthetic imaginations. When it came to art galleries they were both of the opinion that interest and enjoyment were forthcoming with just looking. Generally there was an artist's name and date to read and most often the name meant little to either of them anyway. They enjoyed the architecture and cultural delights of several famous cities but they made sure of enough time for soaking up plenty of sunshine while sitting beside a lakeside swimming pool. Indulging their taste buds was certainly not forgotten, with local ice cream, fresh seasonal fruit and a well-chilled bottle of prosecco and if it was Rhiannon who appeared to gain the greater pleasure from this trio of tastings, she reminded James that it was her particular request for Italy and its justified reputation for sunshine and all the delicious things with which it can be accompanied.

Chapter Forty-Five

Short Story (See chapter two)

'WHO WOULD BE A MEMBER OF PARLIAMENT'

By Jayne St John

When Mr and Mr Chalk, named their only son, Wensley, nobody could say that they didn't have sense of humour, sad that they themselves didn't appreciate the joke, because all they had managed was a misspelling but nobody queried it and Wensley remained Wensley for the rest of his life and when anybody abbreviated it to 'Wes', he always politely offered the correction, no, 'Wens' and ignored any appearances of puzzlement. Wens, or Wes, was a perky little lad, bright, did well at school, passed his eleven plus and went to his local Lincolnshire Grammar School. He remained a little lad and perky with it, after most of his contempories had become six foot giants. He was generally the butt of their jokes but he never felt himself being bullied. Much to everybody's surprise he joined the army when he was seventeen and having reached five foot nine and average weight, he looked more the part. Perhaps it was only in looks he looked the part while his continued perky manner irritated too many squaddies. It was six months later that he went AWOL for the first time. Army Police involved and Army punishment followed as did a second and then a third period of AWOL. Eventually common-sense prevailed and he was discharged and it was if over the next few years his AWOL periods from the army became AWOL periods from life in general. Reasonable employment was followed by poor employment, and then indifferent part-time jobs and then no jobs. That wasn't the end of the sequence and like many before him, drink accompanied his lengthening periods of no jobs.

If the drink dulled his wits just a little, it was a gradual process and the perky personality became something of a Jack Dawkins, 'Artful,' if a somewhat less successful 'Dodger'. Periods of enterprising pick-pocketing became punctuated with periods of boredom while killing time at His Majesty's Pleasure and the punishments were not issued because he had been stealing silk handkerchiefs. For the most part, Wens had sufficient wits to watch into which pocket thoughtless blokes were inclined to drop their wallets. His first attempt, successful as it happened, was after he made the observation in a small shop, followed the guy through the narrow shop doorway, rudely barged into him and as he squeezed past, dipped and picked the wallet as he went. His first brush with the law came when he unwisely allowed himself on his fourth attempt, to be in full view of a security camera mounted on the opposite side of the road and the subsequent picture gave a perfect view of a wallet just making its way into a pocket of Mr Wens Chalk. He was identified because he was well known as one who might be seen sleeping rough in the area. What the camera didn't spot was his well-rehearsed drill of speedily sifting out the best contents as he crossed the road, depositing the unwanted dross from his gloved hand into the nearest waste-paper basket, and then off to spend his winnings, generally on cigarettes and drink. If there were any debit cards he would have a go at swiping with them quickly before any owner had time to contact their bank.

Wens had moved away from Lincolnshire because he never returned home after he left the army. He spent some time in Peterborough but gradually moved further south, Stevenage and finally ended up in the Watford area, he moved around a lot, sometimes sleeping rough but as his skill as a pick-pocket thief improved so did his resources grow. He rented a room, cheapest possible, no questions asked, but it gave him a base, somewhere to keep a few bits and pieces, essential changes of clothes as it was important he could change his appearance easily and quickly. He never kept to one address for long, didn't want people getting familiar with him. Being in Watford meant he could get to London easily, always bought a ticket, never wanted to be caught over something stupid. He soon found that London Train Stations provided rich pickings but he had to keep to the rush hour, good crowds provided good cover. Concourse stalls were useful watching places, guys made quick purchases, kept their wallets handy, handy for them so handy for him.

He didn't like staying very late up in London, never slept rough as he felt there were too many weirdoes. He woke up once when he found himself being groped, defended himself with a well placed kick and then scarpered at speed. He found the theatre land a useful source of temporary wealth, couples were too silly and self-distracted, blokes showing off with eye-candy on their arm. He didn't bother with friends, kept himself to himself, stayed fairly fit in as much as he could run at speed, got him out of uncomfortable situations more than once.

Sometimes his pocket picking gave him more than he expected, most frequent extra was a mobile phone and he started selling these on. He chose seedy looking secondhand shops and he never argued over what he was offered. A deal conducted at speed was best and safest. Very occasionally the wallet was worth more than the contents, nicest one which ever came his way was a brand new crocodile-skin example, must have been an expensive birthday present.

When he was in Watford he frequently spent time keeping warm in big supermarkets. He made sure to look the part, used a trolley, had some shopping in it, not much but bulky items which were useful for hiding something; he always paid for them. Packets of kitchen rolls were often cheapest and best. On these trips he was keeping an eye open for a handbag or a purse; some women he realised were just plain stupid with their security as far as their possessions were concerned. A quick snatch from the top of an open handbag, round the end of the aisle, winnings straight into a shopping bag, next aisle a very speedy change of appearance and he was away. Quick visit to the men's toilets gave him time to look at the contents of any handbag or purse and he stuffed in his pockets money and cards, wrapped what he didn't want in a supermarket bag and that went into the first bin he passed.

After he'd been at his trade for a few years he decided to extend it a bit, develop some new skills, and he hit upon the idea of wrist-watch snatching. This was a greater risk, both to himself and to his victims as they had to be a bit elderly. For his first attempt he chose a crowded shopping area in Watford, a shop doorway and he contrived to knock an old man over, made it look convincing by combining barging into his victim and at the same time using his foot to trip the person over. That second manoeuvre went unnoticed but what was seen was that he was one who bent down to help, bring about a degree of fluster, talk loudly, cause some confusion and just when he thought the person was making moves to get up, reaching a hand down to push up with, that was the moment for the snatch. It had to be a quick powerful tug, sufficient to break from the side of the wrist watch the spindle holding the strap on. His perky nature came in handy as he would help brush the victim down a bit and then he slipped away into the crowd, a bit of speed and he was gone. Older victims were best he found, more likely to have nice watches, they were easy to cause to lose their balance, least expected an attack, always slower to respond and rarely with sufficient presence of mind.

Needless-to-say, it was a watch-snatch which brought to an end the petty crime career of one Wensley Chalk, a few days before Christmas in the busy shopping area of Oxford Street. He had spotted his victim in a large store, holding a couple of shopping bags. The circumstances looked favourable as the man was about seventy years old, using a walking stick, he was on his own and about to leave the store. Preparation complete, Wens got up close as they went through the double doors. Wens leant into the victim's side, placed his foot in front of the guy's nearest leg and down he went; shopping in one direction, his stick rolled out of reach and his hat went flying as he hit his head on the door frame. Wens went into his 'stage' role and was able to complete his snatch straight away but because the victim was a bit stunned he couldn't begin to get up although he was trying to scrabble about, reaching for his stick. At the same time Wens started speaking loudly to a lady who was just beginning to bend down to offer assistance, that she should call an ambulance. Out of the corner of his eye, Wens noticed a police officer pushing through the crowd but his route was blocked by another person claiming to be a first aider. These distractions gave Wens just the opportunity to slip back into the store and speedily get to the back of the ground floor where there was another exit point. He was pleased with his escape as the incident was attracting too much concern on the part of the on-lookers, but unbeknown to Wens, one of them had taken a photograph.

Removing his cloth cap and glasses, Wens made his way to the underground station and started his journey back to Watford. Only after he got back to his room did he inspect the results of the snatch and suddenly was caused to think that he might be in big trouble; he was the temporary owner of a Rolex. He may not have known how valuable it was but he understood sufficient to realise that whoever had lost it would be making a fuss. Up early the next morning he was out to off-load, a major error of judgement on his part. Wens made up some lame excuse about having inherited it from a great uncle, told the second-hand shop owner that he didn't want to keep it so accepted fifty quid for it. He knew it was worth more but short of throwing it away he was keen to part company with it.

Without Wens realising, all the circumstances were now against him. The fellow who had lost his watch was a well-known Home Counties Member of Parliament and because of his being stunned in the fall he was taken to hospital, a move which automatically led to publicity. The bright member of the public who had taken the photograph went to the local police station with the police officer who had witnessed the incident and there the photograph was transferred to official records and to this he added his signature. In hospital a seventy four year old Trent Ravenscroft, M.P. for North.........., was telling a newspaper reporter how upset he was at the loss because the watch had come from his father, a fighter pilot in the second world war who had been shot down and crashed in Kent in 1942. He had been trying to return to base but never made it and the site of his crash and death was not far from the current headquarters of Trent's Kent constituency. Crucial to the speedy enquiry was the second-hand shop dealer who knew far more about Rolex watches than did our villain. After telephoning the U.K. headquarters of Rolex, David Sealing arranged for the watch to be sent to them by special delivery and in a very short space of time the full history of the watch was known, first owner, current owner and address, history of any servicing and repairs undertaken, in fact the watch, a Silver Cased Rolex Oyster from 1941 had a complete 'biography'. A head-line from one of the next day's papers said it all:

'Popular M.P. Mugged for Heroic Father's Rolex'

Wens Chalk had little time to wonder what was going to happen because in less than twelve hours he was arrested and if there was any confusion as to his identity and guilt, Wens was totally unable to explain the presence of his left thumb print on the underside of the watch case. Wens was remanded in custody, put on trial at Watford Crown Court where he pleaded guilty. There was little to be said for him in mitigation, periods when he went AWOL from the army were seen by most people as crimes and not cries for help, so there was absolutely no public sympathy, not that that would have influenced the judge who certainly didn't mince his words in describing the villain in his dock and subsequently sentencing him to eight years in prison. Trent Ravenscroft got his Rolex watch back and was then greeted by fellow M.Ps with enthusiasm when he was able to retake his usual seat in the Commons, while Watford's 'Artful Dodger' went into an extended period of retirement.

As it happened, Retirement was also in the mind of Trent Ravenscroft but he could time his departure according to his own whim and pleasure. When he mentioned this to his family the idea evolved quite quickly that retirement and seventy-fifth birthday celebrations should be combined. Noticed by his wife was that the famous Rolex watch was no longer adorning Trent's wrist; very quietly, he admitted to not wanting to be mugged again. A suggestion from his oldest son, quite unexpected as he was likely to be the eventual recipient of the watch, was that it should be presented to an appropriate Royal Air Force Museum or auctioned and with the proceeds being presented to the Royal British Legion; in the event both suggestions were agreed. A London auction house gave an estimated value of £35000, a private benefactor made an approach bearing a gift of £45000 with a cheque payable to the Royal British Legion, and a famous Second World War Royal Air Force Museum somewhere in Kent received for display, a Silver Cased Rolex Oyster Watch from 1941, once the property of Flight Lieutenant Bentley Ravenscroft, and to this was added his D.F.C. along with other medals, his famous flying jacket, his RAF Pilot's Flying Log, other documents together with many original second world war photographs.

Printed in Poland
by Amazon Fulfillment
Poland Sp. z o.o., Wrocław

88280375R00190